PRAISE

"In *Roam*, C.H. Armstrong sings with a brilliant, powerful youthful voice as she portrays a narrator named Abby who experiences what it's like to be homeless with her family while dealing with the emotional and complex daily challenges of attending a new school. We, her readers, are drawn in from the first page. This lovely book has tremendous heart."

—Brandon Hobson, author of *Where the Dead Sit Talking*

"An empathetic tale that treats homelessness with respect and makes it visible."

—Kirkus Reviews

"In her warm and hopeful novel, C.H. Armstrong has created a spirited heroine who triumphs over her circumstances thanks to those who believe in her; friends, family, teachers and ultimately, herself."

—Lorna Landvik, Author of *Once in A Blue Moon Lodge*

"Roam is a study in empathy, forgiveness, and second chances—an impactful and memorable story of teenage homelessness."

—Foreword Reviews

"C.H. Armstrong's *Roam* is a book we need; too often we look past families like Abby Lunde's who live on the periphery of our lives and our novels. Armstrong's book pays compassionate and eloquent attention to teenage angst and love amidst the backdrop of homelessness."

—Cara Sue Achterberg, author of *Girls' Weekend* and *I'm Not Her*

"*Roam* is a comp_____ ____ look into the life of a homeless teen.
A __ _____ ___ ___ __e to understand the hardship of
____ ___ ___ ____ ___ ·each out to help others."

_____ Lamb, author of *No Place I'd Rather Be*

ROAM

C.H. ARMSTRONG

2019

In Loving Memory of Linda Curtis
December 31, 1941—May 31, 2018

Published by Central Avenue Publishing, an imprint of Central Avenue Marketing Ltd.
www.centralavenuepublishing.com

ROAM

Trade Paperback: 978-1-77168-151-3
Epub: 978-1-77168-152-0
Mobi: 978-1-77168-153-7

Published in Canada
Printed in United States of America

1. YOUNG ADULT FICTION / Social Themes / Homelessness & Poverty

3 5 7 9 10 8 6 4 2

"I've learned that people will forget what you said, people will forget what you did, but people will never forget how you made them feel."

—Dr. Maya Angelou

ROAM

CHAPTER ONE

I HATE THIS TOWN ALREADY.

My stepdad, Nick, drives down the main street of Rochester, pulling even with a car filled with teenagers. I stare at them, thankful for the van's tinted windows, which keep my gaze from catching their attention. The driver is a girl about my age, and the car is a fire-engine red sports car with temporary tags. She and her passengers dance in their seats, singing to the blaring music.

Everywhere I look screams wealth and privilege—from the carefully manicured lawns to the kids in the car next to us. The cost of their clothing alone would probably eat up Nick's whole paycheck—if he still had one. But he doesn't, and neither does Mom.

I wonder about the kids in the sports car. Are they as perfect as they appear, or are their lives secretly as screwed up as mine? Maybe the driver's dad is embezzling money from his company. He'll get caught next week, the scandal will hit the newspapers, and the whole family will be ruined. Or the guy in the passenger seat: maybe he's about to discover his parents are really his grandparents, and his "older sister" is really his mom. Everybody's hiding something. We all have secrets. It can't be just my family.

Angry tears threaten. The kids pull ahead, so Nick holds back, allowing them to pass. What would they think if they knew our secrets? Anger flows like hot lava as I imagine them laughing at our ratty old van with the rusted-out fender on the driver's side. Next to them, we look homeless.

Manic laughter erupts from my belly. I smother it, but not before Mom hears from the front seat. She turns around and shoots me a smile that says, "*Tell me what's so funny*," but I ignore her, turning away and staring out my window. I should feel bad for ignoring Mom but she's pretty much ruined our lives, so I'd call us even.

Seated next to me, my little sister, Amber, taps my arm. "What's so funny, Sister?"

"Nothing." I smile, taking the edge off my short reply.

The sports car disappears around a corner into a residential neighborhood. At the next stoplight, Nick turns into a 24-hour Walmart parking lot, then rolls the windows down about two inches before turning off the engine.

"We'll park it here for tonight," he says. "With so many other cars, nobody will notice an extra van in the lot."

"Is it safe?" Mom scans the parking lot, her expression skeptical.

"Pretty much. The doors'll be locked, so we should be okay."

"I miss BooBoo Bunny," Amber cries.

At six, everything in the last two days has been confusing to her. She's asked endless questions for which none of us have answers—at least not answers you can give a first grader.

Why can't we go home?

Why do we have to sleep in the van?

Why can't I bring my bicycle?

My patience is short and, before I can stop myself, angry words spew out. "None of us like it. Deal with it."

Mom spins in her seat. "Abby, you've made it clear how you feel about this situation, but there's no need to snap at your sister."

I narrow my eyes at Mom. Just as I open my mouth to let her know how I *really* feel about her and this entire messed-up situation she's put us in, Nick turns and catches my eye. His expression says, "*Leave it, Abby. Please.*" I bite down hard on the inside of my cheek and turn to glare out the window. For Nick's sake, I'll shut my mouth—but only because it's Nick asking and, deep down, I'm terrified he'll leave us. Because without Nick, this shit-show our lives have become would be even worse. He's the one who keeps us going—the one who keeps me from strangling Mom—and he's the only one who can help us out of this mess.

Be nice. Be nice. The words scream inside my head like a mantra. I take in a breath and, ignoring Mom, I turn to Nick and ask, "So what do we do now?"

Nick smiles his thanks. "Tomorrow, we get you two started in school, then your mom and I will see what the Salvation Army has to offer." His face flushes. "I hate to ask, but can you help us out?"

I lift an eyebrow. "Sure. What do you need?"

"Can you check out the newspaper office one day this week? If you got a job delivering papers, you could take Amber with you and it'd be a huge help."

"Sure."

Nick's smile is sad—embarrassed, maybe. Asking my help must be a blow to his pride.

"Mommy?" Amber asks. "How're we gonna sleep in the van?"

"It'll be fun." Mom's chipper voice grates on my nerves. "Like camping. We have pillows and blankets, and we've already folded down the rear seats."

"Will we all fit?"

"We should."

Amber frowns. "What if someone sees us?"

"Nobody will see us. They'd have to peek in, and there's no reason for anyone to do that."

"Like a monster?"

"No, baby, we'll be fine. Daddy will protect us."

My face flames red with anger. *Daddy will protect us? Is she serious? How much more weight can Nick's shoulders stand?* I bite my tongue before the words spew out.

We left Omaha this afternoon, just one step ahead of eviction. The landlord visited two days ago, warning us we had seventy-two hours to pay the current and last month's rent or she'd return with a police escort and a locksmith. There was no point in fighting it, Nick said, so we spent all day yesterday packing only our absolute necessities. We left everything else behind—there just wasn't enough room.

Now, with darkness descending, Amber's getting antsy and her whining is playing on our last nerves.

"Why don't we turn in for an early night?" Mom suggests.

"But it's too early," Amber cries. "I wanna watch TV."

"You know the van's TV doesn't work, sweetheart," Nick says. "Just try closing your eyes for a bit."

Amber grumbles but stretches beside me on the hard floorboard in the back of Mom's van. Tossing and turning, she reminds me of a dog turning circles before lying in its bed. Just when I think she's found a comfortable position, she rolls over again.

Oof! A bony elbow gouges my stomach.

"Quit it, Amber," I growl. "Be still!"

"I can't sleep," she whines.

"How about Sister sings to you?" Mom suggests.

I narrow my eyes and shoot Mom a scalding glare.

"Yeah!" Amber agrees. "Sing the rainbow song!"

"Not tonight, Am. I don't feel like it."

"Please, Sister?" Amber begs.

"No."

"Abby." Nick touches my arm. "Please? You know it helps her fall asleep."

"Fine." I blow out a frustrated breath and pull myself to a sitting position beside Amber.

Singing used to be a relaxing outlet for me—something I did effort-

ROAM

lessly and often just to see Mom smile. But making Mom happy isn't at the top of my list anymore and, at the moment, I'm not at all in the mood. Now that Nick's asked, though, I relent. He doesn't ask much of me and I don't want to be the reason he gives up and leaves us. So I close my eyes and disappear inside my head with the first few bars of "Over the Rainbow." With my eyes closed, I imagine myself as Dorothy and almost forget the last six months.

My mind drifts to my old bedroom. Though small and cheaply decorated with frilly old-lady curtains purchased at a garage sale, it was mine. My heart aches for all we've left behind—my books, Amber's collection of stuffed animals, Nick's guitar, and even Mom's Mickey Mouse collection. But we can't go back, so I focus on happier times, like singing on my comfortable old bed while Amber danced around the room pretending she was a famous ballerina. The memory is bittersweet, and I return to the present as I close out the last measures of the song.

Amber breathes a contented sigh, and I smile down at her relaxed features. Sound asleep, her long, dark lashes gently brush her cheek. My heart warms at her sweetness. As angry as I am at everything, I can't stay angry with Amber. I brush her soft blond hair away from her cheek, then crawl under the blanket and rest my head next to hers. With Nick on one end and me on the other, and Mom and Amber sandwiched in between, we settle down to sleep for the night.

"9-1-1, what is your emergency?"

The woman's voice comes through the line as though through a tunnel. My mind goes blank. Cold rain pelts the patio door to my left, while my mother lies on the kitchen floor only inches away. She jerks spasmodically and all I can see are the whites of her eyes as the pupils have rolled into the back of her head. My own body shakes until I almost drop the phone.

"Hello?" the voice says. "This is 9-1-1. What is your emergency?"

An invisible hand squeezes my throat. "My mom."

"Ma'am? Could you please speak louder? What is your emergency?"

I clear my throat. *"My mom. She's—I don't know. She fell down and now she's—I'm not sure! She's shaking—like she's having a seizure or something."*

"What is your address?"

I force myself to think. *"Meadowlark Lane. 1113 Meadowlark Lane."*

"I'm dispatching an ambulance, but I need you to stay with me. Is your mother breathing?"

"I think so." I squat and place my ear near Mom's mouth. A light waft of breath tickles my chin. *"Yes."*

"That's a good sign. What is your name, please?"

"Abby. Abby Lunde."

"Okay, Abby," the operator says, her voice calm. *"My name is Elena and I'm gonna stay with you until the ambulance comes. Is your mother lying on her side or on her back?"*

"On her…" I pause mid-sentence as a dark stain colors the front of her gray pajama bottoms. *"Oh, God. She just—she peed her pants."*

"That's okay, Abby. Now I need you to listen, okay? If she's on her back, I need you to roll her into a side-lying position."

"What does that mean?" Even the smallest instruction confounds me.

"Carefully roll her over so she's lying on her side if you can. Can you do that for me?"

"Yeah." I press the speaker button before setting the phone down and kneel beside my mother. Her body jerks and resists, but after several moments I have her on her side.

"Abby, are you still there?" The voice is tinny through the speaker.

"Yeah. It's just—she's jerking a lot and I don't know if I can keep her in that position."

"The ambulance is two minutes away. Is the front door unlocked?"

"I—I don't know." My eyes flash to the front door. *"No."*

"Okay, Abby. As soon as you have your mom stable on her side, you need

to unlock the front door for the EMTs. Can you do that?"

I reach for a chair, pulling it onto its side and propping it behind Mom's back. I say a silent prayer that it'll stay put and move away slowly. It holds— for the moment, at least. "Yes. I'll do that now."

In my mind, I run to the door, but everything moves in slow motion. My legs shake like they're weighted by cinder blocks. It's all taking too long! I turn the deadbolt and throw the door wide as the sound of sirens reaches my ears.

"Abby?" the voice calls urgently from the phone. "Abby? Abby!"

"Abby!"

I'm jolted awake by Nick's hand on my arm as he shakes me. My eyes flash open and it takes me a second to realize where I am. Amber lies beside me, her thumb resting inside her gaping mouth. My pulse races as the realness of the dream swallows me.

"You okay?" Nick asks.

I nod, my mouth too dry to speak.

"Same dream? The 9-1-1 call?"

I nod again.

Nick smiles sadly, his empathy reaching me through his gaze. "It's gonna be okay, kiddo. I promise."

I moisten my lips with my tongue. "How do you know?"

"Because I do. I swear I won't let anything happen to you girls. The next few weeks are gonna suck, but we'll get through it. Someday you'll look back on everything and a small piece of you will be thankful for it."

"If you say so." I roll my eyes, but temper the sarcasm with a smile.

"I do say so. Now go back to sleep." He squeezes my shoulder twice, something he's always done to spread his confidence to me.

For the next several hours, I lie there in the gray dark of Mom's van. My eyes are closed, but every time I doze off, I'm jolted awake. Voices assault me from outside—a young couple laughing as they carelessly bump the back of our van with a grocery cart. I hold my breath, praying they won't notice us inside the van. They move away until their words are indistinct, then the piercing cry of a young baby echoes through the quiet night. I glance at my watch—3:22 a.m. *Who takes a baby out at this time of night?*

"Breathe, Abby," Nick whispers. "I promised you it'll be okay, and it will."

The parking lot lights shine brightly through the van's windows, revealing Nick's gentle smile as he lies nestled close to Mom.

"What if they saw us?" I whisper.

"They didn't. Go back to sleep."

Anger churns in my belly at the helplessness of our situation, but there's nothing I can do to change it. My home is with my family, which means my home is currently the back of Mom's van. I close my eyes and force myself to sleep.

CHAPTER TWO

I'M SITTING IN MS. RAVEN'S OFFICE, WAITING FOR HER TO RETURN FROM A "QUICK TRIP" TO RETRIEVE MY class schedule from the printer, but it's been at least ten minutes and she's yet to make a reappearance. I look around her office, noticing her degree certificate on the wall with *The University of Minnesota* emblazoned in large letters.

She has all sorts of gadgets on her desk, presumably to reduce her students' anxiety during their visits. I pick up a green stress ball and squish it between my fingers and palm. Do these things really work? I squish it again, and then again. I feel exactly the same: nervous.

"I'm sorry that took so long." Ms. Raven opens her office door and I quickly return the ball to its home on her desk. "There was a paper jam and we had to clear it."

"That's okay." I accept two sheets of paper from her outstretched hand.

"This first page has your class schedule. Since classes have already started, I had difficulty finding an elective for you but there was an opening in vocal music. I hope that's okay?"

I shrug. "Sure. I haven't done much singing except around my family."

"You'll be fine." Miss Raven waves a dismissive hand. "Show up on time, follow directions, and you'll be okay. I've looked at your transcripts, and it looks like you're on track to graduate in June. Have you thought about what you'll do after high school? College, maybe?"

"I haven't thought about it yet," I lie.

Of course I've thought about it—I'm not stupid! Which also means I know we can't afford it. Maybe we could've before Mom screwed everything up, but not now.

"Okay. Let's worry about that another day. Today let's focus on your classes, and then we can revisit your options in a couple of weeks. The second sheet I gave you is a map of the school." Ms. Raven taps the page with a perfectly manicured fingertip. "You'll notice the school is round, so it's difficult to get lost. The classroom number corresponds to the closest door, and those numbers are also marked on the floor near the corresponding stairwells. So, for example, classroom 1-326 is on the first floor closest to Door Three. Does that make sense?"

I nod. "I think so."

"Good. If you get lost, follow the circle of the building and you'll end up back where you started."

"Thank you." Though this school looks easy to navigate, I'm not quite ready to share her optimism.

"You're very welcome. Now, I'll have one of our office aides show you around and take you to your first class. Just give me one minute." She's out the door in a flash, and I hope I'm not in for another long wait.

Moments later Ms. Raven returns with the most attractive guy I've ever seen. He stands at well over six feet tall with eyes the color of melted dark chocolate. He pushes his pitch-black hair away from his forehead and offers me a smile that frames perfect white teeth.

Wow!

"Abby," Ms. Raven interrupts my perusal. "Meet Zach Andrews. Zach is a senior, like you, and he's one of our office aides this period. Zach will give you a quick tour of the building, and then walk you to your first class."

Beautiful and rich. Those are the perfect words to describe Zach Andrews. From his expensive shoes to the Tommy Hilfiger polo, he seems to have wealth, privilege, and "Future GQ Model" tattooed everywhere. He's probably popular, too—anyone who looks like that has to be popular.

I clamp my jaw shut. *Get a grip, Abby! He's out of your league!*

Zach's face lights up in a blinding grin, revealing a dimple in his left cheek. He extends his hand for a handshake. "Nice to meet you, Abby."

"You, too," I say, meeting his hand with my own.

Zach's smile is contagious and my lips tip upward.

He takes my schedule and scans it briefly. "This isn't too bad. You've got some great teachers. You sing?"

"A little, why?" I ask, following him into the hallway.

"You have Mrs. Miner for vocal music. You'll love her."

"You have her?"

"Not this year—it wouldn't fit into my schedule, but I've had her before."

I smile at Zach, but remind myself not to get too keyed up about him. He's attractive, true, and if things were different, we might make perfect sense. But things aren't different, and my secrets would horrify him. I take a breath and focus on the major landmarks of the building as he points them out.

I'm right about one thing: Zach is popular. So far, there isn't anyone who doesn't know him, and I lose count of how many people greet him as we pass. We stop outside a closed door on the third floor. The tour is over, and I stupidly wish for an excuse to extend it.

"Okay, so first period is almost over so there's no point going to that one," Zach says. "This is your history class. Just hang out here until the bell rings, then go on in."

"Thanks."

"No problem. Hey—you have 'A' lunch. So do I. Look for me, okay?"

Um…no! Bad idea.

"Sure," I say instead.

"Okay. I'll catch you later." Zach smiles one last time and heads back down the hall. I watch him go, and my heart does a little flip-flop at the "what-ifs."

I lean against the wall next to the closed classroom door. The halls are quiet, but the peace is short-lived. Within moments the bell rings, and doors on three sides of me are thrown open as students stream out of classrooms like worker ants marching to orders. Dozens of eyes fall on me, all wondering the same things: *Who is she? Where is she from?* But not one person greets me or offers a smile of welcome. And I get it. I'm pretty sure I did the same thing…before.

I busy myself by searching through my nearly empty backpack. When the last two students leave the classroom, I cautiously step inside. Leaning against his desk and glancing over a student's homework is my history teacher, Mr. Hedrick. Dressed impeccably in a suit and tie, he's the epitome of "old school." I groan inwardly at what this means about his teaching style.

He's absorbed in his work, so I study him. His white hair is clipped military short, and his heavy plastic glasses are propped precariously at the tip of his long, straight nose. His thin lips are pressed together in displeasure, and a deep crease forms a crater-like indentation between his nearly transparent eyebrows. He tosses the papers onto his desk, then removes his glasses and massages the bridge of his nose with his thumb and forefinger. I clear my throat, but he doesn't hear me.

"Mr. Hedrick?" I say.

He jerks to attention and replaces his glasses. "Yes?"

"Hi. I'm Abby Lunde. I was assigned to your class."

"Oh yes!" Mr. Hedrick rifles through the mess of papers on his desk. "I just got your registration, Abby. Come in and choose a seat anywhere you'd like."

"Thank you." I select a seat toward the middle-back of the class.

Students trickle into the classroom—sometimes alone, but frequently in groups of twos and threes. Most of them look the same:

name-brand clothing, perfect hair, perfect makeup, perfect everything. I draw a breath and try not to hate them for representing what I no longer have—what I will probably never have again.

As closely as I'm studying them, I know they're doing the same to me. I pretend to ignore the way they look me over, wondering whether I'm worthy of their consideration then deciding not to put forth the effort to find out. The seats around me fill and I sit in the midst of them, invisible.

I open my notebook and doodle in the margins of a clean sheet. If I learned anything at my old school, it's the importance of confidence. In this caste system that is High-School Hell, confidence, or lack thereof, determines social placement, and I will never again allow myself to be a bottom dweller. Apparently, however, someone else has a different idea.

"You can't sit here."

The comment comes from a girl with beautiful long, straight, blond hair. She has the tiniest upturned nose, which matches her petite frame. Though barely five feet tall, she carries herself with the regal bearing of a queen. *Confidence.* This one will be at the top of the food chain. I give her a cursory glance then return my attention to my drawings.

"I said you can't sit here," she repeats. "Are you deaf?"

I finish filling in the three-dimensional box I've drawn, then lift an eyebrow and take her in from head to toe. "Says who?"

"Says me. This is my seat, and I always sit here."

"Well," I smile like I'm talking to a small child, "I was told to sit anywhere I liked. I like this seat."

A few students snigger but are cut off by a sharp glance from the girl in front of me.

"I don't think you understood me," she says. "You need to move."

Instinctively I know the next few moments will define my experience at this school. If I back down today, she'll think she can push me around forever. Been there, done that.

"Oh, I understood you fine." I draw another three-dimensional box. "Sit somewhere else, and you can have this one tomorrow."

"C'mon, Trish," says a pretty girl with auburn hair. "It's not worth it, and Hedrick will count us tardy if we're not in our seats when the bell rings."

"Screw Hedrick. I want this chair."

"You really should take another seat," I suggest. "I'm not moving, and I'd hate to see you counted tardy."

Behind her, Mr. Hedrick clears his throat. "I have to agree, Ms. Landry. Please have a seat. With your attitude, I'm thinking I might have a detention slip with your name on it."

Well played, Mr. Hedrick! I bite my lip to staunch my laughter at Trish's shocked expression.

"Mr. Hedrick! I—" Her jaw flaps open and closed.

"Yes, Ms. Landry?"

"Never mind." She storms off and sits three seats behind me. My first class and I've already made an enemy. What's next?

CHAPTER THREE

HISTORY WITH MR. HEDRICK IS FAR BETTER THAN I EXPECTED. RATHER THAN A TEDIOUS LECTURE FILLED with dates and places, he regales us with stories of historical figures as though retelling humorous anecdotes about old friends. Characters come to life, and I forget to take notes. I'm sitting on the edge of my seat, waiting to learn the ending of a particularly humorous tale he refers to as "The Misadventures of Guy Fawkes," when the bell rings. The entire class groans.

"Ah. Too bad," he says, his gray eyes sparkling with humor. "Guess you'll have to stay awake for another lecture tomorrow to see how it ends."

I smile for a brief second before Trish catches my attention. Her lips form a thin line, and the malice in her expression is unmistakable. She stares at me, daring me to look away first. When I refuse, she flips her long hair over her shoulder and graces me with an evil smile that says, "*Game on.*" If I wondered before, there can be no question now: I'm screwed.

My next class is chemistry with Ms. Burke. Finding the class quickly, I scan the room and discover I'm the second to arrive. The only other student is a tall boy seated near the back. His curly dark hair is a little on the long side, but it suits his boyish features. Peeking out from behind his long lashes are eyes the color of cornflowers. He's beautiful in a masculine way. Our eyes meet and he smiles, his expression open and approachable. I hesitate, hoping I haven't misunderstood his silent welcome, but since there's no one else to witness my humiliation if I'm wrong, I take the desk behind him.

I'm barely seated when he spins around and faces me. "Welcome to chaos. I'm Josh."

"I'm Abby." A smile teases my lips.

"You new to town, or just new to Rochester South?"

"Both, I guess."

"Figured. I've never seen you before." Josh shrugs. "But you could've transferred from one of the other high schools, I guess."

I'm saved from responding when Ms. Burke enters the room. The complete opposite of Mr. Hedrick, she's young with long, platinum-blond hair tipped in black. She wears faded jeans and an even more faded sweatshirt reading *Rochester South* in big gold letters across the front. If I didn't know better, I'd mistake her for a student, but she quickly takes command, erasing any doubt.

I'm not sure why, but I've always sucked at science. You'd think having a mom whose strengths are in math and science, I'd excel, but my strong subject is English. Maybe I take after the sperm donor who is my real dad—who knows? I just don't get science in the same way I do English. It's too bad, though, because I really like science. And I love how, in chemistry, different elements combine to become something completely new without any obvious traits of their origins. But despite how much I like the subject, my nerves are shot after my run-in with Trish and I know I'll never be able to concentrate. The truth is, it's not just Trish I'm worried about, though that tops my list. I'm also worried about how long it'll take us to find a place to live, and whether Mom will screw things up for us again before we do. And *then* there's this school and Trish. If there's one good thing about leaving Omaha, it's that I get a clean slate where nobody knows anything about me. Here, I can be anyone I want…or at least I could've before my exchange with Trish. I can't help wondering how much damage I've already done.

I'm lost in my own worries and miss the direction to move our desks into small groups. As the room erupts around me, I remain in my same position, confused at the disruption. Luckily, Josh is one step ahead and rotates his desk toward mine so I don't need to go anywhere, and maybe don't look as stupid as I feel.

"Wake up, Ariel." Josh snaps his fingers. "We're supposed to be in groups of twos and threes. Wanna be my partner?"

"Abby," I correct. "And I guess."

"You may be Abby, but you look like an Ariel with that red hair of yours."

My face flames. There's no malice in Josh's expression so I stutter out a thanks for what I hope is a compliment, and remind him again my name is Abby.

"If it's all the same to you, I'll just call you Ariel," he says.

And just like that, I have a new identity. I'm no longer Abby—social pariah of Omaha East High School. I'm Ariel, renamed by the weird guy in front of me.

"So what's your story?" Josh asks, skimming through the textbook for our assigned questions.

I think about making up a story, but I've never been a good liar, so I go with the truth. Or mostly the truth, anyway. "I don't have one. You?"

"Everybody has a story, Ariel. Where are you from?"

"Abby," I remind him again, but inside my stomach flutters at the nickname. "I'm from Omaha. We just moved here."

"Let me guess: your dad took a job with IBM or the Clinic." Josh rolls his eyes, as though he's heard this a thousand times.

"The Clinic?"

"Mayo Clinic. That's what we call it here." He makes air quotes with his fingers. "*The Clinic.*"

"Oh. No. He just wanted a change."

"Just like that?"

I snap my fingers. "Just like that."

"Huh. Go figure. So when's your lunch block?"

My stomach clenches. "Block A. I have lunch next. You?"

"Same. I'll walk you down there. You can eat with us."

Relief floods through me. I didn't realize how worried I was about lunch, but now I won't have to decide whether to eat alone or sit with Zach.

"So what about your parents?" I ask. "Where do they work?"

"IBM. They're both computer geeks."

Great—computer geeks. Translated, that means money, and a lot of it.

Our conversation stalls out as we complete our group assignment, then Josh staples the pages together and writes our names at the top of the first page. When he gets to mine, he writes, "Ariel."

I clear my throat. "It's *Abby*. You wrote Ariel."

Josh smiles. Leaving "Ariel" written on the paper, he writes "Abby" beside it in brackets. "That should suffice."

I laugh. "Is this going to be a problem for you—remembering my name, that is?"

"Nope—but you should probably get used to being called Ariel to avoid confusion."

Usually this kind of thing might irritate me, but Josh makes me laugh. Already I love that he's funny and not the least bit pretentious.

"C'mon," Josh says as the bell rings. "Let's head to the lunchroom and see what our esteemed nutrition specialists have created for us today."

"Should I be scared?"

"Very." Josh fakes a shiver of dread.

We approach the cafeteria and my mind races. First, I'm worried about whether my lunch account is set up properly with sufficient funds. The lady at registration promised Nick it would be and that nobody would know I'm on free lunch, but the fear of anyone finding out how poor we are is pervasive. Then there's just being in the cafeteria. I hate cafeterias, and I haven't eaten in one since midway through last school year. I just couldn't. I still don't know if I can. Instead, I spent most of my lunch periods hiding out in the school library. But this place is different. Nobody knows me here. I'm no longer Abby Lunde, I'm Ariel.

My stomach growls, reminding me I haven't eaten since the PB&J sandwich Mom gave us all for dinner last night. I steal a glance at Josh and he smothers a grin.

"Don't say a word!" I warn.

"What? Me?" Josh throws his hands up.

I lift an eyebrow and give him a stern glare, but his laughter makes it impossible to stay serious. My face breaks into its own stupid grin.

"Yeah—you need more practice, Ariel. You're way more Little Mermaid than Sea Witch." He laughs. "C'mon, let's get something to eat before someone mistakes you for a ravenous Simba."

Josh picks up two trays and hands one to me. "Now I know you're hungry, but go slow. The buffet looks really cool, but there are dangers hidden within." He wiggles his eyebrows.

I bump my shoulder against his. "Can you be serious for one minute?"

"I am serious." He waves a hand toward the various food lines like Vanna White presenting letters on *Wheel of Fortune*. In his best game-show-host voice he says, "Over here we have the salad line, and—if your dietary preferences run more toward the carnivorous variety—we offer a burger bar along the back wall on the right side. On the other side of that same wall is today's 'special,' but don't be fooled. The only thing 'special' about it is the hocus-pocus they did to make it look edible. Trust me when I say you're better off with a burger or salad."

I smother a giggle. "Thanks."

I choose the burger bar because it has the shortest line. I select a cheeseburger and add a container of tater tots to my tray.

Josh is waiting for me near the cash register next to a large refrigerator with a selection of fruit drinks and milk. Grabbing a bottle of apple juice, I smile at Josh and join him in line. Piled high on his tray is a small mountain of salad topped with enough croutons and cheese for three people.

"Would you like some salad with your cheese and croutons?" I tease.

He snorts. "Just playing it safe. You can't really ruin salad toppings when they just pour them out of a bag."

Josh hands his card to the woman at the register. In seconds, he's through the line and it's my turn.

"We're back in the far right corner. Round table." Josh nods toward the back of the cafeteria. "I'll save you a seat."

I nod, but my stomach churns and nausea overwhelms me. Where only minutes ago I was hungry, now I can think of only one thing: *Please let my card go through without a problem! Please don't let Josh find out I have no money for lunch.*

The cashier swipes my card and hands it back to me. Moments pass and the machine does nothing. She smiles awkwardly, but still the machine is silent as the seconds tick by.

"Could I have your card again, please?" the woman asks. "It didn't seem to register."

Sweat collects at the nape of my neck, and my hands shake. I hand over my card and she smiles before swiping it a second time. This time, it immediately beeps a confirmation. Relief rushes through me but I'm afraid I'll jumble my words if I speak, so I nod and search the room for Josh.

The cafeteria is packed with students, and it seems every eye is on me. With so many people, it takes me a moment to find Josh but I soon spot him, waving both hands to get my attention. I offer a weak smile, then carry my tray through the ocean of students toward a table where Josh waits beside two girls who are already seated and watching my approach.

I'm almost there when my attention is snagged by three girls to my right. I turn toward them, and they stare at me behind their hands as they giggle and talk to each other in hushed whispers. I can't hear their words, so my imagination takes flight. I have no reason to suspect so, but I know they're talking about me. My skin tingles and anxiety washes over me. I ignore them and continue toward Josh, but my steps are sluggish, as though I'm wading through thick mud. My heart thumps in my chest. The voices buzz around me, indistinct like the hum of bees in a hive. Dread washes over me. I've been here before.

SIX MONTHS EARLIER

"So, then…are we on for Saturday?" Sarah picks at the salad on her lunch tray. "I'll pick you guys up at seven thirty and we can catch the eight ten show."

"I can't," Emma says. "I'm babysitting for the Bendicksons."

"You're always babysitting," Sarah whines. "Can't you skip it this time?"

"I can't. I'm saving money for my prom dress. My mom is only giving me a hundred dollars, and the one I want is almost three times more. I have to make up the difference."

"What about a later show?" I suggest. "Or even Sunday?"

At that moment, our mobile phones ping at the same time—the unmistakable sound of an incoming Snapchat. I take a bite of my pizza then pick up my phone to see what I've been sent. It's a Snap from Alicia, which surprises me. I don't even know why we're on each other's Snapchats. She's hated me since I took her spot on cheerleading squad two years ago, but it's been worse since she failed my mom's AP math class last semester. Like somehow that's my fault. I can't help it if my mom's a teacher, and Alicia is a stupid twit who can't do the coursework. I consider ignoring the Snap, but curiosity won't let me. I touch my finger to the icon and bring up the image.

At first, what I'm seeing doesn't register. The photo is grainy, as though taken at night without a flash. A man and woman stand together, entangled in an intimate embrace. The woman's peach silk blouse is unbuttoned nearly to the navel…and just like that, the image disappears. I touch the icon a second time and the image returns. The woman's white lace bra is nearly covered by the man's large hand as he caresses her through its fabric. Their lips are locked together and I study their faces. Just as recognition sets in, the image disappears again. Frantic now, I touch the icon a third time, hoping to bring it back up—to prove to myself I didn't see what I know I saw. But the image is gone, forever lost in the cybersphere.

Bile rushes from my stomach and I grit my teeth to keep from throwing up. My skin prickles and my head spins. I need to get out of here. I turn to Emma and Sarah with the intent of excusing myself, but am met by two sets of wide eyes, both holding a combination of shock and sympathy.

Emma's mouth opens and closes, but no sound comes out. Sarah, on the other hand, has never been at a loss for words. In a too-loud voice, she says, "Your mom and Coach Hawkins? Did you know?"

My head shakes back and forth in denial—not only at what I've just seen, but that I could ever have known anything about it. My mom—everyone's favorite math teacher—with our high school's football coach. How could they?

Voices hum around me, but I can't make out their words. I can't tell if it's because the words are indistinct, or because I can't hear past the buzzing in my ears. I glance across the cafeteria and almost every set of eyes is on me. Boys send me sly grins that say, "Well, this is an interesting development," while girls whisper behind hands thrown in front of their faces. Only a few people are out of the loop, but they're smart enough to understand something big is going down.

Alicia Fucking Adams. She sent the Snap to almost the entire junior class!

"DAYDREAMING AGAIN, ARIEL?" Josh stands beside me, yanking me back to the present.

"Sorry," I laugh, but the sound is forced. "I just had a weird moment of déjà vu."

"Oh man! I hate that! They give me the creeps." Josh moves back to his table and I follow, the memory of another day and time still racing through my head. He stops at a round table where two other girls are waiting. Like everyone else in the room, they watch me. They don't look *un*friendly, but their curiosity is palpable. I approach the table, then remain standing for a moment as I decide what to do.

Josh rolls his eyes. "Sit down already, Ariel."

"Abby." I sigh and place my tray on the table.

"Oh no! He's done it again!" says the girl closest to Josh.

"Quiet, Tink." Josh grins.

My eyes flash between them. *Tink?*

I study "Tink" and comprehension sets in. With her petite stature, perky upturned nose and pixie haircut, she's the embodiment of Tinker Bell from *Peter Pan*. Weird!

"Have a seat," laughs the girl on the other side of Tink. "Josh has this habit of naming his 'harem' the names of Disney characters. Bet you can't guess who I'm supposed to be."

I study the girl, taking in her long sable hair and almond-shaped eyes the color of burnt umber. Of Middle-Eastern descent, there can be no doubt. I groan. "Jasmine?" I guess, referring to the character from Disney's *Aladdin*.

"Bingo!" Josh confirms.

"Well, if *I'm* Ariel and *they're* Tink and Jasmine, who does that make *you*—Flounder, Mr. Smee, or Abu the monkey?"

Tink barely has time to snort out a laugh when, beside her, blue Gatorade sprays out of Jasmine's nose as she tries to swallow her laughter and her drink at the same time.

"Oh, my God," the Jasmine lookalike gasps, wiping droplets of blue liquid from her nose. "I'm totally calling Iago the parrot for Josh!"

Josh smothers a grin and puffs out his chest. "All right you three, enough. If you must know, I'm the master creator, Walt Disney himself."

"Bullshit," the Tink lookalike coughs into her napkin, earning another round of laughter from everyone but Josh.

"Jasmine" smiles and reaches her hand across the table to shake mine. "I'm Tera. And Tink over here is Wendy."

Just as my hand reaches Tera's, the absurdity hits me and I slap my other hand over my mouth to hide my laughter. "Tink's real name is Wendy? As in Wendy Darling from *Peter Pan*? Wasn't that already Disney enough for you, Josh?"

Josh flushes. "Doesn't Ariel lose her voice in the movie?"

Once again, the three of us burst into a round of laughter. And just like that, the memories and heartache of another lifetime are momentarily erased. Already in just a few hours, I've laughed more today than I have in the last six months.

"So—" I clear my throat. "Do people actually call you by your princess names?"

"No way!" Tera says, her eyes horrified. "Only Josh, thank God. I'd die if anyone else called me Jasmine."

"I can't call you Jasmine?"

The voice comes from behind my right shoulder and the hairs on the back of my neck stand straight up. I don't have to turn around to know who it is. Strangely, I'd already recognize that voice anywhere: Zach. Only a few hours into the day and I already know his voice. This is not good. This is *really* not good.

"Hey, Abby…Josh…*Tink*." Zach grins.

"Ugh!" Wendy rolls her eyes.

"Just kidding, Wen." Zach winks at Wendy, his bright smile almost flirting, then turns to me. "Hey, Abby—I thought you were gonna find me at lunch."

"I'm sorry. Josh was in my last class, so I came down with him," I explain.

"No worries. Another time."

"Sure," I say, but I know better. There won't be another time because I can't let there be. If the pounding of my heart is any indication, I need to keep my distance. It's one thing to make new friends based upon lies, but I can't risk throwing a broken heart into the mix. And Zach Andrews has heartbreak etched all over him.

"Okay, then. I'd better get back to my table. I'll catch you guys around," he says.

He returns to a round table in the middle of the room and sits next to none other than Trish. Beside her is the same girl she was with earlier, along with a posse of preppy rich kids. Trish's eyes meet mine and the malice extends across the distance.

"So…" Josh says. "Zach Andrews, huh?"

"What?" I shrug, hoping he'll let the subject drop. "He was in the office when I registered this morning, and Ms. Raven had him show me around. He seems nice."

"Yeah? Well, be careful. He's actually a really nice guy, but his ex-girlfriend is toxic."

"Who's his ex-girlfriend?"

"See the blonde next to him, shooting daggers at us?" Tera asks.

"Shooting daggers at Abby," Wendy corrects.

"Yeah. She was in my history class. Trish something." I shrug again.

"Landry," Wendy supplies. "She's a real witch. Her daddy's a neurosurgeon at the Clinic and they're super rich. They live out on Pill Hill and she lords it over everyone."

"Pill Hill?" I ask.

"It's the nickname for the housing development where a lot of doctors live. It's a really expensive neighborhood with large, older homes," Tera explains.

"Yup. And it looks like you've already made an enemy of her on your first day." Josh throws an arm around my shoulders. "Nice work, Ariel. It takes most people at least a few days to make an enemy of Trish."

Groaning, I steal another glance at Zach's table. I can't catch a break. Not even half a day at my new school, and already I've made an enemy of Miss Popularity.

CHAPTER FOUR

AFTER LUNCH, I HAVE AN OPEN PERIOD. I
DON'T KNOW ANYONE, SO I MAKE MY WAY TOWARD DOOR SIX
where I remember a large open area with vending machines and high-top
tables. This place is as good as anywhere, I figure. I select a table and pull
out my history homework. In no time, I shut out the world and focus on
the work at hand. It seems like only minutes later when the bell rings for
the next period. I check my schedule: *Vocal Music, Room 1-421*. I study
my map, then set off in what I hope is the right direction.

My teacher, Mrs. Miner, is older than I expected. She wears a pair
of gold granny glasses connected to a beaded chain around her neck,
and her dark brown skin is flawless except for the smattering of freckles
kissing her cheekbones. Something about those freckles brings warmth
to her features, but it's the laugh lines that pull me in. When she smiles,
those tiny wrinkles wink at me from the outer edges of both eyes.

"Abby Lunde!" She greets me with a wide smile. "Welcome! Tell me
about yourself, please."

Standing at the front of the room, I glance around to see who's watching. Students enter from doors located on each side of the large classroom, but they're all focused on their own conversations and don't spare
me a glance. I offer her a tentative smile. "What would you like to know?"

"Tell me about your singing experience."

"I don't really have any."

"Sure ya do! All of us have sung in the shower, or while driving, when nobody's listening," she prompts.

"Well, sure. I mean, who doesn't sing in the shower? But I've never sung in front of anyone except my family."

"Well there ya go—that counts. I knew you had a singer inside you!" Her smile is contagious, and a grin teases the corners of my own lips. "I'll tell ya what: don't think, just answer. Name the first children's song that comes to your mind."

I flounder for the title of *any* song then blurt out, "'Twinkle Twinkle Little Star'?"

"Perfect!" Mrs. Miner beams. "Now, in your best singing voice, sing it to me."

Heat floods my face and my pulse quickens. I scan the room, confirming again that no one is paying attention.

"Don't be shy—just a few notes."

I clear my throat and close my eyes. Like a toddler, I pretend if I can't see them they can't see me. I know it's silly, but it's the only way I'll get through the next few seconds. Tentatively, and with just enough volume that only she can hear, I sing the first several measures of the nursery rhyme. I finish and open my eyes to Mrs. Miner's beaming smile.

"Very nice, Abby. Why, your voice is as lovely as a nightingale's! You'll be perfect for my alto section." She points to a middle row where four other girls are seated and deep in conversation.

My face flushes hot and I select one of three open chairs and smile at the girl seated closest. She returns my smile, but her welcome is tentative and she continues her conversation as though I don't exist. Invisible, I can do.

Vocal music class is far better than I'd imagined. The music is fun and our voices blend together seamlessly until I can't tell where my voice ends and the others begin. In minutes, my anxiety disappears and I'm lost in the music.

Though Mrs. Miner is strict, with a no-nonsense approach to teaching, she's fun. Her demeanor is warm and animated, like she loves what she's doing. She loses her smile only once, and then only after asking the same two girls in the soprano section to pay attention.

"Stop-stop-stop!" She slaps her conductor's wand onto the podium. Her lips draw downward. "Star and Brook-Lynn, since you seem to require our complete attention, we'll stop and give you the consideration you've denied the rest of us. Please put us out of our misery and tell us what y'all two find so amusing."

"Nothing, Mrs. Miner," one of the girls responds, her voice practically a whisper. "We're sorry."

"No, really—please. I'm sorry for interrupting your conversation with my class. It's your turn. Enlighten us."

Students giggle, and the second girl flushes crimson. A heavy silence settles over the room while we wait.

Mrs. Miner lifts an eyebrow. "Are you done now, ladies?"

"Yes, ma'am," they reply in unison.

"Good. Then for the remainder of class, I suggest you two quit your dipsy-doodlin' and humbuggin' and work with me. Otherwise, you'll need to find another class."

At the words *dipsy-doodlin'* and *humbuggin'*, the class roars with laughter. Star and Brook-Lynn stare at spots on the floor, their eyes not meeting each other or Mrs. Miner.

"All right, y'all!" Mrs. Miner claps her hands. "Pay attention! We have a concert comin' up. Don't make me have to give all y'all detention so we can make up after school what you didn't accomplish in class!"

The class quiets and she continues without further interruption. Before long, the bell rings and students fly out of their chairs to leave.

"Okay, y'all. The Fall Concert is November eleventh," Mrs. Miner announces above the commotion. "Attendance is required, so don't y'all tell me later you forgot! Mark your calendars and tell your parents—participation counts toward your final grades."

I enter the hallway and check my schedule for my last class—English with Mr. Thompson. It's not far away and I'm one of the first to arrive. I scan the room for a seat and spot Zach in the middle row, his backpack slung into the chair in front of him. My heart flutters, but I pretend I don't see him. It's too late, though—he's already seen me.

"Abby. I saved you a seat." He waves to the desk in front of him and removes his backpack.

"Oh. Thanks. How'd you know I was in here?"

"I saw your schedule this morning, remember?"

"Oh, yeah. But you didn't say anything."

He shrugs. "I didn't think about it."

I slide into the desk and grab a notebook out of my bag.

"So what do you think?" he asks.

"About what?"

"The school. Your classes. Everything."

"Oh." I squint my eyes in thought. "The school is huge, but the layout makes everything easy to find. My classes are decent—and you were right! I love Mrs. Miner."

"She's great, isn't she?"

I nod. "You couldn't fit her class into your schedule?"

"Nah, and I was bummed. She's the reason I learned guitar. She needed a guitarist for the Fall Concert my freshman year and she loaned me one to learn on. Did you catch her accent?"

"How could I miss it?" I laugh. "What the heck are *dipsy-doodlin'* and *humbuggin'*?"

"Right?" He laughs. "Wait until you hear some of her other favorite phrases."

"Where's she from? Not Minnesota, with that accent."

"Nope." Zach shakes his head. "Oklahoma, I think. At least she's a Sooners fan."

"So how long did you take guitar lessons?" I ask, changing the subject.

"I taught myself, actually."

29

"Really?" I lift a surprised eyebrow. "Do you still play?"

"Every chance I get."

Before we can say more, the bell rings. I turn face-forward as our teacher enters the room.

At roughly thirty-five, Mr. Thompson wears chunky, black-rimmed glasses, and has wavy brown hair combed neatly to the side. Similar to Ms. Burke, he's dressed casually in jeans and a Green Bay Packers sweatshirt.

"Mr. T!" says a blond boy in the front. "The Packers? Seriously? The Vikes are gonna take 'em down this weekend!"

"Oh yeah?" Mr. Thompson smiles. "They're gonna wake up from their nap and finally play a game?"

"Burn!" shouts another kid.

The next several minutes are a pandemonium of ribbing between Mr. Thompson and fans of the Minnesota Vikings. At the center, he deflects barbs and dishes them out in equal measure.

"Okay—okay, enough." He laughs, but his voice holds a note of authority. "We'll continue this discussion next week after my Packers kill the Vikings. Right now we have to start class. With a show of hands, how many of you have read *To Kill a Mockingbird*?"

Only a few hands are raised.

"Okay, then." He raises an eyebrow. "How many of you were *supposed* to read it at some point and didn't?"

This time, nearly every hand rises.

"Good to know." He smiles.

Mr. Thompson weaves through the aisles of desks, passing out copies of the book as he goes. "I realize most of you were assigned this title in eighth grade English, but it's clear most of you also ditched the reading part."

A few students chuckle.

"Over the next several weeks, we'll study it again—this time more closely. We'll examine the lessons Harper Lee gives to readers. Among those are themes of compassion, courage, understanding, and forgiveness. Life lessons, if you will.

"At the end of this section, you'll select one character and write a paper outlining the lessons you've learned from that character. You'll need to identify what those lessons are and how you can apply them in your own lives. Because you're seniors—which implies you have a higher level of understanding than you had a few years ago—I'll expect more than a regurgitation, or retelling, of the story. I'll want to know what you *think*—not what you think I want to hear, but how you *feel* about what you've read. You'll need to know your character so well you can anticipate how he or she might react to various situations. Basically, I'll expect you to know your character as well as you know yourself."

All around me, students groan.

"Okay, okay—enough grumbling. Here's the good news: any student who gets an A will be excused from the final exam at semester's end. Any questions?"

Mr. Thompson glances around the room, making eye contact with each student. Satisfied, he nods. "Okay. You have the rest of this period to get started. Your assignment is to read the first five chapters and be ready to discuss them tomorrow. I'll expect active participation from each of you. Remember: the only wrong answers are those not given, and I'll deduct points from anyone who fails to contribute to our discussion. So get started."

The room is silent, the only sound that of pages crackling as they turn. I study the book's cover, smoothing my fingers over the title and cover art. I've loved this book since the first time I read it years ago. My mind flashes back to the bookcase I left behind. Where is it now? Have my favorite books been given to someone who will love them as I have, or did the landlord dump them in some landfill? I cringe. I left my copy of *To Kill a Mockingbird* on the second shelf, right between copies of

Harry Potter and the Sorcerer's Stone and *Eleanor and Park,* the pages of each novel well-worn and their covers showing the abuse of overuse that stands as a beacon of pride for every well-loved novel.

I look at the copy in my hands, its cover smooth and barely used. Compared to the one on my bookshelf, it looks sad—neglected by those who didn't understand its value. I flip to the first page and savor the first words.

"When he was nearly thirteen my brother Jem got his arm badly broken at the elbow."

Just like that, I'm swallowed into the world of Scout Finch, her brother, Jem, and their summer friend, Dill. A half hour later, I'm so completely absorbed that I resent the bell signaling the end of the school day. Tearing off a piece of notebook paper, I place it between the pages then sling my bag over my back. A rogue hand waves inches from my nose, startling me.

"Earth to Abby." Zach grins.

"I'm sorry?" I offer a distracted smile. "Did you say something?"

"I asked how far you got."

"Oh—almost three chapters. You?"

"Just two. Have you read it before?"

"Yeah." I blush. "A few times at least."

"At least?" He laughs.

"Well, yeah. It's sorta my favorite book."

Zach's forehead creases. "Why?"

"Have you read it yet?" I ask as we enter the hallway.

"Nope. It was assigned in eighth grade, but I never got around to it."

"Then you have no idea what you're missing. Give it a chance. I bet you'll love it." I look up to smile at Zach, but my blood runs cold. Trish is walking straight toward us.

"Hey, Zach." She ignores me and sidles up next to him, weaving an arm through his like she owns him.

Anger colors my vision. For a few short minutes, I allowed myself to feel normal—to forget that nothing will ever be normal again.

"Hey, Trish. Have you met Abby?" Zach asks.

"Um…" She eyes me up and down then turns her attention back to Zach. "Yeah. We have history together."

"Oh, that's right," he says. "I forgot you were in there."

I wish I could forget she's in there.

I tilt my lips in a smile and turn it full-force on Zach. "I gotta run. My little sister is waiting for me. Catch up with you later?"

"Sure," he says. "I'll see you tomorrow."

"Later," Trish coos.

Anger burns inside me and I rush away before I explode. I leave the building and step into the student parking lot where I'm brought up short by an SUV parked about twenty feet in front of me. The vehicle is empty, but what catches my attention is the window paint covering the glass.

Happy Birthday, Kannon!
Happy 18th!
Finally legal!

Other kids might find this flattering, but I can't. The hairs on my neck prickle and, despite the cool outside air, sweat trickles between my breasts. My breath comes in short gasps, and I can't get enough oxygen into my lungs. I try to turn away, but I can't. All I can do is stare at the car in front of me and remember…

FIVE MONTHS EARLIER

I wander down the quiet halls of my high school alone. I'm alone a lot these days. Each day I arrive early and hide in the library until first bell, and return at day's end until the building is mostly empty. It's easier this way and Mrs. Stephenson, the school librarian, doesn't mind. She and Mom were good friends in that period of time I refer to as BS—Before Snapchat. Since then, though, I'm not sure Mom has any friends left. I sure as hell don't—even Emma and Sarah have bailed. They stuck around for a while, but what's that saying about your friends being a representation of yourself? Yeah—neither of them wanted anything to do with me after Mom's scandal. Just like I'm guilty by association with Mom, Emma and Sarah were guilty by association with me. So they left me to fend for myself.

If there's one positive, it's that I don't have to run into Mom at school anymore. When the school board learned about the Snapchat, she and Coach Hawkins were given the "opportunity" to resign. I don't know where he went, but I sure as hell know where Mom is. Right now she's probably sitting at home, scanning the newspapers for a job. What does she think is going to happen? Does she really think people will forget? There's no chance in hell she'll get a teaching job anywhere near here, and nobody else wants a woman who's spent the last fifteen years in the classroom. At this point, I don't even care what she does anymore.

I run the steps from the third floor to the first, then fast-walk to the student parking lot and my outdated Jeep Liberty. The lot is almost empty and, like me, my Jeep stands friendless. I'm about ten feet away when I notice both driver-side tires are flat. My shoulders deflate—I should've expected this. My life has been one big practical joke since that afternoon in the cafeteria. I scan for more damage. As I take in the full picture, my hands shake and my backpack falls to the pavement. It's not just two flat tires, but all four of them—slashed. As if that isn't enough, red window paint covers every inch of the glass with the words, WHORE and SLUT.

"YOU OKAY?"

A hand touches my shoulder, and I swipe at the hot tears racing down my cheeks. I must look like an idiot, crying in a parking lot over someone's car.

"Abby, right?" the voice says.

I swipe again at my eyes then smile up into the concerned brown eyes of Mr. Thompson. I hiccup a laugh. "I'm sorry—I'm fine. Really—I feel stupid. I was just missing my friends. At my old school, ya know? It just sorta hit me all of a sudden."

He smiles. "Ah, yes. It's hard leaving friends behind. Were you at your old school long?"

"My whole life."

"Even harder," he sympathizes. "But how was your first day here? Were the kids good to you?"

"They were great," I say, excluding Trish from the equation. "I think I'll like it here."

He nods. "Good deal. Well, if you're okay, I'll see you tomorrow. Don't forget your *Mockingbird* homework."

"Not a chance," I reply.

He crosses the parking lot and waves as he leaves, but I stand there staring at the window-painted SUV, remembering.

CHAPTER FIVE

AMBER'S SCHOOL IS ONLY A FEW BLOCKS AWAY
AND I ARRIVE WITH TIME TO SPARE. I TAKE A SEAT IN A
chair next to an Asian woman holding a toddler in her arms. The little
guy can't be older than two, but his bright eyes shine with intelligence
and interest. He peers into my green eyes, and I have the sensation he's
trying to discover all my secrets. He pulls his fingers out of his mouth
and reaches his hand toward me, but his mom catches his slobber-cov-
ered fingers and rescues my face from his saliva. She smiles apologeti-
cally, but I give her a smile I hope says, "*It's okay—no apology needed.*"

At exactly three thirty, the bell pierces the silence and the foyer becomes a buzz of activity. Classroom doors are thrown open and students
race into the hallways, eager to escape the school's prison-like walls.

I'm not sure where Amber will emerge, so I'm stationed near the
front doors, forcing her to pass me to get outside. I wait while children
of different sizes rush by, none of them Amber. When I'm about to give
up, I catch sight of her blond head bobbing along behind three boys who
block her path. Our eyes meet and I don't need to see her grin to know
she's happy. She's one of those people whose smile starts with her eyes. I
let out a relieved breath and smile back.

"How was school?" I ask when she stands in front of me.

"Fun! Mrs. Ekman's really nice, and I have a new boyfriend."

"A boyfriend? You're in first grade!"

"I can't help it." She shrugs and beams a toothless grin. "I'm irresistible."

"Uh-huh," I say.

"So where're we going?"

"To the library. Mom and Nick will get us in a couple hours. Do you have homework?"

"Nope."

"Okay, but I do. You can pick out a few books and read quietly while I do mine. Deal?"

"Deal." She holds up a fist and I bump my knuckles against hers.

Amber walks beside me through the parking lot, down the residential streets, and onto the main sidewalk leading to the library. We've barely gone three blocks when she falls behind, her stride now a bizarre sort of hop-walk.

"What are you doing?" I ask.

She frowns. "My toes are squooshed and it hurts to walk."

I blow out a breath of irritation—not at Amber, but on her behalf. Once again, this is Mom's fault. Everything that has brought us to our current situation is part of the spiraling effect of her selfish actions. Mom's affair meant losing her job. Losing her job meant less money for the things we need. And right now Amber needs new shoes. Six-year-olds have a right to shoes that fit!

"Let's sing," I suggest. "It'll make the walk seem faster."

"Can you carry me? Please?"

I breathe in and out to a count of five. Amber weighs roughly fifty pounds and we still have at least another mile to go. If I carry her today, it's a sure bet I'll have to carry her every day. But how can I not? I squat low and put my hands on my knees. "Jump on. I'll carry you until you get too heavy, then you gotta get down. Deal?"

"Will you still sing?"

"Only if you sing with me."

"Deal!" Amber climbs on my back and wraps her arms and legs around my shoulders and waist. When she's firmly anchored, I stand upright and begin walking.

"Okay, then. What're we singing?" I ask.

"How about that song about being free?"

"'We Shall Be Free?'"

"Yeah, that one."

I smile and ruffle Amber's hair. "You're a weird kid, ya know that? You're probably the only six-year-old in the world who even knows who Garth Brooks is, much less a song that old—it's older than I am."

Amber grins. "I learned it from the best!"

I smile down at her, remembering how Nick likes to jack up the stereo to some of the best classic country and rock music—Garth Brooks, George Strait, Johnny Cash, The Beatles, Led Zeppelin, Queen…

"Okay, then. Garth Brooks it is." I belt out the first few bars and Amber's voice joins mine. Together we sing for the next full block then segue into Queen's "Bohemian Rhapsody."

There's no doubt Amber's heavy, but sometimes you have to pick your battles. She's content, so I carry her until two blocks from the library then set her down to walk on her own.

THE ROCHESTER PUBLIC Library is surprisingly busy, with a steady stream of people going in and out its doors. It's larger than expected and I gape at its size. It might be similar in size to our local library in Omaha, but the high ceilings and glass windows around the front side make it feel cavernous.

On the main floor, between the front desk and the children's section, are two rooms located side by side. The first is enclosed in glass walls and features a bank of computers nestled between private carrels. The sign above the door glows with neon letters reading, "Teens." Next door, in another room also enclosed by glass walls, is an arts and crafts room clearly intended for use by children. The two rooms are close enough that I can supervise Amber while doing my homework. This won't be so bad after all.

"Check this out." I point to the arts and crafts room. "Would you rather create or read for a while?"

Amber's eyes light up. "Create!"

"Okay. I'll be in the room next door. Don't go anywhere else, and find me if you need something. Mom and Nick shouldn't be too long."

I leave Amber and find a carrel in the media room next door. I enjoy the room's quiet emptiness for a moment, then pull out the school's copy of *To Kill a Mockingbird* from my backpack. Alone with no distractions, I'm fully immersed in the world of Scout Finch when, what seems like only seconds later, I catch a glimpse of Nick from the corner of my eye. I wave, drawing his attention. He approaches the media room and leans through the doorway.

"Hey," he whispers. "Where's Amber?"

I nod in the direction of the craft room. "Next door."

"Okay—grab her and let's head out. Your mom's waiting in the van."

CHAPTER SIX

"WHERE'RE WE GOING NOW?" I ASK, CLOSING
THE VAN'S DOOR ON MY SIDE.

"Dinner." Nick says. "While you were at school, your mom and I
stopped by the Salvation Army to check out the services they provide.
We're headed back there now for their free dinner. It's first come, first
served so we need to get there early."

"Okay, then what?"

"We have a lot to discuss," Mom interrupts. "Let's get there and we
can talk while we eat."

I'm anxious to know what they discovered, but I bide my time. We
arrive before the doors open and wait near the head of the line. Behind
us, the line grows and extends down the main hall and around a corner. I
wonder where it ends, and whether it continues all the way outside. I'm
surprised at the number of people. How are there so many?

At exactly six p.m. the doors open and we advance to a short assembly line where volunteers serve food. I assess the tray I'm handed:
noodles in some kind of cream sauce with pinkish-brown meat mixed in,
peas, and a hard dinner roll. I can't tell the origin of the mystery meat,
but I'm too embarrassed to ask the server. I guess I'll find out.

"Is there any butter?" Mom asks a volunteer.

"We're out. Sorry," she says with a sympathetic smile.

Mom nods her thanks and follows Nick to a table near the back
of the room. I sit beside Amber and discreetly study the people around

me. The room holds the distinct scent of unwashed bodies and, while the odor itself doesn't surprise me, I'm shocked at the variety of people assembled. I've always imagined homeless people as unkempt vagrants in rags. What I find, instead, is a collection of people who look like us—normal.

At the end of our table, four elderly women huddle together in quiet conversation. Though their clothing is as aged as their wrinkled skin, their appearances are neat and tidy. They don't look homeless, exactly—just tired, maybe, and a little defeated. At the next table is a girl about my age. Her hair is dyed blue and is pulled into a messy bun on top of her head. She wears a Minnesota Wild hockey T-shirt that's seen better days, and she holds an infant in her arms. The baby nurses at his mother's breast from under a bunched-up edge of her T-shirt, and part of me is shocked. I know breastfeeding is natural, and it's not like the girl is flashing anyone. It's just that I've never seen it done in public. I should look away, but part of me is fascinated. The girl, however, seems too tired to care so she feeds her baby while navigating a fork to her mouth, careful not to spill food on her child. She chews as though savoring the meal and, except for her baby, she's alone.

It strikes me that—besides Amber, the girl, her baby, and me—there are no other kids here. It's weird and I want to ask someone about it, but I don't know who or what I'd say, so I file the question away.

My gaze flits around the room and lands on seven adults eating together. Though they sit side by side with shoulders nearly touching, they don't speak. They must know each other—why else would they sit so closely together when there are other tables?—yet they don't interact at all. I wonder what their stories are. Why sit together, but not share conversation?

To my left, a glass falls to the floor and shatters. An old man sits alone at a long table, his long gray hair hanging in matted dreadlocks around his shoulders. His skin is smudged with filth, and his clothing is nothing more than thin rags hanging off his skeletal frame. He rocks in his seat, his eyes dashing around the room. A volunteer with a dustpan and broom steps close, and the man lets out a high-pitched screech. His eyes widen and he whispers to himself, his rotting teeth now biting the nails on his fingers. Like with the nursing mom, I know I should look away, but I can't. He seems so pathetic sitting there all alone. My stomach drops—as bad as I think my life is, his looks so much worse.

The rest of the room is filled with people who look *normal*—reasonably groomed, though clearly struggling. While there are some grizzled vagrants, most aren't too different from me. My face burns and my fingertips tingle with mortification.

"Hey, Abby? You with us?" Mom nudges me.

"Yeah. Sorry," I say. "I just—I was just thinking."

Nick throws me a curious look then picks up the conversation where he left off. "So we have a few options, but it may take time. The Dorothy Day House will take us for two weeks, but they're full right now."

"The Dorothy Day House?" I ask.

"Ah. You're back with us," Nick teases. "The Dorothy Day House is a homeless shelter. If we can get in there, we'll have a place to sleep at night, then we have to leave by nine o'clock each morning. They serve a dinner at night and breakfast in the morning. For lunch, we're allowed to pack our own from what's available in the kitchen. They close the doors from nine to three thirty, and we're supposed to use that time to find jobs."

"What kind of jobs?" I narrow my eyes. "Mom is *not* going back to teaching—not at my school!"

"No." Mom's voice is strained and she looks irritated, as though she is having to explain something to someone who doesn't understand English. "I can't go back to teaching. Not yet anyway. I don't have a Minnesota license, and we don't have the money for me to get one right now. And until we get a cell phone, I can't even substitute teach. With my background, though, I thought I'd look at preschools. It'd be a pay cut, but it's a foot in the door and might help me make connections in the community until I can update my license."

I roll my eyes and my chest tightens with anger. How dare she get angry with *me*! How *dare* she treat me like *I'm* the immature one! It was *her* immaturity—*her* thoughtless and selfish actions—that got us here in the first place!

"Yes, Mother," I bite back. "I am painfully aware of *your* situation."

Nick pinches the bridge of his nose with two fingers and breathes out a long sigh. I'm pushing too hard, so I close my eyes and level my voice into a more conciliatory tone. "So how long until we can get into the…um….Daphne Day House?"

"*Dorothy Day*," Nick corrects. "And hopefully by next week. There are several people whose time is up soon, so maybe as early as Monday or Tuesday."

"So what do we do until then?"

"For now, we sleep in the van. It could be worse," Mom offers, reticent.

I ignore her and direct my next question to Nick. "What about showers? I'm gonna need to wash my hair, and we'll all start smelling soon if we don't bathe."

"We've got that figured out, too," Mom interjects. "Walmart has two family bathrooms with locking doors. We should be able to use the sinks to wash our hair and take sponge baths. That's the best we can do for now. If we're quiet and move quickly, we shouldn't get caught."

"But I don't wanna sleep in the van again," Amber cries. "I wanna go home."

"Honey, we can't go home," Nick says. "This won't last forever, but it's the best we have right now."

"How're we doing on money?" I interrupt.

"We're okay for now, but we have to spend carefully," Nick says. "You girls will get free breakfast and lunch at school, and your mom and

I will get by on PB&J sandwiches until dinner. We'll eat here on week-nights and Sundays. On Saturdays, the Presbyterian Church downtown offers a free meal. We won't starve at least."

I nod. "And laundry?"

"We have enough clothes to see us through a week, then we'll find a laundromat on the weekends," Mom says. "We'll only wash what we have to, so be careful and plan to wear your clothes at least twice."

I scowl at the idea of wearing dirty clothes, but keep my mouth closed.

After dinner, we return to Walmart. Nick parks between two other vans and turns off the engine. We sit quietly for several moments, each lost in our own thoughts.

"Now what're we gonna do?" Amber asks, breaking the silence.

"Why don't we check out the bathrooms and wash up?" Mom suggests.

The last thing I want is to bathe in a Walmart bathroom, but I snatch a tiny bottle of shampoo from Mom's offered hand and toss it into my backpack along with a towel and a washrag.

"Where'd you get the shampoo?" I ask.

"The Salvation Army gave us some provisions to get by," Mom says.

I nod, all kinds of snarky comebacks flying through my brain, but I stomp them down. I'm too tired and just want to get this experience over with.

Together we walk into Walmart, where Nick grabs a cart and pushes it down the aisles. We follow, but none of us places anything into the basket. After awhile, Mom taps my elbow, indicating I should follow. Out loud she says, "Let's go find the bathroom, Amber. It's been a while since you've gone."

To Amber's credit, she doesn't argue but takes Mom's hand and we leave Nick standing in the sporting goods aisle. I assume they've planned this in advance, and Nick will meet back up with us.

Mom leads us to one of two family bathrooms and locks the door. Along one wall are two toilets: a regular-sized one for adults, and a small one for children beside it. Mom flips the faucets on to warm the water, then pulls a large plastic bowl from her backpack and hands it to me.

"What do you want me to do with this?" I ask.

"Use it to rinse your hair, then we'll fill it with water for sponge baths," she explains.

I hate admitting it, but the bowl is a brilliant idea. In no time, we're bathed and ready to leave the bathroom.

"Here." Mom holds out a fleece hat. "Put this on."

"I'm fine," I say, ignoring her and heading toward the exit door.

Mom huffs out an angry breath. "*Why must you argue everything?* It's to hide your wet hair. We can't very well hide the fact we've just bathed in here if we walk out with wet hair. Put it on."

"Whatever." I catch the hat Mom tosses in my direction and tuck my long hair under it, hiding my ginger locks from view. I glance in the mirror to check for stray strands of hair. When we're ready, we step out of the bathroom and head to the van, where Nick will join us.

"I'M COLD," AMBER whines.

"Scoot closer and we can share our warmth," Mom says.

We're settled down for our second night in the van and, though we're all exhausted, none of us can sleep. Besides the bright light streaming through the windows, it's also colder than last night.

"It's only early October," I mumble. "We haven't even seen cold yet."

"That's enough, Abby," Mom scolds.

"It's true, though. Why are you yelling at me? Amber's right—it's friggin' cold and it's only gonna get worse. What'll happen in November or December when it *really* gets cold?"

"We'll have something figured out by then. In the meantime, I'm still your mother and you will *not* use that tone of voice with me. I don't ask much of you, but I expect your respect."

I snort out a bitter laugh. "Respect? You've got to be kidding! How much respect did you give us—give *Nick*—when—"

"Enough, Abby. Not another word." Nick's voice cuts right through me.

"Seriously, Nick? You're going to defend her after—"

"I said enough, and I meant it. It's over. Your mother's apologized countless times. We have to move on if we're going to get through this."

"But—"

"No buts, Abby. If you still need to get this off your chest tomorrow, we can. But we'll find an appropriate place and time. Now is neither, and you know why."

I glance down at Amber, who stares at me with wide eyes, taking in every word. He's right. Now isn't the time. If any of us escaped Mom's humiliation unscathed, it's Amber, and it's unfair to discuss something in front of her she can't understand.

"Fine," I say quietly.

For the next five minutes, the van is silent but the air is thick with anger and unsaid words. I lie beside Amber, seething over everything I wish I could say, when her tiny hand finds mine.

"I love you, Sister," she whispers.

And just like that, my anger lessens and my heart aches with a raw intensity. I look down into Amber's huge blue eyes and smile behind tears. "I love you, too, Am."

CHAPTER SEVEN

"How can you forgive her? Why didn't you leave her when you found out? It's what I would've done."

Nick and I are waiting in the van while Mom and Amber make one last bathroom stop inside Walmart. I barely slept a wink all night, instead seething over my argument with Mom.

Nick runs his fingers through his dark hair. "I was wondering when you'd ask."

"I've been wanting to, but I didn't want to upset you. I hate her, Nick! Everything that's happened—the whole reason we're here today—is because of her."

"You don't really hate her, Abs. You're just angry and deeply hurt."

"Maybe. But right now the anger is still so raw it feels like hate. I can't even look at her without remembering. Why didn't you leave her when you found out? Most people would've."

"It crossed my mind, but I couldn't when it meant leaving you girls behind."

I choke on a sob because he's cut to the heart of my biggest fear—if he leaves, he might take Amber and leave me behind. Though he's the only dad I've ever known, he's not really mine because he's never legally adopted me—and not because he hasn't tried. He wanted to after Amber was born, but Mom wouldn't contact my sperm donor to sign away his rights.

"But how do you stay, knowing what she's done?" I ask. "Especially now. I mean, you could just leave and not have to worry about the rest of us."

"I could never do that, Abby." Nick stares at me until my eyes meet his. "You're my daughter, Abs. Not by blood, but because I love you. I would never leave you behind. When everything first happened—when people found out about your mom—I thought about leaving. But you girls are my family—you're everything to me. So in those first few weeks, I stayed because I couldn't let you go."

"So what happens in a few months when I graduate high school? Will you leave then?"

Nick shakes his head. "No, I won't. Your mom and I have talked a lot since everything happened. Our marriage isn't perfect, but I love your mother and I believe she loves me, too. Sometimes love means swallowing your pride and forgiving, so I'm staying."

"But how could you after what she did?"

Nick blows out a sigh. "I know it's hard for you to understand, Abs, but every situation isn't black and white—there isn't always a right or wrong answer. Sometimes there are shades of gray, and adults aren't perfect. Sometimes we do stupid things for reasons we don't understand. In your mom's case, I think she was flattered by the attention. She'd just turned forty, and that's a hard age for some people to deal with. We'd been arguing about money for weeks after the garage cut my hours, and it was just one of those things that happened. I don't know if I'll ever fully understand how she could do that, but I've forgiven her. And she is sorry, Abs. You need to talk to her and hash this out, because you can't go on like this. You two used to be so close, remember?"

At this, my thoughts drift back to the day I came home with a seven out of twenty-five on a tenth grade science test. Mrs. Monson had used a red marker to write a huge F at the top of the page, a fat circle surrounding it like an exclamation point. I was devastated—not only because I'd studied so hard for that test, but because Alicia Adams had seen it and teased me relentlessly. I was sure Mom, being a teacher at my school, would be livid. My face flaming with shame, I held out the piece of paper, then closed my eyes and waited for the lecture and grounding I was sure would come. Mom studied the paper for a long moment, then set it down on the coffee table between us and took a seat on the sofa. "Sing to me," she said. My eyes widened and I couldn't believe I'd heard her correctly. Where was the yelling? The disappointment? I'd mentally prepared my defense, but I hadn't prepared for *this* reaction. Seeing my confusion, Mom smiled softly at me and said, "You've shown me your weakness, Abby. Now show me your strength."

Nick was still talking. "...so talk to her and fix it while you still can."

I steeled myself. "I don't know how. She didn't just cheat on you—which was bad enough—but she ruined all of our lives in the process. Then she got to quit and walk away as though nothing happened. But I couldn't—I had to stay and face my friends, only to find out I didn't have friends anymore. How can I ever forgive her?"

"That's something you'll have to figure out, and I hope you will. All I can tell you is forgiveness isn't about the other person, it's about ourselves."

"What do you mean?"

Nick studies me, then turns his attention toward the main doors of Walmart. "I think I'll let you think on that awhile. Right now we need to get you girls to school."

THERE ARE COUNTLESS things I never imagined about being homeless—so many things I'd taken for granted. Like having a bathroom available in the middle of the night, running water to brush my teeth, and even a mirror to judge whether my clothes look okay. All of these things are a luxury when your home is your vehicle. Maybe worst of all is the lack of privacy, especially for dressing. We resolve this issue by taking turns inside the van while the rest of us stand guard out-side. For everything else, Nick drops me at school early so I can use the semi-privacy of the school bathrooms. It keeps us from drawing extra attention by reducing our trips inside Walmart.

I close the van door, then enter through the students' entry at Door Six and slip quietly down the empty hallways. I keep my eyes downcast, searching for the bathroom I know is here somewhere. My heart pounds in my ears. We aren't allowed in the building this early without a pass, and the last thing I want is to get caught.

I find the bathroom and sneak inside, where I select the farthest stall and hang my backpack on the hook. I grab my toothbrush, run it under the sink's faucet, squeeze a dab of paste onto the bristles, then secure my-self inside the locked bathroom stall. I'm still brushing when the outer door opens and the chatter of two girls stops my progress.

"You should've seen how she was hanging all over Zach yesterday after school. Like she'd ever have a chance with him!"

Trish! Apparently I'm not the only one who breaks school rules. I'm frozen in place with a mouthful of toothpaste. Spitting will draw attention so I lower myself onto the seat and wait with the minty foam in my mouth.

"She seemed nice enough to me," another girl replies.

"She would. She wasn't coming onto *your* boyfriend! And besides, *everybody* seems nice enough to you, Zoë."

"I thought you and Zach broke up?"

"We're on a *break*. He just hasn't realized how much he misses me yet," Trish coos.

I peek through the crack in the stall door. Trish is peering into the mirror, applying a glob of lip gloss to her full lips. She smacks loudly, then hands the tube to her sidekick from yesterday—Zoë, she called her.

"C'mon," Trish says. "I wanna find Zach before school starts. He still doesn't have a date for Homecoming."

The two girls exit the bathroom and I count to ten before throwing open the stall door and spitting my toothpaste into the sink. I cup my hands and rinse my mouth with water.

Wonderful! Trish really does have it in for me!

A glance at my watch reminds me to hurry—only three minutes until the first bell. I retrieve my brush from my backpack and run it through my hair. When I've brushed the snarls smooth, I separate it into three sections and braid it down the back.

With only one minute remaining, I wait until the high-pitched peal of the bell before opening the bathroom door. At its cue, I step into the mad rush of students, seamlessly blending into their ranks.

MY FIRST CLASS is political science with Mr. Zagan, a class I missed yesterday. I find the room easily and spot Josh seated in a middle row.

"Morning, Ariel." He grins.

"Good morning, Walt. Or is it Flounder? I can't remember." I smile and slide into the open desk beside him.

"Hey now!"

"What? You give everyone else nicknames."

"Humph!" It's the first time I've seen someone scowl through a grin.

The bell rings and Mr. Zagan marches inside like a drill sergeant. Though not a large man, he carries himself with enough arrogance to compensate for his size. His expression is dour with no trace of humor. "If you're out of your seats, come see me now for a detention slip."

Several students groan but approach his desk, where he furiously signs the promised detentions. Slumped over, pen in hand, his orangey-yellow hair falls over his forehead, and I wonder if he's the victim of a bad dye job. He lifts his pale blue eyes as a student asks a question, his expression holding so much malice, goose bumps rise on my arms. I despise him immediately.

When the last student receives a detention slip, Mr. Zagan offers no words of welcome or good morning to the class—he simply stands and begins his lecture as though he's been grievously interrupted mid-sentence. His voice is dry and free of inflection, as though he's bored. It's soon clear Mr. Zagan could make puppies on Christmas morning seem dreadful. The hour drags by, and the monotony of his voice lulls me to sleep. A foot kicks mine—Josh.

"You're snoring," he whispers.

"Was not," I whisper back.

"Okay." He shrugs. "Don't say I didn't tell you."

I pry my heavy eyes open and focus on the lecture, but moments later I'm again jolted awake, this time by the bell to change classes.

"Not sleeping, huh?" Josh laughs.

I'm caught and I know it, but after a mostly sleepless night, I'm not at all in the mood. I shoot Josh a death glare, but he laughs louder. Irritated now, I gather my things and stalk into the hall, where I'm nearly knocked to the ground by the solid body of none other than Zach. My breath whooshes out of me.

"Whoa!" Zach's arm steadies me. "In a hurry for your next class?"

"Nah," I growl and flip my thumb toward Josh as he reaches my side. "He's being a smartass and I needed to escape."

"She fell asleep in Zagan's class." Josh defends himself. "Dude, she snores!"

"Good to know." Zach wiggles his eyebrows, earning himself a snort of laughter from Josh.

"So what are you doing here, anyway?" I ask Zach.

He shrugs. "Came to walk you to your next class."

"Why?"

"Do I need a reason?"

I lift an eyebrow. "Yeah."

"Okay. Because I want to."

"How'd you know I was here?"

"You're not very good at this, Abby. I saw your schedule yesterday. Remember?"

Heat creeps into my cheeks. "I forgot."

"I didn't." He smiles.

Obviously. My heart thumps in my chest. I stare into Zach's nearly black eyes and search desperately for a witty response.

"Hey, you two! I'm still here!" Josh waves a hand between Zach and me. "I hate to interrupt your mating ritual, but a little less rudeness would be appreciated."

"We're not—what?" My face floods with more scorching heat. "Oh shut up, Walt!"

"Good comeback," Zach snorts.

Josh throws his hands palms-up in front of him. "Hey, I just call it like I see it!"

I steal a glance at Zach. His lips twitch. I wince and mentally begin planning my revenge on Josh.

"C'mon, Abby." Zach laughs. "Let's get you out of here before your face goes up in flames. See ya, Josh."

"Later." Josh's voice is singsong, grating on my last nerve.

I'm mortified—so embarrassed I can barely look at Zach. *What's his game?* I wonder. I know I'm not ugly, but I'm not beautiful and I've only been here two days. I eye him suspiciously as he walks beside me, navigating us through the crush of students. We're almost to my next class when he bumps my shoulder with his own.

"Hey—don't be embarrassed. Josh was kidding."

"I know." I can't meet his eyes. "I'm just—why *are* you walking me to class?"

"Because I want to. I want to get to know you better."

"What about Trish?"

Zach's eyebrows draw together. "What about her?"

"She won't be happy to see us together. She's in my next class."

"Okay...and that's a problem...how?"

"Aren't you two a thing?" I challenge.

He laughs. "No—we're not *a thing*. We dated last year, but it's been over forever."

"Does she know that?"

"Yes, she knows. Don't worry about her."

"Easy for you to say," I mumble.

Zach stops outside Mr. Hedrick's classroom and pulls me off to one side, allowing others to pass through. "What are you doing tonight?"

My brain freezes. I can't just say, "*Oh, not much. Just grabbing a free meal with the fam and half the indigent population of Rochester at the Salvation Army. I hear they're having tuna noodle surprise—I can't wait! Then we'll just head over to the Walmart parking lot and have a camp-out in the back of Mom's van. No s'mores this time, though. You know—same ol', same ol'. What about you?*"

"Family stuff," I say instead.

"Wanna go see a movie?"

Oh crap! My mind spins with lies, so I stall. "Why?"

Zach's dimple deepens in his cheek. "Asked and already answered at least once. So what do you say?"

"I—can't. We're still trying to get settled after the move, so my mom expects me home to help out. Maybe another time?"

What the hell, Abs? Another time? If I'm serious about staying away from Zach, there can't be another time.

"Sounds good," he says. "Find me at lunch?"

"I—Josh is expecting me, I think."

"Okay. Tomorrow?"

"Tomorrow." The agreement slips out before I can stop it this time. But really, how many times can a girl be expected to say no when her heart is screaming yes!?

Zach's face lights up. "Tomorrow, then."

"Yeah," I say more firmly, mentally smothering the voice of reason inside my head. "Tomorrow."

Still standing outside of the classroom, we grin stupidly at each other.

I clear my throat. "I—I should probably get to class."

Zach's face flames and he nods. "Oh, yeah. Me too. Tomorrow, then?"

I nod. "Tomorrow."

He winks, then turns away and walks toward his next class. Watching him, my heart races. I lean back against the wall and bite my lip, but I can't suppress my smile as I replay in my head every moment of the last forty-five seconds.

"Best find a seat, Ms. Lunde." Mr. Hedrick startles me and I flinch. "The bell should be ringing soon and I'd hate to give you a tardy on your second day."

"Yes, sir."

I enter the room and scan my surroundings. Trish has arrived ahead of me and is sitting in the seat I took yesterday. Our eyes meet and she smirks. I'm too happy to care so I select a seat near the back, behind a girl with thick brown hair. Her green eyes are hidden behind outdated glasses. With a little makeup and the right haircut, she'd be gorgeous, but her natural, earthy style suits her.

She leans back in her seat and whispers, "Don't let her bother you. Karma's coming for her."

"Thanks. If you find out when that's expected to happen, let me know and I'll add it to my calendar."

The girl laughs. "I'm Amy."

"Abby," I reply.

The bell rings and Mr. Hedrick closes the classroom door. Like last period, my eyes are heavy and sleep calls. I close them, promising myself I won't fall asleep. I'll just rest my eyes while I listen. But I do fall asleep, and the bell to change classes startles me awake once again. I've missed the entire lecture. Now I may never know how the miscreant Guy Fawkes met his demise.

Mr. Hedrick stops me as I leave the room. "You'll need more sleep if you want to make it through this class, Ms. Lunde. I cover a lot of material you won't find in the textbook."

My heart plummets. I bite my lip to stave off the angry tears burning the backs of my eyelids. "I'm sorry. It won't happen again."

I'm almost out the door when Trish's overly-chipper voice reaches me. "You can't hoot with the owls at night, Abby, if you want to soar with the eagles in the morning."

My vision blurred by tears, I rush out of the room and run smack into a rock-hard body for the second time today.

"Whoa! Ariel!" Josh catches my fall. "Who peed in your Froot Loops?"

I glare at him. "Very funny. I've just had a rough day."

"Oh no!" The edges of his lips tip down. "Are you gonna cry?"

I swipe at the lone tear that defies me by escaping and shove past him. "No."

"Yeah, whatever." He races to my side and throws an arm around my shoulders. In his best carnival-barker's voice he continues, "Come with me, Chickadee! I'm a man with a plan! I'll bring your smile back in style. I'll turn your frown upside down."

It's impossible to stay upset around Josh. He makes me laugh when I really want to cry or rage at the world, and I love him just a little bit for doing so. I smile my thanks and match his pace as we walk to our chemistry class. By the time we arrive, I know I've found my first true friend at this school.

"ARE YOU SITTING with us at lunch, or have you got a hot date with Zach?" Josh asks after chemistry.

"No hot date. But he did ask me to have lunch with him. I said you were expecting me. I hope that's okay?"

"Sure, but why would you sit with us when you can sit with Zach? He has a thing for you, ya know."

"I know, but I'm not sure I trust him."

Josh quirks an eyebrow. "Why not?"

"For one, I just got here yesterday. Why would he want to hang out with me? He knows nothing at all about me. And, if I can ignore for a minute that he seems really nice and is completely hot, we really have nothing in common."

"Do you like him?"

I shrug. "I don't know. I mean, I guess—what I know of him, at least. I just don't get what he sees in me."

"Well, that's obvious! You're new and you're cute. Rochester's a small town, and most of us have known each other since preschool. Those things alone are enough to make almost any guy here want to ask you out. And it's not only Zach who's into you; it's just he got there first."

I stop walking and turn to him. "What does that mean?"

"Just what it sounds like. Zach's already shown an interest in you, so other guys will stay away. He's staked his claim."

"Like…what?" I frown and put my fists on my hips. "Like there's a Post-It Note stuck to my forehead reading, 'Property of Zach'?"

He shrugs. "Not exactly, but something like that."

"I'm not property."

"Of course not. It's—a bro code thing. You wouldn't date a guy your best girlfriend liked, would you?"

"Well, no."

"Exactly—bro code or, in your case, girl code. Zach's a good guy. Give him a chance." Josh resumes walking, leaving me behind.

"Okay, fine," I say, catching up. "What about you, then? How do they know *you* haven't staked a claim?"

Josh stops walking again and studies me. "Tell me you don't have a thing for me, Ariel."

I snort out a laugh. "Of course not. I mean—not that you're not—I mean—I already think of you as a friend."

He throws a hand up. "Say no more. We're good."

I let out a relieved breath as we resume walking. "You still haven't answered my question, though. Why doesn't this bro code apply to you?"

Josh laughs. "Seriously, Ariel? You need to swim to the surface and be part of our world. How could you miss knowing I prefer guys?"

I stop walking and my jaw drops. "What? You're gay?"

He touches his forefinger to my chin, pushing it closed. "You're catching flies, Ariel."

"But how? I mean—you don't *look* gay," I blurt out.

Josh lifts an eyebrow. "What is gay supposed to look like?"

"I—I don't know. I've never really known anyone who's gay."

Josh stares at me, his expression guarded. "Well, now you do."

"Wow. But…you're sure? I mean—"

Josh's blue eyes lose their sparkle. He shrugs, but the expression is less "*I don't care,*" and more "*I misjudged you.*" He turns away and continues toward the cafeteria, throwing over his shoulder in a flat voice, "Trust me, I'd know. But, whatever. Are you coming or what, *Abby*?"

His use of my real name is a punch to the gut. I hurry next to him and place my hand on his bicep, halting his progress. "Wait! I'm sorry! Please don't be mad! I didn't mean it like it sounded. I just meant— oh!" I press my palms to my hot cheeks. "I'm making this worse! I just meant—I was surprised. I'm so sorry—I'm such an idiot! I like you, Josh! Dammit—I wish I *did* have fins so I couldn't put my feet in my mouth. Forgive me? Please?"

I wait in agonized silence as he studies me, but a tiny sparkle of humor flashes in his eyes just seconds before a smirk lifts the corners of his lips. "So—does this mean I don't have to find another redhead to play Ariel?"

I gasp. "Don't you dare! The part is mine and I'll drown the girl who thinks she can take my place!"

"Ooh! Savage! I like it!" Josh takes my hand and weaves our fingers together. With a quick squeeze, he says, "If I was straight, we'd make a kick-ass couple."

CHAPTER EIGHT

I CAN'T STOP THINKING ABOUT ZACH. SINCE AGREEING TO HAVE LUNCH WITH HIM TOMORROW, THEN THE discussion with Josh about being "claimed," he's all I can think about. I know I should stay away, but is it wrong to want a little bit of happiness for as long as I can get it?

"Listen up, people!" Mr. Thompson shouts over the shuffle of movement and conversation at the end of class. "Remember to stay current on your reading so we're on the same page when I open discussion tomorrow."

I stand to leave, but Zach stops me. "Can I drive you home?"

I offer an apologetic smile. "No, but thanks. My sister is waiting for me to pick her up, then I'm stopping by the *The Daily* for a job application. After that I'm studying at the library." I blow out a breath—it takes everything in me to say no, when I want more than anything to say yes.

"I'll take you. It'll give us a chance to hang out for a while. What'll your sister do while you're filling out the job application?"

I shrug. "She'll go with me, I guess."

"C'mon." He smiles, showing off the dimple in his cheek. "I'll drive and stay with your sister while you apply for the job."

I should say no, but my lips won't form the word. Taking my silence for a yes, he takes my backpack and throws it over his shoulder.

"Zach...wait." With no other choice, I follow him toward the exit.

"C'mon, Abby. I know you want to say yes. Are you afraid of me?"

He's teasing, but my fight instinct kicks in, taking it as a challenge.

"Hell no, I'm not afraid of you! I'm not afraid of anyone!"

Zach lifts an eyebrow. "You sure?"

I stare at him a moment then blow out a resigned breath. "Fine. But you'll be bored."

"Is that a dare?" He arches an eyebrow again.

"No." I laugh. "It's a fact."

"We'll see."

We reach the parking lot, where the window-painted SUV is in the same spot as before. This time I'm prepared and ignore it. As we approach a black Audi with tinted windows, Zach pulls a key fob from his pocket and presses it twice. The Audi's headlights flash at the same time its horn chirps. I stop in my tracks, gaping stupidly.

"Are you kidding me?" I ask.

"What?" His eyes cloud in confusion.

"An Audi, Zach? Is this your car or your parents'?"

He narrows his eyes, choosing his words carefully. "It's mine. Why?"

Once again reality crashes in on me. I'd figured Zach was rich, but the level of privilege is beyond anything I'd imagined. Even when I had my own car, it was ancient. We never could've afforded an Audi—not for Mom or Nick, and *definitely* not for me.

"You realize most kids don't have Audis, right? I mean, my car is manufactured by Fred Flintstone. It's my feet!"

He shrugs. "Yeah, well—it was a gift for my eighteenth birthday. My parents work hard and don't have a lot of time to spend with me, so sometimes they compensate with big purchases."

"What do they do?"

"What?"

"Your parents. What do they do?" I ask again, slower this time.

"They're both at the Clinic. My mom's an ENT surgeon, and my dad's a pediatrician."

"So your family's rich," I say, my voice flat.

"No, we're not rich, just comfortable. Is this a problem?"

"Well, yeah, Zach. It kinda is." I cross my arms over my chest. "We don't have anything in common, and I can't keep up with your kind of money."

His mouth opens and closes as he searches for a comeback. "Nothing in common? How about the fact I like you and want to get to know you better? I know you feel the same."

"It's been two days, Zach, not two months. You know nothing about me." I yank my backpack from his shoulder and turn to walk away, but he grabs ahold of the strap and stops my progress.

"Wait!" His eyes are pleading. "Tell me you're kidding. It's a car, Abby. Is this, like, reverse snobbery or something?"

"No, it's not snobbery of any kind, Zach. I like you, but I don't see this going anywhere. Why would you want to hang out with me, anyway? Isn't Trish more your style?"

"No." His lips form an angry line. "You don't get to do that—you don't get to bring Trish into this because something else has you spooked. Get this, Abby: I *like* you. I want to spend time with you and get to know you better. How does what I drive have anything to do with whether we can be friends—or more?"

I release a tired sigh. "Because it would never work. I can't afford the things you have, and you'll eventually be embarrassed by what I don't have."

"Stop!" Zach runs a hand through his hair. "You're making assumptions about me when you know almost nothing, and that's not fair. If you don't like me, say so. But if you do—even a little—then I deserve a chance. We'll take it one step at a time and see where it goes. Don't be a snob."

Heat rushes to my face. "I'm not a snob!"

Zach pauses until my eyes meet his. Then, with three words, he issues a dare: "Then prove it."

I square my shoulders, lifting my chin for extra confidence. "Fine."

Zach grins and opens the passenger door. I sigh, then throw my backpack on the floorboard and climb into the seat. He waits until I'm buckled, then closes my door and crosses around to the driver's side.

"Where to?" he asks.

"SISTER!"

Amber waves frantically as her blond head bobs up and down from behind a taller boy. Even from a distance, her giant blue eyes shine, drawing the attention of those nearby. I smile back at her.

"Here she comes." I point her out to Zach.

He lifts an eyebrow. "'Sister?'"

I shrug. "It was her first word. It's the only thing she's ever called me."

"Cute." He grins. "She's adorable—she looks like Tweety Bird."

I roll my eyes. Gosh, I've never heard *that* before!

"Hey, Sister!" Amber throws her arms around me and squeezes. Stepping back, she eyes Zach then offers him her biggest smile. "Are you Sister's boyfriend?"

Zach chokes on a laugh.

"No, Amber." My face flames hot. "This is my friend Zach. Zach, this is Amber."

"Nice to meet you," he says.

Amber's right hand juts out, her arm straight and rigid. "Nice to meet you, too!"

He smiles and meets her hand with his own. When their handshake is complete, she stands on tiptoe and taps my shoulder. I bend down to hear her secret, thankful she's finally showing some discretion, but in a too-loud voice she asks, "If he's not your boyfriend, can he be mine?"

Zach lets out a bark of laughter, and I pray the ground will swallow me whole. I knew this was a bad idea!

I shake my head and stand to my full height. "I thought you had a boyfriend."

Amber shrugs. "That was yesterday. He's dating Alexiya now."

"Dating?" Zach interrupts. "How exactly do you 'date' in first grade?"

Amber gives him her full attention and I groan. In seconds, she'll have him wrapped around her little finger like she has the rest of us. "Well, you know—he sits by me at lunch, and plays with me at recess. When we play tag, he can't chase anyone but me."

"Okay," Zach says. "So why is he 'dating' Alexiya now instead of you?"

"He cheated on me." Amber shrugs again. "He pushed Alexiya on the swings today, so I broke up with him."

Zach chokes on another laugh, then bends over at the waist, his body shaking with mirth.

"And so the string tightens," I whisper under my breath. Hearing me, Amber glows as she realizes she's reeled in another admirer.

Bringing his laughter under control, Zach straightens and wipes a tear from his cheek. "You've got this dating thing figured out, Tweety Bird."

"Tweety Bird?" Amber's eyebrows draw together. "I'm not a Tweety Bird."

"You look like one," he says.

"What's a Tweety Bird look like?"

"Haven't you ever seen that cartoon with Sylvester, the big black cat?" Zach makes claws with his hands and pretends he's creeping up on someone. "He sneaks around the cage of this little yellow bird with giant blue eyes like yours, and the bird says 'I tot I taw a putty tat.'"

Amber rolls her eyes. "That's weird."

"It's not weird." He fakes offense. "The bird's saying, 'I thought I saw a pussy cat.'"

Amber studies him, her brows scrunched up in thought. "Why doesn't he just say that? Why call it a putty tat?"

Zach runs his hands through his hair in mock frustration. "Never mind. Some day I'll rent the old movies and we can watch them together—that is, if you can give your sister some pointers on this dating thing. She's struggling."

"Shut up," I say, kidding.

Amber's eyes widen, the nickname forgotten. "You don't know how it works, Sister? I can teach you."

The ground isn't large enough to swallow me. I need a black hole or, better yet, Harry Potter's Invisibility Cloak. Zach's laughter is back, but he takes Amber's bag and swings it over his shoulder. Somehow seeing him wear a Disney Princess backpack evens the score and I feel a little better. He reaches for my hand then takes Amber's on his other side.

"C'mon, Amber," he says. "Let's get your sister to the *The Daily* before she strangles one of us."

ZACH DRIVES AROUND the building twice, with no luck finding street-side parking.

"Why don't I drop you off here, and Amber and I will circle the block a few times until you're done?" he offers.

"You don't mind?"

"Nope—so long as Amber doesn't mind."

"Oh, I don't mind," she says. "It'll give me a chance to get all my questions answered."

Oh geez! I pinch the bridge of my nose between my thumb and first finger. "Okay. But, Amber, I'm warning you: don't say or do anything to embarrass me. Understand?"

"I won't." She takes her first finger and criss-crosses it over her heart. "I'll just ask what he's looking for in a girlfriend, and what his 'tentions are with my sister."

"No, you will not!"

"Go—we'll be fine." Zach laughs.

"You behave, Am! Don't ask him anything that'll embarrass me when I find out!"

"Who, me?" Her voice drips innocence.

I grumble under my breath, but leave them in the car and enter the newspaper office. A bell on the door chimes and a young woman with red cat-eye glasses greets me from behind a desk.

"Can I help you?" she asks.

"I'd like to fill out an application, please."

"Oh, sure. Let me get one for you. If you have a few minutes, I think Bryan will want to talk to you. We've had a couple of carrier positions open up, and he's trying to get them filled."

"Thanks."

The woman steps away, then returns moments later with an application and pen attached to a clipboard. "If you'll complete this form, Bryan will be out soon."

I take the form, fill out my full name, and then stop cold. The form requires an address, and I can't say, *Green van with the rusted driver-side fender in the Walmart parking lot.* My brain floods with a litany of possible lies. At this rate, I'll have a whole new identity before the day is out.

I clear my throat. "I'm sorry to bother you, but I'm not sure what to write for the address. We just moved here and we're staying at a hotel while my parents find a house. They're looking to buy, but haven't found anything yet."

The woman taps her manicured finger on her top lip. "Just write, 'ask me,' and you can explain it to Bryan. It shouldn't be a problem."

When I complete the application, the woman takes it and disappears. When she returns, an attractive older man in a wrinkled gray suit follows her. His short salt-and-pepper hair is balding on top, and his gray beard is neatly trimmed.

"Abby?" he asks.

"Yes?"

"Bryan Wiewel." He extends his hand to shake mine. "I'm the managing editor. I understand you're looking for a job?"

I nod. "Yes, sir."

"We're currently filling positions for carriers. It's six days per week, Monday through Saturday. Does that appeal to you?"

"Yes. Would you have an open route somewhere between here and Rochester South?"

Bryan smiles and waves an arm toward an open door. "I think we can work something out. Let's talk in my office."

I follow Bryan and take a seat in one of two chairs provided. His desk is cluttered with empty coffee cups and misaligned stacks of newspapers. He walks behind his desk, rearranges several items, then holds his hand across his tie as he takes a seat.

"Maris is the circulation manager and usually does these interviews, but she's out today and we need to get these positions settled," he says, turning his attention to my application.

The room is uncomfortably silent while Bryan scans my personal information. After a moment, he sets my application on his desk and folds his hands.

"Tell me about yourself," he prompts. "Madigan says you've just moved here. Where are you from?"

"Omaha. I just transferred to Rochester South."

"So what brings you to Rochester?"

I'm stumped by the question, but decide to stick as closely to the truth as I can. "My stepdad was looking for better job opportunities."

"I see. And where does he work?"

"I—I don't remember. He just started this week and I don't remember the company name." The lie tastes bitter on my tongue.

Bryan waves his hand in dismissal. "That's okay. So what brings you here today? Why here instead of, say, retail or fast food?"

"Well—" I clear my throat. "I—I have a younger sister I babysit after school. I thought it might be something we could do together until our parents get home."

"I see. How old is your sister?"

"Six."

Bryan taps his forefinger against his upper lip. "It's a lot colder here than Omaha. Are you prepared for the harsh winters?"

I nod. "I think so. We'll dress warmly."

Bryan squints and stares off at some point behind my right shoulder. After a tense several moments, he turns his attention to me and offers a smile. "Okay, Abby. Let's give you a try. You mentioned a route between here and Rochester South; we have two available, so you can take your pick. How does that sound?"

"That sounds great! Thank you!"

Bryan chuckles. "It's nice to see such enthusiasm. Come back tomorrow after school and see Maris. She'll let you pick a route, then walk you through the process and rules."

"Thank you!" I grin.

"It's my pleasure. We'll see you tomorrow, then?"

"Yes, sir!"

I nearly skip out the front door and find Zach parked right in front of the building.

"I got the job!" I squeal before the car door is fully open.

"Way to go!" he replies.

"This calls for a celebration!" Amber's head pops through the middle of us from the back seat. "I think Zach should take me to Dairy Queen!"

Zach laughs. "Sorry, Amber! Dairy Queen closed last week for the winter."

"Aw, man!" Her shoulders slump, then her face brightens. "I'll settle for Flapdoodles?"

"No, you won't," I interrupt. "We've got to get to the library."

"To the library, then." Zach puts the Audi in gear and pulls out of the parallel parking space.

"Yay! Are you going with us?" Amber asks.

Zach glances at me, smiling. "Sure, why not?"

"You really don't have to—" I begin.

"I told you," he interrupts. "I want to hang out with you, and I haven't had a chance yet."

My heart beats frantically and, in spite of myself, I'm giddy. "If you're sure. I'm not doing anything but studying…"

"I can study, too."

"Okay…but don't say I didn't warn you."

ZACH AND I sit side by side in matching carrels inside the library's teen room, each of us working on homework. It's a comfortable silence with both of us engrossed in different assignments, and it feels good knowing he's right beside me. My heart flutters and I peek in his direction only to find him watching me.

"What are you doing?" I ask.

"Just watching you."

"I can see that. Why?"

He grins. "Because I can."

My heart beats so loudly I know he must hear it. I roll my eyes. "Don't you have anything better to do?"

"Nope." He continues staring at me.

I pick up his copy of *To Kill a Mockingbird* and hand it to him. "Here, read this."

"Are you going to the football game tomorrow night?" he asks instead.

"That's random." I laugh. "I hadn't thought about it."

"You should. I'm playing."

"You play football?"

"No." His expression is stoic. "I just thought I'd play this one time to impress you."

I stare at him, not sure if he's kidding.

"Yes, I play!" He laughs. "Come to the game tomorrow night."

"I don't have a pass and I'm broke right now." *And there's no way I can get the money to get in.*

"That's no problem. Josh and the girls always go, so go with them.

They'll go in first, then you meet them halfway down the fence and they'll give you one of their passes. The gate checkers never look at the photo IDs, only the backs to see you have the pass."

I shake my head. "That's stealing."

"Only if you get caught. And besides, everybody does it and they know we do it. C'mon—I want you to see me play."

"Maybe." *Or not.*

"Give me your phone number and I'll call you." Zach pulls out an iPhone and offers it to me.

My brain freezes. My cell phone was one of the first things we cut to save money. "I don't have one. I—dropped it in the sink and we haven't replaced it yet."

"Oh man! I hate that. Did you put it in rice?" he asks.

"Rice?"

"Yeah. They say if you put it in rice, it dries the phone out and sometimes you can still use it."

"Oh." I shake my head. "I didn't think about it, and it's too late now."

"Bummer. Next time, though, remember it. It's a good tip. What about a landline?"

"It...we...it hasn't been hooked up yet," I lie.

Zach pockets his cell phone and offers a sympathetic smile. "That has to suck. I was without my mobile for three days this summer and it felt like I'd been shut off from the rest of the world."

"Yeah...pretty much."

"About the game," Zach presses. "Think about it and you can tell me tomorrow at school. I'd really like you to come."

Before I can answer, Nick walks through the library's front doors and heads in our direction. The moment he realizes Zach's with me, his eyes narrow and his smile disappears.

"We gotta go," I tell Zach.

Nick steps into the room and offers Zach a tentative smile before turning to me. "Where's Amber?"

"In the craft room again."

"Okay. Go get her and we'll meet you in the van. Your mom's had a long day, so we need to get going."

"Okay," I say, and wait for Nick to leave.

But he doesn't leave. In fact, he doesn't move a single inch. He just stands there, his gaze moving between Zach and me. I widen my eyes in an expression I hope reads, "*Okay, Nick…you can go now,*" but he doesn't move. Finally, after what seems the longest time, he blows out a breath and turns back toward the main doors.

"*Now, please, Abby,*" he says over his shoulder. "We need to get going."

When Nick disappears through the exit doors, Zach turns and asks, "Your stepdad?"

"Nope." I shake my head. "Just some guy who comes here often. He likes to tell me it's time to go, and that he's waiting on me."

"Smartass," Zach says.

"Um—hello? Pot? This is the kettle!"

"Fair enough." He grins.

We sit there another moment, neither of us speaking but also not wanting to leave.

"I've gotta go," I finally say. "It's been fun. Thanks for the ride, and for staying with Amber. She likes you already."

"She's funny—almost makes me wish I had a little brother or sister."

"You can have her," I offer.

Zach's eyes widen. "I said 'almost.' I'm not a glutton for punishment."

I snort out a laugh. Being with Zach is so easy. Maybe I can make this work. Maybe, if I'm careful, he'll never know our secrets. Or, if he finds out, maybe he won't know until after our lives are moving in a good direction. By then, maybe it won't matter anymore. Maybe.

CHAPTER NINE

"WHO WAS THAT KID AT THE LIBRARY?" NICK asks, almost the second I step in the van.

"Just a guy from school."

"His name's Zach, and he's Sister's new boyfriend!" Amber supplies.

I shoot Amber a stink eye, but it's too late. Mom turns around and faces me from the front seat. "A boyfriend, Abby? Is that a good idea?"

I narrow my eyes and tilt my head slightly in a gesture I hope reads, "*Seriously, Mom?*" But I say nothing and, after a moment, I roll my eyes and turn my head to stare out the window.

Mom's gaze bores into the back of my head. "Is he a boyfriend, Abby? Or is it moving in that direction?"

"I'm not having this conversation." My inflection is bored but inside I'm seething. "I'm almost eighteen and you've lost the right to counsel me on good relationship decisions."

"Abby." Nick's eyes meet mine in the rearview mirror.

I clench my teeth and throw him a look that says, "*What? Am I wrong?*" He glances away only long enough to check the road, then returns his eyes to mine—a silent warning.

Mom sighs. "You're right, Abby. You're almost eighteen. But we're in an unusual situation, and I'm not sure the kids here would understand. I don't want to see you hurt."

"You weren't worried about that before," I mumble.

If Mom hears me, she lets it go.

Nick clears his throat and our eyes meet again in the rearview mirror. "Your mom has a point, Abs. I'm sure he's a nice kid, but think about what she's saying. Neither of us wants to see you hurt."

"You, too, Nick?" My voice wobbles. "For the first time in almost a year, a guy pays attention to me *because of me!* Not because of Mom, or because he's hedging his bets I'm a slut like…*other people.* And you want me to shut it down? Aren't I allowed to have *any* happiness?"

I don't know why I'm arguing. They're not saying anything I haven't told myself a hundred times, or that I didn't just tell Zach this afternoon in different words. But hearing them say it makes my anger rise and seep out through every pore. I know Zach's a bad idea, but maybe—just maybe—I can make it work. And if I can't, well…maybe the time we spend together and the "normalness" he makes me feel will be worth the pain when he finds out and drops me cold.

"Abby, honey," Mom says. "Of course you're allowed happiness. That's all I've ever wanted for you. Will you just consider what I've said?"

I blow out a breath and stare out my window. "I'm done with this conversation."

Mom remains rear-facing, staring at me while I stare out the window. After the longest time, she turns back in her seat. The subject is dropped—for now, anyway.

SALVATION ARMY DINNER, Day Two. On the menu: meatloaf, dry mashed potatoes, overcooked broccoli and cold dinner rolls—no butter.

I feel like I've been here before. But of course, I have. We sit in the same seats as last night, and are surrounded by many of the same people. The teen mom sits at her same table, this time wearing a man's flannel shirt. Tonight, her dinner remains untouched as she rocks and pats her baby's bottom to console him.

My gaze moves around the room and I realize the old man with the gray dreadlocks is missing. I wonder where he is and whether he'll eat tonight.

The baby at the next table cries harder. The young mom rises and stands behind her seat, patting his butt and swaying in time to a silent metronome. But it doesn't help—the baby cries harder.

"Where are you going?" Nick asks.

I turn my attention toward him and find Mom rising from the table.

"I'm gonna see if I can help her," she responds.

"Claire…" Nick warns.

A look passes between them—a silent communication I can't decode—and Nick nods. Mom moves toward the girl and speaks softly to her. The girl's expression is wary—distrustful. She glances at our table before returning her attention to Mom. A few more words are whispered, and the girl wavers with indecision. A moment later, she hands her baby to Mom as though handing over priceless golden eggs. Mom takes the baby and begins a weird swaying/bouncing combination, then nods at the girl's dinner. Still watchful, the girl sits and lifts her fork while Mom stands within arm's reach and consoles the baby. Mom is like a magician. Within moments the baby's cries cease. Beside me, Amber gets up and moves toward Mom. She peeks at the baby and her blue eyes glisten with excitement. Then, in typical Amber fashion, she plops down in the seat next to the teen mom and begins a one-sided conversation.

"Why does she do that?" I ask Nick.

"Your Mom or Amber?"

"Mom. The girl is a stranger, but she just pushes her way in to help."

"Because that's who she is. If it's within her ability to help another person, she does. That's why she was such a good teacher."

"It's been a long time since I've seen that side of her."

"It's been a long time since you've *looked* for that side of her," he corrects.

Tears cloud my vision and I swallow a lump in my throat. For the next few minutes, we watch as Mom cradles the baby and coos softly to him while Amber continues her monologue with the young mom.

"So tell me about Zach," Nick says.

I shrug. "What do you want to know?"

"Tell me anything."

I think for a second and a smile teases my lips. "Well…he's cute. But more than that, he's really nice. He's on the football team and he plays guitar."

"Guitar, huh?" He smiles. "An honorable hobby. Is he any good?"

"Not sure. I haven't heard him play yet." I smile, but a pang of sadness hits me as I remember the guitar Nick left behind when we moved. He loved that guitar as much as I loved my books.

"There's um…" I clear my throat. "So tomorrow night there's a football game. Zach asked me to go and watch him play."

Nick nods. "And you'd like to go, I assume?"

"I'd like to, but it costs money to get in."

"What did you tell him?"

"Just that I didn't have money for admission. He suggested I could sneak in with someone else's pre-paid pass."

Nick's eyes hold mine. "You know that's stealing, right? We don't do that. It seems like an easy solution when you have nothing—or next to nothing—but it can spiral out of control pretty fast. Doing it just once changes who you are."

I nod. "I know."

Nick rests his elbows on the table and places his chin on top of his folded hands. He's silent for a long moment before asking, "How much is it to get in?"

My eyes widen. "I don't know—probably about the same as it was in Omaha. Student tickets there were five dollars."

He pulls his wallet from his back pocket and riffles around for a few seconds before handing me a ten-dollar bill. "Just in case it's more. Bring me back any change."

"I can go?" I ask, shocked.

"Yes, but only this time. We're down to just over a hundred dollars, and we'll need every penny. We still need to buy a cheap mobile phone for job callbacks." Nick runs his hand through his hair as though hoping he'll find an extra dollar or two hidden within its too-long locks.

"Are you sure? What if we need it for something important?"

"This is important, too, Abs." Nick's eyes hold mine. "You've had a shit year. You're right about what you said earlier—you're due a little bit of happiness. If five dollars will help—even if it's only this one time—then it's yours."

My heart is light in my chest. I can't help myself—I get out of my seat and throw my arms around Nick's neck from behind. "Thank you."

He pats my forearms. "It comes with one condition, Abs."

My heart sinks and I pull away, taking the seat next to him. "What?"

"You have to resolve this situation with your mother. You're both hurting, and I can't let it go on any longer. She's apologized more times than I can count. You made a big point earlier of reminding us you're almost eighteen and you don't always have to do things our way. That's true—you'll graduate in June and be a full-fledged adult with responsibilities. So it's time you start learning to adult, and you do that by learning to forgive, or at least by trying to understand things from other perspectives. And you can start with your mom."

I bite my lip until it stings. He's right—I am hurting. I hurt all over, especially every time I fight with Mom. I don't know if I can forgive her, but if Nick can—and it was his trust she violated more than any of ours—then I can try. For Nick's sake, if not Mom's.

"I'll try." I nod.

"Try hard."

CHAPTER TEN

"THERE'S ZACH!" AMBER SQUEALS AS NICK DRIVES INTO THE HIGH-SCHOOL PARKING LOT.

Tired and grumpy, I shoot her a scowl. It's bad enough we're arriving at school later than I hoped, but now Zach will see me before I've brushed my teeth. At least I've combed the snarls from my hair. Nick stops the van and I jump out, closing the door before Zach sees the clutter of our vagabond lifestyle.

"What are you doing here?" I ask as he approaches me.

"Waiting for you."

"Why?"

"Because I wanted to." He grins and I have to stop myself from touching the divot in his left cheek.

"I gotta run to the bathroom." I avoid talking straight at him with my morning breath.

"I'll wait for you. Have you had breakfast?"

"No, I was planning to grab a bagel here."

"Go to the bathroom, then we'll grab something from the cafeteria. Hurry before all the good stuff is gone," he teases.

In the bathroom, I make short work of my grooming. I wipe my mouth on a paper towel and stare at my reflection in the mirror. My hair is pulled back into another French braid with tiny tendrils escaping on each side, and my green eyes sport circles almost the same color underneath from lack of sleep. Tiny freckles dot my nose, and I wish I had makeup to cover them. But I've never worn much makeup so that's not something I would've had in my cosmetics bag anyway. My lips are pale and a little dry, so I reach into my front pocket for my ever-present tube of lip balm and smooth it on my lips. Much better. I tuck the lip balm away and smile at myself in the mirror. *What does Zach see in me?* With no answers, I blow out a breath and step into the hall.

"Took you long enough," Zach teases as I make my way beside him.

"Whatever." I roll my eyes. "You didn't have to wait."

"Hey." He tugs my arm, pulling me to a stop beside him. "I was kidding."

"I'm sorry. I'm in a bad mood."

"What's wrong?" His eyes narrow.

What's wrong? I can't tell him the hard freeze last night left us so cold we couldn't sleep. Or that when we did find sleep, Nick's snoring was so loud people in Australia needed earplugs. I settle on a lie. "Amber was in rare form this morning."

"Ah. She's definitely unique."

"Yup," I say, refusing to make the lie worse by playing it up.

"So, are you coming to the game tonight?" he asks as we approach the breakfast bar.

"I haven't talked to Josh and the girls yet, but I think so."

"Excellent!"

"What position do you play?"

"Quarterback."

"Oh lovely," I groan. "Rich, popular *and* the star of the football team."

"Hey now!" Zach bumps my shoulder with his.

"I'm teasing," I admit, choosing a cinnamon raisin bagel and a bottle of orange juice from the breakfast bar.

Zach grabs a blueberry bagel and joins me as the cafeteria lady slides my card through the machine. Our cards returned, he selects a table and waves at an empty chair for me to sit.

"So." He wipes his palms on his jeans. "There's something I want to ask you."

Anxiety ripples through me. "What?"

"I'd normally come up with some grand gesture to ask you this, but I'm running out of time so I'm just gonna ask: will you go to Homecoming with me?"

Relief washes over me. My first thought is, "*Thank God he hasn't discovered our living situation.*" My second thought is panic: I can't go to Homecoming! I have nothing to wear, and where would he pick me up?

"Okay…" I stall. "What does that mean?"

"What does what mean?"

"Homecoming. I know what it is in Omaha, but what does it mean here? What do you guys do?"

"Oh." Zach smiles. "It's probably the same as Omaha. The Homecoming Committee decorates the gym with some lame theme for the dance, everybody gets dressed up, I pick you up and take you to dinner, then we go to the dance. It's just a fun excuse to get dressed up and celebrate the big game."

"Isn't it next week?"

"Yeah—next Saturday night," he says.

"Why haven't you asked anyone else?"

Zach shrugs. "There wasn't anyone I wanted to go with, so I was going to skip it. But now you're here, I want to go with you."

"Oh."

"Oh?" he teases. "Does that mean oh-yes or oh-no?"

"I'm not sure. How dressed up do we have to get?"

"It's fancy, but not like prom fancy. Girls usually wear short dresses, some of them frilly or with weird glittery shit all over them."

Okay, so expensive dresses. I pause, trying to come up with any way I can make this work. I can't tell Zach we can't afford a dress, especially knowing how rich his family is. "It doesn't give me much time to buy a dress, and everything's probably been picked through. Can I think about it?"

"Sure, but can you let me know soon?"

"I'll talk to my mom and see if we can go shopping this weekend," I lie. "I'll warn you, though—it's so late, the stores are probably sold out. Can I tell you Monday?"

"Sure." He grins. "But look hard. I really want you to go."

My mind spins. Why didn't I say no? Even if I could find a dress, the logistics of where he'd pick me up and take me home are impossible. And then there's Trish. If she finds out—and there's no way she won't—she'll make my life a living hell. It's decided: I'm a glutton for punishment. Instead of saying no, I've drawn out the inevitable.

My stomach churns so I toss the remainder of my bagel in the garbage and follow Zach through the hallways to my first class—political science with Zagan. *Oh joy! This day just keeps getting better!*

Zach stops outside the classroom door. "Remember: you're having lunch with me today."

I nod. "I'll see you later."

I enter the room and find Josh right away, this time with Tera and Wendy seated next to him. I slide into the seat behind him and across from Wendy. "I didn't know you two were in this class. Where were you yesterday?"

"We came together and Tera's car stalled at a stoplight and wouldn't start," Wendy explains.

"I'm not sure which is worse," I say with a laugh. "Not having a car, or having one that leaves you stranded at a stoplight."

"They both suck. I had to call my older brother to come get us, and he acted like it was a huge hardship. Poor Braden…" Tera's voice drips with mock sympathy. "The poor high-school graduate taking a gap year had to pull his bony ass out of bed to jump-start his sister's car."

Wendy laughs. "You should've seen him, though, Abby. He showed up wearing two different shoes and his sweatshirt inside out. He was half awake and almost connected the cables wrong."

"Right?" Tera laughs. "Thank God you caught him or my car would've been messed up!"

"And to think I had a thing for your brother." Wendy sighs. "He's still cute, though, if he wasn't such an ass."

"So…" Josh interrupts, "talking about cute, what's the story with Zach, Ariel?"

"Oh yeah!" Tera says. "What's going on? I've been dying to ask."

"No story. Why?" I shrug.

"Oh, I dunno," Josh says. "I saw you leave with him yesterday after school, then he walked you to class again today."

"Oh. Well." Heat flushes my face and I tingle with…something. Excitement? "We hung out after school yesterday, then he met me at Door Six this morning."

"Yeah? And…?" Tera prompts.

"And what?"

"You're smiling too big for that to be all," Wendy says. "So what are you not telling us?"

I straighten my face, hoping to hide what I'm sure must be a goofy grin. "He wants me to come watch him play tonight, and he asked me to Homecoming."

"Shut up!" Wendy squeals.

"Yes!" Tera reaches across the aisle and bumps fists with Josh.

"I told you so," Josh says. "The guy likes you."

"Well, it really doesn't matter because I can't go."

"Whoa! What? To Homecoming or the game?" Wendy asks.

"Homecoming."

"Why not?" Tera asks.

Here we go again…

"I don't have a dress and it's probably too late to get one. Not to mention, I think Trish expected Zach to ask her."

"Screw Trish! Why do you even care?" Tera says. "As for a dress, don't you have one at home you've worn before? Nobody will know the difference since you're new."

"I..." My heart races. "I—I might, but most of our stuff is still packed. I don't even know which box it's in."

The lies come easier now and I hate myself for them.

"You don't think you'd find one if we go shopping this weekend?" Wendy asks.

"I doubt it." I shrug. "Everything good is probably gone."

"Fact," Tera says, tapping her finger on her top lip. "You're pretty much screwed if you don't get one by the first week of school."

"What if you borrowed one of Tink or Jasmine's dresses?" Josh turns his attention to the girls. "Didn't you guys keep your dresses from previous years?"

"Oh—I can't..." I begin.

Tera's eyes light up. "Yes! That's it!"

"But—"

"But nothing," Wendy interrupts. "It's a great idea. I have at least two dresses still in my closet. You can pick one."

I take in Wendy's five-foot-nothing frame and estimate her weight at a hundred pounds soaking wet. I have easily six inches and twenty pounds on her. "Sure. I bet your dresses would look spectacular if I could get them past my big toe!"

Wendy laughs. "I'm not that much smaller than you!"

I arch an eyebrow.

"Okay, okay. Fair enough." Wendy turns to Tera. "But you and Tera are about the same size."

"I really can't..."

"Yes, you can," Tera says. "I have three I'm almost certain will fit. You can take your pick. What size shoes do you wear?"

"Six, why?"

"Damn, girl!" Tera says. "I have shoes that match perfectly with each dress, but you have tiny feet!"

Wendy bounces in her seat. "Ooh! Ooh! But I wear a six, and I have dozens of shoes you can choose from."

"You guys are nuts," I say. "I can't borrow your clothes and shoes like that. I'd feel—weird."

"Why?" Tera and Wendy ask in unison, both of them giving me stunned expressions.

"Well—*because*."

Tera shrugs. "We do it all the time, and you better get used to it. It's the membership fee for friendship. Today we loan you an outfit, then we get to raid your closet when everything's unpacked."

I stare at them. They apparently do this all the time, so it's not like they see it as charity. Maybe I can hold off reciprocating until I actually *have* a closet and some clothes to choose from. "Okay—but it might be awhile before *Abby's Apparel* is open for shopping. We have a shitload of things to put away and it might take some time."

Josh rubs his hands together with glee. "Okay, then! It's settled. You're going."

"I guess I am," I say, stunned at how they've railroaded me.

"We should all go together," Wendy says. "Tera and I were going to get ready at my house and have the guys pick us up there, but let's make it a girls' night. We'll all get ready together then crash at my house after the dance. It'll be fun!"

"Ahem." Josh clears his throat. "Don't forget me! We're a foursome, remember?"

Wendy pats his hand. "Ah, is poor Joshy feeling left out?"

"You joke, but the struggle is real," he says.

Wendy laughs. "Okay—you can get ready with us, but my mom would die if I said you were spending the night—gay or not. But we can still all go together."

"Will your parents freak if I bring a date?" he asks.

"Seriously?" Wendy rolls her eyes. "My folks think you walk on water. You think they'd deny you *anything?*"

"Okay!" Josh does a fist pump. "It's a date!"

"Good deal," Tera says, then changes the subject. "Order of business number two: what did you tell Zach about the game tonight?"

"Oh, that." I shrug. "I said I'd check with you guys to make sure you're going and don't mind if I tag along."

"Are you kidding? Of course we're going and you can tag along," Josh says. "Meet us at the main gate at six forty-five?"

"Okay." I smile and relief surges through my veins.

The bell rings and Mr. Zagan closes the door on two late students who try sneaking in. He grins vindictively at the faces on the other side of the skinny window. "My class has started. You'll need a late slip from the office."

"Asshole," Wendy mumbles and I stifle a snort of laughter.

Zagan stalks to his desk and picks up a stack of handouts. "Take one and pass the rest back."

Students grumble as they scan the handout—a pop quiz. I *really* don't like this teacher.

ZACH'S WAITING FOR me when Josh and I walk to the cafeteria. Catching my surprised expression, he laughs. "Just wanted to make sure you don't forget our lunch date."

I roll my eyes.

"So hey! I hear we're all going to Homecoming together?" Josh interjects.

I groan and shoot him a scathing look.

"We are?" Zach's face lights up.

"Maybe," I say. "Tera's gonna loan me a dress so I don't have to worry about finding one on such late notice."

"That's great!"

"Yeah," I say. "And we were thinking the girls and Josh could get ready at Wendy's house and we could all leave from there. That is, if you don't mind?"

"Of course I don't mind," he says. "Does that mean you'll go?"

"So long as my parents don't have a problem with it, but I don't know why they would." I smile.

"Yes!" Zach jumps in the air and does a victory dance. Students pass us on their way into the cafeteria, their snorts of laughter making me flush.

"Thanks, Josh," I whisper. "You have the biggest mouth of anyone I know!"

"Just doing my job, Ariel!" Josh wiggles his fingers in a wave and makes his way to the salad bar. "I'll catch you later. Have fun."

Zach grabs two trays and hands one to me. "C'mon. Let's get lunch."

I take the tray and we separate to get our entrees then meet back at the cashier line. Once we've paid, he leads me through the crowded lunchroom to a table nearly half full of students. Only four seats remain, so Zach pulls one out for me and takes another on my right.

"This must be Abby," says a tall guy with wiry red hair and glasses. "I'm Scott. You're in my chemistry class."

I nod, remembering him vaguely.

Zach points to each person and makes introductions. "That's Nikolai, B. Patrick, Ariyana, Reagan, and—"

"We know each other." Trish sets her tray at one of the two remaining spots, leaving the last one open for Zoë.

"Trish," Zach says anyway. "And Zoë."

"Nice to meet all of you," I say, promising myself I'll be nice to Trish.

"So what's this mean?" she asks. "You two an item now?"

"No," I say.

"I'm working on it," Zach says at the same time.

Trish rolls her eyes. Just when I think my nerves might snap, Zach's hand reaches for mine under the table. He squeezes gently, and I look up into his smiling eyes.

"Relax," he whispers.

I nod and somehow my anxiety melts.

"So, Zach," Trish says. "Are you still planning to skip Homecoming this year?"

"Nope. I've changed my mind."

"Oh yeah?" She smiles. "Do you have a date yet?"

"Yup. I asked Abby this morning."

Trish's mouth twists into an ugly sneer.

"Hey, man!" Scott says. "This'll be fun! We can all go together."

"Maybe, but last I heard you don't have a date," Zach says.

"I'm working on it." Scott's gaze turns to Trish. "Just trying to figure out how to ask the girl."

"Well you'd better do it soon," she says. "Some of us are getting tired of waiting around to be asked. Homecoming is only a week away."

Geez! Obvious much? I bite my tongue to keep the words from spewing out.

Zach squeezes my hand again, and my heart thuds. Maybe this really can work. His friends don't seem freaked out or surprised. In fact, except for Trish, they seem cool with it.

LUNCH WITH TRISH at the same table makes for the longest forty minutes. In fact, if not for Zach, it would be intolerable. Each time I tense up, he reaches for my hand and offers a smile that makes my heart pound so loudly I know he must hear it. But he doesn't comment— he just holds my hand and includes me in conversation when he can.

It turns out Scott and Zach have been best friends since first grade. Like Zach, he's on the football team, but he's also a diver competing on the boys' swim/dive team. I learn Trish and Zoë have been on the same club gymnastics team since they were toddlers, and they compete for our high school in the winter. I did gymnastics for a while, but even before everything happened with Mom, the sport outpriced us and I had to quit.

Zoë is decently nice, but I can't figure out why she's Trish's sidekick and not the other way around. Physically, she's polar opposite and much prettier. Her hair is the color of chestnuts and frames her face in gentle waves, and her eyes are such a pretty shade of brown it's like looking into the eyes of a doe. She's taller than Trish—about my height—but she's slimmer than I am, probably from all the gymnastics.

Zach stands and relief rushes through me. Lunch is over. I've barely contributed ten words, but I've survived Trish. To her credit, she's ignored me, so there wasn't much to survive beyond the awkwardness. In any case, I'm relieved to leave this group behind.

"It was nice meeting you guys—and getting to know you better, Trish," I say, still holding onto my promise to be nice.

Zoë offers me a tentative smile, but Trish still ignores me.

"I'll see you in chemistry tomorrow," Scott says.

I smile. "Sounds good."

Zach weaves his fingers between mine and leads me out of the cafeteria. When we reach Door Six, I throw my books onto a high-top table and take a seat. "Lunch was fun."

Zach lifts an eyebrow but doesn't call me on my lie. "I'll see you in Thompson's class?"

"I'll be there."

"I'll save you a seat." Leaning over, he kisses my cheek then walks away without a backward glance.

Holy crap! He kissed me! My hand flies to my cheek and touches the spot where his lips have been. My concentration is now shot, and I can think of nothing but Zach. I don't know why, but he likes *me*. Not Trish or anyone else—but *me*. Abby Lunde. Instead of working on homework, I spend the hour replaying that two-second kiss in my head.

CHAPTER ELEVEN

I'M STILL GRINNING AS I ENTER MRS. MINER'S CLASSROOM. I TAKE MY ASSIGNED SEAT AND A BURST OF confidence surges through me. In the few days I've been here, I've never spoken to the four girls seated next to me. It's time I step outside my comfort zone.

I square my shoulders and glance at the girl closest to me. She's pretty with long, wavy, dishwater-blond hair and hazel eyes. She wears a letterman's jacket with "Eckhoff" embroidered on the left breast, and a variety of soccer patches cover both arms. I smile. "Hi. I'm Abby."

She returns my smile with a shy one of her own. "Emily."

A light-skinned African-American girl named Kierra introduces herself next. Her voice is wispy, and I'm surprised—it's nothing like the alto of her singing voice. Like Emily, she wears a letterman's jacket, but hers sports patches from diving, cross-country and vocal music.

Next to Kierra is Jordan, whose white-blond hair escapes from a stubby ponytail in small tufts around her face like tiny feathers. Yesterday I heard someone call her "Q-tip," and I realize it's in reference to the color and texture of her hair. She nods. "Hi."

"I'm Paige," says the girl on the end. Her smile is friendly, but guarded, as though trying to figure me out. Fair enough—I've been doing the same to them all week.

"Nice to meet you," I say.

"Rumor says you're going to Homecoming with Zach Andrews,"

Kierra says. "Is it true?"

My eyes widen. "Yeah. How'd you know? He just asked this morning."

"News travels fast. Half the school probably knew within seconds of him asking," Emily says.

"Great," I mutter.

Paige shrugs. "I wouldn't worry about it. It's not like you could've kept it a secret. Besides that, Zach's a great guy—unlike that skank ex-girlfriend of his."

"Trish?"

"You've met her?" Kierra asks.

I roll my eyes. "She was there when Zach announced we were going to Homecoming."

"Shut up!" Emily grins. "I'm sorry I missed that. What'd she do?"

Before I can answer, the bell rings and Mrs. Miner steps to the podium. "Quiet down, class! We have a lot to accomplish today."

I whisper to Emily. "She didn't do anything, but she hates me."

"Don't worry about her," she whispers back. "She won't do anything to make herself look too bad in front of Zach."

"I hope not."

"Emily and Abby!" Mrs. Miner says. "Time to zip your lips! Eyes up here and focused on me!"

My face flushes and I give her my attention. When all eyes are on her, she holds up a clipboard and turns it face-out toward the class. "As I'm sure y'all remember, the Fall Concert is in November. I need two soloists, a male and a female. Auditions are next week, and I have a sign-up here with available times. I'll pass the clipboard around and, if you're interested, select a time and write your name on the schedule. If y'all have questions, see me after class."

She hands the clipboard to a boy on her right then directs the class in a *Do-Re-Me* warm-up. When the clipboard comes to me, I pass it on without a glance. The period flies by as her class always does, and I'm almost to the hallway when she calls out to me. "Abby—could you stay behind for a minute, please?"

Heat floods my cheeks, and I wonder why she's holding me behind and not Emily, too. Embarrassed tears threaten but I choke them back. When the last student leaves, Mrs. Miner glances over the audition form and approaches me. "I don't see your name on this list, Abby. Are you not interested in auditioning?"

What?

"I—no," I say. "I wasn't planning to."

Her eyebrows draw together. "Why not?"

I snort out a laugh. "Rotten fruit doesn't look good on me."

Mrs. Miner's expression changes from confused to understanding. "You don't like your voice?"

"It's okay." I shrug. "But next to everyone else in this class, it sounds…weird."

"No, sweetheart." She laughs. "Your voice isn't weird, it's unique—there's a difference. It's recognizable, like Prince or Ed Sheeran or even Elvis. It's almost hard to believe you haven't had any training."

I blush. "Thank you."

"I'd like you to audition for the soloist part. Do you have time in your schedule?"

"Maybe. What would I have to do?"

"Pick a song you like and be prepared to sing it a cappella. I'll be listening for your ability to stay on pitch in the absence of music."

"Does it matter what I sing?"

"Nope." She shakes her head. "Pick something you like and know the words to. If you feel confident singing it, then you'll do well."

"What happens if I get the part?"

She hands me the clipboard. "Then I'll assign you a few solos and a couple of duets for the program along with one personal choice of your own, then we'll schedule time to practice together before the concert."

I select a time during my open period then hand it back to her. "I can't believe I'm doing this," I mumble.

"Not only should you be doing this, you should also be investigating vocal music programs for college."

"I can't—I don't have money for college." The words slip out and my face flames. I look away, refusing to make eye contact, but she continues as though what I've said is inconsequential.

"Don't dismiss it so easily," she says. "Most students don't have money for college. That's what financial aid is for. My boys couldn't have gone without grants and scholarships."

I lift my eyes. "Don't you have to pay up front?"

"Darlin', if everybody needed money up front, nobody would go at all. You have to look for opportunities. In your case, I think you're a good candidate for a vocal music scholarship, at the very least."

Hope blossoms in my chest. "Really? What would I have to do?"

"I can help with that, and I'm sure Ms. Raven would help you identify other scholarship or grant options. Let's get through this audition, then let's talk in the next couple weeks. Sound good?"

"Yes—thank you!"

"You're welcome." She smiles. "Now scoot before you're late for your next class."

HAPPINESS OVERWHELMS ME until I think I might burst, and I nearly skip the entire way to Mr. Thompson's class.

"What are you grinning about?" Zach is seated in his usual seat, so I slide into the seat beside him.

"Mrs. Miner. She wants me to audition for soloist in the Fall Concert."

"That's great!" He beams. "What are you going to sing?"

"I have no idea! I don't even know where to start."

"I'll help," he offers. "Let's get together this weekend—I can come over with my guitar and we'll work something up for you."

I shake my head as my brain scrambles for an excuse. "That won't work. We—we're still unpacking and our house looks like a bad episode of *Hoarders*."

"Then come to my house." He shrugs. "My folks won't mind."

"Are you sure?"

"Are you kidding? My mom's 'that mom' who would rather I bring friends home than go out. She'll love it."

"Okay," I say. "I'll ask my parents, but I don't think they'll mind."

"Good. Do that." He grins. "Are you picking Amber up today?"

"Yeah. Every day."

"I'll give you a ride, then drop you off at the *The Daily* if you want."

I shake my head. "You don't have to do that."

"I *want* to do that."

"Okay," I say with a laugh. "But if Amber embarrasses me again, it'll have to be the last time."

"Oh, I don't know her well, but I'm sure she'll embarrass you again. I'm looking forward to it. She's funny."

"Yeah, well—you don't have to live with her."

Zach starts to offer another comment but he's cut off as Mr. Thompson enters the room. "If you're not in your seats, you need to get there quickly. We have a lot to get done today."

Mr. Thompson waits until the room settles and every student is seated before continuing. He opens his mouth to make his next statement when two late students slip in and try sneaking into their seats unseen. He catches them and lifts an eyebrow. Unlike Zagan, though, he lets it go and turns his attention to the now quiet classroom.

"You should've all read through chapter fifteen, so let's talk about the main theme of this book, which is when Atticus tells Jem it's a sin to kill a mockingbird. Is everyone caught up through at least chapter ten?" he asks.

Most of the class nods, so he continues. "If you'll remember, Scout says she can't remember another time when Atticus considered something a sin. He tells Jem he can kill all the blue jays he can hit, but to never kill a mockingbird. Why do you think he says that?"

The room is a tomb of silence. Mr. Thompson lifts an eyebrow. "I'm grading on your participation. What did Atticus mean? What is it about killing a mockingbird that makes it a sin?"

A student shifts in her seat and Mr. Thompson's expression takes on a momentary look of relief, but she turns her focus to her desk and refuses to meet his eyes.

"Anyone?" he asks.

A pencil drops to the floor and its owner retrieves it stealthily. A student in the back row clears her throat, but says nothing. Mr. Thompson waits as the clock ticks loudly from its home on the wall above his desk. Time stretches in the silence and he flushes red. Abruptly, he tosses his book onto his desk and unanchored papers scatter to the floor.

"C'mon, people! Wake up," he shouts. "This isn't hard. Does nobody have an answer to this question?"

I glance around, expecting someone to answer, but almost every head is dipped in obvious boredom. I hesitantly raise my hand.

"Abby!" He smiles relief. "You know the answer?"

I clear my throat and my heart beats against my ribs. "I think he means it's wrong to hurt something completely innocent. A mockingbird doesn't do anything but fly around singing and bringing people joy. They take nothing, but give back so much."

"Very good." Mr. Thompson smiles, then addresses the class. "Abby's right. The mockingbird is a metaphor for innocence. It does nothing to harm and, in fact, only brings pleasure to others, so hurting it—killing it—is the worst kind of wrong a person can do. Does anyone else wish to add to that?"

The classroom remains quiet.

"Anyone disagree?" he asks.

Still nobody answers.

Mr. Thompson's face flushes again. "You people need to sit up and pay attention. This is important. This isn't just a good book—it's a life lesson I'm trying to give you for free. Five bonus points to Ms. Lunde for paying attention in class. The rest of you have an assignment due tomorrow: you're to write a two-page, typed and double-spaced paper, giving me one example of a 'mockingbird' today. It can be an example from literature, television, real life—whatever, so long as it fits within the parameters of the description we've discussed today. Tomorrow, I'll expect you ready to discuss through chapter twenty, and I *will not* accept a repeat of today's lack of participation. Abby, you're exempt from the paper. I would also caution each of you to pay close attention to this theme as you continue reading. I'm giving you a heads-up right now—this is a major theme of one of the greatest books in literature, and you will not pass this class without understanding. Now get started."

The room erupts in groans, and my body tingles with mortification. Why did I have to open my big mouth? If I'd kept it shut, I'd be in as much trouble as everyone else but at least nobody would be mad at me. I bury my head in my book, but I'm not reading; I'm hiding. I turn the pages mindlessly until the bell rings at the end of class.

"Abby. Would you mind staying behind a minute?" Mr. Thompson asks as I collect my books.

I shoot Zach a look that says, "*Please don't leave without me,*" then turn back to Mr. Thompson.

"Abby," he says when the last student leaves. "I'm sorry I put you on the spot like that. I realized afterward it wasn't fair to you."

"That's okay." My face flushes. "I can understand why you were frustrated."

"I was, but that's still no excuse. About the book—you have an excellent grasp of the themes."

"Yes, well—I've read it a few times."

"I figured. I knew the second I asked the question you had the answer, but you held back for some reason. It's a great book."

"It's more than that!" Excitement bubbles in my chest. "It's like an instruction manual on how to live life."

He grins. "Elaborate."

"Well, Atticus isn't just giving life lessons to Jem and Scout, he's teaching all of us. He says you don't understand a person until you climb into his skin and walk around in it for a while, and that's true. You have no idea what someone else is going through until you've lived it—until you put yourself in their shoes."

"That's exactly right. It's actually one of the most important lessons from the book I hope to teach my students. If we can walk around in the shoes of others, so to speak, then we can better understand what motivates their actions."

"So, it's like learning empathy?" Zach asks.

Mr. Thompson turns to Zach. "I hadn't thought about it that way, but yeah—it's exactly like learning empathy. When you can understand another person, it's easier to figure out why they do things. And if you can do that then it's easier to forgive their actions."

Somehow it doesn't feel like we're talking about *To Kill a Mockingbird* anymore. I tiptoe back through the last several months in my head, trying to remember if I've tried understanding anything from Mom's point of view. Would it make a difference if I did? If I could understand *why* she cheated on Nick, would I stop being mad?

CHAPTER TWELVE

"ZACH!" AMBER RACES TOWARD US, WEAVING HER TINY BODY BETWEEN OTHER STUDENTS. REACHING OUR side, she throws her arms around him in a tight hug. "I've missed you!"

"Hey, Amber. How was school?" he asks.

"Good!" Her shoulders deflate. "But I have bad news."

My heart drops. "What's wrong?"

"Well, I should really tell Zach first, but since you're here, I'll tell you, too." She turns to Zach, her lips drawn down in a frown. "I'm sorry, Zach, but I have to break up with you."

Zach clutches his chest. "Ouch! That hurts! What'd I do wrong?"

"Nothing." She covers a giggle with her hand. "But Kason and me are back together on account of 'cause he can play with me at recess and you're too old."

"Ow!" He clutches his chest a second time, this time falling to his knees. Amber's giggles echo through the halls, and I bite my lip to hold back my own laughter.

"We can still be friends!" she assures him. "And I know Sister really likes you, so you can be her boyfriend now!"

Zach sits on the floor, his legs bent and his head hanging low between his knees. His shoulders shake as tears of mirth stream down both sides of his face. Heat creeps from my neck to my cheeks. *That's it—I'm going to strangle her!*

"One step at a time." Zach snorts out a laugh and pulls himself to standing. "We still haven't gotten your sister on a first date yet."

"Oh, but she will now that I'm not standin' in her way!" Amber grins and takes his hand as we walk to the parking lot. My face flames, but I bite my tongue. If I engage her, she'll never stop.

We climb into Zach's car and it's only a few minutes before he pulls into a space right in front of the newspaper office. He lets the engine idle while Amber piles out and I collect my things.

"Sure you don't want me to wait for you?" he asks.

"Nah—I don't know how long I'll be."

"Okay, then. See you at the game tonight?"

"I'll be there!"

Zach's dimple deepens in his cheek. "Don't forget to check about this weekend, okay?"

"I won't."

He nods, then catches Amber's eye. "See you later, shortcake!"

She rushes past me, jumps back into the car, and throws her arms around Zach's neck. "Thanks for not being mad. You're the best ex-boyfriend ever."

Zach laughs, then turns his attention to me. He winks. "See you tonight, Abby."

I watch him drive away. When his car disappears from sight, I take Amber's hand and walk into the *The Daily* building. I'm nervous, yet excited, for so many reasons.

"HOW'D SCHOOL GO today?" Nick asks, setting his tray on the table.

We're seated in the same seats we've staked as our own this entire week. On the menu tonight: spaghetti, tossed salad in vinaigrette dressing, and garlic toast. They must've found the butter.

"It was good. Zach asked me to Homecoming next weekend," I say.

Mom flashes me a compassionate frown. "I hope you let him down gently."

"Actually, no. I told him I could go, so long as you two don't have any issues with it."

Mom takes a breath as though gearing up for another fight. "Okay—catch me up on what I'm missing because you know we can't afford to buy you a dress, and I can't even begin to imagine how you plan to manage the pickup and drop-off situation."

"Well." I take a breath. I promised Nick I'd try with Mom and I meant it. Blowing out my breath, I explain our plans then wait while Mom and Nick process all I've said.

"That's...wow," Mom says. "You've certainly figured out the details. I still don't think this Zach is a good idea."

Anger rushes through my veins. I tried—I really tried. I open my mouth to snipe an angry comment, but Nick interrupts before I can get out the first word.

"Sounds like you have a plan," he says. "I'm really proud of you, Abs."

Mom's eyes swing to his and she shoots him an expression I don't need a decoder ring to translate: "*Seriously?*"

I smile, knowing I've won this round. But then Mom opens round two.

"So...okay," she says. "Who is this other boy—Josh? Why's he getting ready with the girls?"

Angry heat climbs to my cheeks. I have no idea what Mom will think of Josh, but I won't let her belittle him.

"Josh is gay." My voice is strong and unapologetic. "He's getting ready with us because that's what friends do—and he's our friend."

Mom blows out a breath. "C'mon, Abby. It was a simple question. You don't have to be so prickly and defensive every time I open my mouth. Do you really think I'm so narrow-minded I would hold your friend's sexuality against him?"

My shoulders slump. "No. It's just…"

My voice trails off because I have no idea what I intended to say. Before I can find the words, Nick stands and takes Amber's hand.

"How about we go say hi to your new friend and her baby?" he asks Amber.

Her eyes light up and she grins. In a heartbeat, she's out of her chair and already seated next to the teen mom and her baby, her mouth moving in excited chatter.

Nick catches my eye and he lifts an eyebrow. "Don't forget our agreement, Abs."

Mom's gaze moves between us, then Nick follows Amber and sits across from the teen mom.

"What's that all about?" Mom asks.

I shrug. "Nothing."

She lets it go and, for the next few minutes, we sit across from each other without speaking. Mom catches my eye and waits until I don't look away.

"What?" I ask.

"Abby, I have to be honest. I don't have a problem with your friend, but I'm worried about you. You've had a rough time these last six months or so, and I'm sorry." She holds up a hand, preventing my interruption. "No—let me finish. You know I take full responsibility for the hell you've lived through. If I could hit a rewind button, I would. But I can't. What I can do is try to keep it from happening to you again."

"Mom—"

"No." She shakes her head. "I need to finish, okay?"

I nod.

"Now I'm worried about your friendship with Josh, even more than I'm worried about whether a romantic relationship with Zach is a good idea. Does the rest of the school know Josh is gay and, if so, how do they treat him? I just—I can't stand the idea of you being on the other end of another situation that brings you pain."

I grind my teeth and count to ten. I want to rail at her—to tell her it's none of her business—but her eyes hold nothing but love and concern. I decide to take Nick's advice and start adulting. I breathe deeply and think through my words as I say them.

"Mom, I know you're concerned. I'm fine. Josh is fine. Everybody knows he's gay, and nobody cares. And even if they didn't know, he's my friend and I wouldn't abandon him to save my own skin like Emma and Sarah did to me. But more than that, even if people *didn't* know—if it getting out were to cause a scandal and put me in the same position as last time—it would be completely different."

"How?"

"Because last time I wasn't given a choice. I was part of the collateral damage of your actions. This time, I'm choosing. This time, if I become a social outcast, it's because I'm *choosing* to stand beside my friend."

Mom's eyes glaze with tears. "But you've only known him a few days."

"I know, but it doesn't feel like that. If I learned anything from what happened, it's that I would never do to my friends what my old friends did to me."

Tears spill over Mom's lashes and she wipes them away with a napkin. "I really am sorry, Abby. I can't even explain my actions because I'm still not sure I completely understand them myself. But I hate this constant fighting between us. I hate that you hate me. I would do anything to change that and earn your forgiveness. Is there anything I can do to get us back where we were before all this happened?"

She reaches out to touch my hand, which rests on the table between us. On reflex, I snatch my hand back and swipe at the tears spilling over my lashes, but it's a futile effort.

"I don't hate you, Mom," I say, my voice barely a whisper. "I thought I did—sometimes I say I do—but I really don't. I'm just so angry and hurt that sometimes it feels like hate. I mean, you spent my first six-teen years cautioning my behavior and reminding me the importance of honor and morals, and then you—it's like you didn't believe the rules you were teaching me. What you did made a mockery of everything you'd taught me. So I can't help it. I'm pissed."

"I'm really sorry, Abs. I'm trying to make it better."

I nod. "I know you are, Mom. I just need more time. The agreement Nick mentioned? He wants me to patch things up with you because my anger is hurting all of us. And he's right—sometimes I'm so mad I can't breathe. So I'm trying to let it go. I don't know if I can ever forgive you, but maybe we can turn to a fresh page and try to move forward."

Mom reaches for my hands again, and this time I allow her to pull them toward the center of the table. "I'd really like that, Abby. Thank you."

Leaving my hands in hers, I nod but don't answer. I can't. I'm two seconds away from an ugly cry. Instead, I gulp hard and offer Mom a tentative smile. Her eyes shine back at me through tears, and I know she understands.

We've said all that can be said for now, so we tuck into our meals and eat quietly. The tension has lifted and my heart is lighter than it's been since—well, since I can't remember when. There's something about letting go of anger that's like losing the weight of heavy cinder blocks. Our silence must be Nick's cue, because only a few minutes pass before he and Amber return to our table.

"Corbin is so sweet," Amber says, taking her seat next to me. "Kat says he's gonna be as big as me pretty soon, and then we can play to-gether."

Mom smiles at Amber, then meets Nick's eyes in another one of those conversations where no words are exchanged. To Amber she says, "It'll be a little while, honey. He's still tiny."

Nick twirls his spaghetti on his fork, then takes a bite and chews slowly before swallowing. "Anything else happen at school today?"

I smile. "I almost forgot. My vocal music teacher wants me to audition for the solo part in the Fall Concert. Zach said he'd help me find a song. He's invited me to his house this weekend to work on it."

Mom swallows hard and pulls her bottom lip between her teeth. To her credit, though, she doesn't say a word.

"What did you tell him?" Nick asks.

"Just that I'd need to ask, but I didn't think you'd care."

"Will his parents be home?" Mom asks.

"I guess so. I mean—I didn't ask, but he mentioned me meeting his mom."

She nods and lifts a questioning eyebrow at Nick.

"I don't see a problem with it," he says.

I smile my thanks. "I'll let him know when I see him tonight."

"Tonight?" Mom asks.

Nick turns to Mom. "I forgot to tell you. I gave Abby permission to go to the football game tonight."

"Oh." Mom's eyebrows crinkle like there's more she wants to say but she resists.

"So what about you two?" I say. "Any news today?"

"Actually, yes." Nick nods. "The Dorothy Day House should be able to take us on Monday. It's first come, first served, so we need to get there as soon as the doors open. With luck, this'll be our last weekend in the van for at least two weeks. Plus, I got a part-time job as night janitor at the Episcopal Church."

"That's great!" I say, meaning it. It's not a full-time job and it won't bring in a lot of money, but it's one step closer to where we need to be.

Mom nudges Amber. "You've been quiet. Everything okay?"

"Yup!" Amber smiles a toothless grin. "I broke up with Zach today, but he took it okay."

"Who's Zach?" Nick asks.

Amber rolls her eyes. *"Sister's boyfriend."*

Mom chokes on her water. "What?"

"Long story, Mom," I say, as a genuine smile stretches across my face.

"SORRY I'M LATE," I tell Josh as I arrive at the football stadium. I'm only five minutes late, but punctuality is one of my compulsions.

"Meh." He shrugs. "No worries. Jasmine and Tink are late, as always."

"Thank goodness. I hate making people wait, but I don't mind waiting on others."

"So the news is all over school. Are you ready for the attention you're about to get for going to Homecoming with Zach?"

"What do you mean?" Dread settles in my stomach.

"Sweetie—" Josh smiles. "Zach's a great guy, but you're about to go under the microscope. He doesn't breathe without the whole school talking about it."

"Oh great. That's the last thing I need."

"You like him, though, right?"

"Well, yeah—he's really sweet."

Josh shrugs. "Then don't worry about it. You'll get lots of attention for a while—maybe a couple of weeks—but they'll get sick of it soon enough. Just be patient and ride it out."

Tera's bright-orange, classic Volkswagen Beetle pulls into the parking lot and emits a scraping sound as its undercarriage grazes the parking bumper. Josh's eyes meet mine and we burst into laughter.

"And she was worried about crossing the jumper cables?" he says.

Wendy and Tera pile out and Josh shouts out to them. "I thought you two would never get here!"

Wendy rolls her eyes. "Tera's car wouldn't start again."

"Well, at least I have a car, loser!" Tera makes an L-formation with her right hand over her forehead. "It's certainly good enough for you to bum rides in when it's working, since you don't even have one."

"Fair enough," Wendy agrees.

We enter through the main gates and find seats in the front row, right behind the players. Zach stands in front of me in his dark green number nine jersey. Next to him is Scott and a man I assume is their coach.

I haven't been to a football game since before everything fell apart at my old school. To be honest, I never thought I'd go to another game. It's different, though. This time I'm in the stands, not cheering from the sidelines. My gaze moves to our cheerleaders as they do their pre-game stretches. Trish is stationed next to Zoë, their legs in full splits. My muscles tense as my body remembers stretching in the same manner.

Josh stands. "I need a soda. You guys wanna come?"

"Nah, I'm good," Tera says.

"Me too," Wendy and I say together.

I'm watching Josh walk away when a crumpled paper cup hits me in the chest.

"What the—" My eyes scan for the culprit and land on Zach, standing below me with a goofy grin on his face.

"You made it!" he says.

I chuck the paper cup back at him and earn a death glare from the coach. He obviously missed his player throwing it at me first. "I said I would."

"I probably won't get a chance to talk to you again, but I wanted to say hi. Did you talk to your folks about this weekend?"

"I did. When do you want me?" I ask.

"Three o'clock on Sunday?"

"That works. Where do you live?"

"413 Charles Mayo Lane. Want me to come get you?"

"Nope." I grab a pen and jot down the address, then click the pen closed. "Got it. I'll see you then."

"Sounds good. And thanks for coming—it means a lot."

He looks like he might say more, but his coach thumps him on the back of his head and tells him to get his head in the game.

I turn to Wendy and show her the address. "Where is this?"

"Um…" She squints her eyes in thought. "Somewhere over in Pill Hill, I think."

My forehead crinkles. "Are you *kidding*?"

"Nope. That Zach's address?"

"Yeah. Didn't you say Trish lives in Pill Hill?"

"Yeah, but it's a big neighborhood." She shrugs. "They could be blocks away from each other."

"But it's a wealthy neighborhood, right?"

"What did you expect?" she asks. "It's Zach Andrews. You've seen what he drives."

"Yeah, but I guess I didn't expect *that*."

"Look, don't worry about it," she says. "He's obviously crazy about you. Don't make a problem where there isn't one."

"If you only knew how many problems this could create," I mumble.

Wendy stares at me, obviously trying to understand my frustration, but her attention turns to the announcer as he calls the starting lineup. Minutes later, the game starts with Zach leading as quarterback. I immerse myself in the chaos that is a high-school football game, cheering along with the Rochester South crowd at every score and booing the refs at every bad call. When the buzzer signals game over, I celebrate as Rochester South brings home a hard-won victory of 28-27.

CHAPTER THIRTEEN

I'M FREEZING. REGARDLESS OF WHICH WAY I
MOVE OR HOW TIGHTLY I PULL THE BLANKETS AROUND ME,
I can't stop shivering. My arms are covered in goose bumps and I clench
my jaw to stop my teeth from chattering. It's no use—they chatter anyway. I snuggle closer to Amber, hoping to soak up some of her warmth,
but it doesn't help. I can't remember ever being so cold. I open my eyes
and the early morning sun peeks through the frost-covered windows of
our van. I let out a breath, and the steam from its warmth hangs in the
air of the cold fall morning. Though still October, we had a hard freeze
last night.

"Mommy, I'm cold," Amber whines.

"I know, baby. Snuggle closer to me and we'll try to warm up,"
Mom says.

"This is not good," I groan. "It's not even November yet."

"Just two more nights," Nick says. "With luck, we'll get into the
Dorothy Day House on Monday."

"Let's get some coffee," Mom says. "McDonald's is cheap and offers
free refills."

"We better not," Nick replies. "The girls don't like coffee, and hot
chocolate's more expensive."

"I'll drink coffee," I say. "And Amber will, too, if we put enough
sugar and cream in it. Please, Nick? We're freezing."

"It would get us out of the cold for a while," Mom says. "The one by the mall has a PlayPlace—Amber could run off some energy."

Nick breathes out a hot breath and its vapor floats in the air. "Okay, but just coffee. We'll have lunch in a few hours at the Presbyterian Church."

"But I'm hungry, too, Daddy!" Amber cries.

"Claire, see if you can give her something to tide her over," he directs.

Mom opens a loaf of bread and spreads peanut butter on a slice while Nick starts the van. Cold air blows from the vents as the engine warms. Amber's quiet only as long as it takes to finish her sandwich, then she wrinkles her nose and complains of thirst until Nick finally pulls into the McDonald's parking lot.

"Why don't you three go on back to the play area," Mom says. "I'll bring the coffee when it's ready."

We follow Nick into the PlayPlace and take in the large, colorful tunnels and slides. I glance around for a place to sit and my heart drops. Sitting near a window is Trish and her sidekick, Zoë. A toddler crawls down from their table and races through the tunnels and up the slides. Before I can look away, Trish spots me and sneers. *Great!*

Nick selects a booth on the opposite side and we slide in while Amber drops to the floor and takes off her shoes. In seconds, she disappears into the maze of tunnels and slides. Mom pushes open the door to the PlayPlace. She carries a tray loaded with four small coffees, a pile of sugar packets, and about twenty sealed creamer cups. Nick stands and takes the tray, an eyebrow raised and a smile teasing the corners of his lips.

"I just wanted to make sure there's enough cream and sugar for the girls," Mom says, but the corners of her own lips form a smile to match Nick's.

I can't help but watch them. Even after everything, they're still in synch with each other. It wasn't always like this, of course. They argued a lot in the first weeks after the scandal, but Mom's seizure brought them together again.

Oh God. That seizure.

FOUR MONTHS AGO

The front door is unlocked. I push it open and take in the destruction of our living room. Everything is chaos. What should be on the shelves is scattered on the floor. The sofa cushions are flung about, and the stuffing from one hemorrhages onto the rug. It's like a mafia movie where the good guys are on the run, but know they're caught when their hotel room is vandalized. The bad guys have been there—searching for a secret recording or flash drive—and left the place in shambles.

My heart races and I reach for Nick's electric guitar. It's a little unwieldy, but is heavy enough to pack a punch. I hope.

The ice dispenser rumbles from the kitchen and I lower the guitar. Someone's in there, and I can't imagine a burglar or mafia hit man taking time to get ice for his drink. But just in case, I move on quiet feet toward the kitchen.

Mom sits at the table in her pajamas. Her dark red hair is pulled up into a messy knot on top of her head, its uncombed strands sticking out where she didn't care enough to fix them properly. She's been like this for weeks, but I thought her doctor had sorted her out with the latest cure-all antidepressant. Apparently not.

Mom tips a glass to her lips and takes a long swallow before placing the drink back on the table. The bottle stands beside her glass and I can just read its label from where I'm standing. Highland Park Single Malt Scotch Whisky. I didn't think it was possible to surprise me anymore, but color me shocked: my mom is drinking all alone at three fifteen in the afternoon. I've never known her to drink except on rare occasions.

"Mom?" I step into the room.

Her head turns toward me in slow motion. Her green eyes are tear-glazed and bloodshot. Almost as though summoned, a fat teardrop falls from her lashes and lands on the gray sweatpants of her pajama set.

"Oh, baby," she whispers. "I'm so sorry."

I back away and lean against the doorframe. I fold my arms across my chest because I've heard "I'm sorry" at least a hundred times. It no longer *means anything to me.*

"What are you sorry for this time?" My voice is cold, brittle. "The living room? I'm not cleaning it up."

Mom's face drops to her hands and she sobs. In that moment, I snap. What the hell does she have to cry about? I stalk to the table and grab the bottle of Highland Park and her half-filled glass, taking them to the sink.

Her head pops up when she hears the ice hit the ceramic basin. "What are you doing?"

My hands shake and I can't even look at her. "I'm pouring this shit out. What the hell are you doing?"

"Oh, Abby." She rises on unsteady feet. "Please don't."

I set the empty glass in the sink and turn to her. "Why are you crying now, Mom? And what's with the booze—and the temper tantrum in the living room? What the hell is wrong with you?"

"I—I heard. I'm so sorry."

My heart flips and I'd swear it bleeds a little at her words. I know exactly what she's talking about, and deep down I hope I'm wrong. But then, I know better than anyone how fast news travels at Omaha East. "You heard what?"

"Erin called me," she says, referring to my cheerleading coach. "She said the girls voted you off the squad. Oh, baby, I'm sorry."

I narrow my eyes. "She called you when? Because I just found out half an hour ago."

"This morning," she admits. "Right after you left for school. The girls did it last night after practice and she planned to tell you before practice today. She wanted to give me a heads-up."

Rage pours through me. "You've known for"—I glance at my watch— "five or six hours and you couldn't give me a heads-up? Are you fucking kidding me? You couldn't call me or come get me out of school? Maybe let me quit so I could save a little bit of pride? Really, Mom?"

Anger blinds me at this last injustice. Though things have been strained with my cheer squad, I thought they were my friends and just needed time to adjust. But when Erin dropped the news, I was blindsided. They'd voted me out. Like I was nothing. Like we hadn't all been friends since elementary school. Like they'd never been to my house, or had Mom carpool them around before we got our drivers' licenses. I clench my fists.

"I—I didn't think," she says.

"That's the problem, Mom. You never think," I yell. "You didn't think before you screwed Coach Hawkins, you probably didn't think when you trashed the living room in a drunken temper tantrum, and you sure as hell didn't think about me and how I was about to be screwed over by the last group of people who were supposed to be my friends. Thanks, Mom!"

I pick up the bottle of Highland Park, pull the cork, and pour its contents down the sink.

"Stop!" Mom screams and trips on her feet as she rushes to my side. "That's nearly a hundred dollars you're pouring down the sink!"

But I can't stop. I want to hurt her any way I can, and the closest thing to my fingertips is the booze she's used to drown her sorrows—my sorrows, really.

We struggle against each other for a few moments, but in the end I win, and the drain swallows the last drop of whisky from the bottle.

"Why would you do that?" she shrieks. "That was expensive Scotch."

"Oh God, Mom. Do you really want to play the 'Why Would You Do That' game?"

She stalks toward me, pulls her arm back, and slaps my cheek with her open palm. "I am still your mother and you will talk to me with respect." Spit sprays from her mouth.

"Then fucking act like it!" I shout as I back away.

She sways, then advances toward me a second time, her face purple with rage. She reaches for my shirt and gathers it into both fists. Then suddenly, she lets go. In slow motion, her eyes roll into the back of her head and she drops to the floor. Her body jerks spasmodically as though she's having a seizure.

"Mom?" I cry and drop to the floor next to her. "Mama!"

But she doesn't answer.

I reach for the phone, and with shaking hands I press the three most important numbers I've committed to memory: 9-1-1.

THE MEMORIES FLOOD back, my reaction so strong it's like it's happening for the first time. I slide out of the booth. "Going to the restroom," I say, keeping my head down so they won't see my expression.

I promised to turn the page with Mom, and I meant it. My heart has been so much lighter since hashing things out with her last night, but now there's an elephant sitting on my chest and I can't breathe.

I throw open the bathroom door and head for the sinks, where I blot my face with cold water. It soothes the heat and somehow tempers the rage. I reach for a paper towel, and the bathroom door swings open.

Trish.

"Abby!" Her smile is fake. "Out for breakfast with the family?"

"Something like that. You?"

"Helping Zoë babysit her cousin."

I nod. "That's nice of you."

Trish steps to the mirror and paints gloss onto her lips. She rubs them together and makes a loud pop, then catches my eye in the reflection. "What can I say? I'm a nice person."

The door opens again, and this time it's Amber with Mom behind her. Mom smiles at Trish, her eyes moving between us. She opens a stall for Amber then turns to Trish.

"You must be Mrs. Lunde." Trish's voice is sugar-sweet.

Mom smiles, but her body language is guarded. "Yes. And you are?"

"Oh," she says. "I'm Trish. Abby and I go to school together."

"How nice." Mom's words are clipped. Not unfriendly, but not exactly warm.

Trish turns to me. "Oh, Abby! I guess I'll see you at Homecoming!

Scott asked me after school yesterday."

"That's nice. I'm sure I'll see a lot of people there."

"Oh, but Zach didn't tell you?" She smirks. "We're all going together."

"How do you figure?"

She shrugs. "Scott and Zach worked it out last night. We're all meeting at Wendy's."

"Oh." I'm shocked and don't know how to respond.

The toilet flushes and Amber emerges. She stares at Trish for a moment before Mom redirects her to wash her hands.

Trish primps in the mirror, straightening a hair that's not out of place, then turns back to Mom and me. "Well, I gotta go. It was nice meeting you, Mrs. Lunde."

Without waiting for a response, she flips her hair over her shoulder and struts out the bathroom door.

"Who was *that*?" Amber's tiny nose is scrunched in distaste.

"Trish Landry. She goes to my school."

"She doesn't like you very much."

"Amber," Mom warns. "That's not very nice."

"No, Mom. It's true. She hates me."

Mom's eyes hold mine while Amber dries her hands. "Are you okay, Abby?"

I nod. "She's Zach's ex-girlfriend, and she expected he'd ask her to Homecoming."

"That'll be awkward then," Mom says, choosing her words carefully. "You sure you still want to go?"

"Positive." I nod. "I've had enough bullying to last a lifetime. I can hold my own with her."

"She has mean eyes," Amber says.

"Yeah, she does," I agree.

WEEKENDS ARE TOUGH when you're homeless—at least for kids. During the week, Amber and I spend the majority of our time at school. Aside from my paper route later in the day, the weekends are a black hole of time with nowhere to go and nothing to do but roam. Even for Mom and Nick, the weekends pose a challenge because most of the places they'd apply for jobs are closed. To fill this never-ending downtime, we return to the library.

Amber and I are now regulars and head to our posts in the teen media and arts-and-crafts rooms. Mom and Nick take the stairs to the second floor where they check the classifieds for job openings.

"Stay close to Sister, and don't go anywhere," Mom warns Amber. "Daddy and I will be upstairs if you need us."

Amber grins at me and rolls her eyes dramatically—a gesture I'm sure she learned from me. I drop her off in the kids' art room, then find a carrel next door with a clear view of her in the adjacent room.

I debate my options. I could do homework, but what I really want is to get on Instagram. I pull up the website and use my old login but, without a phone, there's nothing I can do but comment on the posts of others—and the last thing in the world I want to do is reconnect with my old "friends" from home.

I tap my fingers on the keyboard for several seconds, then type in the web address for Facebook and enter my old login information. I haven't been on Facebook in longer than I can remember, but I'm hoping kids in Rochester still have accounts. I mean, *I* still have an open account, even though I didn't use it as much after I got a phone. While it's not the best, it's a place I can call home—somewhere people can find me until we have a real place to live.

My heart aches as old, familiar names pop up in my feed. Part of me wants to read their status updates, but doing so will only twist the dagger buried deep inside. Instead, I open my friends list, unfriending and blocking everyone from my old school or anyone who had anything to do with

Mom's scandal. When I'm done, I have two friends left—Mom and Nick.

New School, New Me. I say the words like a mantra.

Now with a fresh start, I spend the next twenty minutes finding the accounts of Josh, Wendy, Tera, and Zach. I click the icon to send friend requests, then hesitate over Emily, Jordan, Kierra and Paige from my vocal music class. On a whim, I send them friend requests, too. I'm just logging off when a message pings from Zach.

ZACH: *Hey, you! Facebook? Really? LOL*

ME: *Haha! Yeah—at least until I get a new phone. I was hoping you had an account.*

ZACH: *It's all good. I'll start using it more now I know you're here. We still on for tomorrow?*

ME: *Yup. 3:00?*

ZACH: *Looking forward to it! Wanna do something today?*

ME: *Can't. Family stuff.*

ZACH: *Dang!*

ME: *Gotta run. I was just signing off.*

ZACH: *Later.*

I close the window and smile. I'm sleeping in my mom's van, but I have friends. If I had to choose between having a house and having friends, I'd choose friends every time. I barely survived the alternative.

I open my backpack and begin my homework, but I've barely started when Mom sneaks up behind me and taps my shoulder. "You ready? It's already eleven, and we can go to the church at any time."

"Sure." I toss my things in my backpack and follow her to the van where Nick and Amber are already waiting.

MOM IS GIDDY about the soup kitchen we're headed to for lunch. On the way there, she talks nonstop about how nice it's rumored to be. It's a soup kitchen—how nice can it really be? But Mom won't be deterred.

"It's run entirely on donations with a volunteer staff," she reports.

"How is that different from the Salvation Army?" I ask.

Nick meets my eyes in the rearview mirror and grins. He's apparently asked the same question.

Mom ignores the sarcasm. "The same woman has been running it mostly by herself for more than twenty years. They say it's more personal than the Salvation Army."

Nick pulls into a parking space at the Presbyterian Church, then Mom leads the way through a set of side doors and follows signs directing newcomers to a large dining hall. Scattered throughout the room are round tables, each sporting white linen tablecloths, and formally set for eight people. At each place setting are real dishes, real utensils and paper napkins folded nicely. In the center of each table is a small flower arrangement.

At the front of the room nearest the kitchen are three banquet tables, each laden with appetizers: fresh veggies with dip, bananas, granola bars, single-serving containers of applesauce, and a coffee pot with fresh, hot coffee. Moving in every direction are volunteers preparing for the afternoon meal.

Though we've arrived early, the room is filled with dozens of people. Like at the Salvation Army, each person shows signs of enduring hard times, but that's where the similarities end. There's a feeling of camaraderie in the air, and as I study the people around me, I realize they know and like each other.

At the table nearest me are four adults engaged in conversation. My attention focuses on the oldest of the group—a woman I guess to be in her mid-seventies, her silver hair pulled neatly away from her face in a tight bun. Her attention is focused on a woman to her left, who's waving her hands theatrically as she shares some story with the group. I'm startled by the differences between the two women. The older woman is dressed impeccably in an outdated powder-blue, polyester knit suit and large pearl clip-on earrings. She completes the ensemble with nylon stockings and small heels, reminding me of a Sunday school teacher. The younger woman is her polar opposite and is decorated with piercings through her left eyebrow and septum. Her jeans are frayed at the hem and sport large holes at the knees. Behind her right ear and peeking above the collar of her red flannel shirt is the tattoo of a cobra, its scaly length winding down her arm and below the cuff of her rolled-up sleeves, ending at her wrist with its razor-like fangs bared and ready to strike. Despite these differences, the two women engage in conversation like old friends.

At the same table are two older gentlemen whose appearances are so similar they could be brothers—twins, even. Both men wear too-long gray beards, faded, worn jeans, and nearly identical blue flannel shirts. Rather than appearing homeless, however, they are exactly how I'd imagined my own grandfathers might look if they were alive.

At every table are people talking. I can't understand what I'm seeing—this place is nothing like the Salvation Army, and doesn't resemble any soup kitchen I've imagined. There's a warmth here I never expected.

"Welcome," says a voice to our right. "You're new. I'm Linda Cummings."

The woman offers us a warm smile and extends her hand to shake Nick's. She's an older woman, probably in her late sixties, with short gray hair and a white apron. Her face is flushed, either from heat in the kitchen or from juggling too many things at once, I'm not sure.

"Nick Lunde." He places his arm around Mom. "This is my wife, Claire, and our daughters, Abby and Amber."

"Nice to meet you," the woman says. "Please come in and find a seat. And help yourselves to the appetizers. If there's anything left after lunch, feel free to take what you need, but do please wait until after lunch so everyone has a chance to have some. We serve family-style, so don't be afraid to sit with someone you don't know."

"Thank you," Mom and Nick say in unison.

We sit at the closest table, leaving four seats open for others to join us. A smile is stretched wide across Mom's face.

"You look really happy, Mom," I offer. "How'd you know about this place?"

"The lady I talked to at the Salvation Army that first day mentioned it to me. It sounded too good to be true, so I didn't want to tell you too much and be wrong. What do you think?"

I smile. "It's nice. Is it like this all the time, or are they doing something special?"

"I'm told it's like this every week."

My eyes roam around the room and pause on an older gentleman who swaggers in carrying a bushel of fresh vegetables. He strides directly toward the woman who greeted us and, reaching her side, pulls her into a hug. She smiles and accepts the vegetables he's brought for her. For the next several minutes they relax in conversation like old friends.

"That's Kade," a woman says, stopping beside my chair. "He's sort of the patriarch here. He comes every week and never without a gift for Linda or one of the rest of us. You'll like him."

Mom and Nick stand in greeting.

"I'm Claire," Mom says. "This is my husband, Nick, and our daughters, Abby and Amber."

"Nice to meet you." The woman smiles and the maze of wrinkles pulls on her face. "I'm Ana. Care if I join you?"

"Of course not." Nick pulls out a chair and waves his hand toward it.

"Thank you—and they said chivalry was dead," she teases.

"Have you been coming here long?" Nick asks, resuming his seat.

"About three years. I used to come with my mom, but she died four months ago. It was our one mother-daughter outing every week. Now she's gone, I feel sorta like this is the last of my family, so I keep coming and Linda keeps welcoming me."

"Are you homeless, too?" Amber asks.

"Amber!" Mom's face and neck heat with red splotches.

"No, it's okay." Ana smiles. "No, I'm not homeless—not everyone here is homeless. Some are here because they've been ill or have mental illnesses that make keeping a job difficult; some are recovering from drug or alcohol abuse; and some others have made some bad life decisions that spiraled out of control. The rest of us are just doing the best we can to make ends meet on bad-paying jobs. There's no judgment here. Linda makes everyone welcome, and we take care of each other."

"How do you mean?" Nick asks.

"How do we take care of each other?"

He nods.

"Saturday is our day to network, so to speak. We share information about who's hiring, or where to find cheap housing. Basically, we share information we've learned that might be helpful to others."

"How come there aren't any other kids here?" Amber asks.

Ana exchanges a look with Mom and Nick, then clears her throat. "We get kids here sometimes," she says, carefully choosing her words. "But being poor is very hard, and mommies and daddies always want what's best for their children. So sometimes, they let their children live with other mommies and daddies for a while so they have warm beds and plenty of food."

The blue of Amber's eyes glistens with tears. "You mean they give their children away?"

"No, baby," Mom says quickly. "They just send them to live with someone else for a little while so they can have the things their mommies and daddies can't give them right now."

Amber's bottom lip trembles and a fat tear falls to her cheek. "Are you gonna send me and Sister away?"

"Absolutely not!" Nick's voice is firm, brooking no argument.

The finality of his words leaves an uncomfortable silence. Fear settles in my belly. It's one thing for Nick to say "absolutely not." It'll be another thing for him to follow through if times get too desperate. Mom's eyes meet mine and her gaze reflects the same concerns spinning through my own head.

"Let me introduce you to Kade." Ana's voice is too bright, as though trying to make us forget our dark thoughts. She waves her hand in his direction, and he smiles and approaches our table.

"Good to see you, girl." Kade pulls Ana into a hug. "How're you doing?"

"I'm good." She nods. "Just one day at a time."

"It's hard. I know. We all miss your mom."

"Thank you." Unshed tears glisten in Ana's eyes. Turning to us, she sniffles once then makes introductions. "Kade, meet my new friends."

"Nick and Claire Lunde." Nick stands and extends his hand to Kade. He nods at Amber and me and introduces us next.

"Nice to meet you," Kade says. "Mind if I join you?"

"Of course." Mom gestures at an empty seat.

Kade settles behind the table and to the left of Nick with one chair separating them. "So you're new I take it? What brings you here?"

"Same reason as everyone else, I guess," Nick says. "Bad luck and hoping for a hand up."

"Ain't that the truth? Where're you staying?"

Mom and Nick exchange a look. Before either responds, Amber interrupts.

"In our van." She frowns. "We moved from Omaha last week, and it's cold at night. But I started a new school, and my teacher is really nice, and Sister and me already have boyfriends."

Mom winces. "Sister and I."

"Not you, silly." Amber shakes her head. "You're married to Daddy. Sister and *me* have boyfriends."

Mom opens her mouth, then closes it and shakes her head. Kade and Ana laugh.

"Don't be ashamed, Claire," Kade says. "We've all been there, some of us worse than others. When I first came here, I was living in my car. It took me two years, but now I have a small apartment and a job that pays decent. It's luxurious compared to what I had before."

"How long have you been coming here?" Mom asks.

"Almost ten years. These people are like family—some change and new people move in and out, but there's a core group of us who've been here for years."

Mrs. Cummings moves to the front of the room and raises a hand. "If I could have your attention, please. If everyone would please sit down, I have some announcements before we eat."

The room is a flurry of activity as those standing take seats. After several moments, the room quiets.

"Thank you," she says. "Today we have chicken tetrazzini with salad, garlic toast, and chocolate sheet cake for dessert. We have a few new guests, so please make any unfamiliar faces feel welcome. After grace, our volunteers will bring food to your tables in serving bowls. Please remain seated while the food is served—we don't want to spill on anyone. When the bowls arrive, please serve yourselves and pass the bowls around. If there's anything you need, please ask—we're happy to try to get it for you. Once every table has been served, we can bring you more if there's any available. Any questions?"

The room is quiet and a few heads shake no.

"Okay, then. If you would please bow your heads for grace."

Mrs. Cummings gives the most comprehensive prayer I've ever heard. It's not that she drones on forever, it's that she mentions so many people by name. She asks for prayers for a woman named Jo who hasn't been seen in two weeks, and one for a man named Luke who's in the hospital with pneumonia. She mentions that Amelia is anticipating word on a job interview, and prays it's offered to her. Then, much to my surprise, she mentions our names.

"Please guide and protect our newest guests, Nick and Claire and their two girls. Keep them safe and together, and help them find the resources necessary to see them through this difficult time."

Nick reaches for Mom's hand as tears race unheeded down her cheeks.

"Amen."

A flock of volunteers pushes in trays of food and systematically serves each table. Throughout the meal, they refill our bowls and pitchers of lemonade, and bring carafes of fresh coffee when asked. They treat us like paying customers at a nice restaurant, rather than the destitute partaking of a charity meal.

The food is delicious, but the best part isn't the food—it's how we're treated, like real people, rather than the beggars we are. For an hour, our circumstances are forgotten and we enjoy the meal for the food and conversation around us.

After dinner, Mom and Nick stand talking to several people, so I go in search of Mrs. Cummings. I catch her as she passes by in a flurry of activity. "Mrs. Cummings?"

She stops and her forehead creases. "Yes? Um—Abby?"

I nod. "Yes, ma'am. I wanted to thank you for the meal. This place— it's really special."

"You're welcome." She smiles.

"Could I—I was wondering if you needed help with cleanup?"

"What a kind offer! But no, thank you—you're a guest. Did you get any of the leftover granola bars or applesauce off the table? There's plenty left."

"No ma'am. I'm fine, thank you."

I *am* fine, but it would be nice to take some extra with us, just in case. But I decline so as not to seem greedy.

"No, you're not, and I won't hear another word of it," she huffs. "There are plenty of leftovers and we never let anything go to waste.

Come with me."

Mrs. Cummings walks away, obviously expecting I'll follow. In the kitchen she finds a large Ziploc baggie then stalks out into the dining hall and begins filling it. "This cheese will save well in this weather—keep it in your car and it'll be fine for a few days. These rolls might also come in handy, and you should always have a couple of granola bars on hand."

When she's done packing the bag, it's too full to zip. She shrugs. "Oh well. Take the granola bars out later and seal the cheese and rolls inside so they stay fresh. Be sure to share with your sister and parents. Will we see you next week?"

"I think so." I nod.

"Good."

Tears threaten and I bite my lip to hold them back. I want to tell her how much her kindness means to me, but I'm afraid my tears will spill onto my cheeks. Instead I stand there, awkwardly.

She regards me carefully. "You look like you could use a hug. May I?"

I catch my bottom lip between my teeth and swallow hard as I nod, then step into her open arms and breathe in her scent. She smells like garlic and fresh bread, and my eyes mist again with tears. She's so warm and comfortable—it's like hugging my grandma, except I've never had a grandma. Pieces of the hurt and anger I've been carrying around are chipped away. I want to stay here all day, but that would be weird. So I squeeze one last time and step out of her arms.

"Thank you," I whisper.

She lifts my chin with her right knuckle. "Keep your chin up, sweetheart. What you're going through is especially hard at your age. It's easy to forget you're worthy when you're trying so hard just to make it through each day, but always remember: you are worthy. Never be embarrassed to accept a hand up when someone offers. Today someone helps you, but someday you'll return the favor by helping someone else in kind."

My throat closes and the tears I've tried so hard to hold back, fall. I wipe a hand over my eyes and nod. *You are worthy.* Just three simple words, but they mean everything to me.

CHAPTER FOURTEEN

SUNDAY MORNING ARRIVES AND WE'VE SUR-
VIVED ANOTHER NIGHT IN THE VAN. WE HAVE TWO CHOICES
today, neither of them appealing. We can stay in the van, all four of us
in close quarters and the temperature cold enough to make us miserable,
or we can find a church where hopefully they'll offer refreshments before
services. It's our only real hope for anything to eat before dinner, and it'll
get us out of the cold until the library opens at one o'clock. The decision
is easy: we attend services at the Episcopal Church where Nick's been
hired as the night janitor.

Dressed in our Sunday best—which isn't any better than our Monday, Tuesday or Wednesday best—we're greeted in the narthex by an
elderly woman seated on a mobility walker. She smiles and directs us
toward the refreshments offered for an implied donation.

"Only take what you need," Nick whispers.

I select three mini-muffins then follow Nick and Mom to an empty
table. Amber scarfs down the donut holes she's selected in just a few
bites, but I can't eat. The muffins are like sawdust in my mouth. Crash-
ing the church's Sunday services is the lowest of the low, and I hate myself for being here. I offer my muffins to Amber and pick at a hangnail
on my thumb.

"Nick!"

At the sound of Nick's name, I glance up as a gentleman approaches.
In his early fifties, his thick glasses cover electric-blue eyes. His smile is

genuine and welcoming, but my attention is focused on his short, mostly graying hair. It's cut in military fashion and flat on top like Buzz McCallister's in the *Home Alone* movies. It looks prickly, and I have this insane desire to pat his head to see if his hair pokes my palm.

Nick swallows a bite of muffin and extends his hand in greeting. "Jim. Thanks for the invitation."

"I'm glad you could make it," he says. "This is your family?"

"It is." Nick introduces us and explains that Jim is the Director of Christian Education at the church. He's also the man responsible for hiring him.

"Have you checked out our Sunday school classes?" Jim asks.

Nick shakes his head. "Not yet. We weren't sure where to start."

Jim reaches for a bulletin from the centerpiece display in the middle of our table and hands it to Mom. "This explains a lot, but let me give you the highlights. We have three services, so you can choose the one that best meets your needs. Sunday school classes are offered for adults, teens and children during the nine forty-five service. You've already missed them today, but consider them next week if you return. Tonight at six, we offer three levels of choir practices—again for adults, teens and children—and at seven we offer senior-high youth group."

Mom studies the bulletin. "You're quite busy here. Our church at home didn't offer half as many programs."

Jim smiles. "We're very family-centered here. Not only do we want your family to have opportunities to do things together, we also like to think of ourselves as one big extended family."

"Thank you," Nick says.

Jim glances at his watch and his face falls. "I'm sorry. I'm giving the eleven o'clock sermon and I need to prepare. I'm glad you could come today. Feel free to check out the building if you'd like. I'll be around after services if I can answer any questions for you."

"Thanks," Mom says. "We'll definitely find you later if we have questions."

With those parting words, Jim heads through the mostly-empty sanctuary and toward the pulpit, stopping only a moment to say a word to the sound techs. Watching his guileless interactions, first with us and then with the sound techs, leaves me ashamed. We're frauds and don't deserve his kindness. We didn't attend this morning to worship; we've come to stave off hunger and get out of the cold. Our price for the privilege is sitting through the worship service. I'm horrified at our duplicity. I despise lying, and I wonder whether the level of lying is worse if you tell that lie in church. I can't shake the feeling God is watching and shaking his head in disappointment.

"ABS, WAKE UP."

A voice reaches deep into the cobwebs of my sleep-drugged brain, demanding my attention. I lift my head off my arms and wipe a stream of drool onto the sleeve of my sweatshirt. It takes a second to understand where I am, but a quick scan of the room reminds me I'm sitting in my favorite carrel at the library. I wipe the sleep from my eyes. "What time is it?"

Nick glances at the clock above the doorframe. "It's two thirty. Are you still going to Zach's?"

"Yeah." I cover a yawn with my hand. "I can't believe I fell asleep."

"I can. You almost fell asleep during the church service this morning."

"Yeah," I say. "It was too cold to sleep last night."

Nick looks away and heat creeps up his neck. "I'm sorry, kiddo. This is not the kind of life I imagined for you and your sister."

"I can't imagine it's the kind of life you imagined for yourself, either."

"No." He smiles at me. "You're right about that."

More alert now, I gather my things and zip my backpack closed. "I told Zach I'd be there by three, so I better get going."

"How far away is it?"

"A few blocks, I think, but I'm not good at gauging walking time yet."

Nick nods. "Be safe, and be back here by five thirty when the library closes."

"But that only gives me two hours. Can I just meet you somewhere else?"

Nick blows out a breath. "I guess, but I hate having us separated without a mobile phone. Let's do this: we'll be here until five thirty, then the Salvation Army for dinner at six. After that, we'll jet over to the Episcopal Church for seven o'clock. All of those places are within walking distance, but it's getting dark early these days, so seven is a hard-stop time."

Dread settles over me. "What's at the church?"

"Youth group. Your mom and I want you to go."

"No, Nick." I shake my head. "Please don't make me go. It was bad enough this morning."

"I'm sorry, Abs. It gives us an extra hour or two out of the cold."

"God, Nick. I feel like such a fraud there."

"I know, honey. But this is temporary. Please do this for us until we have a better option?"

Once again, I can't tell Nick no. If not for us, he wouldn't even have to be here right now.

I STUDY THE directions from Google Maps I copied down from the computer at the library. It estimates the distance to Zach's house at 1.2 miles. It's not a bad walk, and the exercise makes the cold less noticeable. I'm approaching the house when a pizza delivery truck backs out of his driveway and misses me by about six inches. Spotting me, the driver slams on his brakes and waves an apology. "You okay?"

"Fine." I wave. "Thanks for asking."

The driver backs down the remainder of the driveway—more slowly this time—and I'm left standing in front of a colonial-style home with a white porch and rock siding. I double-check the address, though I'm sure there's no mistake. The house is huge and I gape at its grandeur. It's easily three times the size of our house in Omaha.

I stand in the driveway contemplating whether I should ring the doorbell or leave, but the door opens and the decision is no longer mine to make. Standing in the doorway in bare feet, faded black sweatpants, and a Rochester South Football T-shirt is Zach. A lock of his dark hair falls over his forehead and he pushes it out of his eyes, then turns his full smile on me. "Are you coming in?

My heart takes off at warp speed. "I'm still deciding."

Zach laughs and steps out of the doorway. He walks toward me, leaving the door open behind him. I wince at his bare feet on the cold concrete. Reaching me, he takes my hand and leads me toward the front door. "It's just a house. I was afraid you'd react like this after you saw my car."

I blush. "Yeah, well—I already told you most kids don't drive the kind of car you drive."

"I remember," he says. "C'mon. My dad's gone, but you can meet my mom."

I remove my shoes at the front door and grit my teeth to keep my jaw from dropping wide open. The house is even more beautiful on the inside! An impressive staircase spirals upward to a second-floor landing with a large railing overlooking the main floor below. To my right is an immaculately decorated formal living room that screams, "*Don't touch anything!*" On my left is a formal dining room with a cherrywood table set for eight. Elegant china sits atop a crisp white tablecloth adorned in the center with a display of fresh flowers.

Wow!

"Are you having guests for dinner tonight?" I ask.

Zach's eyes follow the direction of my gaze. "No—my mom likes to keep the dining room staged. She says it keeps me from throwing my junk on the table."

"Oh."

Zach leads me into the kitchen, where once again I'm awed by the size. On one end is another table, this one seating six. At the other end is an island—at least as long as the table—with a white stone countertop. A built-in double oven occupies the left wall and, directly across from it on the other side of the island, are a wine fridge and *two* dishwashers! At the base of this U-shaped formation is a six-burner cooktop with a built-in griddle.

The cabinets are a brilliant white, and immaculate. Everything is pristine and very modern. *Mom would die for this kitchen!*

Standing at the island cutting vegetables is an elegant woman who can only be Zach's mom. Tall and slim, with dark hair neatly cut into a long bob, she looks at me with the same dark eyes I've admired in Zach. She smiles and wipes her hands on a towel, then walks forward to greet me. "You must be Abby! Zach's told me so much about you. Welcome."

"Thank you, Mrs.—"

"Cherie," she interrupts with a warm smile. "Mrs. Andrews is Zach's grandma."

"Thank you." I smile back.

Cherie goes to a cabinet and pulls out two plates. "I know it seems late for lunch, but Zach ordered pizza so I hope you're hungry. The boy can eat like a horse, so make him slow down and share with you."

"Thanks." I take a plate, then select a slice of pepperoni pizza before sitting across from Zach.

"Zach tells me Mrs. Miner wants you to audition for soloist in the Fall Concert?" she asks.

I swallow a bite of pizza and nod. "Yes. I've never sung in public before, so I'm a little nervous."

"No need to be nervous. Helen Miner knows her music, and she knows talent when she sees it. If she's singled you out, you must be good. I can't wait to hear you."

A heady rush of pleasure washes over me. "Thanks—I hope you're right."

"Oh, I'm always right. Ask Zach," she teases, and a dimple exactly like Zach's deepens her left cheek.

Zach rolls his eyes, but Cherie leans down and hugs his shoulders. "On that note, I have some things I need to finish up for work tomorrow. I'll leave you two to your plans. Zach, there's soda in the fridge. Make sure you offer some to Abby, and make her feel welcome."

"Okay, Mom." His voice is monotone but he grins in her direction.

We finish our pizza and Zach grabs two sodas before leading me up to his room on the second floor. He waves me inside and props open the door. "Gotta leave the door open. My mom is really weird about that."

"Yeah, mine too."

I stand inside Zach's room and take in the sight before me. His bedroom is all teenage boy, and different than anything I've ever seen. In the center of the large room is a queen-sized bed, neatly made with a dark green comforter. Along one wall stands a massive oak desk with a MacBook resting in its center. On the opposite wall is a futon beside two matching oak dressers. The top drawer of one dresser is open and a pair of blue boxer briefs hangs from the drawer's edge.

Following the direction of my gaze, Zach rushes to the dresser and stuffs the article inside, closing it before I can see more. Red creeps up his neck and I smother a giggle.

Along the walls—and strategically placed around the room for best visibility—are shelves of trophies and medals. It seems there's nothing at which Zach doesn't excel.

"Competitive much?" I tease.

"Yeah—about that." His head dips and he peeks at me through the dark hair hanging over his forehead. "My mom had this thing when I was younger that I had to try everything. So I tried hockey, basketball, soccer, swimming, baseball, and wrestling before eventually finding football."

His discomfort makes me smile. "Do you still play these other sports?"

"Not so much. I gave up wrestling and soccer in ninth grade. I never really cared for swimming, so I only did a year of that, but I still play baseball in the spring, and I like to play pickup basketball when I get a chance. If nothing else, trying everything gave me a love for sports, which made it easier to decide what I want to do after high school."

"Let me guess: medical school like your parents?" I grin.

Zach returns my smile. "Not exactly, but close. Guess again."

"I have no idea. Tell me."

"Athletic training. It's like a doctor, but usually without a medical degree. Sports teams from high schools all the way through professional leagues usually have a trainer on staff to take care of their players."

"Huh." I lift a hockey trophy off the shelf and read the inscription: *Supermite Hockey MVP.*

"Huh," he echoes. "What does that mean?"

"Nothing really." I shrug and replace the trophy. "I was just wondering why athletic training instead of, say, a full-fledged Sports Med doctor."

He shakes his head. "Nope—that's not for me. I've seen how much time it takes my parents away, and I want to spend time with my kids when I have them."

"You don't spend much time with your mom and dad?"

"No—I do. But between emergency calls and traveling for medical conferences, I've always felt like second in line. They compensate by throwing money at me."

"Hence the Audi?" I ask.

He nods. "So what about you? Do you play any sports?"

"Not really. I did a few years of ballet and gymnastics, and I was a cheerleader at my old school for a while."

"Oh yeah?" He lifts an eyebrow. "That's pretty cool."

I shrug and push away the painful memories. "It was okay."

Zach picks up his guitar and takes a seat next to his desk. "Have you thought about what you want to sing for Mrs. Miner?"

I shake my head. "I have no idea. I don't even know where to start."

"Okay. What's your favorite song?"

"Right now? Um...'Blackbird?'"

Zach tilts his head to the side, his eyebrows drawn together. "I don't think I'm familiar with it."

"It's an old Beatles song."

"The Beatles?" Zach laughs, and his face lights up with recognition. "Seriously? What are you, fifty?"

"I don't know!" Heat floods my face until my cheeks sting. "It was the first thing that popped into my head!"

"Whoa! Don't be embarrassed!" he says, still laughing. "I'm just kidding with you! I was just surprised—I expected you to name something from this generation. But let's give it a try—I'll see if I can find the chords."

Zach flips open his laptop, and uses a search engine to find the song. He studies it a moment then smiles. "This one's easy. Do you know the words?"

"I think so."

"Okay. I'll play a short intro and nod for your entrance."

I pull in a breath and push my nervousness to a dark corner. At Zach's nod, I close my eyes and sing through the first chorus. And then the guitar stops. I open my eyes and stare at Zach, who stares back at me with an expression I can't read. The room is silent and the hairs on my arms stand up at the same time heat rushes to my face. My heart drops to my stomach and I bite my lip to stop the tears stinging the backs of my eyes.

"Okay. Thanks anyway." The first tear slips over my bottom lash. I wipe it away before he sees, then head for the bedroom door. "I gotta go."

Zach jerks to attention, jumps out of his chair, and grabs my arm as I reach the door. "Whoa! Where are you going? Are you mad because I stopped?"

"Well, yeah. I mean, no. I mean—I don't know who Mrs. Miner

thought she heard, but it wasn't me." I pull at my arm. "I gotta go."

"No!" Zach's hand moves to mine and he sets the guitar down. "I didn't stop because it was bad! I stopped because I was surprised!"

I shrug. "Yeah, well—bad, surprised. Same thing. Thanks, though."

"No, wait!" Zach holds my hand firmly. "Surprised-good. I mean—I knew you had to be at least decent since Mrs. Miner singled you out, but I had no idea how good you'd be. I was shocked, that's all!"

"You—you liked it, then?"

"Liked it? I've never heard anything like it! Your voice is different, but in a good way. You've never done *any* singing?"

I shake my head. "Only for fun, and then just in front of my family."

"Wow!" Zach's smile is like a kid's on Christmas morning. "Okay, then. We need to find you something more challenging—something that really shows off your voice and gives it the justice it deserves." He stares off across the room, his lips pursed in thought. "Adele!"

"Adele?" I nearly shout. "I can't sing Adele! Won't she be overdone? Won't that be too cliché?"

"Exactly!" Proud of his idea, he smiles wider. "There'll be at least two or three girls who'll choose Adele, thinking they can sing her, but they can't. I bet *you* can, though. And if I'm right, you'll blow them out of the water. Do you like Adele?"

I shrug. "Of course—who doesn't?"

"Exactly! Do you have a favorite?"

I think for a second. "Maybe 'Hello?'"

"That would be excellent if you can pull it off. Want to give it a try?"

I gnaw on my bottom lip. "I guess."

Can I really do this? Adele is—Adele! If I don't do this well, I'll be the joke of the entire school. It's a gamble, but Zach's enthusiasm is contagious. Coming to a decision, I say more firmly, "Okay!"

"Do you know the words?"

"Not all of them."

Zach prints the lyrics from an online site and hands the copy to me. Then, resuming his seat, he picks up his guitar and strums the first chords. At his nod, I open my throat and sing the words on the staff. When the song ends, I stand nervously and await his critique.

A slow smile overtakes his face. His dimple deepens in his cheek, and I'm once again struck by the urge to touch the small groove with my fingertip. "I think you've got your song."

"Are you sure?" I raise both eyebrows. "I dunno…"

"Okay, let's do this again, and this time I'll record it." Zach opens GarageBand, then takes out a microphone from the top drawer of his desk. He connects it to his laptop and hands it to me. "Here—sing into the mic. I want you to hear what I hear when you sing."

I don't want to do this. Seriously, who really wants to hear herself sing? But Zach is bubbling with excitement, so I do what he asks. Once again, he plays the opening chords and I enter at his nod. When I finish the last note, he waits only a second then presses a button to stop recording.

"Now listen." He connects a set of speakers to the laptop and clicks the play button. A voice comes through the speakers—clear and pure and unique in a way that raises goose bumps along my arms.

"That's not me," I whisper.

"That *is* you," he whispers back.

My head spins and my knees threaten to give out. I sit on Zach's bed and try to understand what I've just heard. *That can't be me!*

Zach's face is lit up in an excited grin. "I think this is the song. What do you think?"

I swallow hard and my eyes meet his. I nod and my words are barely more than a whisper. "I think so, too."

"You're gonna kill 'em, Abby!"

Zach and I practice for the next two hours, going over the song dozens of times. After the first half hour, he puts the guitar away and insists I sing a cappella while he coaches my performance. Before I realize, it's nearing six thirty. If I hurry, I'll have just enough time to make it to the church.

Zach closes his laptop. "When is your audition?"

"Thursday during my open hour."

"I have chemistry with Burke. I'll see if she'll let me out to watch." He shrugs. "Or I'll just skip if she won't."

"You'd do that for me?"

"Are you kidding?" he asks. "I wouldn't miss it! I'm dying to see Miner's reaction!"

"Thanks—for everything."

"Don't thank me, Abby." His voice sends a shiver through me. "I like you—a lot. I know you can't be surprised, but I want us to be more than friends."

I shake my head. "I don't know—we're so different."

"I don't care. I know you're freaked about how much money my parents have, but that's not me. I'm not responsible for how much my parents have any more than you're responsible for what your parents *don't* have. I want to be with you."

"What does that mean, exactly?" I'm buying time. I know what he means, I just don't know how to respond.

"For starters, it means we go on dates, and we don't date anyone else. We hang out—a lot." He smiles and kneels in front of me on the futon. "I get to kiss you…"

"A lot?" My mind goes blank.

Zach smiles, then leans forward and touches his lips to mine. My heart leaps into my throat and I struggle to breathe. The kiss is short, only a testing of the waters. He leans back on his heels. "A lot."

I shake my head. "I don't know."

He leans forward again, this time holding my face between the palms of his two hands. "I guess I didn't do that right. Let me try again." He touches his lips to mine a second time, this time lingering. His warm breath sends tingles down my arms, and my heart pounds so loudly I know he must hear it. His tongue licks out and tastes mine. "Say yes, Abby."

"Yes," I whisper, not even realizing I've answered.

His kiss deepens until the only thing I can think about is the two of us in this moment. I know this is a bad idea, but he makes me feel like anything is possible—like everything I want is within my grasp. Right now, the only thing I want is Zach. He kisses me until I'm breathless, then leans back and smiles gently. "I knew I'd win you over."

"Oh yeah?" I press my lips together, hiding a smile. "Pretty sure of yourself, were you?"

He sits beside me and lifts my hand, holding it between his own. He smiles. "Absolutely."

I clear my throat. "I hate this, but I gotta go. My parents are meeting me at the Episcopal Church downtown."

He frowns. "Can I give you a ride?"

I nod and his lips meet mine once again.

CHAPTER FIFTEEN

LAST NIGHT I TOSSED AND TURNED—NOT BE-
CAUSE OF THE COLD THIS TIME, BUT BECAUSE OF ZACH. FOR
the first time in ages, I'm happy—really happy. I don't care that I didn't
get much sleep last night. I only care that, in a few minutes, I'll see Zach
again.

"Have a good day, Abby," Nick says as we arrive at Door Six. "It's
good to see you smile, kiddo."

"Thanks, Nick."

In a bubble of euphoria, I step out of the van and find Zach leaning
against the side of the building.

"Waiting for me?" I grin.

He draws his lips together, hiding a smile. "Shh. My girlfriend will
hear you."

I roll my eyes. "You're an idiot."

"Busted." He grins, taking my hand. "You want breakfast?"

I nod. "Yeah, but I need to run to the bathroom first."

"Always the bathroom with you first thing in the morning," he
teases. "You must have the world's smallest bladder."

"I'll be quick." I duck inside the bathroom and emerge several minutes later to find Zach still grinning that wide smile that brings out the
dimple in his cheek.

"You pulled your hair back," he says.

I shrug. "It was in my way."

The cafeteria is offering fresh breakfast burritos today, so we each select one, then eat in comfortable silence. When we finish our last bites, Zach takes our garbage and drops it in the nearest bin. He returns and takes my hand, weaving our fingers together. "I'll walk you to class."

"You don't have to."

"I want to," he says.

My body tingles, and I discreetly pinch myself to confirm I'm not dreaming. Heads turn in our direction as we walk hand in hand down the wide hallway. I hold my breath.

"Relax," he says. "You're tensing up. It's okay."

"Easy for you to say."

"Yup. It is easy for me to say, 'cause I'm with the prettiest girl in school."

My heart melts and I beam at him. When we reach the door to my first class, Zach turns toward me and closes the distance between us. "I'll come back and walk you to your next class."

"You don't have to."

"I want to." He leans down and touches his lips to mine.

"Not in the hall." Mr. Zagan's dry voice reaches us and we jerk apart like opposing magnets. "You know better, Mr. Andrews."

My face flames. "Sorry."

"Don't let me catch you again," Mr. Zagan growls.

"Don't let him embarrass you," Zach says. "He's just a lonely old man, jealous nobody will kiss *him* in the hallways."

I bite my lip and nod.

"I'll see you in an hour." He winks, then turns and walks toward the office.

I enter Zagan's class and find my seat next to Josh. My heart pounds in my chest.

Josh raises an eyebrow. "Hm…seems like I missed a couple chapters of your book. It looks like it's getting steamy."

"Shut up, Walt," I say.

"C'mon, Ariel. Don't take away my fun! Are you dating Zach now?"

I shrug, but my face flames. "I guess."

"What do you mean you guess? You either are or you're not."

"Fine—yes." I roll my eyes. "We're dating."

"Whoa! When did this happen?"

"Yesterday. He invited me over to work on the song for Mrs. Miner's audition. He asked and I—I couldn't say no!"

"Of course you couldn't! I don't know anyone who could say no to Zach!"

I shoot him a "*hands off*" scowl.

"Hey! Don't get mad at me!" He throws his hands up. "I'm just sayin' is all!"

The bell rings, and Tera and Wendy slip inside just seconds before Mr. Zagan closes the door.

"Thank you for joining us, ladies, but you're late," he says.

"Aw, c'mon Mr. Zagan!" Wendy whines. "Please don't count us tardy! We can't help it Tera drives a piece of crap and couldn't get it started again!"

"Does the bus pick up near your house?" he asks.

"Yeah…" Wendy confirms.

Zagan slaps detention slips on their desks. "Then I suggest you start taking advantage of more reliable transportation."

OUR FIRST LUNCH as a couple, my second week at this school and the hundredth time my stomach is in knots. Zach guides me to the same table as Friday where Scott, Trish and Zoë are already seated, along with several others whose names I've forgotten. I take the seat Zach offers and try not to look as nervous as I feel.

"Hey, Abby," Scott says. "I hear you're dating Zach?"

"Um—"

Trish's Gatorade bottle slams on the table in front of me. The fear starts in my hands, which tremble visibly. Dark circles dot my vision and I pinch the inside of my arm to keep from passing out. The memories of another day rush back and I have to remind myself this is nothing like my old school. *I'm just dating Zach. That's all. I've done nothing wrong, and there's no reason for anyone to turn on me.* I repeat these words in my head, but the cafeteria is silent. All eyes are turned to our table.

Trish's voice rings throughout the now-quiet room. "You've *got* to be kidding me! Why would you date her, Zach? Can't you tell she's nothing but trash? A whore? She only likes you because your parents are loaded."

The word *whore* rings through my ears until it's the only word I can focus on. I'm cold all over, yet sweat glistens on my brow. *Hold it together, Abby,* I scream inside my head. Because any minute, I know I'll fall apart.

"That's enough, Trish." Zach's voice is quiet but frigid.

"No, Zach, it's not enough." Her voice is so loud she doesn't need a microphone. "What is it about you guys that you follow your hormones wherever they lead? Has all the blood rushed out of your head and you can't say no to a pretty face? She's using you, Zach. You've known her for, what? Like, a minute? What do you even know about her? Can't you see she's a slut?"

*Slut…Slut…Slut…*the word filters through my head like a chant.

Scott's face turns the same beet color as his hair. "Trish, stop. What's wrong with you?"

"Trish," Zoë whispers. "Don't do this…it's not fa—"

"Not *fair*, Zoë?" Trish's voice is shrill. "Is that what you were about to say? Don't tell me it's not fair. What's not fair is this tramp walks in here a WEEK ago and suddenly thinks she owns the school."

Zoë tries again. "This isn't the time—"

"Really?" Trish yells, her voice almost manic. "When is a good time? I'm only saying out loud what everybody else is thinking!"

Zach and Scott stand at the same time, their bodies forming a wall and shielding me from view. I want to run away, but I'm frozen in place. I'm unable to move or utter a single sound.

"Shut your ugly mouth," Zach says between clenched teeth.

"Or what, Zach? What are you gonna do?"

Zach's hands open and close as though he wants to hit something, but he keeps them at his side.

"Stop it, Trish," Scott says. "You need to sit somewhere else today."

"Gladly!" Trish stands and picks up her tray. "She must have some pretty special 'talents' to keep your attention, Zach. Just make sure you see a doctor when you're done with your trailer trash girlfriend. You don't want to pass along any *diseases* you might pick up while you're slumming."

She turns, then stops and throws over her shoulder, "On second thought, Zach? Don't worry about it—I'm not sure the rest of us will want anything to do with you after she's done with you."

Trish stomps out of the cafeteria. Zoë's face is ghost white and tears rest on the edges of her bottom lashes. She swallows and looks between Zach and me. A moment passes and none of us move.

Zoë stands and picks up her tray. She shakes her head. "I'm sorry. I'm—I—I'm really sorry."

With those words, she returns her tray and leaves the cafeteria. Every eye follows her, and it's another two or three minutes before the room resumes its normal noise level.

When I'm sure everyone's attentions are back on their own business, I excuse myself for the bathroom. The tears I've been holding in are seconds from falling, and I need to escape before I can't stop them. I stand and glance at Zach. "Excuse me. I'll be back in a minute."

He grabs my hand, his eyes pleading. "Don't go. I'm sorry she did that."

I offer him a bright smile, but I'm sure it looks as fake as it feels. "I just need to use the restroom. I'll be right back."

"You sure?" He stares into my eyes.

I nod. "I'm sure."

He releases my hand and I offer him one last smile. Then, leaving my tray on the table, I walk out of the cafeteria the way I have so many other times at my old school—with my head held high and a brittle smile on my face.

"ABBY!" THE BATHROOM door bangs open and Tera's voice echoes inside the tomb-like room. I swipe at my eyes with a wad of toilet paper. I've only been in here about three minutes, but already my tears have soiled half a roll.

"Abby," Tera says again. "Come out. It's just us."

I sniffle. "Give me a minute."

"Don't let her get to you. We told you she's a witch," Wendy says.

"I'm fine. Really—just give me second." I pull another piece of toilet paper from the roll and blow my nose. Already it's congested in that awful way it gets when you cry too hard and too fast.

"Then come out and show us," Josh says.

"Josh!" I gasp. "What are you doing in here? Get out! You'll get in trouble."

"Not until you come out, Ariel," he replies.

"I can't yet." I blot my eyes. "Give me a minute."

"Okay, but the longer you stay in there, the bigger the risk I run of getting into trouble."

"Oh geez—fine!" I open the door and I'm immediately pulled into a group hug.

"Don't let her get to you," Josh says. "She's just jealous. You're prettier than she is, rumor has it you sing better than she does, and now you're dating her ex-boyfriend. You're living her life and she's jealous."

"I've seen her car. If she's jealous of my life, she can have it," I say. "And what about her singing?"

"You haven't heard?" Tera asks. "The whole school is talking about it."

"Talking about what?"

Tera, Josh and Wendy exchange a look.

"What?" I demand. "Now you have to tell me!"

"Hm." Josh turns to Wendy. "Tink?"

Wendy huffs out a breath and rolls her eyes. "Trish is auditioning for soloist in the Fall Concert. She's won every year since ninth grade, so it's always assumed she's unbeatable. But these girls in your vocal music class are running their mouths, telling everyone you're better than she is. Now half the school has bets on which of you will get the part."

"What?" My eyes go wide. "Why does anyone even care?"

Josh snorts out a laugh. "Seriously? Because Trish is a bitch and everyone's dying to finally see her lose. No doubt she's talented, and rumor has it she's been accepted to Juilliard, but it would serve her right if she lost for once."

"But—"

"*Are* you auditioning?" Tera interrupts.

"Yeah—I was planning to."

"Holy crap!" Wendy says. "No wonder she hates you! She's scared."

"Yeah, and totally screwed if Ariel wins. She'll never live it down." Josh laughs then eyes the bathroom door. "C'mon—I gotta jet before I get caught. Plus, I need to place my bet on Ariel."

"Don't you dare!" I exclaim.

He wiggles his eyebrows. "Seriously, Ariel? Why not? I don't care if I win—I just want to bet against Trish!"

I punch him lightly on the arm. "Stop it, Josh—you're not funny."

"Ow!" He rubs his arm. "I'm not trying to be."

"Are we good in here?" Wendy asks. "You okay?"

"Yeah—I'm fine. Just embarrassed." I wipe away the last of my tears and glance in the mirror. My eyes are pink around the rims, but nothing most people would readily notice.

"Don't be. Everyone knows what she is," Tera says. "If people are looking at you, it's because they're awed by your courage."

"I hope you're right."

"I am! So c'mon—let's go finish lunch."

"Thanks, you guys. You're the best friends I've ever had, and I've only known you a week!"

"Of course we are!" Josh holds the door while we file out. "We're awesome!"

When I return to my seat, Zach takes my hand and stares into my eyes. "You okay?"

"I'm good. I just needed a minute."

"Don't worry about Trish," Scott says. "She's made an ass of herself and she knows it."

"Thanks. She's going with our group to Homecoming, though?"

Scott clears his throat and his Adam's apple bobs. "About that—I asked her Friday night. I had no idea she might cause a problem. We'll find a different group."

I shake my head. "No—I'll be okay. We'll just—we'll figure it out that night."

My appetite is gone, so I push my food around on my tray while I wait for the lunch period to end.

CHAPTER SIXTEEN

DINNER AT THE SALVATION ARMY—AGAIN. ON
THE MENU TONIGHT: CHICKEN AND RICE CASSEROLE, PEAS,
and cold rolls. It wouldn't be bad if I had an appetite. Since the scene
with Trish, I've been in a funk. I push my peas into my chicken casserole
and imagine how I might've reacted differently, but every scenario ends
the same: utter humiliation. And not Trish's, but mine.

"Sister's not listening again," Amber says.

"What?" I turn my attention back to my family.

"I said, 'Sister's not listening again.'"

"I'm sorry. My head is somewhere else."

"You okay?" Mom asks.

I shrug. Though I promised to be nicer to Mom, right now I can
only remember she's the reason for our current predicament. If she
hadn't screwed around with Coach Hawkins, none of this would've happened. It's like a freakin' domino effect. Her affair knocked over the first
domino, and they've been falling ever since. I wish we could fast-forward
to the last domino and get it over with.

But if Mom hadn't knocked over the first one, there would be no Zach.
My mind plays a game of mental ping-pong, arguing over which is
worse: being homeless or not having Zach in my life. I don't know the
answer because both scenarios suck.

Mom takes a breath and an invisible shield goes up—the same shield
she pulled down when I called a truce. Great.

Nick clears his throat. "I was saying we got into the Dorothy Day House today. Your mom and I checked us in when they opened at four, so we can go straight there after dinner."

"That's great!" I say, but my voice lacks enthusiasm.

Nick lifts an eyebrow, but I avoid his gaze and focus on my meal.

"So," he continues. "We'll get settled there after dinner, then I have to be at work around eight. I won't be back until after the eleven o'clock curfew, but they've made an exception because of my work schedule."

I spear a pea with my fork and place it on my tongue. I chew once then swallow and spear a second pea.

"Okay, Abby." Nick's eyes lock on mine. "What's wrong?"

I shake my head. "Nothing."

"You're sure?"

"I'm fine, Nick." My voice sounds irritated even to my own ears. "Tell us about the Dorothy Day House. What's it like?"

Mom and Nick exchange one of their long looks, then Mom blows out another breath. The sound grates on my nerves but I bite my tongue. I'm sick of being angry. I just want out of this hellhole that is homeless life and to be normal again.

"I think you'll be pleasantly surprised," Mom says. "From the street, it doesn't even look like a homeless shelter. In fact, it matches every other house in the neighborhood. The best part is they have showers and washing machines."

Despite myself, my lips turn up. It's only been a week since I've had a real shower, but the idea of the hot, sudsy water streaming over my body lifts my spirits. Funny how having almost nothing makes you appreciate the small things. It might as well be Christmas morning for the excitement tingling under my skin.

"Thank God!" I say. "I can't wait to take a real shower again."

"It's a lifesaver for sure—at least for the next two weeks," Nick says.

My eyebrows draw together. "We'll have our own place in another two weeks, won't we?"

"I don't know. We'll need enough money to cover first- and last-month's rent, not to mention utilities. The part-time jobs are a good start, but your mom and I will need to find full-time jobs soon or it'll take forever to put enough money together."

"I can sell my paintings," Amber offers, referring to the artwork she creates every day at the library.

Nick ruffles her hair. "I'll let you know if it comes to that, baby."

"Are we going to be okay?" I ask.

Nick stares at his tray, his Adam's apple bobbing up and down. "It'll be tight, but we'll be fine. We bought a cheap cell phone today for job callbacks, so that set us back some. We'll have to be careful—walk where we can, eat where it's free, and don't use any more gas than necessary."

I do the math in my head—we must be down to around fifty dollars or less. *Please let us get out of this mess soon.*

NICK GUIDES US through a side door of the brown and white two-story house that will be our home for the next two weeks. He stops at a desk and scrawls our names into a thick register, then smiles at the woman behind the desk. "Hi. Nick and Claire Lunde with our children, Abby and Amber—we checked in earlier but needed to get the girls and bring them back?"

The woman sits on a bar stool behind the desk. Her shoulder-length gray hair is pulled back into a low ponytail, and she smiles warmly at Nick's introduction. "Come in, please. I'm Jennie. Since you've already checked in, I assume you've been shown your rooms?"

"Yes," Mom says. "They gave us a single room with four beds, but said it was unusual to put us all together?"

"Yes," Jennie says. "For obvious reasons, we normally split the men and women, but we're at capacity for men and I remember you checking in. The staff discussed it and decided it was ridiculous to turn your husband away when we have a room with four beds and no other woman to take that last bed. Since you're a family, we made an exception."

"Thank you," Nick says. "We appreciate it."

"It's our pleasure." She turns to Amber and me, her expression serious. "We don't get many children, so we have one important rule and I need you girls to pay close attention. You *must* stay with a parent at all times. Our guests are mostly safe—and there's always a volunteer on site—but it's for your protection. Please don't wander off on your own. Do you understand?"

Amber and I assure her we do. She studies us a moment then nods and leads us up a flight of stairs to the second floor and into the third room on the left. Inside is a sparsely furnished bedroom with four narrow beds. The room is small, but there's enough space to navigate in and out. I select the bed farthest from the door and take a seat. The mattress is neither too firm nor too soft, but every movement causes a creaking of the springs.

"There are two showers, one for men and one for women, and they're marked accordingly." Jennie points to two doors in the hall. "Please make your showers short—not more than about five minutes. The hot water tank is small and everyone wants a hot shower."

She leads us down a second set of steps that end outside a small living room. The furniture is dated, but the room is tidy. Even the television is one of those old box styles that weighs about a hundred pounds. It reminds me of an elderly person's home—a grandma, maybe—and I keep expecting someone to offer me cookies and milk.

Around the room are a handful of men and women, some watching television, some in conversation, and others just enjoying the atmosphere of a home, maybe for the first time in recent memory. Jennie doesn't allow us much time to consider them, as she picks up her tour and demands our attention.

"This is our main living room," she says. "It has a television with local channels, and there's a second TV in the basement. Feel free to change channels, but please be respectful of each other and share the remote."

Jennie opens a door off the living room that I've mistaken for a closet, then leads us down a straight flight of stairs into a finished basement. It's cooler down here with a slightly damp odor, but the room is larger than the one upstairs and equally as tidy. Besides the promised second TV, it also hosts a pool table and several card tables, some with half-solved puzzles. An older woman in a faded purple velour tracksuit sits at one table and plays a game of solitaire. She glances at us then turns her attention back to her game. Besides us, she's the only person in the room.

Jennie opens a door to our left. "In here are three washers and dryers. I recommend using the signup sheet on the wall to reserve your spot. It looks open now, so you might put your name on the list before it fills up."

Mom glances at the signup and picks a time. With the tour over, we follow Jennie up to the main floor and make our way back to our room.

"You showering first?" Nick asks me.

"Can I?"

He shrugs. "Might as well."

A smile spreads across my face. I'm sure I appear giddy, but I don't care. I've had a crap day, and this is the best thing to happen in a while. I set off toward the shower with Nick standing guard by the door, while Mom takes Amber down to the laundry to start our wash.

In the bathroom, I turn the shower as hot as I can stand it and enjoy the water's spray. I lather from head to toe, then rinse and lather a second time. I know I'm only supposed to spend five minutes, but—just this once—I cheat by a few extra minutes, promising myself it'll be the only time.

When I finish, Mom and Amber take the shower together while Nick and I watch the laundry, then Nick showers last before heading out to work. By the time he finishes, there's a line of residents waiting at both bathroom doors.

It's now a few minutes after eleven and I smother a yawn.

"Why don't you go to bed," Mom suggests. "I'll wait up for Nick."

I want to wait up for him, but I'm exhausted. When I'm hit with another yawn, I take Mom's suggestion and crawl under the covers. I pull the blankets high over my head and snuggle deep into the bed's warmth where I fall asleep almost immediately.

For the first time in a week, I sleep soundly. There are no bright lights peeking through the windows; the room is kept at a perfect temperature; and my bed, though old and creaky, is more comfortable than anything I can remember. And even though I wake up once to the sound of Nick's chainsaw snoring, my only feeling is relief that he's made it back safely.

CHAPTER SEVENTEEN

I NEVER THOUGHT I'D SAY IT, BUT I'M THANK-
FUL TO CALL A HOMELESS SHELTER "HOME." IT'S NOT FANCY,
and there are a few sketchy people who stay here with us, but it's clean
and the volunteers are nice. And it sure beats living out of Mom's van!

Each day our housemates change, as those whose time has expired
move out and others move in. As warned, Amber and I are the only kids.

Besides a warm bed and meals, the best thing to come out of staying
here is new shoes for Amber. On the third day after we arrived, Jennie
spotted Amber limping and insisted upon knowing why. When she realized the problem, she showed us a storage closet filled with donations
from the community. There she directed Amber to pick out a new pair of
shoes. I was ashamed at the extra charity, but not Amber—she's now the
proud second owner of pink canvas high-tops in nearly new condition.
Though they're a bit too wide for her narrow feet, the length is better and
she once again walks without discomfort.

Now for the bad news: our money is almost gone. Though we walk
almost everywhere, Nick insists on driving us to school because it's the
farthest distance in one shot, and he's adamant we arrive on time. He
reminds us, "An education is your ticket out of poverty."

With all the walking, we're certainly getting our exercise. From the
high school to the library is two miles, broken up by my paper route in
between. Then from the library to the Dorothy Day House is another
half mile. If I kept a log, I'm sure it would reflect at least five miles a day,

not including the normal walking everyone does.

At school, things are better—except for Trish. Though I've done my best to avoid her, there's no escaping her in my history class, where she spends every hour shooting daggers at me or grinning as though she knows my darkest secrets. Thankfully, I'm making friends and kids have begun greeting me much the same as they did Zach that first day. It's now Thursday, and I slide into my seat seconds before the bell rings to start chemistry.

"Made it." I say just loud enough for Josh and Scott to hear.

Since meeting through Zach, Scott and I have become friends and I usually manage to find a seat between him and Josh in our chem class.

"Just barely," Scott jokes. "That's twice this week. What's your excuse today?"

"Zach," I say.

"Ah-gain." Scott laughs. "You ready for Homecoming?"

"I think so. You're still going with Trish?"

"Yeah." He studies his hands for a moment before looking back up at me. "Look, I'm sorry for the way she acted the other day. I don't know what got into her, but I promise to keep her in check."

"Zach will kill you if you don't," Josh interjects.

"Fact," Scott agrees.

"It's okay—it's not your fault," I tell Scott.

He opens his mouth to respond, but Ms. Burke demands our attention and begins her lecture. As hard as I try to pay attention, I can't. Butterflies float in my stomach.

"What's wrong with you, Ariel?" Josh says, as we work with Scott on the day's group assignment. "You're never this off-kilter. Get your head in the game!"

"I'm sorry. I'm just nervous."

"Why?" Scott asks.

"Today's her audition for Mrs. Miner," Josh explains.

Scott's forehead crinkles. "That's today? I forgot. What time?"

"Fifth period," I groan.

"Dang. I'd love to come watch, but I have a class."

"Skip it," Josh says. "That's what a bunch of us are doing."

"I might. It's just art, and my project is almost done."

"You're in art?" I snort out a laugh.

Red heat moves up Scott's neck to his forehead. "Yes—and no, I'm not an artist. I needed a fine arts credit and it was that or pottery."

I glance at his large hands and smother another giggle at the image of him forming tiny clay pots. With effort, I force my attention back to our assignment, and we work wordlessly for the remainder of the class.

"YOU READY?"

I zip my bag closed and stare up into Zach's dark eyes. His smile is warm and my heart beats a staccato as it does every time I see him. I've read sappy romance novels where the heroine pinches herself to confirm she's not dreaming, and I've always thought it was stupid, but at this moment, I get it—I feel like pinching myself. I don't have to, though, because Zach leans down and touches his lips to mine in the briefest peck of a kiss. This is definitely real. I offer him a smile as he takes my bag.

"For lunch, or for my audition?" I ask.

Zach slips his hand into mine. "Both."

"Hm…" I tap a finger on my top lip. "For lunch? I'm starving. For the audition? Can we just skip it?"

"Don't worry. I'll be there, and Josh said he's going." Turning to Josh he asks, "Are Tera and Wendy coming?"

Josh shakes his head. "They can't. They've got Marshall for English and she's giving a test today."

"So, I guess it's just us. Are you coming?" Zach asks Scott.

"I was thinking about it. I'll see if I can talk Mrs. Williams into letting me out of art."

"I'll save you a seat, just in case," Zach tells him.

"Thanks, man!"

We enter the cafeteria and the butterflies in my stomach swarm as if fighting an all-out war. Though I'm hungry, my main concern is not throwing up. I select a plain turkey sandwich and chew slowly, desperately trying to forget my audition in an hour. I swallow my last bite and Josh bumps my shoulder with his own, nearly tossing me into Zach's lap. I glare at him. "What the hell, Josh?"

He shrugs. "You need to get out of your head, Ariel."

"I'm not in my head. I'm minding my own business, eating my sandwich."

"Right." He stretches the word out. "What were you thinking just before I bumped you?"

My face flushes.

"I knew it," he says. "Get the hell out of your head and think of something else."

"Leave her alone," Zach interjects. "She's nervous, but she'll be alright."

"Yeah," Wendy charges. "You try putting yourself up in front of the entire school, with all eyes watching you."

I groan. *Way to get me out of my head, Wendy.*

"That's right!" Tera interjects. "You're one to talk, Josh. Remember in third grade when you did that speech for Mrs. Ellison's class, and you got so scared you peed your pants?"

"I never—" Josh begins.

"Oh yes, you did!" Zach interrupts. "All you had to do was stand up and recite the Pledge of Allegiance by yourself, but you peed your pants. I can't believe I'd forgotten that!"

Josh flushes. "I spilled my milk in my lap."

"Right." Wendy rolls her eyes. "Because the milk carton magically floated off the tray, poured down your pants, then gently set itself back in its normal spot without anyone noticing."

Josh sputters. His face is purple, and I'm laughing so hard tears spill onto my cheeks. Wendy and Tera smile at each other and share a fist bump.

The bell rings, a shrill screech alerting me my time is up. I close my eyes and take a breath while Zach takes our trays to the tray return. My moment of meditation is interrupted when Josh throws an arm around me and pulls me to his side.

"You've got this, Ariel," he says. "And you owe me for taking one for the team." His sapphire eyes twinkle—he did this on purpose, deviously setting himself up for humiliation to redirect my attention.

I throw my arms around his neck and whisper, "I love you, Walt."

"I know you do, Ariel. Now, just in case, make a quick stop in the bathroom and then go kick ass!"

ZACH LEADS ME through the main door of a nearly packed auditorium. I had no idea there would be so many people, and I trip over my own feet and nearly fall to the floor.

"Whoa!" He catches me and pulls me close. "You okay?"

I breathe in the woodsy scent of his cologne and it calms me. "Yeah. I'm—don't these people have class or… *something* better to do?"

"Breathe, Abs." He places an arm around me and leads me to a seat next to Josh.

I collapse into the seat and he takes the open chair on my other side. His palm covers my clenched fists, gently opening one before weaving his fingers between mine. My eyes meet his at the same moment he brings our hands to his lips and kisses my knuckles.

"Close your eyes and tune out everything but you and me and the song you're going to sing," he says.

I follow his direction and take deep, relaxing breaths. When my heart rate slows, I turn my attention back to him.

"You ready now?" he asks.

I swallow the knot in my throat and nod.

There are seven auditions in the lineup, and I'm third on the schedule. Though I want to be polite and give the others my attention, I can't. The more I focus on my turn, the more my stomach revolts. I close my eyes again and concentrate on my breathing until I've blocked out everything around me.

Zach's hand squeezes mine and my eyes flash open. He smiles, his expression encouraging. "You're up, Abs."

"Abby Lunde?" Mrs. Miner says, clearly not for the first time.

Panic charges through me and my heart pounds so hard I think it's going to break a rib. *I can't do this!*

"Hey." Zach squeezes my hand again. "You've got this. Just go up there and do what you've practiced."

"I can't," I whisper. "There're too many people."

"Close your eyes and pretend they're not here. Or pretend you're standing in my room. You can do it—I have faith in you."

Josh squeezes my shoulder. "C'mon, Ariel. You've got this."

I blow out a breath. "Okay—you guys are right. I've got this."

Leaving Zach and Josh behind, I throw my shoulders back and meet Mrs. Miner onstage.

"Are you ready?" Her smile is welcoming.

I shake my head. "No, but here goes nothing."

I scan the audience for faces I recognize. Scott walks in and makes his way toward Zach, taking the seat I vacated. Standing together behind the back row are Mr. Thompson and my school counselor, Ms. Raven. Mr. Thompson winks and throws me a thumbs-up.

I grip the microphone in both hands. My body shakes and I've forgotten the words to the song. I stand there as silence echoes throughout the room. A titter of giggles reaches me from somewhere offstage and I swallow hard. I can't move.

"I'm sorry. I—" What started as barely more than a whisper drifts to nothing as my throat dries up and refuses to release another sound. I stand there, alone, wishing I could be anywhere else.

"Take your time," Mrs. Miner encourages.

Another moment passes, and Zach stands and walks toward the aisle. My heart plummets as he exits his row, then lifts in surprise as he turns and approaches the stage. Now, directly in front of me, though still some distance away, he motions me toward him. My feet won't move. It's as though someone has superglued them to the stage.

Understanding my dilemma, he hops onto the stage, walks toward me, and offers me a water bottle. Then, taking the microphone from my hands, he turns and addresses Mrs. Miner.

"Give me one second?" he asks.

Mrs. Miner nods and Zach flips the microphone to the off position. He takes my hand and leads me just beyond the curtain until we're standing back stage and out of sight. Stepping close until we're only inches apart, he touches his forehead to mine. "Look at me, Abs."

I gaze into his dark eyes and once again breathe in the woodsy scent of his cologne. Like before, a gentle calmness washes over me.

"I'm going to sit right in the front row. Forget everyone else in this room but me. Just look straight ahead and sing to me. Can you do that?"

I nod, but only to please him. I don't know that I can at all. Once again I ask myself why I agreed to this.

"Say it—'I can do this.'"

"Okay," I whisper.

"Not good enough. I want to hear the words—all of them. Say, 'I can do this.'"

"I can do this," I whisper again.

"Not loud enough."

Nervous, I look around to see if anyone sees us.

"Uh-uh." Zach catches my chin with his knuckles. "Ignore everything else but you and me. Now say it."

I close my eyes and take two deep breaths. Then, opening them, I borrow Zach's confidence and say firmly, "I can do this."

A slow smile spreads across his face and he leans forward and kisses my forehead. "Yes—you can! Now kill it!"

Weaving his fingers through mine once again, Zach leads me back onstage where he returns the microphone to my hands. He offers me a wink of encouragement, then turns and jumps off the stage, taking a seat in the front row as promised.

I take a sip of water then set the bottle at my feet. I flip the microphone back on and clear my throat. "I'm sorry. I've never sung in front of anyone before, so I'm a little nervous. I'm ready now."

In the quiet auditorium, I lock eyes with Zach and he nods. With a final breath, I close my eyes until the song plays inside my own head. When I'm ready, I open my throat and sing the first few notes. Before I've even hit the chorus, I forget the audience exists. Nothing remains beyond the music and me. My confidence soars and I release the last note of the song.

The room is silent and, with my eyes still closed, it's as though I'm alone. Slowly I open my eyes and take in the stunned expressions of my classmates. A half second later, the auditorium erupts as students and teachers take to their feet in a standing ovation. They're cheering for me, I realize, and I'm not sure how to react to their acceptance.

As the applause continues, I hand the microphone back to Mrs. Miner. My legs shake as I approach Zach. He closes the distance between us and pulls me into his arms, spinning me around in circles before placing me back on my feet. With the palms of his hands on each side of my face he leans down and kisses me in front of the entire auditorium. The cheering escalates, and catcalls are yelled from a few of the rowdier boys. Even the teachers are in the moment—all except Mr. Zagan, who stands by himself with his arms crossed in front of him, his expression sour.

Zach follows my gaze and lets out a howl of laughter. "What'd I say about being old and jealous?"

I gasp. "Shush! He'll hear you!"

Zach shrugs. "Did I say something that wasn't true?"

I shake my head, but can't hold back a smile. "Can we go now?"

"You don't want to stay to watch the others?"

"Would it be rude if I didn't? I'm too wound up, and I need to get out of here."

He takes my hand and leads me out of the auditorium with Josh and Scott following behind. When we reach the main lobby, Josh grabs ahold of me and squeezes me in a tight hug.

"That was excellent, Ariel!" he says. "And you didn't even pee your pants!"

I let out a groan and gently punch his shoulder before being pulled into Scott's muscular arms.

"I didn't know you could sing like that!" Scott says.

I try, but I can't wipe the smile from my face. Adrenaline pumps through me like I've just run a marathon. My hands shake, but not from fear this time—I'm too pumped to feel fear.

Zach retrieves me from Scott's embrace and kisses my cheek. "I'm really proud of you, Abs."

Happiness surges through me, and I wonder if my friends can feel my joy. "What now?"

He glances at the clock on the wall. "We have about thirty minutes until next period, so there's no point leaving. Wanna get a drink out of the vending machine?"

I nod and the four of us walk to the machines, where Zach empties his pockets of change and punches a button for apple juice. He hands it to me, then fills the machine with more quarters.

"Has Trish auditioned yet?" Josh asks no one in particular.

Scott takes a Gatorade from Zach. "Today after school. She's nervous."

"She should be after that!" Josh says.

"Can we please not talk about Trish?" I plead. "I just—she already hates me enough, and I'd rather not get caught talking about her. Plus, I'm in a really good mood right now."

Josh pantomimes zipping his lips and mumbles something I'm sure is supposed to be, "*Not another word.*"

Grabbing our drinks, we take seats at a high-top table. Scott and Josh talk about the chemistry exam scheduled for Monday while Zach and I sit with our hands clasped together, his thumb caressing the back of my own. Words aren't necessary—we've said everything that needs saying. I killed the audition, and now we wait for Monday to discover the results.

When the bell rings, Zach walks me to my next class as he has every day this past week. I swear I'll never get sick of it.

CHAPTER EIGHTEEN

HOMECOMING IS TOMORROW AND I'M MORE NERVOUS THAN I'VE EVER BEEN. I CAN'T STOP WORRYING that everything might go wrong, from Tera's dresses not fitting to Trish pulling some mean prank to ruin the entire evening. I don't expect perfection, but I just want things to go right.

"Your boy is waiting for you," Nick teases as he pulls into the student parking lot.

I glance out the window and my heart does a drumroll. Zach is leaned against a parking lamp, his dimple evident from thirty feet away. I slide open the rear door and step out of the van. "Thanks, Nick. Bye, Mom. Be good, Am."

The door slides closed only seconds before Zach reaches my side. He waves at Nick and takes my hand. "I have something for you."

I arch an eyebrow. "You do? What?"

He reaches into his backpack and pulls out a plastic store bag and hands it to me.

"What is it?"

"Just open it." He smiles and bounces on his feet.

I open the bag and pull out a dark green football jersey. The front features the words "Rochester South" in gold letters across the chest with the number nine filling in the remainder of real estate. I turn it around, and the back is the same, except instead of reading "Rochester South," the letters spell "Andrews."

"What is this?"

"It's Homecoming tradition for players to give their extra jerseys to their girlfriends on game day," he explains. "I was hoping you'd wear mine."

A smile tugs at my lips but I don't respond immediately.

"Please?" he says.

I nod. "Okay."

I pull my sweatshirt over my head, revealing the University of Nebraska T-shirt I'm wearing underneath, then cover it again with Zach's jersey. It hangs to my thighs like a nightshirt, but it's cozy—like I'm wrapped in Zach's arms. I breathe in the aroma of his cologne.

Zach examines me. "It looks better on you than me."

I roll my eyes. "You're weird."

"Maybe, but I saw you sniff my shirt."

"Did not!"

"Uh-huh." He grins. "I know what I saw."

I groan under my breath as Zach grabs my hand and walks with me to the cafeteria for breakfast. We eat quickly then head toward my political science class, walking slowly to extend our last few minutes together. I'm hoping for a private moment to say goodbye, but Tera and Wendy are waiting for us and, judging by the way Tera bounces from one foot to the other, she has something on her mind.

"Have you seen Trish?" she asks before we've even reached her side.

A line forms between Zach's eyebrows. "No. Why?"

"She is *pissed*!" Wendy supplies.

"About what?" I ask.

"Her audition yesterday," Tera says. "It didn't go well for her."

"What happened?" Zach asks.

Tera shrugs. "It doesn't sound like anything happened—she did her normal thing, but didn't get the love she expected."

"Okay—what did she expect?" I ask.

"Well, ya know how people keep congratulating you on your audition?" Wendy asks.

"Yeah?"

"Well, word's gotten out you got a standing ovation and sang an encore."

"That didn't happen!"

"That's not what we heard," Tera replies.

"Well—I mean—I guess I got a standing ovation, but I didn't sing an encore! Where do people get these stories?"

Zach interrupts. "Go on, I want to hear this."

"Okay, so anyway," Tera continues. "I guess Trish was expecting the same response—or better, even. But she got nada."

"What does that mean? The audience didn't even applaud?" I ask.

"No—they clapped politely, I guess, but they didn't give her the same reaction they gave you," Wendy explains.

"Oh no." Part of me feels sorry for Trish—I know better than anyone what it's like to be humiliated—but the other part of me can't forget how mean she's been.

"Oh yes!" Tera grins. "And now she's on a rampage. The only one who can get near her is Zoë. Everyone else is on her shit list."

"Lovely."

Zach pulls me close to his side. "Hey! Don't let it get to you. You practiced your ass off and deserved that ovation. It's not your fault she didn't perform as well."

"The bell is about to ring, ladies, and I have no patience for tardies today." Mr. Zagan's monotone voice startles us and we spring apart. "And Mr. Andrews, don't you have a class to attend?"

"Office aide this hour," Zach replies.

"Then get to the office," the teacher says.

Zach says goodbye and leaves me to walk in with Tera and Wendy. Josh isn't here yet and I don't envy him having to deal with Zagan if he's late.

The bell rings and Zagan closes the door in the faces of two late students, neither of them Josh. I hate this teacher.

"WHERE'S JOSH?" I ask, setting my lunch tray on the table.

"Haven't seen him at all—he's probably got the flu that's going around," Wendy says.

Tera shivers. "I hope not. I don't need the flu before tomorrow night!"

"Right?" Wendy says. "We only have Homecoming as seniors once!"

Zach smiles down at me. "If you get the flu, Abs, we'll just have our own Homecoming celebration."

"Aw," Tera coos.

Wendy points her index finger at her open mouth, pantomiming that she might puke.

Tera laughs. "You're just jealous, Wen."

"Meh." She shrugs then holds her thumb and index finger about a quarter inch apart. "Maybe a *teensy* bit."

Zach places an arm around me and pulls me closer. Wendy rolls her eyes, but he doesn't remove his arm and spends the remainder of lunch eating one-handed.

AFTER LUNCH, I drop my books at my favorite high-top table near Door Six and head to the bathroom before starting my home-work. I open the door and immediately wish I could push a rewind button and choose a different restroom. There must be at least four rest-rooms on this floor, but I choose "Door Number One" and find myself face to face with Trish, her sidekick, Zoë, with her like an obedient pet.

Trish's face lights up in a malicious smile. She steps back for me to enter, but stands between me and the stalls. Her eyes rove over me, be-ginning at my head and moving down my body, ending at my feet. "So I guess it's true. I'd never have thought it, but look at you. It must be true."

I step to my left, but she steps to her right and blocks my path. I sigh. "What do you want?"

Trish smirks. "You're jealous of me, aren't you? If I let you, you'd take everything of mine. But guess what? I'm not gonna let that happen."

I move to shove past her but she steps forward, making it impossible to do anything but retreat—and I refuse to back down, so I hold my ground. Her eyes narrow. "First my boyfriend, and now my hand-me-downs? There's no end to the sloppy seconds you'll take, is there?"

"What are you talking about?"

"Hand. Me. Downs." Her words are slow, insulting. "The jersey you're wearing? It's mine. Zach gave it to me last year. But you wouldn't know since you're not one of us, are you?"

"What do you want, Trish? Why can't you accept that I'm here and I'm staying? I'm sorry things didn't work out with you and Zach, but that's not my problem. So leave me the hell alone."

"I'll consider leaving you alone when you stop taking what's mine."

"What are you talking about? Zach isn't property. I think you're seriously ill—you should see someone about these psychotic episodes of yours."

I change my mind about using the restroom and turn on my heel, yanking the door open with every ounce of my strength. I'm almost out the door when Trish's parting words pierce straight through my heart. "Oh, I almost forgot! Let me know if you figure out how to get the nail polish off the inside hem of that shirt. I tried just about everything, and never could get it out. I can't believe I was so clumsy! But, oh well—Zach didn't mind. It was *my* jersey, after all."

I let the door float closed behind me and walk away.

I will not look…

I can't help it—I have to know for sure. Flipping the bottom of the shirt over near the hem, I spot it immediately: a smeared blotch of bright red nail polish, about the size of a nickel. The truth slaps me in the face and my fingers tingle as hot blood rushes to my head.

I want to rip the shirt from my body and tear it into pieces, but I resist. I reign in my temper and bite hard on my bottom lip, hoping to keep the tears at bay.

Act normal, Abby. Do not let her know she's hurt you! Sit down and work on homework like you always do—don't let her win this round!

I pull Zach's jersey to my nose and breathe in his scent, hoping it will calm me, but I'm too upset. I dig through my backpack for my copy of *Mockingbird*, but come up empty. I grit my teeth to keep from screaming my frustration.

I decide to work on chemistry homework instead but, ten minutes later, I give up. The only thing I can focus on is that stupid red nail polish. I slam my textbook shut and collect my belongings. If I can escape into the pages of *Mockingbird*, then maybe I'll calm down.

I walk the halls toward my locker and grimace at the irony that surrounds me. You expect when classes are in session, the halls will be empty, but that's never the case. And it's not the case now when I don't want anyone seeing me distraught. I'm especially mindful of this as I wipe another stray tear from my cheek and hope nobody notices.

I find my locker and spin the combination on the lock, but my hands are shaking and I land on a wrong number. It takes me two more tries before the lock pops open. Finally! I yank open the narrow door and a cascade of red falls like a waterfall out of my locker and onto the floor around me.

"SHIT!" My voice echoes off the walls and once again I'm thrown back in time to another lifetime and another instance of things falling on me from inside my locker.

FIVE MONTHS EARLIER

I'm late for class, but I always am these days. If there's one good thing that's come out of Mom's resignation, it's that the teachers are nicer to me.

The truth is they pity me. They see Mom's humiliation has led to my own destruction and, while they don't step in to stop the bullying, they give me extra leeway they don't give other students. These people were once Mom's friends. Some were regular guests at our house for Book Club or Bunco Night. Now, I don't know if they're still her friends or not—I only care that they give me the space I need to navigate my new reality.

I can't stand walking down the busy halls between classes anymore. Doing so exposes me to the bullying and jeers, so I hide during passing time then do my passing once the halls are silent. It's easier to ignore a few people calling me whore or slut than it is to ignore large pockets of them all at the same time. Waiting means entering class late, but by silent agreement my teachers don't count me tardy and my classmates don't dare say anything in front of our teachers.

I arrive at my locker and spin the combination until the lock releases, then open the door. I'm confused at first as foil wrappers of red, white, blue, green and gold are vomited from my locker. With them comes small squares of paper the size of Post-It Notes. They float weightlessly through the air before landing on the floor around me. It takes me a moment to understand what I'm seeing and, in that same moment, the fire alarm sounds. Classroom doors are thrown open as students and teachers rush out. But I can't move. I pick off a gold square packet from my shoulder and read the logo: MAGNUM by Trojan. Condoms. In every color imaginable. They're on my shoulders and at my feet, surrounding me on the floor. Hundreds of them, maybe thousands. I step away and my shoe crushes them under my feet, along with the small slips of paper. I don't have to pick them up to see what they are—the image has been burned in my brain for weeks. I catch one in midair and rip the xeroxed photo of Mom and Coach Hawkins into pieces.

I turn to run, but the hall is a crush of people. Even if I barrel through their ranks and make it outside, there'll still be hundreds more students there to witness my humiliation. I'm trapped.

"ABBY?" THE VOICE comes through a tunnel as I frantically shove the little red things back in my locker. My mind doesn't register what they are—I just need them hidden before anyone sees. Hot tears flood down my cheeks and I can't breathe. Each time I try, the air gets stuck near my throat.

"Abby—stop! *Stop!*"

A pair of firm hands holds my shoulders and I slump over until I'm kneeling on the floor. The tears are coming fast now.

"Abby, honey. Calm down. It's okay. Whatever you thought it is, it isn't. Look."

Through tear-fogged eyes, I look at Ms. Burke. She's squatting next to me. Her blond hair with black tips swings forward and she tucks it behind her ears. In one hand she holds a dozen of the little red things. She brings them to her nose and sniffs, then holds them out for me to smell. "It's rose petals, sweetheart," she says. "Someone likes you very much to fill your locker with these."

I stare at her. "Rose petals?"

She nods and smiles. "Yes, and I think I can guess who they're from."

My tears slow and comprehension sets in. *They're not condoms. This is Rochester South, not Omaha East. I have friends here, a boyfriend. Zach.*

"Are you okay?" she asks.

I shake my head. "I—I need to—I need some space for a few minutes."

"Is this your open period?"

I nod.

"Let's do this: go collect yourself—use the staff bathroom." She points at a door almost directly across from us. "I'll take care of the rose petals. I'll scoop them into a bag and put them in your locker, and you can deal with them when you're ready. Okay?"

I bite my bottom lip and nod. "Thank you."

"It's okay. I'm here if you need to talk, or we can get Ms. Raven."

"No. I'm fine."

Her eyes narrow. "Abby, something triggered strong emotions for you. If you're not comfortable talking to me or Ms. Raven, promise me you'll talk to someone else, okay?"

I nod then pull myself to a standing position. Taking my bag, I escape to the staff restroom and lock myself behind the safety of a stall. *Rose petals. Not condoms. Kindness. Not meanness.* I can't wrap my head around it. Humiliation floods through me as I remember the condoms from so long ago—the memory is still as real as the three rose petals I hold between my fingers. They're so delicate—they would bruise if mistreated. I wonder if Zach plucked from the stem himself, or if he bought them that way. And also, how many roses were used. Judging by what I remember, it must've taken dozens of stems.

A bubble of manic laughter belches out of me at the irony of finding rose petals on the heels of my run-in with Trish. If not for the flashback to the condoms, the rose petals would've completely overshadowed the nail polish. But now my head is so screwed up I can't sort it all out. My tears fall unheeded in the quiet bathroom and, though I mean only to allow myself a few minutes, I cry until my body runs dry.

The bell rings to change classes, but I'm not ready to give up my solitude, so I stay hidden behind the stall doors as first one, and then another teacher enters to use the facilities. When the room is empty again, I blow out a breath. What I need is Josh. He could talk me through this and have me laughing in seconds. But I'm alone. It's okay—I've gone it alone before.

It takes me most of the next hour to put things in perspective. Zach was thoughtless in not telling me Trish had worn his jersey, but it wasn't malicious. And his heart was in the right place when he left me the rose petals. He couldn't have known the memories they would trigger, so I can't fault him for that. In fact, I decide, I won't fault him for the jersey either. If it's a tradition for players to give their jerseys to girlfriends, then it probably never occurred to him to tell me. He probably assumed I'd know, since he dated Trish last year.

By the time the bell rings for the last class, I'm composed enough to emerge, but I'm still not sure what I'll say to Zach.

A SUBSTITUTE TEACHER greets me at Mr. Thompson's class. I take a seat and wait for Zach, the entire time running a mental dialogue of what I'll say when I see him. Time ticks by, and the tardy bell rings. Just as the sub closes the door, Zach slides in and shoots her a sheepish look. "I'm sorry I'm tardy. I—um—lost something in the hall and couldn't find it."

"Please take your seat," she directs. "I haven't taken roll yet, so we'll let this one pass."

Zach sits beside me and tips his head to the side, raising an eyebrow. I still don't know what to say, so I ignore him.

The sub, a graying woman in a retro 1980s acid-washed denim skirt writes her name on the SMART Board then turns toward us with a nervous smile. "Good afternoon, I'm Mrs. Figgs. Mr. Thompson is out today, but he left instructions for you to form small groups and work on a list of study questions. So if you would form your groups, you can get started while I take roll."

Zach turns his desk toward mine, his fierce expression forbidding anyone from joining us. "What's going on?"

I stare at my hands. "It's nothing. I'm just trying to work through some things in my head."

"By ignoring me? I looked for you at Door Six to walk you to your vocal music class, and you weren't there. Then I waited outside after your class, and you didn't come out. Mrs. Miner said you never showed up. What gives?"

"I know. I just—I needed some time alone."

Zach's gaze burns, but I refuse to look at him.

"How much of this has to do with Trish?" he asks.

My head snaps up and our eyes lock. "What makes you think it has anything to do with Trish?"

"Because I passed her and Zoë in the hall on my way here. She was giddy, like she had a secret, then asked if you'd gone home. When I said I didn't know, she said she'd seen you in the bathroom and thought you looked upset."

"Oh." I stare at my hands.

Zach lifts my chin with his knuckles, refusing my attempt to look away. "So how much of this has to do with Trish?"

"She said something that upset me. It's—no big deal."

"It's big enough you avoided me and skipped your favorite class. Why? If it has anything to do with me, I have a right to know."

I place my hand over his and lower it to the desk. "It's nothing, Zach, okay? She said something about hand-me-downs, and reminded me you two have a history."

I don't dare tell him about the roses—there's no way he'd understand that, too.

Zach's eyebrows form a straight line then his eyes flash wide. He runs a hand through his dark hair. "Oh geez, Abs—I'm sorry. I didn't think. Trish and I dated, and I let her wear my jersey. It didn't occur to me you'd be bothered by it or I would've said something. Dammit—I'm really sorry."

"I'm not really bothered by it. It's just that she has a way of getting to me."

"Are you mad? I didn't mean to lie to you."

I shake my head. "No, I'm not mad. I'm just sick of her. Every time I turn around, she says something hateful, and I'm beginning to dislike her."

"Just beginning?" he asks.

I laugh. "Okay, no—not just beginning. I've hated her since the first time I met her. I don't know why I let her get to me."

"You shouldn't, you know. If I wanted to be with her, I would. I'd rather be with you."

"I know." I nod. "Sometimes I just need a reminder."

"Are we good, then?"

"Yeah," I say. "By the way? Thanks for the rose petals."

Zach's face lights up. "You got them already? I was hoping to be there when you opened your locker."

Thank God he wasn't!

"Yeah. I got them. Thank you. You put a lot of time and thought into them, and I really appreciate it."

Zach's dimple deepens as his smile grows. "I'm glad. I wanted to surprise you and do something special. You know, since Homecoming is tomorrow and all."

"You definitely surprised me. How'd you get my locker combination?"

Zach wiggles his eyebrows. "There are benefits to be had as an office aide."

CHAPTER NINETEEN

"ARE YOU GONNA KISS ZACH TONIGHT?"

"Amber! That's a completely inappropriate question!" Mom scolds.

Next to her in the front seat, Nick smothers a grin. My face flushes and I wish he'd drive faster so I can escape. Though he's decreed the van "parked," he's agreed to drive me to Wendy's so I don't look like a hobo dragging my gear behind me.

"Well, *is* she?" Amber asks.

"That's not a question you ask, peanut," Nick answers.

Amber turns and stares at me. The seconds tick by and Nick's eyes catch mine in the rearview mirror. His lips tip up into a smirk that reads, "*Well? Are you?*"

"Stop it! I'm not answering that question!" I say.

"I would!" Amber announces.

I blow out a breath. "What do you know about kissing?"

"I know lots about kissing! I know how to French kiss. Kason showed me. Wanna see?"

Mom's head whips around to the back seat, her eyes ping-ponging between Amber and me. *Great. Now I have everybody's attention.* I turn to Amber, intent on telling her to shut up, but my nose pinches in disgust. Her lips are pursed together while tiny bubbles of saliva foam over her lips and drip down her chin. She looks like a cross between a goldfish and a rabid dog.

I shrink away from her. "What the—GROSS! *What are you doing?*

That's disgusting!"

Amber wipes her chin on her sleeve then blows out a few more tiny bubbles. "*They* don't think it's disgusting."

"Seriously, Amber," Mom interrupts. "Sister's right—that's gross. Wipe your chin. And anyway, *who* doesn't think it's disgusting?"

She wipes away the last of the slobber and lifts a shoulder. "The French people!"

"What French people?" Nick interjects, his voice half-distracted as he navigates traffic.

Amber makes a loud *hmph* sound. "The *French* people!"

"Who?" he asks.

"The *kissing* French people! I was showing Sister how to French kiss!"

Nick chokes on a laugh and Mom turns face forward in the van, her shoulders shaking with laughter.

"Thank you, peanut, but I think Sister will be fine without any extra help," Nick says.

Mom clears her throat. "On a different note, what time do you think you'll be ready to leave your friend's house tomorrow?"

"I'm not sure," I say. "Can I just hang out at Wendy's until late afternoon, or when Tera leaves—whichever comes first?"

"I guess that's as good a place as any," Nick says. "We'll take Amber to church then head to the library afterwards. Why don't you plan to meet us by four o'clock."

"Okay."

Nick turns into a residential neighborhood and follows the street a few blocks before stopping in front of an impressive colonial-style home with four large pillars framing the front.

"You memorized the new phone number in case of emergency, right?" Mom asks.

I roll my eyes. "Yes, Mom. You only made me repeat it back to you a dozen times."

Nick laughs. "Okay, then. Call if you have an emergency, but *only* for an emergency. We can't afford more minutes right now."

I slide the door open and jump out before either can offer more advice or edicts. "Will do. Thanks for the ride."

"I'M SO EXCITED you're here!" Wendy beams.

She swings open the heavy white door and steps aside for me to enter. When I step into the foyer, she throws her arms around me in a hug that startles me with its warmth and honesty. "Tera's here already, and she brought the dresses she promised."

"I hope they fit," I say, pulling out of her hug. "Is Josh here yet?"

"Not yet, but he's always running late."

"I thought that was yours and Tera's M-O."

Wendy lets out a bark of laughter then grabs my hand and leads me through the front hall and into the family room. Though prepared for its size, I'm still astonished. In the center of the room is a matching sofa and love seat in mahogany leather, set off by a glass-top coffee table with matching end tables parked on each side of the sofa. Centered in front of the furniture and mounted high above a gas fireplace is a big-screen TV. My jaw drops—the TV is easily the size of our van.

"Oh." Wendy frowns. "I thought my dad would be in here—I was going to introduce you."

I tell her it's okay, but I can't stop staring at the TV.

Wendy reroutes us back through the foyer and up the stairs toward the second level, where we run into her mom on the stairs. She's a replica of Wendy, only older. They share the same petite figure, but what sets them apart as mother and daughter instead of sisters are the tiny smile lines beside her eyes.

"You must be Abby," she says.

"Yes, ma'am."

"Welcome." Her eyes smile like Wendy's. "I'm Karyn. I've been looking forward to meeting you."

"Thank you. It's nice to meet you, too."

Karyn pats my arm as she passes. "I'll let you girls do your thing, but call me if you need anything, okay?"

"Thanks, Mom—we will," Wendy assures her.

Wendy's room is at the end of a long hall. On each side are framed photographs in various sizes, a shrine to her family. I stop at a photo of a toddler with two older boys. They're sitting on a sandy beach with a blue ocean behind them. Catching my gaze, Wendy removes the photo from the wall and her lips tilt upward. She runs a finger over the photo, and a thin layer of dust lifts from its surface.

"West Palm Beach, Florida," she explains. "I think I was three or four. I really only remember the ocean and building sand castles."

"And the two boys?"

"My brothers, Declan and Drew." She points to their images as she says their names. "They're six and nine years older than I am. Declan's in law school at the University of South Dakota, and Drew is doing his residency at the Clinic."

"His residency?" I ask.

"Yeah. To be a doctor? He wants to be an oncologist. He graduated with his medical degree from The U, so now he's working on his residency—six years, I think, on top of the eight and a half he's already done. We're lucky he got accepted back here at home."

"Wow. That's a lot of school."

"Right?" Wendy replaces the photo on the wall. "But Drew's always loved school, so it's a natural fit for him."

We continue down the hall and stop at the last door on the left. Inside Tera gazes at her reflection in a floor mirror. She turns from side to side, gauging her appearance. Seeing us, she bounces toward us. "You made it! Are you ready for this?"

"Ready as I'll ever be!" I say.

Tera loops her arm through mine and pulls me toward a large bed in the center of the room. "Well, c'mere and let me show you the dresses!"

Wendy's bed is queen-sized with tall oak bedposts. It's so beautiful I catch myself staring again. One side is a mess of rumpled bedsheets, while the other side is neatly made with a cotton-candy-colored comforter, proving the bed is large enough for her to sleep on one side without mussing the other. On the made-up side are three semi-formal dresses, laid out side by side.

"Oh wow." My jaw drops. "These are gorgeous—they must've cost a fortune. I'm not sure I should borrow any of them."

Tera waves a hand in dismissal. "Don't worry. We'll have our chance to shop in your closet soon, and these will only go to waste if you don't wear one. C'mon—try one on."

Tera picks up a strapless dress in dark green. The bodice is covered from the sweetheart neckline to its waist in glittering rhinestones that sparkle when it moves. The skirt is short and flares from the waist with a sheer overlay threaded at the hem with an invisible wire, causing it to curl rather than lay flat. "Try this one—it'll go great with your hair."

"Are you sure?" I ask.

"Of course I'm sure! I wore this one our freshman year, so I'm pretty sure nobody will remember it."

I take the dress and walk to the full-length mirror, looping the hanger over my head so it hangs in front of me. My breath catches and my nose tickles with the beginning of tears. I bite down hard on my bottom lip—I will not let them see me cry.

"Try it on already," Tera orders.

I move toward Wendy's en-suite bathroom, and a surge of panic flashes through me. "Oh no—I didn't bring a strapless bra!"

"No worries—I've got lots of them," Wendy says. "Try one of mine."

She opens a dresser drawer that's stuffed to overflowing. A few garments fall to the floor, while another catches on a corner and dangles over its edge. I gape at the mess and wonder how she finds anything, but she seems to know exactly where to look.

"Found them!" She holds out three strapless bras.

"Thanks." I lift an eyebrow, giving her a look that reads: "*Why do you have three strapless bras?*"

Wendy shrugs. "I can't ever find one when I need it, so I keep having to buy new ones."

Taking the bras, I shake my head and step into the bathroom. I replace my bra with a beige strapless one and pull the dress over my head until it falls to just above my knees. I can't zip it myself, so I poke my head into the bedroom and come nose to nose with Tera. I let out a gasp. "Oh, hello!"

Tera reddens. "Er…sorry. I was just excited to see how it looks."

"Perfect. You can be the first. Can you zip me up?"

Tera steps inside the bathroom then turns me toward the mirror. She beams at my reflection and slides the zipper home. "Perfect fit—I knew it!"

I study myself. The dress is not only a perfect fit but, with my wavy red hair billowing out over my shoulders, I feel like a princess. It's beyond anything I ever imagined.

"Wow!" Tera blows out a gush of air. "It looks better on you than it ever did on me."

Tears blur my vision, but again I bite my lip to staunch their flow.

Wendy knocks twice and opens the door without waiting for a response. Seeing me, her eyes widen. "You look amazing! And I have just the shoes!"

She races back into the bedroom where she forages through the mess of her closet until only her tiny rear end pokes out from beyond its open doors. When she emerges, she offers me a pair of strappy silver high-heeled shoes. She holds them by the straps, extending them toward me. "Try these."

"Um." My eyebrows rise to my hairline. "How tall are those heels?"

She purses her lips and squints her eyes. "Maybe four inches? Give 'em a try."

I step into the shoes and grab for the doorframe while my ankles wobble precariously. When I'm steady, Wendy bends down and fastens the straps at my ankles. Now standing, she looks me over from head to toe. "Wow!"

Tera studies me. "What are you gonna do with your hair?"

I turn to the mirror and lift my hair off my neck, then let it fall back to my shoulders and down to my waist. "I hadn't thought about it."

"Ooh! Let me do it!" Wendy's eyes sparkle. "Zach's eyes will bug out when he sees you!"

I pause, not sure how to respond.

"C'mon, Abs. I'm good with hair. Please?"

"You should, Abby," Tera interjects. "She's great with hair. And I'll do your makeup."

I shake my head, but Tera's face is already lit with excitement.

"I—I didn't bring any makeup," I stutter.

"Are you kidding?" Tera says. "Wendy has enough for an entire department store. I'll do your makeup and she'll do your hair. Please, Abs?"

I waver, my brain scrambling for how to say no.

"It's decided," Wendy says.

Tera races to the bathroom and grabs a tray of makeup from the counter, then rummages through the drawers for more.

I nod slowly. "Okay…"

"Relax, dah-ling." Wendy imitates an English accent. "When we're done with you, you shall look simply mah-velous. Trust us."

My stomach flip-flops, but I take a seat on the barstool Wendy stole from the kitchen earlier. I inhale a breath but it catches in my throat.

Wendy pulls out a curling iron. "Seriously, Abs. Relax. We promise you'll love what we do."

With those words, she takes a small section of hair and winds it around the iron's hot barrel. I bide my time by studying the images of perfection that are Tera and Wendy.

Wendy's short hair is styled half up and half down with tiny ringlets escaping around her face. It's the perfect accompaniment to the black strapless cocktail dress she's chosen for the evening. Tera, on the other hand, has styled her much longer sable locks into large waves of curls that cascade over her right shoulder and nearly to her waist. It's secured with a small comb embedded with rhinestones matching the sparkling jewels on her teal satin dress. Both girls are stunning, and I know I must look like a charity case standing between them.

"Wow! Your wavy hair is easy to curl!" Wendy says, interrupting my thoughts. "I bet the curls stay and don't fall out after fifteen minutes like mine. If I had hair like yours, I'd grow mine out."

I'm turned away from the mirror, so I twist my neck to sneak a peek but Wendy thumps me on the head with her comb. "Uh-uh! You'll ruin the surprise."

Facing the center of the room again, butterflies flit in my stomach— I hope they know what they're doing!

After a long while, Tera steps back and surveys me through narrowed eyes. The edges of her mouth slide up. "Close your eyes and I'll help you turn around to see the mirror."

"Why do I have to close my eyes?" I laugh.

"Because we want to see your expression when you see the new you!" Wendy interjects. "Now c'mon, Abs. Do as you're told."

With my eyes closed, Tera helps me turn around until I'm facing the full-length mirror.

"Okay," Wendy says. "On the count of three, open your eyes! One...two—"

But I don't wait for three. I open my eyes and blink hard at the image before me. I work my throat, trying to form saliva, but my eyes have a monopoly on moisture. The room is silent as a rush of emotions flows through me. I open my mouth, but no words come out. My heart clenches and the first rogue teardrop falls.

"No!" Tera grabs for a tissue and shoves it at me. "Don't cry! You'll ruin your makeup!"

Wendy studies me, her eyebrows drawn together. "Do the tears mean you're happy, or that you hate it?"

"Are you kidding?" I blow out a breath. "I love it. I—I don't even know what to say. It looks like me, but it doesn't look at all like me."

I turn back to the mirror and study myself. My copper hair is arranged in loose, wavy curls that hang down to my waist. On the left side, a delicate French braid extends across the top of my head and disappears on the other side beneath a rhinestone-studded hair clip complementing the jewels on my dress. My makeup is impeccable. Natural shades of beige and brown are blended seamlessly to color my lids, and my green eyes are made huge with carefully applied eyeliner and mascara. Instead of lipstick, I wear a shimmery gloss with only a hint of pink to enhance the natural color of my lips. I can't believe it's me staring back from the mirror.

"I don't know what to say," I admit. "Thank you!"

Wendy shrugs. "We're friends—it's what friends do!"

"Speaking of friends…" Tera glances at her wristwatch. "I almost forgot about Josh! Where is he, anyway?"

"Have you called him?" I ask.

"I will." Wendy scans the room for her mobile phone. It takes several minutes, but she locates it under a pile of blankets on her bed. "It's already after five—he should've been here two hours ago."

While Wendy dials Josh, Tera retouches her own makeup and I take one last look in the mirror. The transformation astounds me.

"He's not answering," Wendy says.

"He's probably on his way and not picking up 'cause he's driving," says Tera.

Wendy tosses her phone onto the bed then nudges me aside to share the mirror. She adjusts the bodice of her dress, then the skirt, then applies another coat of lip gloss. "I'm going to try Josh again. He should've been here by now."

"It's only been five minutes, Wen," Tera says.

A knock sounds on the door and Wendy's hand flies to her heart. "Finally!" She pulls the door open, but her face drops when she finds her mom on the other side.

"Why don't you girls come down and have some cheese and crackers?" Karyn suggests. "You three must be starving."

"You guys go ahead," Wendy tells us. "I'm gonna call Josh one more time."

Tera and I find the kitchen and scarf down most of the cheese before Wendy joins us.

"He's still not answering," she reports.

"Did you leave a message?" I ask.

"Yeah. And on his mom's phone, too."

"He probably had a family emergency," Tera says.

The doorbell rings and the first of the boys arrive—Tera's and Wendy's dates. Another ten minutes pass and the doorbell chimes again. Knowing it must be Zach or Josh, I answer while Wendy's parents are distracted by Wendy and her date.

Standing before me in black dress pants, a shimmery gray dress shirt, and a green tie the exact color of my dress is Zach. He stares at me, his dark eyes holding an emotion I can't read. After a few seconds, his lips split into a grin so wide the dimple in his cheek draws my eye. Before I can stop myself, I reach out and press my index finger into the divot on his cheek. His hand snatches mine, weaving our fingers together.

"Abby," he says. "You're always beautiful, but this—I hadn't expected this at all."

I release his hand and do a tiny twirl. "You like it, then?"

"Like it? I love it."

Zach tugs me into a kiss, careful not to smudge my makeup. "I'm glad I changed my mind about going tonight."

I step back and touch his green tie. "It matches my dress exactly. How'd you know?"

"Tera," he says. "She made me go tie shopping with her this week and insisted I buy three—one for each of the dresses she had for you to choose from. Wendy texted me the color about an hour ago."

Heat flushes my face. "I'm sorry—you didn't have to do that."

"I wanted to," he says. "I'll just take the other two back next week, but I'll keep this one for a souvenir."

My eyes catch a flash of movement over Zach's shoulder and his mom approaches.

"Zachary Michael Andrews—quit staring at that girl and get her inside the house. It's cold out here," Cherie scolds, but her mouth is stretched wide in a smile. She embraces me and I breathe in the gentle floral scent of her perfume. "Abby, you look beautiful."

"Thank you," I say, closing the door behind us.

"I'm so glad Zach changed his mind about Homecoming. And he couldn't have found a lovelier date," she says.

My face heats again as I show her into Wendy's living room where parents are exchanging phone numbers. The doorbell rings again, but nobody makes a move to answer it, so I head back into the foyer and greet our next guest.

"Abby?" Mom stands on the front porch, her eyes wide. "Oh my goodness, sweetheart. You look stunning."

I smile back and search over her shoulder for the rest of my family. "Where are Nick and Amber?"

Mom clears her throat. "Nick thought it would be good for you and I to share this experience together. You know—after everything. He stayed behind with Amber."

Mom dabs the corner of her eye with a tissue, and for a moment everything in the past is forgotten. I step into her arms and she hugs me close.

"Thanks for coming, Mom."

"I can't get over how beautiful you look," she whispers. "But please be careful with that dress. It must've cost a fortune and we can't afford to replace it."

I roll my eyes and step out of her arms. "Of course, Mom."

Zach winds an arm around my waist and extends his hand to Mom. "Mrs. Lunde? I'm Zach. It's nice to meet you."

Mom smiles and shakes his hand. "Nice to finally meet you, Zach."

He turns to me and holds up a clear box with a gardenia corsage inside. "For you."

"Oh. Thank you! I'm sorry—I didn't even think about a boutonniere for you!"

"No worries. I don't like them anyway." He slides the ivory-petaled flower onto my right wrist and smiles. "There! A wrist corsage means no nasty pins!"

"Zach?" Wendy wrings her hands. "Have you talked to Josh? He was supposed to be here hours ago."

"No—have you called him?"

"Several times, but I'll try again." Her face is flushed and a crease forms between her brows. She scurries away.

"She's really worried," Zach says. "What time was he supposed to be here?"

"Three o'clock," I say.

"He'll be okay. I'll bet he shows up at the dance, 'fashionably late.'" Zach makes air quotes with his fingers.

"Maybe," I say. "Speaking of late, where's Trish and Scott?"

Zach smiles. "They're going with a different group. Scott and I talked about it last night and decided it's better if they go with Zoë's group. Trish will be happier anyway."

My shoulders slump in relief. "Are you okay with that? I know you'd hoped Scott would go with us."

"It's okay," he says. "He's happy, I'm happy, you're happy. It's all good."

Taking my hand, he leads me into the chaos that once was Wendy's living room. We've barely stepped over the threshold when Tera grabs my arm.

"We still can't get ahold of Josh," she says. "Wendy's freaking, and I don't know what to do."

"This isn't like him," Wendy says, joining us. "He wasn't at school yesterday, we didn't talk last night, and he hasn't shown up. Josh would call if he couldn't make it."

"What do you want to do?" Zach asks. "Should we wait for him?"

Wendy gnaws on her bottom lip but shakes her head. "No. I've left several messages already. I guess he'll call us when he gets a chance. But I swear I'm going to throat punch him when I see him for making us worry."

"MY FACE HURTS from smiling." Zach pulls the seatbelt across his chest and starts the car. "I thought they'd never stop taking pictures!"

I laugh. "How many do you think they took?"

"At least a thousand, I'd bet."

"I wish Josh had made it. It doesn't seem right without him."

"You worried?" he asks.

I lift a shoulder. "Yeah—I guess. I haven't known him that long, but it doesn't seem like Josh to stand us up."

He nods. "I'm sure he has a good excuse."

"He better," I say. "Otherwise he's in big trouble with Wendy!"

"Now that would be fun to watch." Zach parks in front of Victoria's, a locally owned Italian restaurant in the heart of downtown Rochester. He opens his door, then flashes me a severe look. "Stay there."

My stomach flip-flops as he walks around and opens my door. He takes my hand and helps me out of the car, then holds the restaurant door for me to enter first before stepping in behind me.

The scents of garlic and fresh-baked bread waft toward me. My stomach grumbles, but I pause long enough to snap mental photographs of the Italian decor. I want to remember every second of this night for the rest of my life.

The hostess greets us and escorts us to a round table for eight behind a private wall. Tera, Wendy, and their dates are already seated, so we take the spots closest to Tera. The two empty seats for Josh and his date stare back at me, and I wonder again why he didn't let us know he wasn't coming.

"Order anything you want," Zach says as we glance over the menus.

Here's the truth: I've never been on a date. I'm seventeen years old, so that's embarrassing to admit, but Mom and Nick wouldn't let me date until I was sixteen, and then I didn't have much chance before everything unraveled with Mom.

I scan the menu and can't decide. After the third time going through every item on the list, I feel Zach's eyes on me.

"What?" Embarrassment creeps up my neck and to my cheeks.

"You look like you're about to order your last meal, and your entire life depends on ordering the right thing," he says with a laugh.

"I give up." I place the menu on the table. "Everything looks good. Just when I decide on one thing, my eye catches on something else. You order for me."

"Really?" Zach's eyes light up.

"Sure. Go for it."

The waiter comes back and Zach begins by ordering virgin strawberry daiquiris.

"Good choice, sir." The waiter scribbles in his notepad. "Would you like to order any appetizers, or would you prefer to skip to the main meal?"

Zach's lips twitch and he turns to the waiter. "We'll start with an order of calamari *fritti*, and then we'll each have an order of gnocchi *alla Romana*."

"Excellent," says the waiter. "And would you like a salad with those orders?"

I shake my head, but Zach winks and turns his attention to the waiter. "We'll each have an order of carpaccio *di manzo*."

"Very good." The waiter takes our menus then moves around the table and takes orders from our dinner mates.

"What in the world, Zach?" I say. "I can't eat all that! And isn't calamari another word for *octopus*?"

"Octopus. Squid." Zach shrugs. "They're both the same. You'll like it."

My face must signal my disgust because Zach reaches for my hand and squeezes gently. "Trust me, okay?"

I nod. "And what about the carpaccio *di*—whatever it was? What is that?"

"It's a salad—you'll like it. It has little pieces of beef, capers and arugula."

"I don't even know what capers are, and I'm pretty sure I've had arugula and didn't like it."

Zach laughs. "You're being difficult, Abs. Trust me. We still have dessert to order."

"Oh no," I tell him, but I can't keep the smile from my face.

In the end, I try—and like—everything Zach orders. The calamari reminds me of fried clams, and the salad is the best I've ever tasted. When our main meals arrive, I'm too stuffed and only eat a few bites before setting my fork down.

"Is that all you're going to eat?" Zach lifts an eyebrow.

"What do you mean, *all?*" My eyes are wide. "I've never eaten so much food at one sitting in my life!"

Zach shoves another forkful of pasta in his mouth and chews, relishing every bite. "You're missing out. Do you want to take it with you for later?"

I do, and the waiter returns with a "to go" box. He transfers the food to the container then asks, "Will you be having dessert tonight?"

"She'll have—" Zach begins.

"Absolutely not!" I interject. "Where do you think I'll put dessert when I couldn't even finish my dinner?"

Zach clears his throat. "*I'll* have the five-layer chocolate cake, and we'll take a second one to go."

"Zach…"

"For after the dance," he says. "You can take it home with you. You can't come here and not get dessert!"

I give him my best evil glare, but there's no heat behind it.

The waiter returns with Zach's cake and another "to go" box, presumably with my dessert inside. He places a leather folder on the table. "Is there anything else I can get you?"

Zach shakes his head. "Thank you, no."

"Thank you," I tell the waiter.

When the waiter leaves, Zach shovels a bite of chocolate cake into his mouth. "Sure you don't want some?"

I smile and shake my head.

He scans the bill between bites and slips a credit card from his pocket, enclosing it inside the folder. Around the table, Tera's and Wendy's dates do the same. A shot of envy thrusts through me at the nonchalance of their actions, but I quickly stomp it down—I will not let jealousy or self-consciousness ruin my night.

THE LOUD THUMPING of bass reaches our ears from the parking lot even with the car windows closed. Again, I wait at Zach's insistence as he circles the car and opens my door.

"Ooh la la! Aren't you the gentleman tonight, Zach," Tera teases as she approaches with her date.

Embarrassment stains her date's face, a striking contrast to his white-blond hair and black button-down shirt. I struggle to remember his name but it escapes me. He shoots me an apologetic smile then leans over and whispers something into Tera's ear. Her eyes flash wide and pink creeps into her cheeks.

Wendy joins us with her date. "I don't even *want* to know what he said to make you blush like that!"

Tera giggles. "You know I'll tell you later. I always do."

Her date frowns, but she steps up on her tiptoes and kisses his cheek. "Just kidding."

Her date smiles down at her. "Right—as if you can keep any secrets from Wendy!"

Wendy's date—whose name I also can't remember—laughs and gives Tera's date a playful shove. "I told you, Kyle, girls are tight and can't keep secrets. Don't do it or say it if you don't want them all to know."

"Fact." Zach laughs and the three boys bump fists.

Okay, then. White hair equals Kyle. Got it.

Zach takes my hand and leads me into the school where we hand over our tickets and join the crush of sweaty bodies inside the gymnasium. My shoulders ache with tension, and I wonder how much money they've spent just on decorations.

The gym is decorated with an oasis of palm trees and sea life painted onto wooden cutouts. Heavy crepe paper drapes from the ceiling and swoops low like waves from above, giving the illusion of a more intimate setting. Blue and green strobe lights ricochet off a mirrored disco ball in the center of the room and, except for the basketball court beneath our feet, it looks nothing like a gymnasium.

The room is filled to capacity with teens dressed in extravagant evening wear. Some girls wear floor-length gowns, but most opt for dresses similar to the one I've borrowed from Tera—knee length and either skintight or pouffy with a sheer or tulle overlay. But one thing is consistent: though not quite elegant enough for prom, there's no doubt each person has spent a lot of time and money trying to outdress everyone else. In my head, I say a silent thanks to Tera for her generosity and pray she never comprehends how much I needed it.

The DJ slows the music and the dance floor empties until only couples remain. The clear strains of "Stand By Me" from generations ago echo through the large room and I wince at the irony. Would Zach stand by me if he knew my secrets?

He squeezes my hand. "Dance with me."

I swallow a knot in my throat and nod as he leads me onto the dance floor. There he pulls me close and we sway together to the music. The song ends and a more current ballad is queued up. Zach pulls me closer and I rest my head on his chest.

"Thank you," he whispers.

I lift my head and look up into his eyes. "For what?"

"For coming with me tonight."

I bite my lip for all the things I'm not telling Zach, then lay my head back against his chest and whisper, "Thank *you*."

We dance the remainder of the song in silence, just enjoying the feel of being in each other's arms, and I'm almost disappointed when the classic Village People song, "YMCA" begins playing. We pull apart just as Wendy and Tera bounce to our sides with their dates, both girls singing at the top of their lungs as they dance to the music.

The six of us dance to nearly every song—all in a group for the fast songs, and partnered off for the slow ones. When the final song ends, my feet are blistered and I've ditched my shoes, but I remain in Zach's embrace as we dance, even as the lights around us brighten the room.

"Um—hello? The music ended eons ago," Tera says from behind me.

Zach sighs. "I guess we better go, huh?"

I purse my lips in a mock pout. "Do we have to?"

"Afraid so. C'mon." He pecks my pouted lips with his own.

We find my shoes on the chair where I abandoned them and Zach leads me out of the gymnasium, his arm wrapped around my waist and Wendy's four-inch strappy heels dangling from his fingers. I limp slightly, but I'm so happy I can barely feel the pain.

"I can carry those." I reach for the shoes.

"You could, but I've got 'em. Plus, you're limping," Zach says.

I smile and glance down at my sore feet. "Only a little. I'm not used to wearing high heels and dancing all night."

Before I can stop him, he scoops me into his arms.

"What are you doing?" I gasp.

"Your feet are important. I'm just gonna carry you out to the car so you don't damage them any more."

Behind me are the unmistakable giggles and snorts of Tera and Wendy.

WE ARRIVE BACK at Wendy's house just minutes after they and their dates pull into her driveway. Zach and I have driven separately for the sake of room, but I'm glad because it gives us a few extra minutes alone.

He flips off the headlights but keeps the motor running for warmth, then reaches between us into the backseat where he gropes in the darkness. He finds what he seeks and holds up the take-home bag from Victoria's restaurant. "You ready for dessert?"

I laugh. "Zach, there's no way I'll ever eat that whole piece of cake by myself."

"I was hoping you'd say that." He winks, then forages through the bag and pulls out two plastic forks. "Guess I'll have to help you."

My lips tilt up and I take the extra fork from his hand. "I'm pretty sure you planned that on purpose."

"I'm pretty sure you're right," he says.

Within moments, the entire piece is gone and Zach offers me a sincere look. "Thanks for going with me tonight."

"You've already thanked me," I say softly.

He nods. "You looked beautiful. You still do. And I had a great time."

Butterflies race in my stomach and heat creeps up my neck. "Me, too. It's already one of my best memories ever."

Zach leans toward me and across the center console. "I'm glad." He cups my cheek in his hand and places his lips over mine. One kiss turns into two, and then three, until I completely lose track of time. I don't know if we've been sitting in the car for five minutes or five hours. I only know I don't want to be anywhere else.

"Come over tomorrow?" he whispers, his lips still so close I can feel his warm breath.

I nod. "What time?"

"Noon? We can go for lunch first."

"Okay."

"Want me to pick you up?"

I shake my head. "I'm not sure where I'll be. I might still be here."

"Okay. Tomorrow, then."

"I have to meet my folks at the library by four," I say.

"We'll make it work."

Zach's lips meet mine one last time, then with a heart-stopping smile, he opens his car door and gets out. Before I can find the handle to release the latch, my own door is opened and Zach holds his hand out for me. When I'm standing at full height, he reaches back inside and retrieves Wendy's shoes and the leftovers from Victoria's, then removes his jacket and places it around my shoulders. "It's too cold out for the way you're dressed. But you still look beautiful."

I snuggle into his side as he leads me up the steps to Wendy's front door. He pulls me close one last time, this time leaving a chaste kiss on my forehead. "Tomorrow, Abs?"

I nod. "Tomorrow."

I take the shoes and carryout bag from Zach's hands and step inside Wendy's house, but stand in the open doorway as he returns to his car and pulls out of the driveway. When his rear lights disappear into the distance, I step back and push the door closed. Now alone, I realize I'm still wearing his jacket. I snuggle deeper inside its warmth and breathe in his scent, then turn to enter the foyer.

"Geez! It took you guys long enough!"

"Aah!" I yelp at Tera's greeting as she steps out from behind the drapes.

"Oh my God! You scared me!" I cover my racing heart with my hand. "We were just saying goodbye."

"We could see that," Wendy teases.

"You were watching the whole time? From behind the drapes?"

"Well, of course we were! What were we supposed to do? We had to make sure Zach didn't take advantage of you!" Tera wiggles her eyebrows suggestively.

Embarrassment washes over me and I follow the two girls up to Wendy's room.

"So spill!" Wendy says. "What were you doing in that dark car for so long?"

"Eating chocolate cake," I answer.

"Uh-huh," Tera says.

Changing the subject, I ask, "So what's up with you and…um… dammit! I still can't remember his name!" I say to Wendy, referring to her date.

"Travis?" She ducks her head, her eyelashes hiding her eyes. "I'm not sure yet. We're just testing the waters."

Tera snorts. "If by 'testing the waters' you mean dancing so close we couldn't slip a piece of paper between you, I'd say the water is a perfect temperature."

Wendy laughs. "There might be *some* chemistry there."

"*Some?*" Tera accuses. "I was afraid to touch either of you for fear of getting scalded by the heat!"

Mission accomplished. Tera and Wendy banter for some time, and I listen without contributing—I'm enjoying it way too much to intervene.

I realize I've never had friends like Tera and Wendy. Even when Sarah and Emma were my best friends, it wasn't the same. I can't explain how it's different, but I know my friendship with them is far better than any I've ever had. It seems weird to be thankful for all the crap I went through, and even that we're homeless at the moment, but without those things, tonight would never have happened.

Wendy and Tera tease each other long into the night until we each drift off to sleep on the floor of Wendy's bedroom. First Tera slips off to sleep, then Wendy, and soon my own eyes close.

CHAPTER TWENTY

"GIRLS." WENDY'S MOM KNOCKS ON THE BED-
ROOM DOOR. "WAKE UP AND COME DOWN FOR BREAKFAST."

Wendy groans and pulls a pillow over her head. "What time is it?"

"9:37," I croak, shielding my eyes from the sun spilling in through a gap in the blackout blinds.

Tera nudges Wendy with her foot. "C'mon, Wen. I'm hungry."

"You guys go without me," she whines.

"No way. C'mon." Tera pulls the blanket off of Wendy. "Get up."

"Fine. I'm coming." She throws her pillow in Tera's direction but misses. "You owe me, though. I had at least another hour of sleep coming."

Groggy and still wearing our pajamas, we trudge downstairs to the kitchen. The table is set with Nutella, whipped cream, sliced strawberries, chocolate chips, peanut butter, and maple syrup. My stomach rumbles.

Karyn sets a plate piled high with Belgian waffles in the center of the table. "Help yourselves, girls."

I mouth the word wow, then say out loud, "Thanks. These look great."

We scarf down breakfast then I draw the long straw for the first shower. I'm rinsing my hair when the doorframe shakes with frantic pounding.

"Abby!" Tera calls out. "You have to get out! We gotta go!"

"What's wrong?" I flip the nozzle to off and reach for a towel.

"Josh's mom called. Hurry and get out so I can tell you."

I don't bother drying off properly, instead throwing clean clothes on my still-damp body. When I emerge, I find Wendy standing beside her bed, tossing things into a book bag.

"What's wrong?" I rush to her side.

Tera catches my arm and shakes her head. "Josh is in the hospital."

My eyes go wide. "What? How? When?"

Wendy swipes at the tears on her cheeks. "We're not sure. His mom called and said he's in the ICU. She said flu, but that doesn't make any sense."

I grab for a chair and fall into it. "ICU? Is he okay?"

"Not sure," Tera says. "They admitted him Thursday night."

My eyes flash back to Wendy. She moves on autopilot, still throwing random things into her backpack. I nod in her direction. "Is she okay?"

"She's pretty shaken up," Tera says. "She and Josh have been friends longer than any of us."

"So what do we do? Can we go to the hospital? Will they let us in to see him?"

"That's why his mom called," Tera says. "She wants us to come see him. Are you in?"

"Of course I'm in." I grab my bag off the floor and throw my dirty clothes inside. "I need to let Zach know. I'm supposed to meet him at—"

"You can call him from the car," Wendy interrupts. "But we gotta get going."

I turn to Tera, my eyes pleading. "I can't call him. I don't have his number."

"Why not?" she asks.

"I just don't, but I can message him through Facebook."

"Want me to text him for you?"

"Yeah—that would be great," I say.

"I'll do it at the hospital. Right now we gotta go."

Wendy's out the door first, sprinting to Tera's VW. She taps her foot, impatient for Tera to unlock the doors. "This piece of crap better start this time."

"Ya know what, Wen?" Tera says. "You need to knock this crap off. We're doing our best to get there as fast as we can."

Wendy's shoulders slump and she bursts into sobs. "I'm sorry. I know. I'm just so worried."

"We know you are, Wen," I say softly. "But his mom says he's better, right? He must be, or she wouldn't let us see him. You need to settle down or they'll never let us go in. Okay?"

Wendy nods and pulls the passenger door open. I squeeze into the back, giving her the front seat. With only a mild stutter, Tera's car starts. Moments later we drive out of the subdivision and through the streets of downtown Rochester. It's only five or six blocks to the hospital, but we hit every stoplight on the way. Anxiety weighs heavily inside the small car.

Tera pulls into the underground parking adjacent to St. Marys Hospital then follows the circular maze in search of an open spot. The first two levels are filled with spaces reserved for "consultants" which Tera informs me is a fancy word for "important doctor." On the fourth level, she finds a space and pulls in. Wendy jumps out before the car is fully in park, leaving Tera and me running to catch up. I'm breathing heavily when we hit the elevators. As the car carries us to the fifth floor Pediatric ICU, I rest against the back wall and catch my breath.

The doors open and we walk-run through the main foyer where a severe woman behind a tall desk stops us. "Ladies, stop—you have to sign in. Who are you here to see?"

"Josh Bryant," Wendy says.

The woman's closely clipped fingernail scans down a list. She stops and writes "Bryant" on three name tag stickers. Handing them to us, she points to her right. "Room 517, but slow down. You can't be rushing through here like this."

We apologize and follow the corridor until we're standing outside Josh's room. The sliding glass door is partially open, but the privacy curtain is closed. The smell of cleaning solution reaches my nose and my head spins. Sweat drips from my forehead, but I'm chilled to the bone. My knees shake and my fingers tingle. I lean against a wall to steady myself. Memories float behind my eyes and I squeeze them shut, hoping to block them out. But it's no use. The room is nearly identical to the one in Omaha where Mom was taken after her episode.

Wendy knocks and steps through the glass door, entering the room with Tera behind her. I try to follow, but my feet won't move.

Tera turns back, her forehead wrinkled. "Are you coming, Abby?"

Her voice is so far away—like she's speaking through a tunnel. I shake my head. "No. Go ahead. I—I need a quick second."

Tera studies me then says, "Come in when you're ready."

I nod, but I'm no longer thinking about Tera or Wendy, or even Josh behind the sliding glass door. The only thing I can think about is Mom in her own hospital bed only a few months ago.

A chair sits outside Josh's door and I collapse into it. The tears come swiftly, but I barely notice. I tuck my head between my knees and sing silently inside my head, but there is no distracting myself—the memories come rushing back like a tsunami and there's no time to run.

FOUR MONTHS EARLIER

Mom lies peacefully in the narrow hospital bed, wires connected to her in more places than I can count. A machine above her head beeps steadily to what I think is her heartbeat. I can't believe how much better she looks now—almost normal. Just hours ago I was sure she was dying, and now she lies there content, with Nick hovering over her and catering to her every need as though the last several weeks never happened. Typical.

I vacillate between anger and fear. Part of me is still furious over all that's happened, but another part of me is scared Mom might die. When she collapsed, I kept thinking I'd done something—that somehow it was my fault—but I can't figure out a single way I could've caused her to have a seizure.

"Feeling better?" Nick asks her.

Mom nods. *"Just ready to figure out what's wrong with me and get out of here."*

No word about the fight we had in the kitchen, and not a single hint of the fact she was drunk. It's like that never happened.

I've been sitting on a cold folding chair so long my butt is numb and they've forgotten I'm here. The curtain outside the sliding glass door ruffles to the side and Dr. Bates walks in. He's so tall I expect him to duck his head as he steps through the doorway, but he clears it easily.

"How're we feeling?" He smiles at Mom.

"Much better," she says. *"Still a little weak, though."*

Dr. Bates studies Mom's chart then his eyes peek over the top at me. *"Young lady, why don't you step outside for a few minutes so I can talk with your mom and dad."*

And just like that, I'm dismissed. I'm the one who was with her when she fell. I'm the one who called 9-1-1 and stayed on the line until the paramedics came. And I'm the one being ejected from the room. Like I said, I'm forgotten. I grab my jacket off the back of the chair and make my way into the hall. My intention is to go somewhere quiet—somewhere I can be alone—but Dr. Bates's voice reaches me in the hall and I realize nobody bothered to close the door behind me. I glance around and the hall is empty, so I slide down the wall until my butt reaches the tile floor. I'm not invisible, but I also think I look less conspicuous than I would be standing with my ear to the door. I close my eyes and tune everything out but the sound of the doctor's voice.

"So your tests came back with good results," Dr. Bates says, *"But we need to talk about the seizure and what caused it. Your chart indicates you've been struggling with depression and anxiety?"*

"Yes," Mom says. *"The last couple months have been really stressful. I was just in to see Dr. Heusman and he put me on an antidepressant that's supposed to help."*

"Right. My notes show at your last visit…four weeks ago…he put you on Bupropion for anxiety."

"That's right," Mom says.

"Has it helped?"

She pauses. "I think so. I've been under so much pressure lately it's hard to tell."

The doctor clears his throat. "Your seizure could be caused by a couple of things, but what I'm most concerned about is your toxicology report, which showed elevated levels of alcohol in your bloodstream."

"I wasn't drunk," Mom interjects. "Or—I might've been a little buzzed, but I'm not a regular drinker. It was a one-off thing."

"Mrs. Lunde, I'm not here to judge you. I'm only here to tell you what I believe happened. Mixing antidepressants with alcohol places a patient at a substantially high risk of seizure. Bupropion, especially, is known to cause seizures in patients who mix it with alcohol. Did Dr. Heusman caution you against using alcohol while taking this medication?"

"No, but I'm not a regular drinker."

He ignores Mom's comment and continues. "In any case, we'll keep you here overnight for observation, but I can't stress enough the dangers of mixing any drugs with alcohol, especially antidepressants. I'll also want you to follow up with Dr. Heusman within a week for him to evaluate your medications and determine if there's a better solution for you."

I stand and step away from Mom's room. Rage flows through me until I'm shaking. What the hell was she thinking? How many classes has she led on the dangers of mixing drugs and alcohol? How many times has she cautioned me about the hazards of drinking too much? She could've died, and why? Because, like sneaking around with Coach Hawkins, she didn't give a damn about anyone but herself.

I don't know where I'm going, but I have to get away. I find the front doors and I'm at a sprint before the automatic sensor has them fully opened. I'm not even a runner, but my legs carry me full throttle. I just can't be here anymore.

I'M STILL SEATED outside Josh's room when Wendy and Tera emerge with his mom. I stand and wipe away the wet tears covering my cheeks.

"Abby, you okay?" Wendy asks.

I force a smile. "I'm fine. I—hospitals are hard for me sometimes."

Mrs. Bryant places an arm around my shoulders and offers a sympathetic smile. "I've been looking forward to meeting you, Abby. Josh speaks highly of you. Thanks for coming."

I nod and swallow a knot in my throat.

"Josh is sleeping," Tera says. "We were headed to the waiting room to talk. Come with us?"

I nod again and follow them down a series of hallways to a waiting room with a television, reclining chairs, a bank of computers and phones, and a play area for children. I sit in the closest chair and Tera plops down beside me. Across from us are Mrs. Bryant and Wendy, their hands clasped together.

Mrs. Bryant clears her throat. "I appreciate you girls coming. I know Josh looks bad, but he's much better than he was Thursday night when they admitted him."

Tera cuts to the chase. "What happened? You said flu, but that doesn't make any sense."

"Not just flu, but flu combined with pneumonia," Mrs. Bryant says. "With Josh's medical history, it makes perfect sense."

"How?" Wendy asks.

"You know Josh has asthma, right?"

Wendy nods. "Sorta—I mean, he used to have an inhaler but I haven't seen it in a long time. He said he outgrew it."

"We thought that—or maybe we just became complacent since it's been under control for so long," Mrs. Bryant says. "At any rate, asthmatics are at an increased risk of respiratory problems associated with the flu. That's why we always get his flu shot early, but we haven't done it yet this year. Getting the shot might not have prevented the flu, but it might've kept the symptoms minimal."

"But it's just the flu," Wendy says.

Mrs. Bryant nods. "Yes, it was 'just' the flu at first, but it worsened quickly to pneumonia. So he has influenza with the complication of pneumonia added. Either one by itself is bad—especially for an asthmatic—but together they're dangerous."

"Okay…" Tera says. "I still don't get it, though. Everybody gets the flu. How did it get so serious?"

"Flu can be serious for anyone—even you girls. Usually, you just get sick and stay home for a few days feeling miserable, then you go back to school. That's how most of us handle it. But Josh's asthma makes him predisposed to pneumonia. If we'd realized his asthma was still active, we would've started him on an albuterol regimen as a preemptive measure, but he hadn't used an inhaler in so long, we didn't even have a current prescription. When I left for work Thursday morning, I didn't think too much of it—he was just running a low-grade fever and felt achy. But by Thursday night his fever had spiked to 102 and he was having trouble catching his breath, so we brought him to the ER."

"Oh my gosh," Wendy whispers.

Mrs. Bryant nods. "We didn't realize how serious it was. We figured they might give him a nebulizer treatment and send him home with a new inhaler and a short supply of steroids. But when they tested his oxygen level, it was dangerously low."

"What's that mean?" I ask.

"Usually anywhere in the ninety percent range or higher is acceptable. Josh came in at seventy-two percent."

"Wow," Tera says.

"Yeah—wow. It was pretty scary. They admitted him immediately and he's been in the ICU since. He's much better than he was, thank God, but he'll be here for a while. They removed the tube from his throat this morning, so his voice is raspy, and he's on regular nebulizer treatments around the clock. If he responds well today, they're talking about moving him to a room in a regular unit tomorrow. So he *is* getting better, but he's still very sick."

"Why didn't you call us before this morning?" Wendy asks. "We could've been here."

Mrs. Bryant shakes her head. "You couldn't have done anything, and I knew you had Homecoming last night. Plus Josh wasn't in any shape for company anyway. It's only been today he's looked strong enough for visitors, though he's still sleeping a lot. I should warn you: his breathing is labored, so he's speaking in fragmented sentences. Don't let that scare you—he just has to catch his breath in between. But also, it helps if you girls will carry the conversation as much as you can so he doesn't wear out."

Wendy places her arms around Josh's mom and hugs her hard. "We're here for anything you need. Just tell us and it's done."

Mrs. Bryant's eyes glaze over but she smiles. "Thank you. I think just seeing you three will go a long way to making him better."

"Good—then let's go back and see him," Wendy says. "Do you think he'll be awake?"

"Maybe." Mrs. Bryant looks at her watch. "He's been sleeping a little over an hour. We should go check."

We stand and my attention turns to the bank of telephones. "You guys go ahead. I need to call my parents."

Mrs. Bryant nods and leads the way back to Josh's room. I lift the receiver and call the number Mom made me memorize for emergencies.

BEEP... BEEP... BEEP...

Josh sleeps in the small room as a machine next to his bed keeps time like a metronome. A tangle of wires leads from under his hospital gown to a machine above his head, its face lit up with red numbers registering what I'm guessing is his heart rate. On his right index finger is a white clip measuring his oxygen level, and on the back of his hand an IV needle is connected to a tiny tube leading to a clear bag of fluid hanging high on a rack. His eyes are closed and his skin so pale I notice a dusting of freckles across his nose. *How have I not seen those freckles before?* My eyes move to his lips and I touch my own in empathy. His are too dry. I want to reach for my lip balm and give them some moisture, but I don't dare. I don't know what his mom would say.

I've been sitting for almost three hours watching Josh sleep. He's so peaceful lying there, only the heavy rasp of his breathing and an occasional barking cough to indicate how sick he really is. The idea of losing him floats through my mind and I have to squash it or cry. I haven't known him long, but the idea of a world without him is unbearable.

The sliding glass door opens and the curtain is pushed to the side as a nurse enters, carrying a mask connected to a small vial of liquid. She offers us a smile. "Time for his breathing treatment."

"Do you have to do that now?" Tera asks. "He's sleeping so peacefully."

"I'm sorry," she replies. "Every four hours. Sometimes they sleep through it, though."

The nurse connects a tube to a spigot on the wall and steam billows from the mask connected to the tube. Then, with Josh still sleeping, she removes the oxygen tubes away from his face and places the mask over his nose and mouth, securing it with an elastic band behind his head.

Josh's eyes flutter open and he looks around the room. His hand moves to the mask, stretching it away from his mouth. "Hey."

The nurse guides the mask back to his face. "Let's leave this on for right now, okay? It's only about fifteen minutes and then you can talk to your friends."

Josh nods and his eyes close to half-mast. He rests a moment then coughs into the mask for long seconds, making my own chest hurt with each deep bark. His mother sits beside him and brushes his hair away from his face.

"You slept a long time," she says. "Feeling any better?"

He cocks his head to the side and lifts a shoulder as if to say, "*Meh—maybe a little.*"

"Why don't you close your eyes and rest while the nebulizer works," she says. "The girls will still be here when it's done."

Josh nods and closes his eyes, then is wracked by another deep cough before settling back under the covers.

The machine takes forever to finish, but after a while the steam lessens and disappears. The nurse removes the mask and replaces it with the oxygen tubes at his nose. She smiles and closes the spigot on the wall. "There you go. Now you can talk."

Wendy and Tera take seats on each side of Josh, so I pull my chair closer to his bedside.

"Hey." His voice is deep and scratchy. "What're you...doing here?"

"The better question," Wendy says, her tone barely disguising her concern, "is what are *you* doing here?"

"I missed...Homecoming," he says.

"We were worried about you," Tera says. "But we never thought you might be seriously sick. We thought you had a family emergency or something."

"How...was it?"

"We missed you," I say.

Josh smiles his cracked lips at me and I can't stand it anymore. I reach into my pocket and hand him my lip balm.

"Thanks." Shaking slightly, he dabs it over his lips.

We spend the next hour telling him about Homecoming, but he doesn't have the stamina to stay awake. After a while, his eyes drift closed and he falls into a deep slumber. We stay until after seven thirty but Josh only awakens twice more, and then only long enough for his breathing treatments.

"Can we come again tomorrow?" Wendy asks.

Mrs. Bryant nods. "Call me first, so if they move him, I can tell you where he is."

"Sounds good," Wendy says.

"Do you need a ride home, Abs?" Tera asks as we leave Josh's room.

I pause. I hate having Nick waste gas, but I also don't want Tera dropping me off at the homeless shelter. "No, thanks. I'll call my step-dad."

"You're sure?" she asks. "It's no problem."

"No problem if it starts," Wendy says under her breath, but smiles.

Tera narrows her eyes.

"I'm sure," I tell her.

"Okay, then. We'll see you at school tomorrow," Wendy says.

I nod and stop at the bank of telephones while the two girls step into the elevator. I dial the number and let it ring twice before hanging up—a code we'd worked out when I called earlier. They don't answer, and I don't expect them to. The CallerID will read Mayo Clinic, alerting them I need a ride, and we won't waste valuable minutes by answering the phone.

NICK IS WAITING for me under the canopy of the St. Marys building when I leave Josh's room.

"Hey." I slide into the passenger seat. "Thanks for picking me up."

"It's fine. I didn't want you walking in the dark. What's the word on your friend?"

"They'll keep him in ICU tonight then probably transfer him to a regular unit tomorrow."

"That's good."

"Yeah."

Nick glances at me before making a right turn. "You missed dinner. Check with your mom—I think she put some aside for you."

"Thanks."

We slow for a red light, pulling to a stop behind a U-Haul truck.

"How much longer are we going to live like this, Nick?" I ask. "I mean, I know you're doing everything you can to get things straightened out, but do you have any guesses?"

He blows out a breath, his expression more defeated than I've ever seen. "I knew that was coming."

"Oh, God. What?" Tendrils of fear crawl up my spine. "Has something worse happened?"

Nick puts his hand over mine and squeezes twice. "No. It's just—your mom and I are getting nervous. We've been out every day looking for anything to bring in more money, and every lead results in a dead end. Sunday is our last night at the Dorothy Day House, and we're not sure what to do. It's getting too cold to sleep in the van, but we don't have another option."

"Is there anything I can do?"

Nick turns and smiles at me. "No, you're doing enough with the paper route and keeping an eye on Amber. If you have any ideas, though, let us know."

CHAPTER TWENTY-ONE

"ABBY." MS. RAVEN SMILES FROM BEHIND HER DESK. "THANKS FOR COMING DOWN."

"Sure. Is everything okay?"

She waves at a seat. I choose one of two open chairs and wait while she turns her attention to the mess of paperwork on her desk. She selects a document and her eyes move over the page. With the sun shining onto the paper through the window, the words *Abby Lunde* are visible from the front side.

"Tell me how classes are going. You're adjusting well?"

"I think so." I nod.

"That's good to hear. I saw your audition—I was impressed. When do you hear the results?"

"At the end of school today, actually. They're supposed to announce it over the intercom."

"Good luck to you."

"Thanks."

Ms. Raven picks up a pencil and taps it on the document in front of her. "Abby, now that you're settled in here, I thought we'd talk about your plans for after high school. Have you given any thought to what you'd like to do?"

I shrug. "I guess I'll probably get a job."

"Have you thought about college? I've looked at your transcripts and your grades are competitive. Mrs. Miner mentioned she thinks you might qualify for a vocal music scholarship. Does that interest you at all?"

"Yeah, but what would I have to do?"

"For starters, you'll need to fill out an application and submit a copy of your transcript with your ACT scores. Additionally, you'll probably need an audition tape, but we can research that more once we've identified a few scholarships. Have you taken your ACT yet?"

I shake my head.

"Okay, let's get that out of the way first. There's a test on October 29th." Ms. Raven reaches inside her desk and pulls out a form, handing it to me. "The fee is forty dollars, and you can pay online with a credit card. Once we get that out of the way, we can start the application process."

My shoulders slump and the futility of it all smothers me. *Forty dollars.* It might as well be *forty million* dollars.

"Is something wrong, Abby?" she asks.

"No. I mean—no. Yes. No." *How can I tell her I can't find a measly forty dollars?*

Ms. Raven studies me then clears her throat. "Abby, I'm going to ask you a sensitive question and I need you to answer me truthfully: will finding forty dollars be a problem?"

My face flushes and I can't meet her eyes. "I—we can't afford it."

She nods then opens her desk drawer again. Her fingers walk through a series of files until she finds what she seeks. She removes a single sheet of paper and hands it to me. "Don't be embarrassed, Abby. You'd be surprised how many families can't afford the test fee. That's why they offer a fee waiver to families who need it. Are you enrolled in the school's free lunch program?"

My face floods with heat again. I nod.

"I didn't mean to embarrass you. I ask because qualifying for our free lunch program means your financial need is already established. It helps us cut through the red tape. Complete that form and return it tomorrow, then we'll get you registered. Okay?"

"Then I can take the ACT?"

She smiles. "Yes, and afterwards we can begin looking at schools and scholarship programs while we wait for your scores."

"But even with a scholarship, isn't college expensive?"

"It can be," she admits. "It depends upon the university you choose and how aggressive you are about finding scholarships and grants. I think we can get you started with some really nice scholarships and you'd probably qualify for a couple of federal grants. If those fail us, then there's always the federal loan option."

My shoulders drop. "A loan?"

"It's not what you think. They're government subsidized with low interest, and payments don't kick in until six months after you graduate college."

Whoa! Information overload!

Ms. Raven laughs. "One thing at a time. Let's get the ACT done and we'll go from there."

IT'S FINALLY LAST period, and I swear I never thought three o'clock would arrive—the day has dragged endlessly as it always does when you're forced to wait.

The intercom crackles and the disembodied voice of Principal Bartlett comes through the speakers: "*If I could have your attention, please, for these announcements…*"

Zach spins in his chair and faces me. "This is it, Abs!"

"Sh." I smile. "I can't hear."

"*…has been cancelled. It will take place next Monday at its normal time. At this time, we will announce the soloists for the Fall Concert.*"

My heart catches as I wait for Mr. Bartlett's next words.

"*Congratulations to Keaton Garner and Abby Lunde, who have been selected as soloists for this year's Fall Concert. Please see Mrs. Miner after school for further instructions.*"

"WHOOP!" Zach's victory shout rings through the room and the class becomes a frenzy of cheers and congratulations.

My face flushes. I did it! I got the part!

My fingertips tingle and my ears buzz. My classmates speak over each other, the roar of their voices competing with the buzzing in my ears. My mouth is stretched into a wide smile. Finally some good news!

"Okay, folks. Settle down," Mr. Thompson calls from the front of the room. "Congratulations, Abby. We may have the next Rochester South celebrity right here in our class."

I nod my thanks—I couldn't form words if I tried.

"I knew you'd do it!" Zach says.

The bell rings and I remain sitting, my head still spinning. Zach grabs my backpack and stuffs my books inside, then grins and grabs my hand. "C'mon Abby. Time to meet your public."

I roll my eyes and walk with him toward Mrs. Miner's classroom. The halls are crowded, and kids I've noticed before call out congratulations—it's like the entire school is on my side. The entire school minus Trish, that is.

From the other end of the hall, Trish walks straight toward me, her stride determined as though she's a charging bull. Her eyes are like chips of ice and my skin prickles. Beside her is Scott. He shouts his congratulations across the distance, oblivious to her agitation. They continue toward us, Trish's body in a direct line with mine. I crowd Zach to avoid her but she anticipates my move and adjusts her path. Just before she plows into me, Scott yanks her toward him. She grazes my elbow, but not enough to injure.

"Hey!" Zach shouts.

Scott's face is purple. He shoots me an apologetic look, then leans close to Trish and says something into her ear. She jerks away and shoves him into a locker, then stomps away. Scott turns to me and mouths, I'm sorry.

I shake my head, hoping he understands I mean, "*It's not your fault.*"

"Are you okay?" Zach examines my elbow. "What the hell is wrong with her? She better get herself in check—that's seriously not cool!"

I bite my tongue. "C'mon, Zach. Let's not let her ruin our day."

He nods, but his eyes are still clouded with anger. We continue to Mrs. Miner's room, then wait while she finishes speaking with Keaton Garner.

"Hey, Abby! Congrats!" Keaton says as we pass in the doorway.

"Thanks. You too!"

Mrs. Miner meets me at the door, her face beaming. "Abby! Congratulations."

Heat rises to my cheeks. "Thank you."

"C'mon in and let's talk about the next few weeks." She waves toward the open chairs. Zach and I sit as she hands me a folder. "I've put together a few solos and duets you'll sing with Keaton. I've highlighted where your parts begin and end, so look them over tonight. I'd like to start meeting with you tomorrow during your open period, if that works for you."

I nod. "That's fine."

"Good. I'll also need a list of times you're available to practice with Keaton. If you can get that to me tomorrow, I'll compare your calendars and come up with a schedule that works for both of you. Sound good?"

"Yes!"

"Now for the fun part. Take this week and select a song for your featured solo. This is your time to shine, and you can choose anything you like so long as I approve it first. If you need piano accompaniment, I'm happy to provide it, but I have an idea that might be better."

"What's that?"

Mrs. Miner's attention turns to Zach. "I'd love to see Zach accompany you on guitar. You two have wonderful chemistry together, and I think it would help your stage fright to have someone nearby to calm your nerves. It's your decision—"

"That's a great idea," I interrupt. "If Zach doesn't mind."

"Mind?" He laughs. "I'd love to!"

Mrs. Miner smiles. "It's a plan, then. Let's talk next week and you can show me what you've come up with. Any questions?"

"No. Thank you, Mrs. Miner," I say. "I won't let you down!"

CHAPTER TWENTY-TWO

THE WEEK FLIES AND BEFORE I KNOW IT, THE NEXT WEEKEND HAS COME AND GONE. JOSH IS STILL IN THE hospital, and Tera, Wendy and I have visited him every day after my paper route. He's much improved and the doctor expects he'll go home tomorrow, but cautions he won't return to school right away.

It's now Monday again and I spent my entire weekend praying for divine intervention—a reprieve to save us from leaving the Dorothy Day House. It never came. I awoke this morning, packed my few things, and said goodbye to the homeless shelter.

Despite finding ourselves back in the van, things are marginally better than the Monday before. Last Wednesday, Nick was offered a second job at a vet clinic, where he cleans the kennels and the outside yard after the dogs have playtime. He hates it, but the pay is decent and we need it. Plus, he can take Amber, if necessary. Then on Friday, Mom started her new job at Hamburger Hut, so we barely saw her all weekend. Otherwise, Saturday and Sunday were predictably the same. We returned to the Presbyterian Church for lunch on Saturday, then I spent Sunday at Zach's, working on my solo for the Fall Concert. We've agreed on another Adele song and Zach has become a relentless taskmaster, making me practice so many times I sometimes wake up to find I've been humming in my sleep. Truthfully, the extra practice has helped my confidence and I'm not as nervous as I was.

I glance at my watch and groan. It's 3:27 a.m. and I can't sleep. It's our first night back in the van and it's every bit as awful as I remember, only worse—the temperature has dropped considerably. I pull my blankets around me and scoot closer to Amber. My nose is so cold it's numb, and I grit my teeth to stop their chattering. Beside me Amber sleeps soundly, probably warmer from the combined heat of Mom's body and mine. On the other side of Mom, Nick's chainsaw snores echo through the van. It wouldn't be so bad if it wasn't so cold, and I wonder if I'll ever be warm again.

MOM RUNS HER hand over Amber's forehead and studies her fever-dulled eyes. We've spent four nights in the van, and each one has left us more exhausted than the last—and now Amber's sick.

"What do we do?" Mom looks at Nick. "She can't go to school."

"I'll stay with her," I offer.

Mom and Nick argue silently with their eyes, their frustration louder than words.

"C'mon," I say. "What other choice do we have? If one of you stays, you'll lose your job—and we need that money. I won't miss much at school and you'll be back early enough for me to do the paper route."

They stare at each other another moment, then Nick shrugs as if to say, "*Fine. Whatever.*"

Mom blows out a breath. "I don't like it, either, Nick, but what choice do we have?"

"You're right—we don't have a choice," he says, then mumbles under his breath, "We never have choices these days."

Tears glisten in Mom's eyes but she turns to me and pulls a smile across her face. "Will you be okay, Abs?"

"Geez, Mom!" I retort, aggravated she'd ask after everything we've been through. "I'm grown up now, you know. I have a job, I've been looking after Amber every day since we got here, and I'm just as capable as you of taking care of this family."

Mom's head snaps back as though I've slapped her. *Dammit—I've been so good at checking my temper!*

Straightening her shoulders, Mom shoots Nick one last look. He nods, then she kisses Amber's forehead and snugs the blankets around her. "We'll get home early if we can."

Home? Who does she think she's kidding?

JUST WHEN YOU think things can't get worse, they do. Until now, I'd thought sleeping in the van at night was as bad as things could get. Oh, how wrong I was! Being stuck in the van all day is worse. Last night's temperatures dropped into the single digits, and it's barely warmed up since. My fingers are red and stiff from the cold, and bending them is painful. My nose is a block of ice, and my lips are so numb I can't enunciate my words. I breathe hot air onto my hands and a puff of steam lingers in the air. It seems only yesterday when watching the vapor from my breath was fun, but this isn't fun at all.

Beside me, Amber's face is flushed but she vibrates with shivers. I've wrapped my body as tightly around her as I can, but it's not enough. Somehow I have to warm her up.

My eyes scan inside the van, searching for anything to provide extra warmth, but there's nothing. And then my attention lands on Mom's keys—they left them in the cup holder between the driver and passenger seats, reminding me, "*For an emergency.*" I study them as my mind races through the pros and cons of heating the van. Coming to a decision, I pull away from Amber and reach for the keys.

"Sister?" Amber's lashes flutter and she gazes at me through fever-glazed eyes. "Please don't go. I'm so cold."

"Sh." I wrap my discarded blankets over her then run my palm along her forehead and down her cheek. "I'm just going to warm the van up for a few minutes, okay?"

Amber closes her eyes and nods.

Careful not to disturb her further, I climb over the center console and squeeze into the driver's seat. I blow out another puff of hot, white air into my hands then slide the key into the ignition and start the van. Frigid air blows from the vents and I turn the knob as hot as it will go. A cold shiver rushes through me. I flip the fan to high then crawl back over the console and under the blankets with Amber.

"It's cold," she whines.

"I know. It'll warm up in a minute."

On the back of the center console above our heads is an air vent. Somehow I have to trap the heat.

"Amber, let me have this top blanket," I say, tugging at the bedspread I've tucked around her.

Freeing the blanket, I cover the air vent and drape the ends through the armrests of the two front seats. I look around for a way to secure the bottom, but my options are limited. With no other choice, I crack the wing windows just enough to slide a piece of fabric through, then close them once again. The effect is a fort that hangs about eight inches above our heads, trapping the heat under the blanket.

After about fifteen minutes, I turn off the ignition. The van is toasty warm—and it's even warmer under our fort—but I know it won't last. I slide back under my makeshift tent and wrap my body around Amber's.

"Thank you," she says, closing her eyes as sleep claims her.

I kiss her forehead and regard her tiny face, her cute upturned nose, and the long eyelashes that hide her brilliant blue eyes. She lets out a long, rattling cough, then settles down until all I can hear is a faint wheeze each time she breathes in. The sound terrifies me—it's too much like the sound Josh made in the hospital when he was hooked up to all those machines. What if Amber needs to be in a hospital? We don't have the money to pay for the ER—would they turn her away? And if they did, would she die? A million truly scary scenarios race through my mind, each one worse than the last. I'm startled back to reality when a tear splashes onto the pillow beside Amber's head.

I don't want to be a grown-up any more!

Another tear escapes and I lay my head next to my baby sister's.

Please let me wake up and discover this has all been a dream.

BANG! I'M JOLTED awake as the van is struck by the door of another vehicle.

"Dammit, Kristina!" a man's voice calls out. "I told you to be careful!"

"Not my fault!" a woman argues. "I told you—you parked too damned close and the wind blew the door right out of my hand!"

I listen as the man and woman argue over who's at fault and whether to leave a note, praying the whole time they just leave. And that's exactly what they do. I'm relieved we've remained undetected, but irritated at their disregard for our property.

I glance at my watch—4:12 p.m. Somehow I've managed to sleep most of the day. Beside me, Amber sleeps peacefully. I test her temperature with my palm and find her still hot to the touch.

My stomach rumbles and I debate waking her. Neither of us has eaten today, but I'm hesitant to wake her when she's probably too sick to eat. Pulling my body away from hers, I escape the homemade fort. Outside the cocoon of my makeshift tent, the air is frigid. All the warmth of a few hours ago is gone. I tuck the blanket's edges around Amber, trapping what little warmth is left. I crawl into the front seat and start the van again. The fuel gage hovers just below a quarter of a tank so I can't let it run long.

While the vehicle warms, I find a stash of granola bars in the glove box and say a silent prayer of thanks to Mrs. Cummings, who never lets us leave Saturday dinner without taking extras. There's seven granola bars and I'm starving, but I don't dare eat more than one.

The next hour moves slowly and my bladder aches for release, but I can't even relieve myself because Amber's too sick to go with me and

I can't leave her alone. I debate squatting beside the van, but the fear of getting caught is real so I squeeze my knees together and pray the sensation passes. The walls close in around me and I count down the minutes until Mom and Nick return. They can't be much longer.

I drift off to sleep, but the urge to pee wakes me again. I peek my head out from under the heavy blanket. Darkness and a blast of cold greet me. I glance at my watch: 7:37 p.m. I've slept more than two hours and Mom and Nick still haven't returned.

Fear races through me. They've been late before, but never this late, and never both at the same time. Not only that, but now I've missed my delivery route! My mind spins through a series of awful scenarios and, just when my anxiety hits its peak, the van's locks pop open and Nick slides into the driver's seat.

"Thank God you're back," I whisper. "Where've you been? I missed my paper route!"

Nick glances at my makeshift tent and his eyebrows draw together. "What? Where's your mom? I got held up at work."

"She's not back yet. And I have to pee really bad."

"Dammit, Abs. I'm sorry. Have you at least had something to eat?"

"A granola bar a couple hours ago." I sit up and my bladder screams for release. "I really have to pee right now."

"Sorry." He waves a hand. "Go—I'll stay with Amber."

I hop out of the van and my bladder nearly releases its contents. I give myself a second to gain control then walk-run into the empty Walmart bathrooms. When I've finished, I stop at the customer service desk and ask for a job application. I don't intend to apply here, but asking for the application makes my quick in-and-out look less suspicious. I hope.

Mom's back when I return. She's brought with her two burgers from work that she sneaked into her purse instead of discarding when a customer's order was filled incorrectly. I've never been so grateful for a cold, greasy burger, and I scarf down my half in only a few bites.

Amber sleeps through our meager dinner and the line of worry crossing Mom's forehead deepens. She runs her palm over Amber's forehead. "I wish I had a thermometer…"

Nick and I don't respond—there's nothing we can say.

"We need to figure out a plan for tomorrow," Mom continues. "I work eight to five."

"Abs, will you be okay with Amber until I get back from the kennel?" Nick asks.

My stomach churns. "I have the ACT tomorrow morning. Please—I can't miss it."

"Shit." Nick pinches the bridge of his nose between his thumb and first finger. "What time?"

"Seven thirty. But I should get done by noon."

He nods and the silence is thick while we wait for him to think through our options.

"Okay," he finally says. "I think I have some flexibility at the kennel. Take your test in the morning, and I'll stay with Amber until you get back. I'll leave a message letting them know I won't be in until after lunch."

"Can you do that?" Mom asks.

Nick shrugs. "What other choice do I have?"

"And my paper route?" I ask. "What do we do about that?"

Nick's shoulders fall. "I'm sorry, kiddo. We need you here. You'll need to call them before your test in the morning—I don't imagine they'd still be there tonight. Explain to them about today, and let them know why you can't make it tomorrow. If we're lucky, they'll be understanding. When you're done with your test tomorrow, head straight over to the Presbyterian Church and try to make it in time for the Community Kitchen. It might be all you get tomorrow."

CHAPTER TWENTY-THREE

MY EYES BLUR AT THE TEST IN FRONT OF ME AND I SMOTHER A YAWN WITH MY FIST. WITH AS MUCH AS I slept yesterday, I'm surprised I'm still tired today. The clock ticks from above the door, its *tick-tick-tick* competing with the frantic scratches of pencils on paper as students complete the ACT in the otherwise silent classroom. It's already 11:53 a.m. and I still have five remaining questions. I don't have time to work them all out, so I fill in random ovals and hope for the best. I blow out a breath and close the booklet before handing it to the proxy on my way out the door. She smiles and nods, careful not to disrupt those still working through the remaining three minutes.

My feet trudge tiredly through the quiet school halls, and frigid air hits me the second I step outside. I wrap my arms around myself for warmth, but it doesn't help much. The lining in my jacket is insufficient, and the cold wind blows straight through as though I'm not wearing a jacket at all. I shiver and increase my pace. I have to hurry—I can't miss lunch.

Icy slush swallows my canvas shoes with what remains of last night's four inches of snow. Cold, wet earth seeps through the fabric until my feet are blocks of ice and prickle with pain. But I can't stop or even slow down. I pick up my pace and arrive at the church out of breath and sweating despite the cold in my bones. I race into the building then stumble to a stop as my eyes find the clock in the hallway: 12:37 p.m. My heart sinks. If lunch isn't over, it will be soon. Can I still participate when arriving so late?

My stomach lets out a growl and I know I have to take a chance. Slower now, I follow the hallway past the kitchen and toward the dining hall.

"Abby?"

I stop and turn back toward Mrs. Cummings's voice, finding her seated at a food preparation bar in the kitchen with two other women, each enjoying what remains of today's meal. My heart sinks. If Mrs. Cummings has time to eat, they must've stopped serving. Tears sting my eyes and I swallow hard. "Hi, Mrs. Cummings."

The elderly woman stands and walks toward me, her smile warm. "I thought that was you. Did you just get here?"

"Yes. I'm—I'm late." Heat creeps into my cheeks.

Mrs. Cummings stretches her neck to see over my shoulder. "Where's the rest of your family?"

"At home—well, actually, Amber and Nick are home. Amber's sick today, and I had the ACT this morning, so Nick's staying with her. Mom's at work." My shoulders fall. "I hurried to get here, but my test took longer than I expected. Can I still eat?"

"Of course!" She waves her hand in dismissal. "Our guests are almost done eating but let's get you a plate."

"You don't mind? I'm really sorry I'm late."

"Sounds like you had a good excuse." Mrs. Cummings bustles around the kitchen, weaving between volunteers working on cleanup. "What will your parents and Amber do for dinner?"

"I—I'm not sure. Amber's too sick to eat, though."

"Well, she's in luck. We had chicken noodle soup with lunch, and we have plenty left. We'll make up four meals and you can take them back with you."

More tears build and sneak out from the corners of my eyes. I swipe at them, hoping she won't see. "Thank you."

Mrs. Cummings tsk-tsks sympathetically as she fills a plate with food, then turns to a lady helping with cleanup. "Nancy, please make up four plates to go with this young lady. Make sure to add plenty of soup, and some extra rolls. If there's any left, put some granola bars or snacks in a Ziploc baggie—anything that will keep well. We'll be back."

Mrs. Cummings takes my arm and hands me the plate piled high with food. Then, picking up the meal she abandoned, she leads me to a preschool room with tiny tables and chairs set up. She waves at a chair and sits. "Let's you and I eat in here."

I take a breath and paste on a smile before bringing my eyes to hers. She hands me a box of tissues.

"You okay?" she asks.

I nod. "I'm fine, thank you."

"Do you want to talk about it?"

I shake my head. "Not really."

She nods and a comfortable silence settles over us as we eat our meals. When I finish, I meet her eyes and ask the question that's been bothering me since the first time we met. "Why do you do this?"

"Feed people?" she asks.

"Yes. You're here every week. Does anyone ever thank you?"

"You did," she reminds me.

"Yeah, but I didn't mean me. I meant everyone else. Does anyone else ever say thank you?"

She nods. "Occasionally. That's not why I do it, though."

"Why then?"

Mrs. Cummings shrugs. "Because I have to. I mean, I'm called to do it. So many people just need a helping hand, and I have a need to provide it—to give them the hand up when they're down."

"But why?"

She shakes her head. "I'm not sure. I guess I feel so blessed for all I have; it's my way of saying thank you for all I've been given. It could be any of us out there on the street. Poverty shows no prejudice."

I ponder her words, remembering how much this one meal each week helps my outlook for the week ahead. It gives me hope. "I'm gonna do this," I blurt out. "When I'm in a better place, I want to come back and help you."

"I'd like that," she says.

With our meals completed, we return to the kitchen where the volunteer has a grocery sack of food ready for me.

"There's plenty in there for dinner tonight, and I threw in some extras for breakfast tomorrow," she says, handing the bag to me.

"Thank you." Then—without any forethought—I throw my arms around both ladies in a hug, saying once more, "Thank you."

CHAPTER TWENTY-FOUR

SUNLIGHT POURS THROUGH THE VAN'S WIN-
DOWS, AND ANOTHER COLD NIGHT HAS PASSED. I OPEN MY
eyes but my head feels like it's splitting open with pain. I close them immediately. I don't remember waking last night so I should be well-rested,
but my body is heavy and craves more sleep. I swallow and it's as if sharp
razors slice the back of my throat. A soft hand feels my forehead and
Mom clucks her tongue. "You have a fever, Abby."

I nod. "My head and throat hurt, too."

"I wish I had a thermometer—you're burning up."

I crack open my eyes. "How's Amber?"

"Still sick, but her fever's down some. I don't think we should leave
you girls alone today."

"We'll be okay," I croak. "We'll sleep, anyway—there's not much
you can do."

Mom looks at Nick and he shrugs. "I hate it, but she's right."

"But Abby can't take care of herself, much less Amber," Mom argues,
her brow etched in indecision as though grappling with what she *wants*
to do versus what she *has* to do.

Nick sighs. "I'll check in on them. I thought I'd try panhandling at
the turn-in to Walmart, so I can peek in every couple hours."

Mom turns her attention back to me, her eyebrows scrunched together. She brushes the hair away from my face. "Sure you'll be okay?"

I nod, but cringe as I swallow. "Yup. We need the money."

Mom studies me then leans down and kisses my forehead. "I love you. Try to get some rest."

Nick grabs a piece of cardboard with large black letters drawn on its surface, and opens the side door. I'm too groggy to read the words, but it isn't necessary—I know what it is. Nick's once-proud shoulders are stooped in defeat but he pulls his lips into a half smile and squeezes my foot twice as he jumps out of the van. "I'll check in on you in an hour or so, okay?"

I don't have the energy to respond. I'm so exhausted I don't even hear the van door close behind him.

"ABS." A HAND shakes me gently. "Abby, wake up."

"I'm awake." My head beats like a bass drum and I know better than to open my eyes again. "What time is it?"

"A little after two."

"Two?" My mind is scrambled. I can't understand how it was early morning only a few minutes ago.

"You've been sleeping all day," Nick says. "You need some soup to warm you up."

I pry open my eyes and find the sun less blinding this time. My head throbs, so I carefully pull myself to a sitting position. Beside me is Amber, already awake and sipping at a steaming cup. My brow wrinkles. "How—? I thought we ate all the soup last night."

"A lady stopped and gave it to me. She'd stopped earlier and asked if I needed anything, and I mentioned having two sick daughters. She left, then returned with two containers of soup and a large cup of coffee from Panera."

"Really?"

"Yeah." Nick nods. "She didn't even stick around to hear my thanks."

"Why would she do that?"

Nick shrugs and sips at his coffee. The soup is still hot and it eases the rawness in my throat, but I can't eat. I secure the lid and hand it back to him. "I'm sorry…"

"It's okay, kiddo."

Guilt washes over me at the waste. Now that I've eaten from it, Nick and Mom can't or they'll risk becoming sick themselves. My head swims. I crawl back under the covers and rest my heavy eyes. A moment passes and Nick's strong hands tuck the blanket's edges around me, trapping the heat. I'm so exhausted—I want to sleep, but shivers wrack my body and I'm cold everywhere.

I don't hear Nick move, but a moment later the van starts and cold air blows through the vents. It won't help, though. Even when it warms, the cold is coming from so deep inside me I know I'll never be warm again. I lie there and drift in and out of consciousness until exhaustion finally wins.

"DADDY, I'M SO cold!" Amber's voice comes to me through a long tunnel. I'm at that in-between stage of asleep and awake where I can hear everything around me, but I can't make my eyes open.

"I know, baby," he whispers.

"There's got to be something we can do." Mom's voice is an angry whisper. "Can we try going back to the Dorothy Day House? If they're not full, maybe they'll let us stay."

Nick sighs. "I've already tried. Their rules are strict—two weeks there, a month away, then we can return for two weeks."

"What about the church?" she whispers. "Couldn't we go there just for tonight? The girls are freezing. You've got the keys, and we'd be out before anyone arrives in the morning."

"I hadn't thought of that," he says. "If we get caught, I'll lose my job."

"Dammit, Nick. What good is a job if we're freezing and the girls are sick? If we don't get them warmed up, it won't matter if you still have a job because we won't have the girls."

"Shit!" Nick croaks out. "Just let me think, okay? I need a minute to think!"

Silence envelops us and I hear the unmistakable sniffle of someone crying.

"Sh…it's okay, Nick," Mom soothes.

My heart races. *Nick* is crying?

"Fuck!" Nick's fist pounds the floorboard and, next to me, Amber cries.

"It's okay, honey," Mom says. "We'll figure something out."

"No, Claire. It's not okay," he says through gritted teeth. "This is not what I wanted for my family. What kind of life is this?"

"We'll get through it. Let's just focus on tonight. What can we do right this minute?"

He doesn't answer for the longest time, then he blows out a breath. "The church is really large—big enough I think we could pull it off without getting caught, at least for one night. There's a storage room in the basement adjacent to the gym. If we slept there, we'd be hidden from sight. There're also two locker rooms with toilets and showers. We'd have to be out early in the morning, though. I don't think the staff comes in before eight, but there's a daycare on the other side of the basement and they probably open by seven, I'd think."

"And the church office is upstairs?" Mom asks.

"Right. Everything should be locked up but, even if someone comes in, there's no reason for them to come downstairs to the storage room—especially at night."

"So what if we stay there tonight and leave early tomorrow morning before anyone gets there? Who would know?"

"It's risky," he warns.

"I know. But it's too cold to stay in this van when we have other options. What if the girls get pneumonia, and we have to add another hospital visit to our list? Could you forgive yourself if something happened to them? I know I couldn't!"

"Fine." Nick's voice is resigned. "But we have to be out early. I'll park the van in the neighborhood behind the church so it doesn't draw attention."

Nick opens the sliding door on his side and pops into the driver's seat. I doze as he drives to the church, only awakening when Mom nudges my shoulder.

"C'mere, my sweet girl," she says to me, helping me sit up. "You're too big for me to carry anymore, but lean on me and I'll help you."

Mom locks an arm around my waist, bearing the burden of my weight as she leads me into the building. Her body is so familiar and sturdy—I wish I could crawl into her lap like I did when I was Amber's age.

Ahead of us, Nick carries Amber cradled in his arms. We follow him down a long hallway and descend a set of stairs before turning left through a set of double doors into the gymnasium. Another set of double doors is located along one wall and leads to a large storage room filled with daycare cots, chairs, tables and other items, all stacked high one atop the other. On an adjacent wall is a shelf holding about a dozen braided rugs. Nick reaches for a cot with one arm and sets it on the floor, then places Amber's body gently atop it. Once she's settled, he pulls a rug from the shelf, unrolls it onto a wide space on the floor, and places a blanket on top of it before nodding at Mom.

"Abby, honey," Mom says. "Lie down on this pallet and get comfortable."

I do as she instructs and curl into a tight ball. Seconds later, the weight of another blanket settles over me.

"What now?" Mom's voice is distant, as though coming through a tunnel. I realize I'm slipping into sleep and defiantly pry my eyes open and watch them.

"I'm gonna move the van," Nick answers. "You go ahead and find a comfortable spot—I'll be back shortly."

Mom puts her arms around Nick's neck. "Thank you," she says, touching her lips to his.

The kiss is short but elicits a smile from Nick. "I won't be long."

CHAPTER TWENTY-FIVE

"ABBY, WAKE UP." MOM'S VOICE ECHOES
THROUGH MY SLEEP-MUDDLED BRAIN. "ABBY, HONEY. YOU
need to wake up."

I open my eyes and swallow the barbed wire in my throat. "I don't
feel good."

"I know, sweetheart. But it's five thirty and we need to get out. I
thought you might want to take a shower first."

"Where are we going?"

"Back to the van. The daycare people will be here soon."

"No, Mom—please." I choke on a sob. "Can't we stay here? We'll be
so quiet they'll never know we're here. Don't make us go!"

"Honey, we can't. If we get caught, Nick'll lose his job." Mom runs
the palm of her hand over my forehead and sighs. "Your fever is up
again."

I pull myself to standing and swipe at the tears leaking from my
eyes. A wave of dizziness washes over me and my head pounds like a
subwoofer. I can't remember a time I've felt so awful.

"Mama, please don't make me go back out there." My words are
nearly indistinguishable through my heavy sobs. I don't even know why
I'm crying. Maybe it's everything, or maybe it's nothing at all. The only
thing I know is I hate this life and I want to go home. Not home to the
van, but home to Omaha—back to a time before everything fell apart.

Mom pulls me into her arms and rocks me back and forth, making my vertigo worse. "I'm sorry, sweet girl. We don't have another choice."

I step out of Mom's arms and rock back against a shelf for support. I try squaring my shoulders and lifting my chin, but I don't have the energy. "I'm not going back out there. I'll go to school instead."

"Sit down, Abby." Nick's voice is a command.

"No," I croak.

"Please, Abs," he says. "Sit down, okay?"

Deflated, I obey.

Nick squats next to me and pushes a strand of hair behind my ear. "Sweetheart, you can't go to school—they wouldn't let you even if you tried."

"Please, Nick." I swipe at a tear with the sleeve of my shirt.

He closes his eyes and pinches the bridge of his nose between two fingers. "Hear me out, okay? You're right—you're too sick to go anywhere." He huffs out a sigh, then opens his eyes and stares into mine. "So I need you to listen carefully. If we let you stay here with Amber, you have to be quieter than you've ever been. You can't leave the storage room except to use the bathroom, and then only if you can't hold it. If you get caught, we'll be in big trouble."

"We can stay, then?" Tears drip off my chin, but I don't care. "They'll never know we're here—I promise."

Mom and Nick exchange glances, once again having an entire conversation without uttering a word. He breathes out a sigh. "I don't see that we have another choice. Let's give it a try. It'll be late before we can get back—maybe as late as eight. We'll have to wait until everyone leaves the church for the day. Can you handle that?"

"Yes! Thank you, Nick! We won't let anyone see us—I promise!"

Before leaving, Mom and Nick forage through the kitchen adjacent to the gym where they find several containers of mini muffins, three bags of frozen rolls, a half-used gallon of orange juice, and a large half-used package of American cheese. Mom pours two glasses of orange juice and hands both to me with a container of mini-muffins. "Share these with Amber when she wakes up, then the rolls and cheese will tide you over if you get hungry for lunch. We'll bring back something for dinner, and I'm leaving a pitcher of water in case you get thirsty. We'll replace the food we've borrowed—somehow."

I nod.

"Are you sure you'll be okay?" she asks.

"We'll be fine."

Mom glances at Amber's sleeping form. She hesitates, then nods at Nick and gathers her things.

"We're counting on you, Abby," Nick says.

"I know. I won't let you down."

He squats next to me and squeezes my shoulder twice. "We know you won't, kiddo. Get some sleep and feel better. We'll see you tonight."

I SLEEP UNTIL nearly ten, when Amber begins stirring. I offer her the juice and muffins, then we crawl back under the covers and sleep until around two o'clock when she wakes again.

"Sister."

I crack my eyes open. Amber sits with her legs folded like a pretzel, her eyes bright and expectant. I close my eyes again and pull my blanket tighter around my shoulders. "You're feeling better?"

"Uh-huh. But I gotta pee."

"Can you hold it?"

She shakes her head. "Uh-uh. I gotta go now."

I blow out a sigh and rub the sleep from my eyes. My head still aches, but the pounding has dulled. "Okay. Give me a sec."

"No, Sister. I gotta go now," she repeats, her voice whiny.

"Okay. Just—hang on!"

I take a second to calculate our options. We're so far removed from the rest of the building it's impossible to know whether anyone else is around. I place my finger over my lips to signal "quiet" and listen for sounds from beyond the storage room doors.

Nothing.

"Okay," I say. "We have to be quiet as mice so we don't get caught. Pretend you're Jack and you're trying to steal the harp from the sleeping giant. Only instead of stealing the harp, we have to make it to the bathroom and back without him catching us. Can you do that?"

Amber grins, her sparkling eyes proving she feels better. "Don't worry, Sister. I'll tiptoe."

Despite how sick I am, her excitement makes me smile. Taking her hand, I lead her to the storage room doors and again place my finger over my lips before cracking the door open an inch. Dust motes hang in the air of the dimly lit gym and my heart pounds in the silence around us.

I open the door another six inches and survey the landscape. The locker rooms are about twenty yards away and marked appropriately for men and women—we should make it without issue. I tug on Amber's hand. "Okay. Let's go, but be quiet."

We sprint on quiet feet across the gym floor and push open the locker room door. I feel for a light switch and find one inside to my right. The room glows under the fluorescent lights.

"Hurry," I whisper.

Amber finds a stall and I take the one next to her. Adrenalin races through me—we're too exposed here with the lights on. The stall next to me flushes and I do the same, meeting Amber at the sink. In no time, we're back behind the safety of the storage room doors.

I've barely crawled under the covers and closed my eyes when Amber's tiny fingers pull at my eyelids, prying them apart. "I'm bored."

I swipe her hands away. "Stop. I don't feel good and I need sleep."

"Can I play with the basketballs?" She points to a rack of balls by the doors.

"No. You have to stay here and be quiet. Pretend we're hiding from the giant, okay? Use the flashlight to read or color, but you can't leave the room."

Amber huffs out a loud sigh. "Fine."

I pull my blankets around my chin and, within seconds, I drift off to sleep.

A FLY LANDS on my nose and I swipe at it with my hand. A moment later, it lands near my upper lip and I swipe again. Within seconds, it's back on my nose. Without opening my eyes, I reach out to trap it but, instead, my hand wraps around the soft tufts of a feather. My eyes flash open. In front of me is Amber, her eyes twinkling as she snatches the feather out of my hand.

"What are you doing?" I groan.

"I'm hungry."

I glance at my watch—it's already after six and I've slept through most of the day. I cover a yawn with my hand and stretch under the blanket. "Give me a second, okay?"

I sit up and relief washes over me. My headache is gone and my throat is less raw than earlier. Even the dizziness has disappeared. I locate the rolls and cheese Mom left behind and assemble them into sandwiches, offering one to Amber. The rolls have freezer burn, but it might be a feast for how quickly we scarf them down.

"When are Daddy and Mommy coming back?" Amber asks, her mouth stuffed with sandwich.

"A couple more hours."

"Why do we have to stay in here? Why can't we go play basketball in the gym?"

"We can't let anyone know we're here, or Nick will lose his job. We have to be very quiet until they get back."

"How much longer?" She frowns. "I'm bored."

"Better bored than cold." I ruffle her hair and feel her forehead for fever. She's cool to the touch. "You're feeling better?"

"Yeah." She nods. "I don't feel sick any more."

"I'm glad. But I need you to be patient. Just a couple more hours, okay?"

Amber sighs. "But there's nothing to do."

"You can read."

"I did that already."

I finish off the last of my sandwich and brush the crumbs from my lap. Standing, I survey the room. Boxes labeled "Christmas" line one wall. On the adjacent wall is a metal cabinet labeled "Supplies." I open it and find organized stacks of construction paper, white painting paper, a can of scissors, and several boxes with half-used watercolor palettes. I pull several paint sheets from the stack and a tin of watercolors from the cabinet. "Want to paint?"

Amber's eyes light up, and for the next two hours I lie beside her as she paints like a pro. Just when I close my eyes and doze off again, the doors to the storage closet creak. My eyes open and my heart races before I realize there's no threat.

"How'd it go?" Nick asks.

I sit up, relief washing over me as Mom steps in behind Nick. "Fine. We didn't see anyone all day. Amber's feeling better, but she's restless."

"And you?" he asks.

"Much better. Still weak, but I think I'll be okay to go to school tomorrow."

Mom sets a paper grocery bag in front of me, the red letters of Hy-Vee emblazoned across its front begging me to tear it open. She kneels next to me. "We brought you something."

"You went grocery shopping? How?"

Mom pulls out several cans of chicken noodle soup, a half-gallon of milk, a jar of peanut butter, and a loaf of bread. "Nick did some pan-handling today. He brought in twenty-seven dollars, so we picked up a few groceries."

"You got milk?" Amber exclaims.

Mom holds up a bag of store brand Cheerios. "And cereal!"

Amber reaches for the bag. "Can we have it now?"

"Not for dinner." Mom smiles and pulls the bag out of her reach. "But you can have a glass of milk with dinner, and cereal in the morning before school."

"One problem," I interrupt. "Bowls and spoons?"

"There are plenty in the cabinets here. We'll wash and put them away before we leave in the morning," Nick says.

"Wait. What?" My insides jump. "You mean—are we gonna stay here another night?"

Nick leans against the wall and folds his arms over his chest. He smiles, but lifts both eyebrows in warning. "We can't go back to the van. It's too cold and we can't take the chance of you girls getting sick again. I've been thinking on this all day, and I think we can stay here at night if we're careful and clean up after ourselves every morning. It's risky and we'll need to be out by six to avoid the daycare, but the setup is ideal. Besides the kitchen, we can use the locker room showers, and the daycare has a washer and dryer."

I'm giddy with relief. It's been a week since I've had a real shower, and I've run out of clean clothes. I swipe at a tear before it falls.

CHAPTER TWENTY-SIX

ZACH'S WAITING FOR ME AT THE DROP-OFF TO
DOOR SIX. SPOTTING OUR VAN, HIS EYES LIGHT UP AND THE
door is barely closed before he pulls me into his arms. "Where've you
been? Are you okay?"

I breathe in his scent. "I'm sorry I bailed on you last weekend. I was
really sick and couldn't even get out of bed."

Zach pulls away, his eyes studying me. "You're okay now?"

"Much better!"

"It's good to have you back," he says, placing a kiss on our joined
hands.

My heart flutters. "Anything new while I was gone?"

"Josh is back," he says, opening the door for me.

"He is?" I scan the foyer. "Where is he?"

"I haven't seen him yet this morning, but I'm sure he's around here
somewhere. You want breakfast?"

"Definitely!" I grin.

Zach pulls me to a stop and tugs me into his arms. "I'm glad you're back."

"Me too."

"Mr. Andrews and Ms. Lunde." Mr. Zagan's brittle voice jolts us
apart. "I believe we've already talked about this. Stop by my classroom
for detention slips before first period."

My face flames.

"I seriously hate that man," Zach groans.

"You and pretty much everyone else," I agree.

Zach squeezes my hand and leads me to the cafeteria where we pick up bagels to eat on our way to Zagan's class. Predictably, Zagan is waiting for us when we arrive, his cold blue eyes gleaming cruelly.

"I trust you won't be late," he says.

Zach rolls his eyes discreetly and takes both slips, handing one to me. Satisfied, Zagan steps back into the classroom.

"I trust you won't be late," Zach mimics in a nasally voice.

I bite my lip to keep from laughing. "See you at lunch?"

He grins then glances around to see if Mr. Zagan is spying. Finding his back turned to us, Zach leans in and kisses the tip of my nose. "Not if I see you first."

With those words, he smirks and leaves me standing outside the classroom. My heart is full. A grin teases the corners of my lips as I find my seat behind Josh.

"Ariel!" He jumps up and throws his arms around me. "Where the hell have you been? I've been worried sick!"

"Walt!" I laugh. "How're you feeling?"

"Much better." He tightens his arms around me and squeezes like he never intends to let go. "But you didn't answer my question. Where've you been? You've been gone for days and we had no way to get ahold of you. Even Zach didn't have a clue."

"I'm sorry." I can't help but grin as I step out of his arms. "I was sick. But I'm back now and I'm better."

"Still no phone?" he asks.

"Not yet—soon, though."

Josh wags a finger in front of my nose. "Don't ever do that again! Next time, find a way to get ahold of someone!"

Tera steps between us and pulls me into a hug. "What he means to say is, he's glad you're back."

"At least it's good to know I've been missed," I say with a laugh.

I step out of Tera's embrace and am enveloped into Wendy's. "That's an understatement. Josh about drove us nuts wondering about you. Was it the flu?"

I nod, stepping back once again. "I think so. Not as bad as Josh's, thank goodness, but I was pretty sick."

"I think I'm half jealous," Wendy says. "I could use a couple sick days to cozy up under the covers and catch up on some TV."

Before we can say more, the bell rings and Mr. Zagan promptly closes the classroom door. "Pop quiz," he announces to the groans of the class.

As he nears my desk, I raise my hand. "Mr. Zagan, could I please make an appointment to take the quiz later this week? I've been out sick for several days."

Zagan eyes me. "I'm sorry to hear that, Ms. Lunde, but no. My expectations are clearly outlined in my syllabus. If you've done as expected, you'll have read ahead and should do fine."

He slaps the quiz on my desk and walks away. Great—I did not need this today. *What is his problem? Does he enjoy making people miserable?*

I scan the quiz and find mostly multiple choice and true/false questions. Some of the answers are obvious, even though I haven't read the material, but most of it requires my best guess. My best guess is that I'll fail it.

THE BELL SOUNDS for lunch and I race to meet Zach in the hall. He smiles and takes my hand, and together we walk toward the cafeteria with Scott and Josh flanking us on each side.

"You're coming over on Sunday?" Zach asks.

My excitement bursts. "I can't."

"Why not?"

"My folks have to work, so I'm stuck with Amber all day."

"Then I'll come to your house and hang out. I've missed you."

I shake my head. "My folks would freak. I can't have guys over when they aren't home."

"Then bring Amber to my house. She can hang out with us, or watch TV, or something. My mom won't mind."

"Are you sure?"

"Yeah."

"Okay." I grin.

"So what's the plan after school?" he asks. "Can I give you a ride?"

"I have to pick up Amber, so that would be great. But—" I pause, not sure how to continue.

Zach slows his stride and turns toward me. "What's wrong?"

"You're not the only one I didn't call this weekend." I frown. "I wasn't able to reach work this weekend to let them know I was sick."

"You didn't even call them?" He asks.

"No, I did. I tried Saturday morning, but all I got was an answering machine and I wasn't sure what to say. I was going to call them again later, but then I felt so awful that—"

"You were sick—they'll understand."

"Maybe. But could you sit with Amber while I talk to them? I don't want her to see me get fired."

"You think they'll fire you for that? It's not like it was your fault."

"I missed three straight days without calling in," I say. "Yeah, I'm pretty sure they will."

"It'll be their loss." He shrugs. "But sure—no problem."

Josh interrupts. "Do you realize you have less than two weeks until the Fall Concert?"

"Don't remind me," I groan. "I've only practiced with Keaton a few times and I'm nervous."

"Don't be," Scott says. "You've got this."

"I hope so."

"You do! Do you think I'd hang out with a loser who couldn't sing?" Josh teases.

"Oh, I might." Zach wiggles his eyebrows. "She's pretty cute, after all."

"Ha-ha." I poke him in the ribs.

"What are you singing?" Josh asks.

"Not telling. You'll have to wait until the concert."

Josh pushes his bottom lip out. "You're mean."

My grin spreads to a full smile. As much as I hate being homeless, moving to Rochester is the best thing we've ever done.

MRS. MINER IS waiting for me when I arrive at her classroom after lunch. "You're back! I was worried—everything okay?"

I nod. "Yup. I just had the flu or something."

"Glad you're feeling better." Mrs. Miner sets her granny glasses firmly on her nose. "We're doing something different today. Ms. Raven found two vocal music scholarships offered by in-state schools—Mankato State and St. Cloud State. Are you still interested?"

My eyes pop wide. "Do you think I have a chance?"

"I do," she says. "But we won't know until we try. Are you ready to try?"

I pull my bottom lip between my teeth and nod.

"Good." Mrs. Miner's eyes smile. "Both schools have the same audition requirements, and we can use your solos from the Fall Concert. I want to run through them a couple of times, then I'll videotape you performing them."

"That's all? I mean—is it that easy?"

"Pretty much." She nods. "You'll need to complete the applications and get three letters of recommendation, but you shouldn't have any problem. Ms. Raven and I are both happy to write letters for you. Do you have another teacher you can ask?"

I think for a moment. "Maybe Mr. Thompson?"

"He'd be an excellent choice. I heard you took the ACT last weekend?"

I nod.

"How'd it go?"

I shrug. "Okay, I think."

"What did you put down as your top three schools?"

"Mankato, St. Cloud, and Eau Claire."

"Good." She nods again. "One less thing to worry about—they'll send the scores directly to the schools you listed. So, let's get started."

I have three solos plus the one I selected with Zach. Mrs. Miner chooses two and I practice them three times each before she's satisfied. Next she coaches me through my introduction, explaining she'll add it to the video during editing. The only part she can't edit are the solos themselves, and it takes about twenty tries before I get through both songs without mistakes. We finish about two minutes before the bell to change classes.

Mrs. Miner presses stop on the recording. "I'll take care of this. Now, you take the applications and talk to Mr. Thompson about a recommendation. See Ms. Raven if you have questions, otherwise return them Friday and we'll get them mailed off."

"Thank you," I say. "I really appreciate your help."

"It's my pleasure." She smiles. "Now scoot before you're late for your next class."

"ZACH!" AMBER WEAVES between students, racing toward us at the end of her school day. Reaching us, she flies into Zach's arms, wrapping her limbs around him like a spider monkey. "I've missed you!"

"Oh yeah?" He grins. "I've missed you, too."

"Are you gonna deliver newspapers with us?"

"We'll see—I'll give you a ride for sure."

"Can I sit in front this time?"

"No you cannot," I interrupt. "You'll sit in back and wait with Zach while I go in. And don't embarrass me this time. Got it?"

Amber sighs. "Fine."

I smile and take her hand. "I'm sorry, Am. I'm just nervous. I didn't mean to hurt your feelings."

Amber's eyes sparkle. "Does that mean I can sit in front?"

"No," I say, giving her a mock scowl.

The drive only takes a few minutes, and Zach finds a parking spot right in front of the building. "Want me to go in with you?"

I shake my head and open the passenger-side door. "No, but thanks anyway. I need to do this myself."

I draw in a deep breath then close my door and open the heavy glass doors of the newspaper building. Madigan guards the lobby as she did the day I was hired. I offer a tentative smile. "Hi, Madigan. Is Maris in?"

Madigan scowls. "She's not. Where've you been? You've been out three days."

My eyes drop and I study my cuticles. "I was sick."

"And you couldn't call?"

I open my mouth to respond, but I'm not sure what to say. Before I can find the words, she rolls her eyes and turns away from me.

"Whatever. I have your check, but Bryan wants to talk to you."

I swallow hard and wait in the empty lobby for her return. Moments later, she reappears holding an envelope, with Bryan on her heels.

"Abby." Bryan's eyes are piercing, displeased. "Want to step into my office?"

My heart thuds and my stomach does a flip-flop. I draw a shallow breath and follow Bryan, taking the same seat I used when I interviewed.

"Feel like telling me what's going on, Abby?" he asks. "You missed three straight days without any word. Maris had to scramble to cover your route."

"I'm sorry, Bryan. I—"

"This is completely unacceptable. Three days, Abby. What kind of work ethic is that? I suggest you examine your priorities."

"I'm really sorry," I whisper. "I was sick until late last night."

His lips form a thin line. "And you couldn't call?"

"I tried, but I just got an answering machine. I didn't know what to say," I whisper.

Bryan shrugs. "Not good enough. You're a senior now, and you should have at least left a message instead of leaving us hanging."

"I'm sorry." I stare at my hands.

Bryan's nostrils flare as he blows out a breath. "Thank you. I accept your apology, but I'm afraid your route has been assigned to someone else."

"So—I'm fired?"

"Yes." He nods. "I'm sorry, Abby."

I roll my lips inward and nod. There's no point arguing. He's angry and at least some of his anger is valid. I stand, my brain screaming all the things I want to say, but say instead, "Thanks, Bryan—for giving me a chance." Tears sting the backs of my eyes and shame smothers me. "Is there anything else you need from me?"

"No. I think we're good." Bryan stands and extends his hand. "I wish you luck, Abby."

We shake hands, but I can't speak. I know if I try, the tears will never stop. With my head down, I clutch my paycheck to my chest and escape through the main lobby.

ZACH'S CAR IS parked where I left him. I yank open the door and slam it shut once I'm seated.

"Whoa! You okay?" He arches an eyebrow.

Tears spill from my eyes and I wipe them away. "I'm fine. Can we just go?"

"Yeah, okay. Do you want to talk about it?"

"No. I just want to go," I snap. "Can you take us to the library?"

"Sure. Mind if I tag along?"

I shrug and stare out the passenger window. "I don't care."

I don't speak again on the drive to the library, and the only words I speak after we arrive are to remind Amber not to wander from the craft room. Zach disappears into another part of the library, leaving me alone with my thoughts in the Teen Room. I settle at a carrel and pull out my homework. I've barely worked three problems of my history homework when Zach returns with a handful of DVDs.

"What's that?" I ask, still sullen.

"For Amber."

He flips over the top DVD, showing the cover.

"What in the world?" I laugh at the *Sylvester and Tweety Bird* images.

"For when you bring her over this weekend," he explains. "I thought she'd enjoy them since she looks so much like Tweety Bird."

"Awww!" I stand and place my arms around Zach, laying my head on his chest. "That's the sweetest thing ever!"

His fingers tangle in my hair and he tugs my head back until I'm looking at him. "If I'd known all I needed to do for affection was to be nice to your sister, I'd've done it sooner."

I laugh and accept his kiss, my anger forgotten.

"I gotta head home," he says when we pull apart. "See you at school tomorrow?"

I bite back a smile. "Not if I see you first."

"Ouch!" Zach taps my nose with his forefinger then says, this time like a command, "I'll see you tomorrow."

He leaves me standing next to my carrel, a much-needed smile on my face and my heart happier than it was only an hour ago.

WE WAIT UNTIL Nick's night shift at the church before returning. In the short time he's worked there, he's always found the church empty, so our odds of remaining undetected are good.

"I want to show you something." He leads us to the basement, but stops in the Senior High Sunday School Room. He opens the door and flips on the light. "What do you think?"

I shrug. "I've seen it before. This is the room they use for youth group."

"Is that all you see?" Mom asks.

Amber and I study the room—it's a rainbow of colors, beginning with a plum-colored velvet couch, a second couch in black leather, and a yellow faux leather futon with six fabric cushions along the back with seats in red, green, and blue. The three pieces are arranged in a U-formation with the black sofa at its center facing the opposite wall, where an old-fashioned box television with a built-in DVD player occupies space next to an equally outdated tower stereo system. On both sides of the black sofa are twin white end tables with pink and purple lava lamps glowing on top of each. In the center of the room is a shag rug of primary colors made from mismatched carpet samples. The walls are painted sunshine yellow and decorated with posters containing inspirational quotes and religious scriptures. It looks like a Crayola box threw up, yet it's strangely welcoming.

"I like it," Amber says.

Mom grins and turns her attention to me. "Abs?"

"It's colorful." I shrug again. "But what am I supposed to see?"

"Well," Nick grins. "If there's nobody in the building until early morning, then maybe we could sleep here instead of the storage room. It'll be more comfortable. We could throw a blanket on the floor for Amber, or pull one of the cots from the storage room for her. What do you think?"

"Yes!" Amber screeches. "Can we watch TV, too?"

"One thing at a time," Mom says.

"But what about getting caught?" I ask.

"We shouldn't be careless, but we should be okay so long as we leave everything immaculate every morning when we leave. Wanna give it a try?"

Amber hops from one foot to the other. "Yes! Yes! Yes!"

I don't have to answer—Amber's answered for both of us. Instead I smile and plop down on the futon. "I call dibs on this one."

CHAPTER TWENTY-SEVEN

IT'S BEEN ELEVEN DAYS SINCE WE MADE OUR HOME IN THE BASEMENT OF EVANGEL EPISCOPAL CHURCH. Each morning we rise by four thirty and stow our belongings in a cardboard box in the supply closet, then clean up meticulously before the daycare workers arrive between six thirty and six forty-five. Though the first few days were scary, we've settled into a pattern. We shower in the locker rooms, cook in the kitchen adjacent to the gym when we can't eat at the Salvation Army, and use the daycare's washer and dryer to do laundry. The church is creepy at night, but we stay together and almost feel normal again.

"Daddy's here," Amber calls through the library's bathroom door where I've been primping for the last twenty minutes.

"Okay. Tell him I'm almost ready," I say.

The door closes and I take one last look at myself in the mirror, studying my black knee-length skirt and white rayon blouse with flared sleeves. The shoes are white-on-black strappy heels with an open toe. The ensemble is compliments of Tera's and Wendy's closets. The Fall Concert starts in an hour and butterflies sword-fight in my stomach.

I push a lock of hair behind my ear and fluff my long waves. With one last glance in the mirror, I pull in a breath and step out of the bathroom. *Here goes nothing!*

"Wow!" Amber's eyes pop wide. "You look beautiful."

I smooth an invisible wrinkle on my skirt. "Ya think?"

"Uh-huh." She nods. "Like a movie star."

She might be only six, but her words lend me confidence. "Thanks, Am. You ready?"

"Uh-huh." Amber grins and takes my hand, leading me toward the exit doors where Mom and Nick wait in the van. "You've got this, Sister."

THE DRIVE TO the high school is quiet, allowing me to practice my solos in my head. When we arrive, the lot is packed with cars—far more than on a normal school day. Nick stops at the front door, letting Mom, Amber and me out.

"Go ahead in," he says. "I'll park and catch you inside."

"Thanks, Nick," I say, knowing I won't see him again before I perform.

"No problem, kiddo. Break a leg."

I close the van door and follow Mom and Amber into the foyer. "I gotta get ready," I say. "See you later?"

Mom nods. "Go ahead. We'll wait here for Nick. Good luck."

Amber throws her arms around my waist. "Bye, Sister!"

"I'm only going onstage for an hour," I say.

"I know," she says. "But I don't want you to forget me when you're famous."

I give her a squeeze and let go. "Never! I only have one sister."

Amber beams as I leave her behind and head toward the backstage area. Waiting for me, Zach scrolls through messages on his iPhone. He's leaned against a cinder block wall with one long leg propped behind him. I clear my throat and his phone is forgotten.

"Wow!" he says. "You look—wow!"

I do a slow twirl. "You like?"

"I do! Are you ready?"

I blow out a breath. "Ready as I'll ever be, I guess."

"You're beautiful, Abs." He takes my hand. "You're gonna knock 'em dead."

"Thanks—I needed to hear that."

Zach steps forward and rests his forehead against mine. "You can do this."

I close my eyes and swallow hard. "Okay. I can do this."

He leans in and kisses me, just a touch of the lips, and then pulls back. "That's for luck." He smiles, then leans in a second time, this time allowing his lips to linger.

All thoughts fly out of my head until the only thing I can think about is Zach and the feel of his lips on mine. Before I'm ready, he ends the kiss and pulls away again.

I open my eyes. "What was that one for?"

He grins. "That one was for me."

"Are you freakin' kidding me?" Josh teases as he approaches us with Wendy and Tera. "Seriously, guys, you disgust me."

"Or make you jealous," Tera says.

"Yeah, that too," he says.

"We're just going in," I say. "I'm glad you came!"

Josh pulls me into a hug, sweeping me off my feet and around in a circle. "We wouldn't miss it for the world, Ariel!"

"Hey! She's mine," Zach teases. "Get your own."

"Yeah?" Josh lifts a challenging eyebrow. "Well—I saw her first."

"Yeah?" Zach puffs out his chest. "Well—you bat for the other team."

"Damn." Josh laughs and sets me on my feet. "Good point!"

"Okay, guys," I interrupt. "If you're done comparing testosterone levels, we gotta go."

Zach snorts and throws an arm around me. "Really, Abs...there's no comparison."

"Zach!" I elbow him and he lets out a gush of air. "That's not nice."

"No worries." Josh laughs. "In a fight between myself and Gaston over here, he may have more testosterone but I've got more charm—and charm trumps braggadocio every time."

"Ouch!" Zach laughs.

"Burn!" Tera and Wendy say together.

I pull a straight face but a smile still teases my lips. "C'mon you guys. Zach and I are gonna be late. See you after?"

"You know it," Wendy says.

"Break a leg," Tera adds.

Josh grins. "We'll see you on the flip side, Ariel. And Gaston?" he says to Zach with a lift of one eyebrow, "Your good looks and testosterone might pull in the ladies, but *charm* is key to keeping them—or the gents, whichever you prefer."

Zach laughs and bumps fists with Josh. "Thanks for the tip, man."

I roll my eyes and pull Zach along with me. "Later, you guys!"

The moment we enter the stage, my stomach flip-flops like an elite gymnast. I roll my shoulders and let go of the tension.

"Hey." Zach squeezes my hand. "You're gonna be fine."

"Yeah." I take another breath and let it out slowly. "I'm gonna be fine."

He brings our joined hands to his lips and kisses the back of mine. "Let's go."

Zach leaves me with the choir and takes his seat beside the piano. Moments later, the lights dim and Mrs. Miner takes the stage.

"Welcome, families and friends!" she begins. "I'm happy to see so much support for our talented students, and I thank you for coming. We have an exciting treat for you this evening, so get comfortable and enjoy the performance!"

The audience applauds and Mrs. Miner ascends the podium, her conductor's wand in hand. She smiles and offers the chorus a wink, then counts under her breath so only we can hear. She cues the piano player.

The first two songs fly by and I'm next up with my first short solo. It's only a few lines and backed up by the chorus, so I don't miss a beat.

I'm totally in the moment without a single thought for the audience. Adrenaline races through me, but not out of fear. Instead, I'm elated. Keaton's voice joins with mine, and we sing song after song together, then with the entire chorus, then independently as soloists.

Nearly a full hour goes by and the program has only two remaining selections: Keaton's choice solo followed by mine. I focus on Keaton as he takes the stage, his deep baritone ringing through the auditorium. For the next three minutes, he holds the audience spellbound. At song's end, he drops his last note and takes a deep bow. When he rises, the auditorium erupts into deafening cheers. My voice joins with others as we stand and offer praise for his stunning performance.

"Thank you, Keaton!" Mrs. Miner says into the microphone. "For our last performance tonight, please allow me to introduce you to Abby Lunde. Abby is new to Rochester South this year, and has been a wonderful addition to our vocal music department, bringing with her an exceptional talent that every music teacher hopes to find. Tonight is her debut as a solo performer, and she's a little nervous. So let's help put her at ease and give a warm welcome for Abby Lunde as she performs for you Adele's 'All I Ask.'"

Oh shit! I'm up!

The audience cheers and my knees rattle against each other. Bile rises, but I breathe in and out slowly, pushing it away. As silence swallows the room, I stand and approach center stage.

A blinding light pours down on me, its heat scalding. Though I can't see the audience, I know they're out there. My brain freezes. I close my eyes and meditate ten seconds, but it doesn't help. My eyes flash to Zach's.

Help!

He stands. Wrapping one hand around the neck of his guitar, he curls the other around the seat of a tall stool and approaches me. He reaches my side and sets the stool down, leaning his guitar against it. He steps close to me and lifts the microphone from the stand, placing it in my hand and wrapping my fingers around it. "Breathe."

Our eyes meet and his confidence seeps into me. I nod as he leans down and kisses my cheek. Then, with a gallant bow, he steps away and takes a seat atop the stool as though his every step was practiced for precision.

I breathe deeply, this time with my diaphragm. Bringing the microphone to my mouth, I wait for the opening strains of Zach's guitar. When it's time for my entrance, I open my throat and allow my voice free rein, forcing myself to forget I'm Abby Lunde, homeless girl. In this moment, I'm confident, talented, and respected. A sense of peace settles over me, and my confidence soars until everything feels so "right" I never want to leave the stage. This is my moment and I wish it could last forever.

Too soon, the song ends and I release the last note, and listen as my voice echoes over the audience. Then, opening my eyes, I smile and dip into a deep bow. The audience erupts in applause and nearly everyone rises to their feet.

"OH MY GOSH, Abby! That was amazing!" Tera squeals as she, Wendy, and Josh storm the stage. "I'd heard you were good, but wow!"

"Thanks." My face hurts from smiling, but it's a wonderful kind of hurt.

"That was—I have no words!" Wendy chimes in.

"You kicked ass, Ariel!" Josh says. "Did you see Trish's face? I wish I'd taken a picture!"

"I didn't see anything—I had my eyes closed," I admit.

"It was hilarious!" Tera laughs. "Her jaw dropped wide open. Karma, baby!"

"Watch your back, Ariel," Josh warns. "She was totally humiliated and will be out for blood."

"I've got your back." Zach pulls me to his side. "Don't worry about Trish."

Before I can respond, a tiny body flies at me, knocking me off balance and out of Zach's embrace. I stagger backward, grabbing ahold of Josh and pulling him with me, his body cushioning my fall as we slide into a heap on the floor.

"Sister!" Amber's tiny body is wrapped entirely around mine.

"Whoa!" Josh laughs, his voice muffled by my armpit. "This must be Elsa."

Amber eyes Josh and scowls. "Am not! I'm Amber!"

"Just go with it," I say.

"Nuh-uh!" She stands tall and places her fists on her hips, her chin high and defiant.

"Get up, Ariel," Josh groans. "You're killing me. And seriously—did you put on deodorant?"

"Very funny." I scoot onto the floor beside him.

"She's not Ariel!" Amber tips her chin and looks at Josh down her tiny nose. "Who are you?"

Mom and Nick approach, and Nick extends his hand to help me stand then does the same for Josh. Standing to his full height, Josh puffs out his chest and puts his fists on his hips in an imitation of Amber.

"I'm Walt," he says.

I blurt out a laugh.

Amber rolls her eyes. "You're weird, Walt."

"Abby, honey!" Mom interrupts, her eyes filled with tears. "That was—I don't know what to say! I've never heard you sing like that! I mean, I've heard you sing dozens of times, but never like *that*! It was… *special*."

Nick hands Mom a tissue and offers me a grin that says, "*That's your mom for you*." He pulls me into a hug. "I'm proud of you, kiddo. You did good."

Nick's eyes are suspiciously wet and the defeat he's carried around for weeks is missing. Though he's always treated me like his own, it's the first time I fully understand that, to him, I *am* his daughter—not just because he married my mom.

I swallow a lump in my throat. "Thanks, Nick."

"It's getting late and we need to get Amber home." Mom wipes away her tears. "Are you about ready?"

"One second." I turn back to my friends. "See you guys tomorrow?"

Josh, Tera and Wendy say goodbye, leaving me standing with my family and Zach.

"Can I walk you out?" Zach asks.

I nod. "I was hoping you would."

None of us say anything as we walk to the van. None of us except Amber, that is, who pleads with Zach for a piggyback ride. Never able to tell her no, he crouches low and she climbs on, choking his neck as he carries her to the van.

"Giddyup, horsey!" she cries.

Mom rolls her eyes and lets out a sigh. "Amber, get in the van, please, and give Sister a minute to say goodbye to Zach."

Zach crouches low and Amber jumps down. "Aw, man! That wasn't a very long ride!"

"Catch me tomorrow and I'll make it up to you," he tells her.

"Deal!" she says, climbing into the van.

I close her door and turn to Zach. "Thank you."

He lifts an eyebrow. "For what?"

"For everything. For practicing with me, for standing by me, for keeping me grounded so I didn't freak out. Everything."

Zach squeezes my hands. "I told you I have your back."

I bite my lip. "See you tomorrow?"

"Not if I see you first." He pulls me in for a kiss.

CHAPTER TWENTY-EIGHT

MOM AND I STAND IN THE KITCHEN, WAITING ON A FROZEN PIZZA IN THE OVEN. WHEN WE RETURNED from the concert, Nick and Amber headed straight to the showers, leaving us to worry about dinner. Adrenaline has been my constant companion since we left the school, and I've been unable to come back down from my high. Thankfully, the ice of the last six months has thawed considerably between Mom and me, and—much like the old days before everything fell apart—she insists on experiencing the evening vicariously through my eyes. I'm not sure which of us I'm humoring as I relate to her every moment of the last two hours.

"I can't even describe it in words!" I say. "I couldn't see the audience, but I could feel their energy—their support!"

Mom reaches into the oven and removes the pizza. A flash of color catches my attention. "Nick—" I begin, but my voice dies in my throat. My body trembles and my heart thuds like a stampede of horses. The large body filling the doorway isn't Nick's. I open my mouth, but no sound follows. Mom hasn't seen him yet, but Jim Kaspar, Director of Christian Education, stands six feet away in the kitchen doorway.

Some people refer to Jim as the Associate Pastor. He's second in command and knows everything that happens in this church. Except, of course, that we've been squatting in the basement. His eyes are wide, his expression one of shock.

"Excuse me," he says.

Mom turns and drops the pan on the floor. She ignores it and stares at Jim, her eyes wide and her hands shaking. She sways on her feet. Jim leaps toward her and leads her to a chair.

"Sit, please," he says, helping her into the chair. "I didn't mean to scare you. I—I didn't expect to find anyone here."

Mom stares at him and I worry she might go into shock.

"Mom?" I say.

Jim takes the oven mitts from her hands and picks up the pizza pan from the floor. The pizza is still edible, but I doubt any of us will be hungry tonight.

Jim returns to her side and runs a hand through the stubble of his hair. "I left some paperwork on my desk and came back to get it. I heard voices—I guess I didn't know *what* I expected to find. Are you okay?"

Mom nods, but her eyes are vacant. She stares at Jim without speaking. Beside her, I'm rooted to the floor, mute in my own shock.

"Claire, I think?" he asks. "We met several weeks ago. You're Nick's wife—our janitor?"

"Yes." Mom nods.

"I'm sorry I startled you. Where's Nick?"

"He—he's taking a shower."

He nods. "I see. Why don't we sit down and talk."

"I need…" Mom scans the room. "I need to get Nick."

"Okay. Why don't you go find him, and I'll wait here. Your daughter can keep me company while we wait."

Mom stands, her movements stiff as though sleepwalking. "I—I'll get him."

When she disappears into the men's locker room, Jim turns to me. "Let's chat while we wait."

I follow him to a long table inside the gym and sit across from him. I'm at a loss for words. He's being so polite—too polite for having found a family squatting in the basement. I stare at the table and examine my fingernails.

"How long have you been here?" he asks gently.

"Almost two weeks."

He nods. "What did you do before that?"

I clear my throat, pausing while my mind searches for the right words.

Jim's eyes hold mine. "I need you to trust me because I'd like to help if I can."

I take a breath and wipe away the first of many tears that will fall this night. I surprise myself at how swiftly the words come rushing out. I tell Jim how we were so cold sleeping in the van, and what a luxury it felt like to have a hot shower at the Dorothy Day House before they kicked us out at the end of our two weeks. How I worry every day whether my lunch card will work at school, and whether my friends will abandon me if they ever find out. I cry as I tell him how sick Amber and I were, and how scared I was the day we shivered alone in the van. I explain how living here has been so much better, even though we have to wake up when it's still dark outside so we don't get caught. And I tell him how none of this was supposed to happen, how we're roaming around from place to place and it all just seems to be getting worse and I don't see when or how we'll ever get out of it.

I finish, with my head down, tears falling into my lap. When I look up, Jim's eyes are filled with tears, and Mom, Amber, and Nick stand like statues in the doorway. Nick's hair is wet and drops of water seep through his T-shirt where he hasn't dried off properly. His eyebrows are scrunched together and his lips are drawn down at the corners. He straightens his shoulders and approaches us. "Jim, I—"

Jim holds up a hand. "Let's sit down and talk about it. Your daughter explained quite a bit, but I have some questions about how you came to be…"

"Homeless," Nick supplies. "You can say it, Jim. It's too late for embarrassment or offense. It is what it is."

He nods. "Homeless."

Nick and Mom take seats next to me, and Nick tells Jim the parts I left out. Again, Jim allows Nick the dignity of telling his whole story. I space out, tiptoeing back in time.

THREE WEEKS BEFORE THE MOVE

Mom's sobs bleed through the thin walls of my bedroom, distracting me from the book I'm reading. I glance at the clock—11:47 p.m. I should've been asleep by now, but I kept telling myself, "Just one more chapter." Another sob reaches my ears and I huff out a breath. It's not the first time I've heard Mom cry lately, and the sound grates on me.

I push my feet from under the covers and creep toward the door. Turning the knob, I ease it open and peek through the narrow slit. Nick holds Mom in his arms, rubbing her back in a soothing motion. His flannel shirt muffles her words, so I open the door wider and squat low so they don't see me.

"They just closed the doors and turned everybody away?" Mom cries. "Without notice—without telling anyone?"

"That's exactly what they did." Nick's body screams defeat. "Twelve years I've worked for them—ten more for some of the guys—and this is how they treat us."

"How did you not know?" Mom asked. "There must've been signs."

"Only when they cut my hours, but it was supposed to be temporary."

"Did they say anything?" she asks.

Nick shakes his head. "Not a word. We showed up to open the garage this morning and found a Post-it Note on the door saying they'd filed for bankruptcy."

Mom chokes on another sob. "What are we going to do? We've already sold everything of value, and we still owe thousands to the hospital. Not to mention the rent—Chloye's already been here twice to collect."

"Twice?" Nick's shock is evident.

Mom won't meet his eyes. "Last week when the girls were home alone was the second time. I was going to tell you, but I didn't know how. I thought I'd have a job by now and could fix it, leaving you one less thing to worry about."

"Dammit, Claire! This is something I needed to know."

"I know. I'm sorry."

He runs his fingers through his hair.

"What do we do now?" Mom asks.

"I don't know. But this is bad. They've warned us twice, and that's more than enough notice for eviction."

"What are you saying?" Mom asks. "They can't just throw us out!"

"They can and they will. They're only required to give us a three days' notice. Even if we fight it, we're only buying—at most—two weeks. Nebraska law has no tolerance for unpaid rent—they almost always favor the landlord."

"How do you know that?" she asks.

"I told you I was homeless before, right after high school when my parents died. I swore I'd never be here again."

"I'm so sorry, Nick," Mom says. "This whole thing is my fault—everything that's happened since that damned Snapchat."

Nick breathes out. "It's done, Claire. We can play the blame game, but right now we gotta get our ducks in a row."

"What do we do?"

He shrugs. "We plan for the future as best we can."

"Which means…?"

"I don't know—maybe we move to Rochester."

"Minnesota?" she asks. "How does that help?"

Nick blows out a breath. "We can't stay here—there's nothing left for us here anymore. Abby's miserable, and you'll never get another teaching job anywhere near this area. After everything that's happened, maybe a new start would be best for all of us."

"Okay, fine—but why Rochester? It's at least a five-hour drive and the

winters are even worse than here."

"I grew up near there, so I know the community reasonably well. Unless things have changed, they have established programs to help us get back on our feet. Plus, if I'm gonna be homeless again, I'd rather choose where."

Silence echoes like a tomb. I cover my mouth with both hands, holding in a gasp of disbelief. Scalding tears race down my face and drop onto my nightshirt. Using the doorframe for support, I stand and slip back into my bedroom.

NICK FINISHES HIS explanation, and Jim's forehead crinkles. Silence echoes in the cavernous gym.

"What are you going to do?" Mom asks.

Jim shakes his head. "I can't send you back to your van. Not tonight in this weather, at least. I know you, Nick, and I couldn't do that to you. I couldn't do that to anyone."

"And tomorrow?" Nick asks. "What happens then?"

Jim sighs. "We come up with a better solution."

"We can't go back out there. Please—" Nick's voice is desperate, and I hate the begging quality in his tone. Nick's always been a proud man, and nobody should ever have to beg for shelter.

"No, I agree." Jim massages his temples with two fingers. "Our first priority is getting your family out of the cold. I'll make some calls in the morning. Evangel is part of an interfaith hospitality network with fourteen other churches. Together, we find solutions for homeless families. I'll start there and see if I can get you enrolled in it."

"What is it, exactly?" Nick asks.

"It's a program where we rotate the 'hosting' of homeless families. Each church handles it a little differently but, generally speaking, your family is invited to live at one of the churches for a week. A family from that church is assigned as your hosts, and they provide food and cook meals with you, their kids play with your kids, and sometimes they even help with homework. They basically try to provide a normal family experience. When the week is over, the guest families rotate together to the next church for one week, and so on until we can help you find permanent housing."

"Why didn't they tell us this at the Salvation Army when they gave us a list of services?" Mom asks.

"Because space is limited, and it's by clergy recommendation only. In most cases, the families come from within our own congregations. If we'd known earlier, we could've recommended your family for the program."

"I—it's not something I wanted to tell more people than we had to," Nick says.

Jim nods. "I can understand that. There's one more thing—and I don't want you to get your hopes up—but it's something we can look into. This same network of churches owns a few single-family transitional homes and four units at Winter Resort apartments. I'll need to look into the details but, if memory serves and if you qualify, they're rent-free and you can stay for four months. If we can work that out for you, we can use that time to help you find better jobs while you save money for a deposit on something more permanent."

Mom's eyes glisten. "Thank you."

"Don't thank me yet," Jim says. "I'll make calls and see what I can set up. Once your housing is figured out, then we can work on helping you find jobs that you're trained to do—something with benefits. I hear you're a teacher, Claire?"

Mom nods. "Yes, but I'm not licensed in Minnesota. I thought maybe I could work in a daycare, but I haven't had any luck. I have other skills, though. I can type, and maybe I could use my math background in some capacity."

"That helps to know." Jim turns his attention to Nick. "And you were a mechanic with the same company for more than ten years, Nick?"

Nick nods. "Twelve years, until I was let go without notice."

"Okay. Let's see what we can do with that. I think a temporary agency might be where we start for Claire until she can get her state teaching credentials established. I'll have to think on yours a little longer, Nick. I'm certain we must have someone in our congregation with ties to a local repair shop. Maybe we could approach them discreetly to see if they have anything that might be a good fit for you."

"I don't know how to thank you," Nick says.

Jim smiles. "You thank me by finding a way to return the favor to someone else when you're better established."

"Absolutely," Nick agrees.

Jim stands and shakes Nick's hand. When he extends that same hand to Mom, however, she ignores it, instead wrapping her arms around him.

"Thank you so much," she says through tears.

Jim smiles and hugs her close. "You're welcome, Claire."

We're left subdued after Jim's departure, and my earlier excitement has vanished. Though he was more than kind, in a strange way it feels as though we've somehow cheated him. I think Mom and Nick feel the same way.

CHAPTER TWENTY-NINE

BETWEEN THE FALL CONCERT AND JIM DIS-
COVERING US IN THE CHURCH BASEMENT, OUR LIVES HAVE
reached a turning point. When I returned to school the next day, nearly
every kid I passed in the halls knew me. Where before they might nod
or say hi when they'd see me with Zach, now kids I don't even know call
me by name. Surprisingly, when kids found out I was on Facebook, my
friends list exploded from about ten to nearly four hundred. I've gone
from being popular as Zach's girlfriend to popular for being me.

Despite my new notoriety, my core group of friends is the same:
Zach, Scott, Josh, Wendy, and Tera. We eat lunch together most days,
and hang out between classes. I even went on a group date with them last
weekend, ending in another sleepover—this time at Tera's.

With Jim's help, we joined the multi-church interfaith hospitality
program. This week we're guests of the St. Catherine's Catholic Church,
and we'll move to Glory Lutheran Church next week. For the first time
since becoming homeless, I'm seeing other homeless kids, but so far
they're all closer in age to Amber than me.

Mom followed Jim's advice and listed with a temporary agency, but
it was mostly a bust. On the plus side, she scored two interviews through
Jim's contacts and was offered the office manager position at the law of-
fices of Hammert, Howard and Higdon. She starts next week, and I'm
secretly thankful she won't be teaching at my school.

Nick still doesn't have any new job leads, but he and Jim meet regularly to explore his options. Yesterday, at Jim's suggestion, Nick dropped his application at a car dealership, an auto parts store, and an appliance repair company. Changing directions seems to have pulled him out of his rut and his mood is so much better.

It's now the Saturday following Thanksgiving. We spent the holiday with our host family at St. Catherine's where we helped prepare a turkey with all the dressings. That night, twelve inches of snow dumped on Rochester, and the temperature has dropped again into the single digits. If not for the many churches of the interfaith network, we'd still be in the van. I know we wouldn't survive.

I'm excited to be back at the Presbyterian Church for the Saturday Community Kitchen. In the last six weeks, these people have become more than friends—they've become extended family.

"Happy Thanksgiving!" Mrs. Cummings greets us, her smile warm. She holds her arms open for Amber, who wraps her arms around the older woman's waist. "Well hello, Miss Amber! I'm so glad you made it!"

"Happy Thanksgiving, Linda," Nick says.

Amber pulls out of Mrs. Cummings's arms and beams up at her. "What's for lunch, Mrs. Cummings?"

"I'm so glad you asked." She ruffles Amber's hair and turns her attention to Mom, Nick and me. Her smile lights up her whole face. "We have turkey and dressing on the menu today. Eight turkeys were donated, so I've been scrounging around these last few days looking for roasters so we could cook them all at the same time. I don't know how we did it, but we did!"

"It smells wonderful," Mom says.

"It does, doesn't it?" Mrs. Cummings agrees. "In twenty-two years, this is only the second time we've been able to provide turkey for Thanksgiving—and today we have eight!"

"We better get out of your way, then." Nick laughs.

Mrs. Cummings pats his arm. "Yes—I have some things to finish up, but you're never in the way. Go—find a table and enjoy dinner."

We select a table in the middle of the room, and Mom and Nick greet people as they stop to say hello. Among them is Mrs. Mowdy, an elderly woman who is a complete enigma to me. She attends most weeks with her granddaughter and she's always dressed impeccably without a stain or wrinkle in sight. Her face is a roadmap of lines, but her clear green eyes shine from behind a set of nondescript glasses. Her granddaughter seats her in one of the empty chairs at our table and her smile warms me.

"It's good to see you, Abby," she says. "How's school?"

"Good, thank you," I tell her.

Before we can say more, Mrs. Cummings calls us to attention. "If everyone would please find a seat. I have a couple of announcements then we'll serve dinner." The room quiets and she continues. "First and most important, Katrina, Rian, and Karolyne are celebrating birthdays this week, so we have a small gift for each of you. Please come see me after dinner, and I'll make sure to get those to you."

Katrina, a middle-aged woman with long gray hair tied back in a low ponytail, smiles her thanks. Two tables over, Rian—a man I guess to be in his thirties—raises a work-calloused hand and waves. Next to him and about his age, Karolyne's face flushes red. She dips her head until her long brown hair cascades around her, hiding her features from view.

"In addition," Mrs. Cummings continues, "I'm pleased to announce that Alisa had her baby on Thursday morning—a little girl she's named Nevaeh. Mom and baby are doing well and expect to be back with us next week. And finally, Landyn, Wesley, and Jacksyn have leads on seasonal work for the holidays, so see them after dinner for more information."

At the table to my left, one of three brothers waves a hand in the air. "We'll set up over in the east corner, Linda."

Mrs. Cummings nods. "Thank you, Landyn. Now, as I've already mentioned to many of you, we're serving turkey with all the fixings.

There's plenty for everyone, so enjoy yourselves and see me after if you'd like leftovers to take with you."

The room buzzes with excitement. For some, this will be the only meal they'll get all day. Others might not have had a real Thanksgiving meal in years. This is a big deal.

Mrs. Cummings smiles. "If you'll give me your attention for one more minute, I'll introduce you to our servers, then we can say grace and begin. With us today are members of the Rochester South High School Key Club, who are fulfilling their club's service requirements by assisting with today's meal. Please make them feel welcome."

My heart stops and fear races through me. *No! Please not now!*

I stare at my lap, terrified to discover whether I know any of the volunteers. It's not that I know everyone at school—far from it. But the Fall Concert drew a lot of attention, and the odds of someone recognizing me are high.

I sit statue-still while Mrs. Cummings leads grace, but my ears buzz with dread. When I'm sure all heads are bowed, I lift my own and peek around the room. I almost sag with relief until my roving eye stops and backtracks four faces. The first tendrils of panic slither below my skin and I can't breathe. My heart skips several beats and bile rises until I taste nausea on my tongue. Directly across from me are two girls. One has her head bowed politely in prayer, but the other has no respect for anyone or anything. Trish's eyes meet mine. She lifts an eyebrow that clearly says, "*Well, this is interesting.*"

The buzzing in my ears increases until it eviscerates all other sound. Heads lift around me, and lips move in what can only be "amen," but it's inaudible above the buzzing. I'm paralyzed and can't move my gaze away from Trish's wicked smirk.

Amber nudges me. Her lips move, but I can't understand her words. Instead, I'm focused on Trish as she releases my gaze and begins serving a nearby table. My trance lifts and I bow my head, close my eyes tight, and pray dinner will end quickly.

A hand lands on my shoulder and squeezes gently. Lifting my head, I gaze into the sympathetic eyes of Zoë. "I'm sorry. I didn't know."

My face flames. I open my mouth to respond, but no words escape. So I nod and look back down at my lap. Though I was hungry ten minutes ago, the idea of food makes my stomach revolt. I push the food around my plate as guilt at the waste wars with humiliation.

"Abby?" Nick touches my arm and my eyes meet his. "You okay?"

I shake my head.

"Claire?" he says, getting my mother's attention.

Mom looks at me and her eyebrows draw together. "Abby?"

My eyes go wide and I shake my head to stop her questions. She studies me then looks to Nick for direction.

He takes my hand under the table and gives it two gentle squeezes. "Do we need to go?"

Finding my voice, I whisper, "No. Please—just try to be normal."

Nick releases my hand then turns to Mom and says softly, "Let's eat and go."

We focus on our meals while Amber, completely oblivious to my distress, keeps a running monologue. The second dinner is over, Nick stands and pulls my chair out for me, then does the same for Mom.

"I'm sorry to rush you," he says casually, but loud enough for those around us to hear, "but I have to get to work early."

Mom and Amber gather their things, and move toward the exit doors. We've almost escaped when Mrs. Cummings stalls us.

"You're leaving?" she asks, surprised.

"Yes," Mom says. "Nick has to be at work early. Thank you for the meal, it was delicious."

"You're welcome. Did you want to take some leftovers?"

"No thank you!" My abrupt interruption startles Mrs. Cummings. "I mean—Nick always says to take only what we need, and I'm sure there are people who need it more than us."

Mom smiles. "Abby's right—we're good. Thank you, Linda, for a delicious meal."

"Okay, then—if you're sure. We'll see you next week?"

Nick grins. "Wouldn't miss it."

We bid her goodbye and walk the maze of quiet hallways to the van. Nobody speaks until we're safe behind the locked van doors.

Mom spins around and faces the back seat. "Abby! What is going on?"

"Remember Trish from McDonald's?" I say. "She was here and she hates me. It'll be all over school by tomorrow."

"Surely not," Mom scoffs. "I can't imagine the administration would stand for that."

"Really, Mom? Like the administration didn't stand for the bullying I got when you were caught with Coach Hawkins?"

Mom's face flames and she swallows hard. "You're right. I'm sorry."

I bite my lip and shrug. "It's whatever. It was bound to happen—I just wish I'd had more time. We were almost there…"

"Can we do anything?" Nick asks.

"No." I shake my head. "Let's just go."

Nick drives to the library, where he and Mom deviate from their pattern and take Amber to a presentation in the auditorium. I escape to the only place I know—the teen media room.

My entire body is stiff and my head thrums with a headache. I'm awash with anxiety and can't pull in a deep breath. It's like having a panic attack in slow motion—except instead of outright hyperventilating, I can't breathe at all. Somehow I have to head this off—run interference and tell my story before Trish does. I sit at my favorite carrel and log onto Facebook, wishing once again I could post on Instagram. Twenty-seven new notices await my attention, along with three new friend requests. I open the first notice and find I've been tagged in a photo. I click the link and I'm taken to Trish's Facebook wall. My heart squeezes and I gasp. The first post at the top of the page is a picture of me sitting with my family at the church only an hour earlier.

It's too late—it's already out there!

The image is panned out to include several of the surrounding tables and there can be no mistake: I'm sitting square in the middle of the town's most needy. Beside the image, the caption reads: *"Abby Lunde eating at a soup kitchen? Is Rochester South's new 'It Girl' homeless? Has she lied to us all along?"*

Zach. It's the first thing that pops into my head. *What will he say?* I'm supposed to hang out with him tomorrow, but there's no way I can go now. I never told him we're homeless, and my omission is as much a lie as lying outright. There's no way he'll forgive me—I can barely forgive myself! I can't see him tomorrow—I need time. Time to decide how to handle the situation.

I pull up his Facebook page and find the same photo of me at the top of his timeline. Someone has shared the link on his wall, so there's no way he'll miss it.

Oh no! This isn't happening! My body erupts like an earthquake and I shake so violently the mouse pointer jumps all over the screen. I find the message link and write only one line.

MESSAGE TO ZACH: *I can't come tomorrow. I'll explain later. I'm sorry.*

I log off before he sees and responds. I'm not sure how soon he'll see it; I only know I can't talk to him right now.

My head falls onto my folded arms and I sob. Will he ever forgive me? What about Josh? Or Tera and Wendy? Why didn't I tell them? But I know exactly why I didn't tell them. There was never a way to tell them because they'd hate me like the kids in Omaha hated me when Mom screwed up. And like last time, they'll hate me for what isn't my fault. Only this time it'll be worse because I deliberately kept it secret.

I'm thankful for the empty room and the seclusion offered by the study carrel. I cry until my body runs dry, then wipe away the last of my tears. A hand touches my shoulder. I turn and Zach stares back at me through eyes the color of onyx. His eyebrows are drawn together, his expression holding a mixture of hurt and anger.

My heart thuds hard in my chest. I knew this day would come: the day when Zach would find out and he'd drop me in disgust. I just hadn't planned on it happening so soon. Just a few more weeks and we'd have been in the clear.

I open and close my mouth several times as I search for the right words. Finally, I settle on only one: "Zach."

He stares at me. "Wanna tell me what's going on?"

"How'd you know I was here?"

He breathes out a sigh. "You're always here. I guess now I know why."

I stare at him. I won't lie to him again, but the truth seems much worse. So I just look at him and say nothing.

"Where do you live, Abby?" he asks.

I open my mouth but shake my head. I have no defense.

"Where does Nick work?" he demands. "Your mom?"

I stare at my lap, hoping the words will come easier if I don't have to see the hurt in his eyes. "Why are you asking?"

"Why do you think I'm asking?" he demands. "Social media has blown up! I want to know what's going on. Why've I never been to your house?"

"I—I don't know what to say. I don't even know where to start."

"Why don't you start at the truth? I can't even defend you if I don't know what that is."

I gawk at him. "Why would you defend me? I don't need to be defended!"

Zach's eyes go round and glisten with unshed tears. "Why would I defend you? Seriously, Abby? How can you ask me that? I love you!"

He loves me? No! He's lying! He pities me!

"No you don't," I say, my voice flat.

He runs his fingers through his hair and clutches his head. "We need to get out of here. We need to talk."

"I don't want to talk. I just want you to go."

"That's a bad idea, Abby." Mom stands in the doorway, her lips drawn down. "I think you should talk to him. He obviously cares, and your whole world is about to fall apart. Again. Go—talk to him."

I'm startled by Mom's presence. How much has she heard?

I shake my head. "Mom! I—I—I can't."

She moves away from the doorframe, picks up my backpack and hands it to Zach. "Bring her back to St. Catherine's Church when you're done? She knows where it is."

"I will." Zach nods.

"Wait!" I gasp. "No! I'm not going! I can't."

"Yes, you are." Mom's voice is a command. "Learn from my mistakes, sweetheart. Dishonesty only breeds distrust. Tell him the truth—all of it. You'll thank me later."

Zach throws my backpack over his shoulder and reaches for my hand. "Thanks," he tells Mom.

Reluctantly, I allow him to lead me out of the library, but my eyes shoot daggers at Mom until we step out of the building. When we reach his car, Zach opens the passenger door and waits for me to be seated and buckled before walking around and getting in on his side. Though he says nothing, his body radiates tension. He looks through the rearview mirror then pulls away from the curb and into the flow of traffic. Silence stretches between us, but is interrupted briefly by the insistent buzzing of his phone. Zach glances at the CallerID then buries it deep in his pocket. I attempt a deep breath, but my chest is constricted and I can barely breathe at all.

He drives to the north side of town and pulls into an empty parking lot overlooking a series of soccer fields. Throwing the gearshift into park, he leaves the engine running for heat. I wait for him to say something—anything—but he doesn't even turn to look at me. His phone buzzes again, and he reaches inside his pocket, sending the caller to voicemail.

Silence envelops us, broken only by the tapping of his fingers on the steering wheel in rapid staccato. I hate the guilt that swallows me. I turn my head and stare out the passenger window through a thick film of unshed tears.

"Tell me," he finally says. "I want to know everything."

I take a shallow breath and swallow through a lump in my throat. "You already know everything there is to know. What more can I say?"

Zach stares out the front window, refusing to look at me. His phone buzzes again, but he ignores it this time. "Why didn't you tell me?"

My eyes shoot wide open and raw anger displaces my fear. I turn toward him. "You're kidding, right? What would you have said if I'd told you we were homeless—that we were sleeping in our van or at the local homeless shelter? That I ate breakfast at school because I'd go hungry otherwise? What would you have said if I'd told you we were squatting in the basement of a church, or that we've been floating from church to church these last few weeks just so we'd have a warm place to sleep? What would you have said, Zach?"

His anger meets my own and he turns to face me. "I don't know what I would've said, but I wouldn't have abandoned you!"

"How do you know, Zach?" I shout. "And even if you didn't, I don't need your pity!"

"I know because I know who I am—and I thought you did, too. And don't worry, Abs—the last thing I'm feeling right now is pity."

"Thanks," I say, dryly.

Zach pulls in a breath. "Who else knows?"

"Apparently everyone, thanks to Trish."

"Did you tell anyone? Josh?"

I shake my head. "No. Nobody."

"So you've been living a lie for what—since you got here? How do you think that makes me feel, Abby? How do you think it feels knowing you didn't trust me? I thought we were more than that."

"I *do* trust you, Zach. I didn't tell you because—because I was embarrassed." My voice trails off to a whisper.

He lifts an eyebrow. "Explain that to me. What do you have to be embarrassed about, except lying to me all this time? It's not your fault you're homeless."

"I don't know. You just—you treated me so well. You have everything: a big house, a nice car, money—I have nothing, and I was embarrassed."

Zach doesn't respond, almost as though he's not sure what to say. Several moments of tense silence pass, and twice more his phone buzzes. He ignores it.

"How long?" he finally asks.

I swallow hard. "Since we moved to Rochester."

"How? How does that happen?"

I explain the series of events, beginning with the Snapchat of Mom. His eyes soften as I explain about her forced resignation, the bullying at my old school, her seizure, Nick's layoff, the mounting medical bills and debt, and finally the almost-eviction that precipitated our move.

"There wasn't anyone who could help you?" he asks. "Grandparents, or your parents' friends?"

I shake my head. "Mom and Nick were both only children. Nick's parents died right after he graduated high school. My mom's mother died of breast cancer when I was a baby, then my grandfather died a month later. As far as I know, they were our only family. As for friends..." I shrug. "They all abandoned us after Mom's affair."

"But what about after you moved here? I would've helped you."

"You don't get it, Zach. I couldn't tell you—I couldn't tell anyone! I'd already been humiliated at my old school for something that wasn't my fault, and I couldn't go through that again. And . . ." I swallow hard, my next words barely a whisper. "I was afraid you'd hate me if you found out."

He ignores my last words and my heart drops to my stomach. *I knew it—he hates me!* I bite my lip. *Don't you dare cry, Abby! Don't you dare let him see you cry!*

Once again his phone buzzes. I want to scream at him—yell at him to shut the damned thing off—but I'm scared. So I do my best to ignore it, instead clearing my throat. "What are you thinking?"

Still Zach doesn't respond. He just stares out the front window as though I don't exist. Minutes pass, and then he punches the steering wheel and shouts, "I'm fucking furious!"

The steering wheel vibrates, the sound echoing in the quiet car. I shrink back against the passenger door as a wave of tears rushes from my eyes. This time I don't even try to stop them. I couldn't if I wanted to.

"I'm sorry," I whisper.

He grinds his teeth. "How could you be with me for two months and not tell me? Don't you trust me?"

"No! Yes! I mean—I *do* trust you, Zach!" I touch his arm but he shrugs me off. The simple gesture is almost my undoing and my heart tingles like it's breaking into pieces.

"Why, Abs?" His voice is quiet.

"Why what?"

"Why didn't you tell me?"

"I told you—I was scared. My best friends at my old school completely abandoned me. I was afraid you guys would do the same. I was scared you'd hate me if you knew. I mean, you have *everything*."

"Yeah," he scoffs. "Everything but your trust. I don't know, Abs—if we don't have trust, then what do we have?"

I stare out the passenger window and another sob wracks my body. I close my eyes, hoping Zach will throw the car in reverse and take me back. Instead, he slowly breathes in and out as though counting to ten before each inhale.

His eyes on me burn, but I refuse to meet them with my own. A moment passes, and he reaches out and pushes a stray hair behind my ear. "Hey. Look at me, Abs."

I wipe my eyes with the sleeve of my sweatshirt and turn my head in his direction, but stare at my lap.

"I'm sorry," he says. "Please don't cry. I'm not really angry with you. More than anything, I'm hurt. I'm sorry I yelled. It's just that it stings that you didn't trust me enough to tell me. And, I guess if I'm angry, I'm really angry at the situation and at Trish. No—I'm livid. I can't believe she'd out you like that. She has everything, and still she's so petty she'd humiliate you for something outside your control."

Zach's words soothe some of my pain and my tears slow. "I'm really sorry."

"I know you are, and I am, too. I didn't handle this well. I was surprised and didn't know how to react."

I nod.

"Abby, look at me." Zach lifts my chin with his knuckles until my eyes meet his. Yet again, his phone vibrates but he ignores it. "This isn't your fault, you know. I'm not even sure it's your parents' fault. Remember when I said I had your back? I meant that. I'm not going to make you go through this alone like your shit friends at your old school. I'm here and I'm not going anywhere."

"You're not?" I ask.

"No." He smiles softly. "I meant what I said earlier. I love you. I have, almost since the first moment I saw you, but I knew it the first time I heard you sing. I love you, and I'm going to stick this out with you. However it turns out, we're a team."

I sit in stunned silence. Deep down, I know I love Zach, too, but I'm not ready to say the words. Especially after all that's happened, saying the words is too much like expressing gratitude. When I finally say them, I want there to be no mistake I mean them, and not because I'm grateful.

"Thank you." I smile through the last of my tears.

Zach cups the back of my head then leans across the console and presses his lips to mine. In seconds, my heart stops aching and soars with relief. I meet his lips with mine as one kiss becomes two, then three. After several long moments, he pulls away and smiles. "Are you okay?"

I nod. "I think so, but what do we do now? I mean—"

"The only thing we can do. Forge ahead. We go to school on Monday, and we face everyone. You don't run away because, if you do, Trish wins. You go in with your head high and confident. And you don't say you're sorry because there's nothing to be sorry for. I'll be right beside you, and so will Josh, Tera, and Wendy. And Scott, too."

"Are you sure?" I ask. "I don't know if I can."

"Absolutely certain. And not only can you, but you will. Between Josh and me, we'll be with you at all times. We won't let you face this alone."

"Thank you."

"Don't thank me. I should be thanking *you* for being with me. I don't care how much money your family has or doesn't have. I just want to be with you."

The first trace of a smile makes its way to my lips. "I want that, too."

"Good, because you're stuck with me for a while."

Zach leans over the console once again and pulls me into his embrace. His lips are firm, as though trying to convey how much he means what he's said. I return his kiss until we're interrupted once again by the insistent buzzing of his phone.

"Aren't you going to get that?" I ask.

His mouth finds mine once again. "It's not for me," he says between kisses.

I pull back and give him a confused look. "Who's it for, then?"

Zach pulls the phone from his pocket, glances at it, then hands it to me. "It's for you."

Surprised, I take the phone from him and read the display. Thirty-four missed calls—all from Josh.

CHAPTER THIRTY

I SPENT THE REMAINDER OF THE WEEKEND DREADING TODAY—DREADING GOING BACK TO SCHOOL AND facing everyone. I've even avoided Facebook because I can't bring myself to look at the comments. I've never been a coward before, but I'm teetering on the edge.

"You ready, kiddo?" Nick asks as he stops at Door Six.

I dry my sweaty palms on my jeans. "No."

"I'm sorry, Abs." Mom turns in her seat and places a hand on my knee. "Maybe this time will be different. Your friends are different, if Zach and Josh are any indication."

I swallow the lump in my throat and nod.

"Keep your chin up, okay?" Nick's eyes meet mine in the rearview mirror. "Don't let them see you stagger. You have no reason to be ashamed."

I close my eyes, pull in a deep breath, and let it out slowly. "Here goes nothing."

My door is barely opened when Zach steps out of Door Six with Josh, Tera, and Wendy at his side. He and Josh smile, but Tera's and Wendy's expressions are unreadable. When they reach my side, Zach pulls me into his strong arms. I take a second to hide in the fabric of his jacket.

"You ready?" he asks.

I nod and pull away, facing Josh and the girls.

Without a word, Josh pulls me into a hug. He says nothing at first—

he just holds me and lends me his strength. "I've got your back, Ariel."

I bury my face further in his sweater. "I know. Thank you."

I pull away and rub hands over my eyes, wiping away the start of tears. There are tears in Josh's eyes, too, but he ignores them. I turn to Wendy and Tera who stand behind him waiting their turns. Tera opens her arms first, and I step into them. Wendy joins us and we stand together in a group hug.

"I—" I begin.

"No," Tera interrupts. "No apologies. No explanations. No embarrassment. I'm sorry you didn't tell us, but we get it."

"You do?"

"Of course we do," Wendy says.

"You're not mad?"

Tera bites her lip, holding back a smile. "For, like, a minute. And then Josh and Wendy smacked me on the head and reminded me it wasn't about us and, if we're really your friends, our job is to support you."

I swipe at another tear. "You're the best friends I've ever had."

"Of course we are. We're awesome." Wendy grins and loops her arm through mine. "Enough procrastinating, though. Let's show 'em what we got."

Tera loops my other arm through hers. "Anybody says anything to you, they'll have to go through us first."

"Damn straight." Zach takes a position on the other side of Tera.

Josh grabs Wendy's empty hand. "Let's go kick some ass."

With me in the middle, and my friends on each side, we're an unbreakable chain, like a team of Red Rover players. Nobody will break our ranks today.

STUNNED IS THE only word I have for the reaction I'm receiving. Stunned because there's been no reaction. None. It's third period already, and not a single person has mentioned the photo. It's almost like it never happened.

I find my desk behind Scott in chemistry and slide into my seat. Beside me, Josh bounces in his chair like a child waiting to visit Santa for the first time. His eyes sparkle.

"What?" I ask.

"Oh man!" He rubs his hands together. "You're gonna love this!"

"Love what?"

Josh turns to Scott and lifts an eyebrow. "Are you going to tell her, or can I?"

Scott laughs. "Oh no. This is mine to tell!"

"Well, would you two tell me already?"

"Okay," Scott says. "First, I'm sorry I missed walking in with you this morning. Zach called me yesterday and filled me in, but I overslept. I barely made it to first period in time."

Josh blows out a sigh. "Okay, okay. Now just tell her!"

"Fine!" Scott rolls his eyes. "So this morning I got here late. I guess because I wasn't part of your 'human chain'"—Scott makes air quotes with his fingers—"a few people didn't realize we were good friends."

"Oh for God's sake!" Josh whines. "Get to the point!"

Scott glares at him. "As I was saying…have you noticed nobody's talking about the photo Trish shared on Instagram?"

"It was on Instagram, too?" I say.

Scott offers an embarrassed smile. "Trish has her Instagram account linked to Facebook. Most of us do. If you post to Instagram, it automatically goes up on Facebook."

"Okay, okay." Josh waves a dismissive hand. "She knows how it works. Would you just get on with the story, please?"

"Anyway . . ." Scott narrows his eyes at Josh. "As I was saying, haven't you found it weird that nobody's said anything?"

"Yeah." I nod slowly. "It's really weird."

"Right? Here's why: a group of kids are pissed at Trish and organized a protest when they found out what happened."

"A protest of what?"

"Trish's bullying," Josh interrupts.

Scott throws another glare at Josh and clears his throat. "Right—Trish's bullying."

My forehead crinkles. "What? How?"

"Apparently, they're sick of it," Scott continues. "Someone started a text chain making sure everyone knew what went down, and calling on them to protest with their silence."

"Okay. That's weird. But why didn't we know?" I ask.

Still bouncing in his seat, Josh interrupts again. "They didn't want you to know—I guess they were afraid you'd feel pitied, so they excluded all of us from the text chain. When Scott wasn't part of our line this morning, a few people forgot how close he is to us and they were talking about it in front of him."

"Weird! What'd they say?" I ask.

Scott shrugs. "Just that they were silently protesting by not acknowledging Trish's post. It was reported to Instagram or Facebook—I'm not sure which—and, soon after, both of her accounts were closed. A text chain was started suggesting everyone pretend it never happened. Someone even sent out a series of tweets under #TeamAbby."

My jaw drops. "No way! It's on Twitter, too?"

Josh grabs my hand. "Focus, Abs!"

"But I don't get it. Why ignore it? And how were they able to keep it from us—did either of you know?"

Scott shakes his head. "Not until this morning, and that's what's brilliant. Trish does things for a reaction, so the idea was to ignore it and not give her the reaction she wanted. They kept it a tight secret and excluded all of us because they were afraid we'd tell you. I never would've known if I hadn't been late this morning."

"Wow!" I blow out a breath.

"That's not even the best part," Josh interrupts. "Mr. Bartlett knows, and Trish has been in his office since first period. Her parents showed up about an hour ago, and they've all been locked in there since."

"No way! That explains why she wasn't in my history class."

"Yup," he says. "Maleficent's rule is about to end. I'd be surprised if even Zoë stands by her now."

Scott rolls his eyes. "You and your Disney references."

"What?" Josh throws his palms in the air. "You're telling me Trish doesn't remind you of Snow White's evil step-monster?"

"Sure." Scott shrugs. "But why Maleficent and not Ursula—you know, since Abby's nickname is Ariel?"

I wave my hand in front of both boys. "Hey guys—your turn to focus here! So what's all this mean?"

Josh shrugs. "Not sure. I'd bet she gets expelled—or suspended at least. There goes Juilliard."

"What? Why?" I ask.

Scott frowns and throws a dirty look at Josh. "The school has a strict no-bullying policy and cyberbullying falls under that category. If she gets expelled or suspended, Juilliard won't take her, regardless of how talented she is."

"Wow. I'm sorry you're in the middle like this. I know you like her."

Scott lifts a shoulder but doesn't meet my eyes. "It is what it is. It was a stupid thing to do and she had to know it."

I'm at a loss for words but am saved from commenting as Ms. Burke enters the room and returns our graded tests from last week. I sit in a daze as waves of disbelief wash over me. Nothing has turned out as I expected. Trish is in serious trouble, and the weirdest thing is I almost feel sorry for her.

At ten minutes before the bell, a knock sounds at the classroom door. Ms. Raven stands in the doorway. Ms. Burke greets her and the two women converse in quiet whispers before Ms. Burke returns her attention to the class.

"Abby," she says. "Ms. Raven needs you for a few minutes. Go ahead and gather your things since it's so close to the bell."

Scared, I collect my books and turn to Josh. "Tell Zach where I am if I don't get back in time for lunch?"

He nods and I meet Ms. Raven in the hall. She smiles and offers polite greetings, but gives no indication of why I've been summoned until we reach her office.

"Have a seat, Abby." She motions toward two empty chairs then sits behind her desk "You've had a rough weekend."

"I guess you heard?"

"About Trish and the soup kitchen?"

I nod. "Yeah."

"I did. I'm sorry—that was a crummy thing to do. Mr. Bartlett is dealing with it, but I wanted to see how you're holding up."

"I'm fine. It's—nothing has turned out like I expected."

She smiles. "I heard about the text chain. That's rather impressive—we have some great kids here."

"Yeah. It was—wow!" I shake my head and search for a way to ask the question burning the back of my brain. There's no good way to ask, so I blurt out, "What will happen to Trish?"

Ms. Raven lifts an eyebrow and sits back in her chair. "I can't comment on her situation, but I will say our entire staff is committed to ensuring a bully-free environment, so I have faith it will be resolved appropriately."

I pause, understanding Ms. Raven is limited in what she can say, but I push anyway. "I heard Trish might get expelled—or at least suspended—and also that she's applied to Juilliard. Could she still get accepted with that on her record?"

"I don't know, but that's not something you need to worry about.

You're not responsible for Trish's actions and, if her punishment is that severe, then it's a good learning experience."

I nod. "Okay. I guess. But can I just say one more thing?"

"Go ahead," Ms. Raven says. "But I won't guarantee I can answer."

"I know I should be happy to see Trish punished. I mean, she's been awful to me since I came here. But…" I pause and search for the right words. "Well, I know what it's like to have everything taken away from you, and also what it's like to be the outcast. I don't like Trish, but I don't want to see something like Juilliard taken away from her. I mean, it seems like a really harsh penalty."

"I see. Unfortunately, it's not my decision, but I'll mention your concerns to Mr. Bartlett."

"Thanks."

Ms. Raven studies me until I squirm. "You're an unusual girl, Abby. And I mean that in a good way. You're far more empathetic than most girls your age. I don't know of another student who would be thinking about Trish right now instead of her own worries. In fact, most students would be screaming for her punishment."

"Yeah. Well…" I shrug. "I'm not sure what it proves to take away her chance at everything she's worked for, even if she is rude and doesn't deserve it. What if Juilliard is her path to greatness? If I'm somehow responsible for taking that opportunity away from her, I'm not sure I could live with myself. You know?"

"I do. And I thank you for your empathy. So!" she says, changing the subject. "Back to *you*. Are you doing okay, Abby? Do you need anything? Where are you staying?"

I assure Ms. Raven we're fine and explain about the interfaith hospitality and meals at the Salvation Army.

"I'm relieved to hear it," she says. "You know you can come to me at any time. I can't fix everything, but I'll give it my best shot."

"I appreciate that."

"Okay, then." Ms. Raven stands. "If there's nothing you need, I'll let you go. Just remember where my office is. The door is always open."

TRISH IS ABSENT from school for three days and the teachers are tight-lipped. Nobody knows what happened or whether she was punished, but when she returns, she seems like a different person. Gone is the arrogance and supercilious behavior, and in its place is a much-subdued Trish who avoids me completely. She's even been moved out of my history class, leaving our only interactions at passing time—and even then she keeps her head down.

With my secret out, I'm free to spend more time with Zach. In the following weeks, we study together after school and even go on a few real dates. Most nights, though, we just watch movies at his house or with the other families at whichever church is hosting us. Though our living situation is still unique, it's a huge improvement and I'm optimistic things will only get better.

Maybe the best news is that Nick finally has a job. Jim Kaspar put in a good word for him with the owner of Hamilton's Chrysler, calling him personally to recommended Nick for the job. After an interview with Mr. Hamilton himself, Nick was offered a position in new car sales. Though he's never worked on commission before, Mr. Hamilton is gambling that Nick's overall knowledge under the hood will translate well to the sales floor. He's finished out his first week and reports he not only enjoys the customer interaction, but he's sold two cars and his manager thinks he shows promise. He's still not making the six-sale minimum before commission kicks in, but it's a start.

With Mom and Nick now both employed, we're finally on the road to normal. In the meantime, one of the transition homes owned by the combined churches has become vacant and, at Jim Kaspar's recommendation, we've been approved and move in on December 28th. We'll be in a real home in time for the New Year!

It's now two days before Christmas, and the last day of school before winter break. I'm studying Mr. Thompson's newest reading assignment when a tap sounds on his classroom door. Standing there is Ms. Raven—I haven't seen her since the day I returned after Trish's social media post. Mr. Thompson leaves his desk and the two speak quietly. Now smiling, he turns back to the class.

"Abby?" he says. "Ms. Raven would like to see you for a few minutes."

I glance at Zach and return his surprised frown. I can't imagine what Ms. Raven needs with me this time. My stomach flip-flops, but I collect my books and meet her in the hall.

"Don't look so serious, Abby," she teases. "It's not bad."

I smile sheepishly. "I'm not used to getting called out of class, and I feel like I've done something wrong."

"Not at all. I just need to meet with you for a few minutes before you head off for winter break."

We step into her office and I'm surprised to find Mrs. Miner waiting for us. I shoot her a confused look and her eyes twinkle with mischief.

"Hi, Abby," she says. "I hope you don't mind my joining you."

"No," I say cautiously. "I don't *think* I mind."

Ms. Raven waves me to a seat then sits behind her desk. "Helen? Would you like to begin?"

Mrs. Miner's eyes crinkle as she smiles. "Thank you, I would, actually."

I look between the two women and my head spins. *What in the world is going on?*

"Abby," Mrs. Miner begins, "did you mail your applications to both of the universities we discussed?"

I nod. "Yes. I've been watching the status online and it shows I've been accepted to St. Cloud, but no word on Mankato yet."

"Wonderful," she says. "Did you have a preference between the two?"

I lift a shoulder. "Not really—they both seem so much alike."

"Well, then. This might make your decision easier."

"How do you mean?" I glance between the two women.

Mrs. Miner raises an eyebrow at Ms. Raven, who nods enthusiastically. "We have great news for you. A letter came today from the Vocal Music Department at St. Cloud State University. As your music teacher, it was addressed to me, but the letter was regarding your scholarship audition."

Goose bumps pop out on my arms. "What did it say?"

"You've been offered a scholarship in vocal music. It covers almost everything—your tuition plus room and board. It's renewable for four years so long as you maintain a three-point-zero GPA and stay in the program."

I sit in a stupor, confused. "What does that mean?"

Ms. Raven grins. "It means if you choose St. Cloud, everything is paid for except your books."

My hands shake and my pulse races. "How much are books?"

"They can be pretty pricey but, if that's all you have to pay for, it's not too bad. A part-time job over the summer should cover books for two semesters." Ms. Raven explains.

My fingers tingle. I open my mouth, but no words come out.

"Well, say something, child!" Mrs. Miner teases. "Congratulations!"

My face flushes hot and I find my voice. "Thank you. I—I couldn't have done it without you both. I'd never even have known it was available."

"It's our pleasure," Mrs. Miner says.

"We're very proud of you, Abby," Ms. Raven adds, then changes the subject. "Now, there're two more things I need to discuss with you while you're here. First, there's another scholarship we think you'd qualify for. It's two thousand dollars, also renewable for four years with good grades and, if you get it, it should easily cover your books. It's offered to students who've experienced tremendous financial hardship, and your family's recent circumstances make you a good candidate. Are you interested?"

I nod. "Definitely. How do I apply?"

"You don't apply *per se*. It's based upon school counselor or teacher recommendation. Mrs. Miner and I could recommend you, but it would mean sharing sensitive information about your family's hardships. In light of everything that's happened, we wanted to ask you before submitting the application."

I don't even have to think about it. Yes! Though we're still homeless, my classmates' reaction has taken the sting out of others knowing. I nod. "Yes—please!"

"Good." Ms. Raven smiles. "Now one last thing before you go. I don't need an answer today, but I'd like you to think on it."

"Okay?"

"Every spring, we host an assembly recognizing significant issues facing our students. A committee of seven seniors decides the topics, then votes on which students should be invited to present. It's titled 'In My Shoes,' and this year they'd like you to be one of their presenters." Ms. Raven's voice gentles. "I know it's still sensitive for you, but they'd like you to talk about your experiences in the homeless community."

My heart races. "Oh—wow. Do I know any of the other presenters?"

"Actually, Josh Bryant accepted about fifteen minutes before we brought you down. He'll talk about his decision to be open regarding his sexual identity. You weren't here when he came out, but it was a difficult decision—as it is for most LGBTQ students. He'll talk about his fears, any hurdles he's overcome, and offer advice for those facing similar decisions."

"Did he—I mean, was it hard for him?" I ask, dreading her answer.

She smiles gently. "I'll let Josh field those questions, but I can say that our school is becoming more accepting of differences, and Josh is a big part of the reason why."

"Can I think about it?"

"The presentation isn't until March 31st, so you can think on it over winter break. If you'll let me know by mid-January, that should be plenty of time."

I nod. "I will. I'll let you know."

CHAPTER THIRTY-ONE

NEVER AGAIN WILL I TAKE FOR GRANTED HAVING OUR OWN REFRIGERATOR AND PANTRY, NOT TO MENTION a roof over our heads. We moved into transition housing last night, and this is our first shopping trip for groceries. We're doing better, but money is still tight. I expect this trip for a dozen or so items to take forever as Mom compares prices and consults her fistful of coupons. We're saving every extra penny to rent our own house and, with Mom and Nick now having a more normal work schedule, I'm looking for a part-time job after school. With luck, I'll have one soon and—between the three of us—we'll be able to afford the first- and last-months' rent before the end of the school year.

I'm standing in the produce aisle, helping Mom select apples, when the hairs rise on the back of my neck. I look up and lock eyes with Trish. She wears a white button-down shirt with a name tag indicating she's a store employee. *Lovely! Of all the grocery stores, we pick the one where Trish works. Note to self: scratch the grocery store off my list of job possibilities.* I turn my back and study the apples. I have no idea what I'm looking for, but it beats interacting with Trish.

"Abby?" she says. "I was hoping we could talk."

I ignore her.

"Abby," she says again. "Can we talk?"

Mom looks up from selecting apples and glances between Trish and me. "Abby? She wants to talk to you."

Thanks, Mom!

I turn to Trish, ready with a scathing comment, but something in the way she looks at me stalls my words. I study her, and her demeanor confuses me. Her eyes are pleading and she picks nervously at a hangnail on her left hand. I want to tell her off, but she looks like a harsh word might shatter her.

"What do you want?" I ask, my voice resigned.

"Can we go somewhere to talk? The snack bar, maybe? I'll buy you a soda." Trish looks sheepish as she stares at the floor. "I'm on a break."

Really? A soda? As if a soda is an enticement or something? I blow out a breath and turn to Mom. "I'll be back in a minute, okay?"

A line forms between Mom's brows, but she nods. "Okay."

"Thanks," Trish says, leading the way to the snack bar. "Do you— can I buy you a soda or something?"

"I'm fine," I say.

"I don't mind. Really."

I shake my head. "No, thanks."

Trish nods and we bypass the snack bar and select a booth. I slide into the seat across from her and wait.

"I'm sorry," she says simply.

My body stills. I don't know what game she's playing, but I won't be drawn in so she can kick me around. I nod and slide toward the edge of the seat to stand. "It's okay. Is that all?"

"No—wait." She grabs my hand and I snatch it away. Her face flames. "I—I wanted to explain."

Trish's eyes are pleading and I hate myself for giving in, but I blow out a breath and settle back into my seat. "It's okay. It's over—you're forgiven."

"Abby, please let me explain," she says.

I close my eyes and count to ten. "Fine. What?"

"I really am sorry. I know I've been awful to you. I don't have a good excuse, but the truth is—everything I did was because I was jealous."

"Jealous," I say. Not a question, but a statement.

"Yeah. I know you don't believe me, but hear me out. Please?"

I nod. "Okay."

"That first day, I saw Zach walk you to class. I saw the way he looked at you and—I won't lie—it made me mad. You have this beautiful red hair and incredible eyes, and I knew right away he was into you. I screwed up when we dated, and I'd been trying to win him back. But the second I saw him with you, I knew it was useless. I didn't think—I just reacted. And the more I saw you with him, the more insecure I felt until I blamed you for taking him away from me."

"So you made my life a living hell? Because you were *jealous*?" I grit my teeth so hard they ache.

Trish stares at the table. "Yeah. And I'm sorry."

I close my eyes and take a minute to process this new information. It's almost too much to understand and I need time to think. I move to stand. "It's fine."

"No, wait! Please don't go!"

The panic in her voice stalls me. I blow out a breath and settle into my seat again.

"It's not fine, Abby, and I know that," she says. "I was unforgivably mean. And—I owe you more than an apology. Mr. Bartlett told me what you said to Ms. Raven—about not wanting my punishment to keep me from getting into Juilliard. I don't know why you'd do that after how awful I was, but I really appreciate what you said."

I shrug. "Like I said—it's fine."

"No, it's not. What I did was horrible. I was so angry I didn't consider the consequences of my actions, or what it meant to you and your family. I was only thinking about myself, and I was so angry I didn't think it through."

"And now you have?" I lift an eyebrow. "How is today different?"

Trish's eyes brim with tears. "I've had a lot of time to think the last few weeks. My parents were irate—I've never seen them so angry and disappointed. They took away my phone and all of my social media the second they found out, and they still haven't given them back. Then they put me in counseling twice a week, which, honestly, has really helped me not only understand my motives, but especially how wrong it was. My counselor is helping me with coping strategies for my anger."

"Well, I guess something good came out of it if it makes you a better person in the long run."

Trish nods but stares at her lap, her bottom lip between her teeth. "I'm trying to change, Abby. I still don't know how I got so screwed up, but I'm trying to be better. I mean it."

I've been angry at Trish for a long time—hated her, even—but at the moment, I pity her. Her words ring sincere, and I realize I have it within me to be a better person. I can carry around my anger and hate, but doing so makes me no better than she's been. In this moment, I finally understand what Nick meant about forgiveness. He meant that withholding it is like taking poison and expecting the other person to die—the anger ends up hurting me more than it hurts the other person. Plus, I can't find it in me to withhold forgiveness when she looks so broken. "It's over. I appreciate your apology. It's all good."

"Yeah." Trish lifts a shoulder. "It sure didn't end up the way I thought it would."

"How did it end up? For you, I mean?"

She swipes at a tear. "The whole school hates me—"

"I'm sure that's not true."

She smiles self-deprecatingly. "No. It's true. Even Zoë won't talk to me. I have no friends—none. It's like I'm a social reject."

"I've been there."

"Yeah?" she says. "Mr. Bartlett suspended me for three days, but because of what you told Ms. Raven, he agreed to keep it off my transcripts if my behavior changes."

"So, Juilliard?" I ask.

"So long as a suspension doesn't show on my record—which it won't, thanks to you—I'll be okay. I owe you for that."

"No, you don't." I shake my head. "I just did the right thing."

"But why? Why would you do that for me?"

"I didn't do it for you. I did it for me."

Trish's eyebrows draw together. "I don't understand."

I study Trish then release a deep breath. "I'm not sure I can help you understand, but this is why. Being homeless is the most helpless feeling in the world. One minute our lives were normal—we were completely in control of our destinies. The next minute, circumstances were thrown at us that took everything away. Everything fell apart—our whole lives changed. I couldn't stop wondering what would happen if you lost Juilliard like we lost our opportunities. Would it change your future? I didn't want to be the reason you lost something that might make that kind of difference."

Trish blinks. "Wow. I don't know what to say."

"It's okay." I shrug. "Let's just move on."

"Just like that?"

"Yeah. Just like that. I wish you hadn't done it, but it showed me a lot about my friends and myself. And it sounds like the therapy is helping you, so it all worked out."

"So we're good?"

"I'm not mad anymore," I say. "But I don't think we can ever be friends. We weren't headed that way anyway, but I don't hate you."

Trish smiles shyly. "Thanks, Abby."

CHAPTER THIRTY-TWO

IF I'VE LEARNED ANYTHING ABOUT MINNE-
SOTA, IT'S THAT THE WINTER LASTS *FOREVER*. IT'S MARCH
31st and everywhere *except* Minnesota, kids are dressed in shorts and
T-shirts. But not us—we got twenty-two inches of snow this week, causing the district to cancel school for two days. Since then I've vacillated
between frustration at the closing and hopeful expectation of one more
snow day—because one more snow day would delay today's "In My
Shoes" program, and I'm having second thoughts about presenting. But
I'm not so lucky. I woke up this morning and checked for school clos-
ings, but there were none.

Resigned to my fate, I apply a light coat of mascara and study myself
in the bathroom mirror. My face is too pale, but I don't dare apply more
makeup. I flash my teeth. Though I've just brushed them, I double-check
for anything in between them. Finding nothing, I close my eyes, inhale
deeply and count to ten before releasing my breath. It doesn't help—I'm
far more nervous today than I was for the Fall Concert.

"Zach's here!" Amber shouts from another room.

My heart races—I'm not ready!

"Sister!" Amber shouts again. "Zach's here!"

"Tell him I'm coming!"

With one last glance in the mirror, I flip the light switch off and grab
my backpack beside the door. I'm as ready as I'll ever be, I guess.

"I'm leaving!" I call out to Nick. He'll walk Amber to school in an hour then take the city bus into work, since Mom leaves by six thirty to be home when Amber gets out of school.

"Good luck!" he shouts back from the kitchen.

I close the front door behind me and zip my coat up to my chin. I frown at the winter wonderland surrounding me. We'd thought the snow had melted for the season, but the berm between the street and sidewalk is piled with snow again. *Does the winter here ever end?*

Zach steps out of the car dressed in khakis, a teal dress shirt, and a matching tie.

"Wow—you clean up well!" I say, reaching his side.

"It's a special day for you." He kisses my cheek and I settle into the front seat. Sliding into his own seat, he asks, "You ready for today?"

"I'm nervous!" I hold up a shaking hand for his inspection.

He takes my hand and gives it a squeeze. "You'll be fine. Remember to breathe."

"Breathe. Right." I breathe in and out to a count of ten. "I can't believe you dressed up."

He doesn't comment, but offers a smile so wide it shows off the dimple in his cheek. We reach the high school and he parks in the student lot near Door Six. The program begins in an hour but Ms. Raven wants the presenters to meet during first period for a dry run, so Zach walks me to the backstage entrance where he pulls me close and rests his chin on my head.

"Knock 'em dead," he says.

I lean back and scowl. "You're supposed to say 'Break a leg.'"

"Yeah, but you might and then I'll feel responsible."

"Ha-ha. Very funny." I step out of his arms.

Zach grins and gives me a peck on the cheek. "Break a leg, Abs," he says before leaving me to walk into the auditorium alone.

I barely step through the backstage doors before Josh rushes to my side. "You made it!"

"Of course I did! I said I'd be here!"

"Yeah, but I know how nervous you've been. I was afraid you'd start puking or something and I'd be on my own."

"Never!" I hold up three fingers in the formation of a Girl Scout pledge. "I solemnly swear that I will not abandon you. If I get sick or die before the program begins, I will rally or rise from the dead long enough to present and provide you moral support."

Josh rolls his eyes. "You are seriously weird, Ariel."

"Yeah? You should see my friends."

"Ha!"

We find our seats and Ms. Raven demands our attention. She walks us through the program in order of appearance. First up is Josh, followed by an eleventh-grade girl named Adelyne who will talk about her struggle with depression. I'm last up, and I'm not sure if I'm glad to be last or nervous that I'll have to wait. My stomach twists and I put a hand over it.

"Don't you dare puke, Ariel," Josh teases.

"If I do, I'll be sure to turn in your direction," I joke back.

The bell rings and my stomach flip-flops again.

"It's showtime!" Ms. Raven says. "Any questions before we get this show on the road?"

We shake our heads. Ms. Raven nods and takes her seat next to Adelyne. Moments later, students and teachers file into the auditorium. There's not enough room for the entire school, so the counselors have devised a rotation that should allow every student to attend at least once before graduating. Additionally, any student with a strong interest is excused from classes to attend.

The auditorium is nearly half full when Zach walks in with Wendy, Tera, and Scott. They're joking around with each other, and I wish I were down there with them instead of sitting on this stage. At almost the same time, Trish enters from a second set of double doors. She's completely alone, and it's impossible to ignore the defeated slump of her shoulders.

Gone is the confidence that's always been the defining characteristic of Trish Landry. Our eyes meet and she smiles cautiously. I smile back and nod, and her smile widens a smidge.

When nearly every seat is taken, Ms. Raven steps to the microphone and the auditorium quiets. "Good morning, and welcome to 'In My Shoes.' This morning we have three important topics presented by three of your classmates, who will share with you a little about the difficult experiences they've encountered as high-school students. Though their stories are uniquely their own, we hope they can provide comfort to other students facing similar challenges. To those of you who cannot relate, personally, we hope their stories will encourage empathy and a better understanding for the experiences of others.

"Our first presenter is Josh Bryant. Many of you know Josh as our resident Disney Expert. A senior this year, Josh is a two-year member of the National Honor Society, Vice President of the Drama Club, and starred as Sky Masterson in last year's Stage Door production of *Guys and Dolls*. He currently serves as President of Rochester South's chapter of the Gay-Straight Alliance and will speak about his unique journey toward finding his sexual identity, and the challenges and rewards he faces as a teen in the LGBTQ community."

Josh stands and takes the mic. In the next ten minutes, he details his confusion as an adolescent, and his "light bulb moment" when he realized how and why he differed from many of his peers. I'm awestruck as he talks about his courage in telling his family, coming out in social settings, and the support he's received from family and friends. He holds the audience entranced, and it's impossible not to find empathy in his experiences and pride in his journey. His cheeks flush with pleasure as he finishes to rousing applause.

I space out during Adelyne's presentation as I practice my own speech in my head. I know I should give her my full attention, but I'm on the verge of freaking out and can only concentrate on one thing at a time. In what seems like only seconds, she finishes her presentation and I'm called to the mic.

The shaking intensifies as Ms. Raven introduces me. My knees rattle. Josh grabs my hand and squeezes.

"You're up, Ariel," he says. "You can do this."

I nod and stand to take my place behind the mic at Ms. Raven's welcome. I smile, but it feels forced—unnatural. I clear my throat, and the mic's feedback squeals throughout the auditorium. I groan with the audience, and somehow it makes me feel a little less alone. I close my eyes and fill my lungs, letting the air out slowly. More relaxed now, I open my eyes and notice a stirring in the back of the auditorium. To my surprise, Mom and Nick enter and take seats beside Principal Bartlett. My heart flips, and a swell of pride rushes through me. They didn't tell me they were coming, and I almost cry knowing how hard it must've been for them to leave their new jobs to attend. I smile in their direction and Mom nods, a look of pure pride shining in her eyes. I clear my throat again and begin.

"Good morning. Some of you know me, but many of you don't. Maybe those of you who don't know me will recognize my story. My name is Abby Lunde, and until a few days before New Year's, I was homeless. Today, I'm ready to tell you my story.

"In her epic novel, *To Kill a Mockingbird*, Harper Lee uses the voice of Atticus Finch to impart an important lesson to his children. He tells them, 'You never really understand a person until you consider things from his point of view—until you climb into his skin and walk around in it.' Basically, Harper Lee says through Atticus the same thing we've all heard countless times, and it's the theme of today's program. She means the only way to understand a person is to see the world as he sees it—as he experiences it.

"With that in mind, and in keeping with the theme of today's program, I'd like to let you walk around 'In My Shoes' for a little bit.

"My shoes are dirty and worn through. I do a lot of walking. It costs too much to put gas in the van, so we walk everywhere we need to go. Until recently, I walked from school to the library most days. That's two miles, in case you wanted to know. I wish my shoes were snow boots because it's cold outside, and canvas sneakers aren't suited for snow. By the time I reach my destination, my feet are wet and freezing. But, hey—I have shoes. Not everyone does.

"My sister is six and growing fast. She needs new shoes frequently, but we can't always afford it. As a result, she's sometimes left wearing too-small shoes that squish her toes. But again, at least she has shoes. Not snow boots or shoes that fit properly, but they protect her feet.

"My mom's and stepdad's shoes are worn thin. Nick's have a hole on the right foot where his little toe pokes through, and the soles of Mom's shoes have come loose. When she walks, the bottoms flap against the tops like they're talking to you. She used the last of Amber's school glue trying to fix them, but it wasn't strong enough. Her shoes still talk when she walks.

"You might wonder how we ever got into this position—how we became homeless. What did we do wrong? I can assure you it's not something we ever imagined would happen. But I've learned it can happen to anyone. We were lucky, though. My stepdad knew Rochester had programs to help us, so he moved us here where people have been kind and have kept us from starving.

"I didn't want to move here—in fact, I hated it at first. But then I met many of you, and my life changed. I met the best friends I've ever had, and I met a girl I thought I hated who also hated me. Talking to her, though, helped me understand that everyone has her own issues, and knowing her story helped me to forgive."

I look out into the audience and my eyes meet Trish's. Several heads follow the direction of my gaze and I smile softly, hoping my expression conveys forgiveness. Trish smiles in return, her expression both contrite and hopeful.

"We all do things we regret, but it takes a big person to say she's sorry, and she's done that. It takes an equally big person to forgive, and so I have."

About half the audience stares at Trish, and I hope I've done the right thing—but I couldn't help it. As awful as she's been, she seems truly sorry and I can't stand to see anyone so defeated. I know better than most what a lonely existence school is with no one to claim as a friend. I hope my statement will heal some of the anger directed at her.

As I continue my speech, Zoë stands and takes the empty seat on one side of Trish. The shy smile on Trish's face is almost heartbreaking.

"So, being homeless wasn't fun. When we first moved here, we lived in my mom's van in the parking lot of Walmart. You might've seen us. We were the dark green van with the rusted-out fender on the driver's side, always parked in the last space closest to Broadway. Each night before bed, we'd pretend to go shopping so we'd have an excuse to sneak into their bathrooms to wash our hair in the sink, brush our teeth, and sponge ourselves off. You never understand how much you love a hot shower until you can't get one.

"Over the last six months, we've lived a variety of places. We even squatted in a church basement. That is, until we got caught.

"You might think getting caught was a bad thing, but it wasn't. The pastor at the church didn't pity us; he was empathetic to our circumstances. He helped us get into a program offering temporary housing, and he used his connections to help my parents get interviews. Those interviews led to jobs with real money coming in that will allow us the means to rent our own home. More than anything, he offered us kindness, understanding, and a helping hand.

"Throughout the time we were homeless, all of our meals were given to us through charity. My sister and I got free breakfast and lunch at school, and we ate dinner at the Salvation Army. On Saturdays, there was the 'soup kitchen' I'm sure you've all heard about. It's called the Saturday

Community Kitchen, by the way, and it's the farthest thing from a soup kitchen I've ever seen. There we were treated as guests instead of beggars. For one day each week, we felt valued and accepted. Normal.

"I've learned a lot during this time, but the most important thing I've learned is to never give up—and for every bad thing that happens, something good happens, too. Though I lived in my parents' van, I made the best friends I've ever known, went to Homecoming, and was given the lead solo in the school concert. I met adults who noticed my circumstances—if not the severity of those circumstances—and extended themselves to help. My school counselor encouraged me to take the ACT and apply to colleges and, together with my vocal music teacher, helped me find scholarships. I thought college was impossible, but I've been accepted to two state universities and offered a significant scholarship to one. Between them, Ms. Raven and Mrs. Miner helped me see that *nothing* is impossible.

"I'm not homeless anymore. We moved into a temporary home just after Christmas, and I have my own bedroom once again. It's not as spectacular as some of yours, I know, but it's mine for now, and I love it.

"Six months ago I felt so helpless—hopeless, even—but today I feel empowered. Today I have a game plan: I'll go to college and someday find a way to give back to the same community that has helped me so much.

"I was reluctant to speak at today's assembly. I'm not good in front of crowds, and being homeless isn't something I'm proud of. But the truth is, despite being homeless, I'm not so different from all of you. I have a family who loves me, great friends who support me, wonderful teachers who inspire and guide me, and a plan for my future. My life isn't perfect, but is anyone's, really?

"So, yeah—my shoes are nothing special, and there are days when I hate them and wish for something a little warmer, and definitely more stylish. But they're my shoes, and I think I'll keep them."

The audience erupts in applause, and I step away from the podium.

Mom throws me a thumbs-up and I beam a smile at her. The applause continues and I take my seat next to Josh. He pulls my hand into his own, squeezing it gently. My eyes meet his and I let out a loud swoosh of air.

EPILOGUE

GRADUATION IS THREE DAYS AWAY, AND I'M
BOTH EXCITED AND SAD. JOSH HAS BEEN ACCEPTED TO THE
University of Minnesota in the Twin Cities, and Tera and Wendy will be
roommates at the University of Wisconsin-Eau Claire. At senior night,
I was shocked to learn I'd won the hardship scholarship Ms. Raven and
Mrs. Miner had recommended me for, so my expenses are covered at
St. Cloud State so long as I keep my grades up. Amber's already crying
about my moving three hours away, but Mom and Nick are elated for
me. We've all tried to distract Amber from her worries by allowing her
to choose her bedroom at the new house Mom and Nick rented in late
April. We're finally standing on our own, and Mom plans to get her
Minnesota teaching license over the summer. Though I've forgiven her,
I'm also glad she doesn't teach college level.

Surprising all of us, Scott received a diving scholarship to the University of Arizona. I had no idea he was so talented. As for Zach, he was
offered two full-ride football scholarships—one to Minnesota State University at Mankato and the second to St. Cloud State University. It was a
tense two weeks while he considered his choices, but he finally opted for
St. Cloud—not because of me, but because they offer the athletic training program he plans to pursue.

This past year has been one of roaming—from bed to bed, from
school to school, and from old friends to new friends. Reflecting back, I
realize the worst parts weren't the cold, the hunger, or even the anxiety.

It was the lack of being grounded—the untethered feeling of wandering without direction—that bothered me the most.

I still don't know what my future holds, but I know I'm no longer lost. I've learned that sometimes we have to roam in order to find the place that feels most like home.

ACKNOWLEDGEMENTS

It's been said, "It takes a village to raise a child." The same is true of writing a novel, and *Roam* is no exception. From the very inception of this novel, and through the countless rewrites and final edits, there was a village of good friends and people in the publishing community who provided invaluable assistance. To the following people, I send my most heartfelt "thanks."

To my family, Troy, Amber, and Braden: you will never fully understand how much your support is appreciated. I love you to the moon and back!

To my agent, Tina Purcell Schwartz: thank you for your belief in this novel! I'm so blessed to have you.

To my publisher, Michelle Halket: you absolutely rock! Thank you for your incredible editing expertise and for helping me take *Roam* to the next level!

To Taylor Hein whose incredibly astute last-minute editing suggestions were spot-on! I'm awed by your insight and grateful for your input.

To Mrs. Helen Miner, retired vocal music teacher at El Reno High School in El Reno, Oklahoma, and 2017 inductee into the Oklahoma African American Educators Inc. Hall of Fame, for inspiring the character of Mrs. Miner. You are one of those teachers who touches the lives of every student. Thank you for loving and inspiring so many of us!

To Linda Curtis, and the Curtis family, who loaned this amazing woman to the Rochester, Minnesota, community for so many years. Thank you for your love and service to the community through your work with the Saturday Noon Meals. Meeting you changed my life, and I'm so blessed to have known you. Rest in peace, dear lady, and know your legacy lives on through those whose lives you touched.

To my mother, Marion Hedrick, and my inlaws, Nancy and Doyle Armstrong, for your endless support and belief in my abilities.

To my "Book Besties"—authors Amanda Linsmeier, Kelly Cain, Jamie McLachlan, and Bianca Schwarz. Thank you for keeping me from losing my mind through this entire process. I'm so grateful for your friendship—and for Amanda's mad titling skills!

To fellow authors Cara Sue Achterberg, Cathy Lamb, Lorna Landvik and Brandon Hobson for your friendship, mentoring and endless encouragement. I owe you each a debt of gratitude and I'm thankful to call you my friends.

To Dr. Catrina Bitner Bourne and Annamaria Williams Hager, Family Nurse Practitioner, for answering my countless medical questions related to medications and seizures. Any errors are entirely mine. Also to Jim Klepper for your spiritual guidance related to the character Jim Kaspar.

To Mayo High School teachers Pattie Ekman and Amy Monson for your edits on the earliest drafts and for the sensitivity reads related to Josh. I love you both and am so grateful to count you as friends.

To Laura DeVilbiss whose skill with voice acting brought Abby to life for the video trailer.

And finally, to my early readers who provided feedback, suggestions, and critique on the overall story and characters. Among those amazing people are Laura Thomas, Sara Hill Bendickson, Terry Johnsen, Donna Cole, Julie Lingo, and Juliana Lee. I couldn't have done this without your help!

The inspiration for *Roam* was borne out of a 2014 feature article about a "soup kitchen" I was assigned to write for *Rochester Women* magazine. Known as the Saturday Noon Meals, this weekly offering was run almost entirely by the organizer, Linda Curtis, with the assistance of community volunteers and donations. There, the most needy in the community were not only provided a weekly meal, but they were treated as human beings and valued members of the community. To say this experience was life-altering to me is not an exaggeration, and I am incredibly grateful to Linda Curtis and her weekly guests for opening my eyes to the needs of the poverty-stricken in my community.

ROAM BY C.H. ARMSTRONG

DISCUSSION

We learn in the first few chapters that Abby's friends ditch her after they find out about her mom's scandal. How do you feel about her friends' actions? Was there another way they could've handled it to stand by Abby without getting burned by the situation themselves? What would you have done?

In the first several chapters, Abby is furious with her mom, blaming her for their living situation. But is blaming her mother fair? Is she too harsh?

When Abby wanted to go to the football game to watch Zach play, Nick gives her some of what little money they have left, saying it was important that she be able to go. Do you think that was a good use of that money? Why or why not?

When Abby finds herself homeless, she guards her secret closely. Was this the right decision? How would you have handled this situation if you were Abby.

When Abby and her family visit the Community Kitchen and meet Mrs. Cummings, they find the camaraderie of the people much different than at the Salvation Army. What thing(s) do you think are responsible for that difference?

Forgiveness is a central part of the characters' lives. Nick must forgive Claire, Abby must forgive her mother and Trish. In Chapter 7, Nick counsels, "Forgiveness isn't about the other person, it's about ourselves." What do you think he meant?

Nick makes the decision to break the law and 'squat' in the basement of the church. Do you think he did the right thing? Why?

Abby's family is experiencing what they hope is a temporary situation. Are there different types of homelessness that people could endure? If there are, do you think it is important to differentiate between different types of homelessness?

Is homelessness a problem in the town or city where you live? How does it make you feel when think about it?

C.H. ARMSTRONG WRITES ISSUE-
DRIVEN YOUNG ADULT AND WOMEN'S FICTION,
and freelances part time as a magazine columnist. An
assignment to cover the twenty-year anniversary of a
local soup kitchen piqued her interest in the homeless
community and inspired *Roam*. She is also the author of
The Edge of Nowhere.

charmstrongbooks.com
@C_H_Armstrong

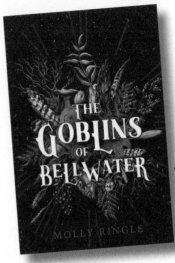

THE GOBLINS OF BELLWATER

Molly Ringle

New Adult - 978-1-77168-117-9

Most people have no idea goblins live in the woods around the small town of Bellwater, Washington. But some are about to find out.

Skye, a young barista and artist, falls victim to a goblin curse in the forest one winter night, rendering her depressed and silenced, unable to speak of what happened. Her older sister, Livy, is at wit's end trying to understand what's wrong with her. Local mechanic Kit would know, but he doesn't talk of such things: he's the human liaison for the goblin tribe, a job he keeps secret and never wanted, thrust on him by an ancient family contract.

Unaware of what's happened to Skye, Kit starts dating Livy, trying to keep it casual to protect her from the attention of the goblins. Meanwhile, unbeknownst to Kit, Skye draws his cousin Grady into the spell through an enchanted kiss in the woods, dooming Grady and Skye both to become goblins and disappear from humankind forever.

It's a midwinter night's enchantment as Livy, the only one untainted by a spell, sets out to save them on a dangerous magical path of her own.

"...something wholly unexpected and fresh." Publishers Weekly

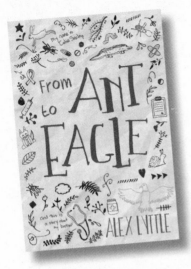

FROM ANT TO EAGLE

Alex Lyttle

Middle Grade - 978-1-77168-111-7

It's the summer before grade six and Calvin Sinclair is bored to tears. He's recently moved from a big city to a small town and there's nothing to do. It's hot, he has no friends and the only kid around is his six-year-old brother, Sammy, who can barely throw a basketball as high as the hoop. Cal occupies his time by getting his brother to do almost anything: from collecting ants to doing Calvin's chores. And Sammy is all too eager - as long as it means getting a "Level" and moving one step closer to his brother's Eagle status.

When Calvin meets Aleta Alvarado, a new girl who shares his love for *Goosebumps* books and adventure, Sammy is pushed aside. Cal feels guilty but not enough to change. At least not until a diagnosis makes things at home start falling apart and he's left wondering whether Sammy will ever complete his own journey…

From Ant to Eagle.

"Tender, direct, honest." Kirkus Reviews

"A moving and ultimately hopeful book." Booklist